Praise for *This Spells Love*

"*This Spells Love* is a romcom-meets-magic delight, and absolutely perfect for the friends-to-lovers enthusiasts who are looking for something unique! Dax is my new book boyfriend and no one else can have him."
— Sarah Adams, *New York Times* bestselling author of *Practice Makes Perfect*

"I am absolutely in love with this book. An addicting page-turner, I could not put it down until I knew how Gemma's journey ended— I feel like my heart was in my throat the entire time. A brilliant, moving, masterfully plotted friends-to-lovers romance (Dax is EVERYTHING) with a splash of magic, Robb's debut is definitely going in my All-Time-Favorites pile."
— Sarah Hogle, author of *Just Like Magic*

"*This Spells Love* is the smart, funny, spicy, heartfelt romcom I've been waiting for. Kate Robb's writing is a delight, her pacing is perfect, and she has created an unforgettable romance that gave me all the feels. This novel is a feat. Emily Henry and Mhairi McFarlane fans take note: you will be utterly charmed by this marvelous debut!"
— Marissa Stapley, *New York Times* bestselling author of *Lucky*

"Kate Robb's enchanting debut, *This Spells Love*, hits all the right beats for a can't-put-it-down romcom: sparkling humor, satisfying heat, and characters you'll fall in love with. This book was a joy to read!"
— Karma Brown, #1 international bestselling author of *Recipe for a Perfect Wife*

"*This Spells Love* is a delightful debut! Kate Robb's writing is as smooth as an oat milk latte and sweet as a donut, giving us characters to love and to root for, no matter which timeline they're in. While Gemma gets to explore life if she had made different choices, love in all its forms—family, sisterly, romantic—remains a constant. We should all be so lucky if we get the chance for a do-over!"
— Jen DeLuca, nationally bestselling author of *Well Met*

This Spells Love

A Novel

Kate Robb

The Dial Press
New York

A Dial Press Trade Paperback Original

Published in the United States by The Dial Press, an imprint of Random House, a division of Penguin Random House LLC, New York.

THE DIAL PRESS is a registered trademark and the colophon is a trademark of Penguin Random House LLC.

DIAL DELIGHTS and colophon are trademarks of Penguin Random House LLC.

Library of Congress Cataloging-in-Publication Data
Names: Robb, Kate, author.
Title: This spells love: a novel / Kate Robb.
Description: New York: The Dial Press, [2023]
Identifiers: LCCN 2022055075 (print) | LCCN 2022055076 (ebook) |
ISBN 9780593596531 (trade paperback; acid-free paper) |
ISBN 9780593596548 (ebook)
Subjects: LCSH: Magic—Fiction. | LCGFT: Romance fiction. | Novels.
Classification: LCC PR9199.4.R5735 L68 2023 (print) |
LCC PR9199.4.R5735 (ebook) | DDC 813/.6—dc23/eng/20230112
LC record available at https://lccn.loc.gov/2022055075
LC ebook record available at https://lccn.loc.gov/2022055076

Printed in the United States of America on acid-free paper

randomhousebooks.com

9 8 7 6 5 4 3 2 1

Book design by Diane Hobbing

To my favorite Hamiltonian, Kath:
When I write the parts I hope are funny,
it's your laugh I hear in my head.

This Spells Love

Chapter 1

"So, ARE WE solving the day's problems with sugar or alcohol?"

It's a great question. The same one I've been debating for the last eighteen minutes, standing on the exact spot on the sidewalk that is equidistant from the front door of Nana's Old-Fashioned Doughnuts and the liquor store.

"You look better today." My older sister, Kiersten, tucks a strand of strawberry-blond hair behind my ear. I'd argue that the hair wasn't out of place, seeing as the best I could do this morning was an intentionally messy bun, but Kierst is used to acting like a mama hen, given our ten-year age difference.

"I feel good," I lie. She knows it, I know it. But to be fair, today, I'm showered, dressed, and wearing clean underwear, a significant improvement from the last three stinky, wallowy, underwear-optional weeks.

"I think Nana's is probably the right life choice." I step toward the clear glass door of the doughnut shop. Kiersten follows behind me. As the door swings open, we are blasted with the sweet scent of sugar and yeast and happiness. Yes. This is the exact type of comfort I need.

We take our place in line behind a handful of other hungry

Hamiltonians who have excellent taste in morning pastries and eye the double-wide glass case hosting dozens of artisanal doughnuts handcrafted with Nana's love.

"What are you getting?" Kiersten nudges me with her elbow as her eyes lock onto a row of Coconut Dreams. Her question is more of a formality. A Wilde sister ritual. To say we come here often is an understatement. A gross understatement.

"Half a dozen Classic Fritters," I tell both Kierst and the little old lady working the cash register, who is not the real Nana. It's my order. The one I give every Saturday morning when we meet for our weekly walk-and-talks, or on a random July Monday when my life has fallen apart.

Beside me, my sister sighs.

"You could branch out, you know." She points to a pink-frosted doughnut. "That one says Wine and Sunshine. Try it with me? I'm conducting serious doughnut research."

She looks over at me with a hopeful raise of her brows. Still, I shake my head and take my doughnut box from the cashier, who gives me a polite smile before reaching for another box and filling it with Kiersten's signature order of *Surprise me*.

The cashier hands the box to Kiersten, who doesn't even bother to wait until we've paid to bite into a dark-pink one and moan. "Oh sweet baby J, this thing is better than an orgasm. You have to try a bite." She holds the cream-filled confection up to my mouth.

"I'm good." I hold up my doughnut box. "Team fritter, remember?"

She takes another big bite and, after yet another head-turning moan, rolls her eyes overdramatically. "I would never knock Nana's fritters. But aren't you ever worried you're missing out on something incredible?"

I'm not.

Or at least not worried enough to order anything but my tried and true.

"Fritters are delicious," I tell her. "They've never left me disappointed."

My intention was not to use my doughnut-purchasing habits as a metaphor for my life. But at the word *disappointed*, something clicks in my brain, and the tears that I have managed to keep inside since the thirty designated minutes of cry-time I allow myself every morning make an unscripted appearance, rolling down my cheeks like midsummer raindrops.

"Stuart was supposed to be my apple fritter." My heart squeezes at the mention of my ex. *Why did I go and do that?* Say out loud, he-who-shall-not-be-named? It's the catalyst that turns my cute summer tears into an ugly thunderstorm. And it takes all of my self-restraint to stand there, avoiding the pitying looks of the cashier while Kierst pulls out her Visa card and pays. The moment the receipt is in her hand, I bolt back out to the sidewalk, where a real-estate-flyer box gives me enough support to close my eyes, turn my head to the sun, and try to forget the clusterfuck that is my love life.

"You okay, Gems?" My sister's hand finds the small of my back. This time, I don't mind so much the motherly circles of her palm over my denim jacket.

"He was supposed to be my future," I say between sobs. "We were gonna get a dog. Maybe a house. Or at least a really great condo with a walk-in closet. And now . . ."

Now he's my ex. An ex that didn't even have the common courtesy to give me the *it's not you, it's me* speech. In fact, he cited me and my dying enthusiasm for our relationship as the number one reason for ending the four years we invested in each other, surprising me in a way I didn't think he was capable of.

"I know this part really sucks." Kiersten wraps her arm around my shoulders and pulls my head to her boobs. "And aside from pumping you full of sugar, there's absolutely nothing I can say or do to make you feel better. But when your heart has had the chance to heal a little bit, I think you're going to see that Stuart was . . ." She hesitates for a moment. "Well, he kind of had the personality of a cardboard box, and you're way better off without him."

I'm about to defend my newly ex. Or maybe myself for staying with him for so long. But my phone vibrates in my pocket. And when I check the screen, the little dark cloud that's been following me around for the past three weeks is cut by a bright ray of sunshine.

Dax: Cool if we push back our hangout by an hour tonight? Got someone coming by. Kind of a big deal.

My heart gives a weird twitch.

Me: Date with the vet?

There's a long string of seconds before my phone pings back.

Dax: Nope canceled that so we could hang. Big client. At least I think it is. It's all very vague. I've been talking to his people all week.

Me: Your client has people? Look at you go!

Dax: Yeah. Maybe after we wallow for a bit tonight we can celebrate

Me: You get enough wine into me, I'm up for almost anything

I watch as three dots appear in our conversation bubble, disappear, then reappear and disappear again. When he does finally message back, all I get is a party hat.

My sister leans in, resting her chin on the little dip of my shoulder.

"If you're texting Stuart, so help me god, I'm taking back the pity fritters."

I hold up my phone as evidence. "Not Stuart. Just Dax. We're hanging out after work."

At the mention of Dax's name, Kiersten's eyebrows hitch up a good inch. "I thought you told me Daxon had a date tonight. With the vet?"

"She's a veterinarian's assistant," I counter. "And Stuart picked his stuff up today. Dax offered to cancel and hang out because he thought I might be upset."

Kiersten responds with an *mmmm-hmmm,* and I prepare for some sort of follow-up comment. Instead, she turns away, and we walk in silence in the direction of my condo. By the third block, I assume the subject has been dropped. Then she stops and fishes out a second doughnut from her box, but before she takes a bite, she pauses. "It was the third date if I recall. That's the sex date. He canceled his sex date for you."

"It's not that big of a deal."

Kierst bites into her doughnut, watching me.

"Stop giving me that look."

She holds up her hands. "This is how I look at everyone. If you are interpreting anything other than sisterly concern, that's on you."

My phone vibrates. It's Dax again. I ignore Kierst and text him back, letting him know he can come over whenever he finishes. The entire time, I can feel her eyes on me.

"You know what I think you should do tonight?" she asks.

My text whooshes out into cyberspace. "I have a very good idea *who* you think I should do."

Kiersten shrugs innocently. "He canceled his date for you. Plus, he's a total babe. I'd be all over that if I wasn't married."

"Kiersten."

"Seriously, the man wears jeans that leave nothing about that ass to the imagination."

"I don't know what that means."

"It means instead of waking up tomorrow morning to your

three alarm clocks, you could be waking up with whisker-burned thighs."

I don't know how to respond. So I stand, mouth still open in shock, as she licks a smudge of abandoned pink frosting from the corner of her lip and starts walking. Her extra three inches in height require me to run-walk to catch up.

"He's my best friend," I tell her, waving my hand in front of my currently non-whisker-burned region. "Doing *that* is not a friend activity."

She eyes my crotch. "Why not? I'd bet the rest of this dough-nut that Daxon McGuire is a generous lover."

My mouth drops open a second time. "Now you're making things up."

Kiersten pops what remains of the gambled doughnut into her mouth. "What did he bring you last month when you were in bed with strep throat?"

I know exactly where she is trying to go. He brought me soup. Homemade. It was delicious. "He got a Crock-Pot for Christmas, and he hadn't used it yet."

She lifts her chin, a huge smile spreading across her face be-cause she thinks she's won our argument. "Make all the excuses you want, Gemma. He wants you. And I think, once your heart has had a little bit more time to realize that Stuart was the fucking worst and you dodged a massive bullet, you'll realize that friends can easily become lovers."

Before I can tell her all of the flaws in her shoddy argument, my phone rings. Kiersten's eyebrows waggle as if she's anticipat-ing more evidence of her wild theory. I get a small sense of satis-faction in holding up my phone and showing her our elderly aunt's name flashing across the screen.

"What's up, Aunt Livi?" I press the phone to my ear and turn my back to my sister.

"Hello, poodle. Just checking in to see how the heart is healing today."

I swallow the lump that has suddenly appeared in my throat at the reminder that my love life is in shambles. "I'm attempting to cope with sugar, but it's not working so well."

There's a soft tinkle of wind chimes in the background on her end of the line. I know the sound well enough to tell that my aunt is in her bookshop and has either opened her front door or has her first customer of the day.

"Well, I called to tell you I have the perfect answer to all of your heart troubles. Why don't you come by for a visit tonight?"

I brace for her new age brand of weird. I've been the recipient of one too many of her healing tonics and cleansing teas not to have developed a healthy skepticism.

"Swing by around seven?" she asks.

"I'm supposed to hang out with Dax tonight."

"Perfect, the more the merrier. Bring your sister too."

I cover the microphone with my palm and turn back to face Kierst. "What are you up to tonight?"

She shrugs. "Watching *The Bachelor* so I can tell you who got kicked off, since you're a weirdo."

It's true. I can't watch that show without knowing who gets a rose. One of my many endearing quirks.

"Come to Aunt Livi's after the kiddos are in bed. She's gonna cure me."

She doesn't agree but instead opens her doughnut box for the third time, then snaps it shut and clutches her stomach. "Fine. I'll come. But if she suggests naked chanting again, I'm leaving."

I wave her off and return my attention to my aunt. "Need me to pick up anything?"

There is a short pause before she speaks. "Actually, yes. If you get a chance. We will need coarse salt, two Scotch bonnet peppers, and four triple-A batteries."

"Sounds good," I say, unsure how afraid I should be of this evening's plans.

I hang up the phone and realize that we are walking not back to my condo but to Kiersten's white minivan parked on a side street. She clicks her key fob, and the back door automatically slides open. She tosses her doughnut box onto a Cheerio-covered car seat and then reaches for the passenger door.

"Want a ride home?"

I shake my head. "I'm gonna walk. I won't get a Peloton workout in before Aunt Livi's. I have a six o'clock with some company in Shanghai that wants me to buy their revolutionary new dandruff shampoo. I'm dreading it already."

"Anytime you want to trade jobs, say the word. Although I recommend you sit through one of Riley's softball games first. Or a PTA meeting. Or what feels like monthly dentist appointments, as all three of my children seem to have inherited Trent's weak teeth. But today is not about my clusterfuck." She holds out her arms, and I let her envelop me in one last hug. She squeezes me tightly before pulling back and cupping my face with her hands.

"I'm glad you're coming tonight," I tell her. "I think a night with you, Aunt Livi, and Dax is exactly what I need."

She walks around to the driver's side, climbs in, and, as she's fastening her seatbelt, hits the button to roll down the passenger window. "You know what they say, Gems, breakups are hard." She winks. "But you know what else is hard?"

I shake my head.

"Dax's dick."

With that, she pulls out into the road. I can hear her laughing all the way to the four-way stop.

Chapter 2

MARGARITAS ARE NOT meant for Monday nights.

There's a reason why that old country song is famous. Tequila does indeed have the tendency to make your clothes fall off, or your lips say things they shouldn't, or, in my case, a combo of the two.

But I considered myself lucky that Aunt Livi's perfect cure for my aching heart turned out to be just her infamous margarita mix. Well, maybe I won't be so lucky tomorrow when I face the almost inevitable hangover that will hit me in the morning, but it could have been a lot worse. The peppers and salt were for the pot of chili she plans on serving for her Tuesday night book club. I have yet to learn the purpose of the batteries. And frankly, I'm too afraid of the answer to ask.

"I think that's the door." Kiersten lifts her head from the well-loved velvet fainting couch across from me, just enough to see over her margarita glass sitting on the coffee table between us.

I strain my ears to hear anything other than the Jimmy Buffett album *Songs You Know by Heart* blasting through Aunt Livi's ancient eighties stereo.

Sure enough, there's a soft *tap, tap, tap* coming from the apartment door. I swing my feet to the floor and decide, since I'm already sitting up, to reach for the coffee table and empty my glass of the remaining sloppy green liquid. The world spins a little as I stand, but I quickly right myself, giddiness flooding my stomach as I run to greet my best friend.

"Daxon McGuire, nice of you to show up!" I shout as I fling the door open to find him leaning on the doorframe, his non-leaning hand curled into a fist, ready to knock again.

His hair is wet from the rain, which curls the ends and turns its normal chestnut color a darker brown. He holds out his arms, and I immediately fold into the little nook under his chin. His henley is damp as he pulls me to his chest. But as his arms wrap around me, I feel this sense of comfort. Of familiarity. I breathe in his scent, Irish Spring soap and the faintest hint of something spicy.

"You smell good," I tell him.

He pulls away, and the loss of support makes me teeter a little. But his hands cup my shoulders, steadying me.

"You smell like you got the party started without me." His face cracks into a wide smile, and it makes me note the stubble on his cheeks. Dax always has stubble. I accuse him, almost daily, of being afraid of the razor. However, tonight it looks a little longer. As if he's let it go an extra day. My fingers find his cheek as if to confirm what my brain is thinking: that his face is not its usual scratchy texture.

"You a little drunk there, Gems?"

I become acutely aware that my face-touching is not normal for us—and possibly creepy. But when his palm covers mine and holds it against his cheek, I forget why this isn't something we do.

"It was an accident. Kiersten keeps doing this thing where she fills my glass up before it's empty. I lost count somewhere between two and a half and three and three-quarters. Jose Cuervo was not made for fractions. Then the ceiling started to get all spinny and . . ." I look down, only now fully realizing that I'm no longer wearing pants. "I got really hot."

Dax's eyes briefly sweep south before returning to my face. "Yeah, I was going to ask what happened there."

My memories are feeling a little fuzzy, but I distinctly remember having a perfectly rational reason for shedding my jeans. "I think I took them off to make a point. Something about turning over a new leaf. You are looking at wild and unpredictable Gemma. She drinks tequila on a work night. She doesn't need pants, or Stuart, for that matter."

I'm aware that I've named he-who-shall-not-be-named yet again, but Aunt Livi's margaritas seem to be doing the trick, and it doesn't sting so much to say it this time.

"I like pantsless Gemma"—Dax's gaze does another sweep—"but part of me wonders." He reaches past me to the pocket of my trench hanging next to the door, pulls out my phone, and swipes it open. Scrolling through the apps, he stops on the alarm clock and clicks. "Ah, just as I suspected. My predictable Gemma is still in there, setting her three backup alarms for the morning."

I grab the phone from his hand and attempt a scowl. But he's right. My leaf is still the same side up as always. "I also texted my concierge and bribed him with apple fritters to be my morning wake-up call," I tell him. "All of the Beauty Buyers have eight straight hours of quarterly sales and ops meetings tomorrow, and if I miss it, I'm gonna be totally fucked for Q3."

"You two gonna make googly eyes at each other all night, or are you gonna help me with this pitcher?"

Kiersten's voice both acts as a reminder that Dax and I are not alone and clears the brain fog enough to make me note that we're standing unnaturally close.

I take a step back, putting a normal friendship amount of distance between us, and gesture for him to take a seat.

Kiersten has my glass refilled and Dax's poured by the time we get to the couch. I take a sip of my half-melted drink, but Dax politely shakes his head. "I drove over here tonight."

Kiersten shrugs and takes the glass, turning toward Aunt Livi. "Need a refill?"

My elderly aunt is asleep on her La-Z-Boy, her mouth half-open, looking a tad bit deceased as her ancient corgi, Dr. Snuggles, curls in her lap.

"Is she okay?" Dax asks.

"Oh, she's fine," answers Kiersten, "just a one-margarita kind of woman, that's all. Hey, Aunt Livi—"

Kierst grabs the broken corner of a Cool Ranch Dorito from the bowl next to the margarita blender and chucks it at my aunt's open mouth.

Even though Kiersten was cut from her beer league softball team, the chip finds its target perfectly. There's a horrific thirty seconds where Aunt Livi breathes in and the chip sort of catches in her throat. Her eyes fly open as she makes this half-startled, half-scared face before Kiersten's mother-of-three instincts kick into action.

She pulls Aunt Livi to her feet while slapping her hard on the back. It takes three hard smacks before the chip flies out of Aunt Livi's mouth and across the living room to be forever lost in the orange shag carpeting.

"Good grief, what in the heck was that?" My aunt's face looks like an overripe tomato.

Kiersten hands her the margarita with a face of pure inno-
cence. "I think a paint chip fell from the ceiling and landed in
your mouth while you were snoring."

My aunt's eyes skim the peeling white paint above her as she
takes a long drink.

"Well, thanks, pudding." Aunt Livi hands Kiersten the now-
empty glass. "I owe you one."

She looks around her living room, her eyes stopping on Dax,
who was not there when she fell asleep. "Oh, Daxon, it's lovely to
see you. You're looking as dapper as always."

Dax blushes and gets up from his seat to give her a kiss on the
cheek. I catch Kiersten enjoying her view of Dax's ass as he bends
over. She catches my eye and winks, and I feel my own cheeks
heating.

"You woke up just in time, Aunt Livi," Kiersten says. "We
were just about to start the part of the night where we roast Stuart mercilessly."

My aunt looks over at me as if asking if I've signed on to this
activity. I shrug, figuring it's cheaper than therapy.

"Do you want to start us off?" Kierst asks Dax.

He shakes his head, also eyeing me. "Ladies first."

Kiersten licks the salted rim of her glass, then sits on the lounger,
flopping her head in my direction. "Before I say what I'm going
to say, you're absolutely sure you and Stu aren't going to kiss and
make up, right?"

My mind drifts back to our breakup three weeks ago. "I threw
a full glass of merlot on his blue Tom Ford suit. He didn't speak
to me for three days after that time when I had a bloody nose,
and some droplets splattered on his khakis. And they were only
J.Crew and it was an accident."

Kiersten snorts. Likely because she has always thought Stuart was too precious. I purposely kept the nosebleed story from her because of it.

"I think you were more in love with the idea of Stuart than the actual person," she says.

My urge to glare at her is stifled by the realization that her words eerily echo Stuart's from our breakup.

"You liked Stu because he had his life together," she continues. "And a swanky apartment."

This time, I do glare. "You make me sound like a heartless gold digger."

Kiersten takes a long sip of her drink. "That's not what I meant. At least not like a money gold digger. But maybe an emotional one."

I'm too angry to respond. Or maybe too drunk. Either way, Kiersten takes my silence as a license to continue.

"Stuart was safe. He was easy. He gave you the predictability you craved. He was the human equivalent of toast and butter, but you can only live off of toast and butter for so long." She gets up from her spot on the lounger and moves to wedge herself between Daxon and me on the couch, taking my hand in hers.

"I get your need for toast and butter, Gems. Hell, with the winners we scored as parents, I understand it completely. But I think you've swung the pendulum a little too far in the opposite direction. You need a little spice in your life."

Kiersten thinks that all her time spent in therapy qualifies her to psychoanalyze me and my life. Our parents were, to put it simply, duds. Married young, my mom was often off finding herself, leaving Kierst and me to source our own dinners. My dad flipped between being unemployed with a regular seat at the local bar to rather gainfully employed at a remote oil field camp in Northern Alberta. So maybe she's not too far off in her theory that their emotional damage drove me to someone so predictable and consistent. I liked how Stuart would drive in from Toronto every Friday night to take me to Fornello's Italian Eatery. He'd have the grilled chicken and merlot and always offer to share. After dinner, we'd have mediocre missionary sex because every other position aggravated his old soccer hip injury, but he'd tell me it was because he liked looking in my eyes when I came. I always knew what to expect with Stu. A cashmere crewneck every Christmas, a *You look great* whether I showed up in lululemon or a negligee. You could give the man thirty-one flavors of ice cream, and he'd always choose vanilla. I know it's messed up, but I found the monotony comforting.

Kierst squeezes my hands. "Think of it this way. You and Stu were done years ago, but you were too set in your ways to admit it. This is good. For both of you. Eventually, you need to stop watering dead plants."

Again I don't say anything. I avoid her eyes, and Dax's, for that matter, wondering how the fuck this turned from roasting Stuart into an intervention. Tonight was supposed to be fun.

"You're mad at me." She says it like a statement.

I pull my hands from hers. "I think you should stick to analyzing your own life and leaving mine alone."

She crosses her arms over her chest. "You're probably right. And I'm done. Said my piece. Over to you, Dax."

She stands, picks up the empty glasses from the coffee table, and takes them to the kitchen. I'm left with the option to stare at my hands or meet Dax's green eyes, which I do.

"Do your worst," I say, but inside I think I'm done with this activity. It's starting to seep in. That sinking feeling you get when you've made a mistake but then gained enough perspective to overanalyze every wrong turn or poor life decision. All of the wrongs that led you to invest four years in a man who irons his boxer briefs. Yes, Stuart kind of sucked. I'm starting to see that more and more. Still, I'm the sucker who stayed with him for so long. Doesn't that mean, by default, that I sort of suck too?

"Well . . ." Dax clears his throat, looking as uncomfortable with all of this as I am. "I think Stuart's an idiot. He never appreciated what he had, and I think you deserve someone better." I've heard this statement before. From friends. From my sister. It's a canned response for anyone who has taken a flying elbow to the heart. But the way Dax says it makes me believe that I deserve more than a man who left my twenty-seventh birthday party after an hour because it conflicted with his CrossFit.

Our conversation is interrupted by the aggressively loud buzzing of Aunt Livi's doorbell announcing the arrival of the pizza.

"I'll get that." I get to my feet, grab my wallet, and move as fast as my tequila-fueled body can take me out Livi's apartment door and down the stairs that lead to the back door to her bookshop. I return a few moments later with a steaming cardboard box that makes drool pool beneath my tongue.

The living room is empty. The sounds in the six-hundred-square-foot apartment hint that Kiersten is on the phone in the bedroom and Dax is in the bathroom. Aunt Livi is in the kitchen, pulling plates from the cupboard. I set the pizza down on the counter beside her. Before I can remove my hand, she covers it with one of hers and squeezes. "How are you holding up there, poodle?" She opens the pizza box, loads a slice onto a plate, and hands it to me.

I take it and walk around to the living-room side of the two-stooled galley window that separates the little kitchenette from her living room.

"Heart is numb thanks to Kiersten's bartending skills. The rest of me wishes I could go back to the night I met Stuart so I could tell him to fuck right off."

As the words leave my mouth, I feel it. That pang of anger,

deep within my chest, aimed not at Stuart but myself. It grows and grows until it becomes so heavy it snaps, then drops to the pit of my stomach, where it acts as a solid reminder of all the times I knew Stu and I weren't meant for forever and ignored it. A reminder of all the other things I could have done if only I would have had the guts to walk away from the relationship.

Aunt Livi shakes her head and tuts. "Oh, you don't mean that." She opens the box and pulls out her own slice of pizza, her gray eyes assessing me with concern.

I take a bite. The hot cheese burns the tender skin on the roof of my mouth, forcing me to *hiffaw* until it cools enough to swallow.

"I do. If you told me your Prius had a flux capacitor, I'd be hauling my ass back to the night I met Stuart at that bar, where I'd tell him to move right along."

Kiersten appears at my side at the same time Dax enters the kitchen. My sister hands me another margarita. A peace offering. I take a long sip and sigh into my once-again half-empty cup. "I gave four of my prettiest years to that man and have zero to show for it."

"You have me." Dax says it so quietly from the corner of the kitchen that I almost don't hear him. "We met that night as well, remember?"

Yes, we did. I almost forgot. Dax was there that night too. It was Stuart's birthday party, but Dax had tagged along with a high school friend who was a co-worker of Stu's. We had a few fleeting moments together before Stuart swept in, ready to woo.

"You were the best thing to happen to me that night, Daxon B.," I tell him. "Too bad it took me four years to see it."

I mean it as a joke. Or a slight at Stuart. But Dax doesn't laugh or smile.

"Well, I don't have a time machine," Aunt Livi muses, "but I did get a rather interesting book in the donation bin this week. Maybe it could help?"

A book.

I guess I should be grateful it's not another aura-cleansing bubble bath.

I love my aunt and her unwavering belief that all of the world's problems can be solved with the right book, but I don't foresee how any work of literature will help me tonight. I'm beyond self-help.

But I'm also too drunk to argue. So I shrug and shovel one last piece of veggie-lover's pizza into my stomach in hopes that it will make for a more bearable morning tomorrow.

The three of us follow Aunt Livi down the back steps to her store, which is less of a traditional bookshop and more of a curated collection of weird and wonderful things. She claims to have the biggest collection of monster erotica in the northern hemisphere. But if you're not into milking minotaurs or dendrophilia (I once made the mistake of googling that—do not recommend), you can also find healing crystals, ancestral incense, and salts of the black, pink, Himalayan, or table variety.

It was my favorite place in the world as a kid.

When my homelife sucked, it offered refuge and familiarity. Its dark corners provided a place to escape and its owner a source of constant and unconditional love. As my high school years approached, the store became more of a humiliating secret. My tween-aged heart longed to be anything but the girl whose parents abandoned her to that weird-smelling shop on James. Now, as a partially functioning adult, I have enough perspective to appreciate it, as well as my Aunt Livi. It's confident in what it is, unapologetic about what it's not, and the one and only place on earth that has ever felt like home.

The store is completely dark until Aunt Livi flips a light switch, illuminating the chandelier-like light fixture that hangs in the middle of the ceiling. It's just a series of colored bulbs hanging from wires, like an eighth-grade science diorama of our solar system, but I've always sworn that the bulbs shift and move when you're not looking.

"Now, where is that book?" Aunt Livi places her hands on her hips and turns a slow 360 on the spot. "I was reading it earlier, but then I did something with it, and I can't for the life of me remember what." She makes eye contact with me and points toward a dark corner of the store. "Why don't you and Daxon check that section? If I shelved it already, it would be down there. Kiersten can take that pile near the front door. I'll check around the cash register."

I eye the floor-to-ceiling shelves that divide the store like a garden maze.

"What exactly are we looking for?"

Aunt Livi waves me off. "I can't quite remember the cover. It's a book. Big. You'll know it when you see it."

There are at least a hundred books down that dark corridor. But I've learned over the years to pick my battles with my eccentric aunt, and I'm two tequilas too far in to win this one. So I follow Dax as he weaves his way toward the back, scanning the shelves for nothing in particular, until he reaches a dead end and turns around.

"Any ideas on how to find this thing?"

I shrug, but as I do, a very Aunt Livi–like thought occurs.

"I think we should listen to the books. Let them speak to us."

Dax, who is the most practical human I've ever known but also the first to agree to anything that could be ridiculous fun, reaches his hand up to the shelf, letting his fingers run along the spines of the books. He closes his eyes and hums in a monotone voice.

"The book that will cure Gemma Wilde of all her problems

is . . ." He pulls a thick white-covered book from the shelf and holds it up. "*Healing Your Inner Child in Ten Easy Steps.*"

He turns it over to examine its cover, which shows a tiny blond girl, eerily similar to an eight-year-old me.

"That's disturbingly accurate." I take the book from his hands and shove it back on the shelf. "But I need at least fourteen steps to cover all of my daddy issues. We better skip to your turn." I close my eyes and let my fingers roam over the shelves, just as Dax did a moment ago, until I feel a sudden urge to stop. "What book will solve all Daxon McGuire's problems?" I blindly pull a large hardcover from the shelf. As I hold it up, my eyes skim the title. My cheeks heat as I realize my fuckup.

"*101 Mind-Blowing Tantric Sex Positions.*" Dax's eyebrows lift as he reads the title.

Dax and I rarely talk about our sex lives. We make jokes about sex, in the general sense. But in the world of Dax and Gemma, real talk on the subject is taboo.

"Interesting choice. Maybe we should . . ." His voice trails off as he takes the book from my hands.

For a split second, I interpret the ending as a "Maybe we should try out position forty-three? Or maybe a twenty-seven if you're up for it?"

I can actually feel the sensation of my blood draining from my face as the image of a naked, sweaty Dax flashes in my vision.

Until Dax places the book back in its spot and nods at something over my shoulder. "Head back? I think your aunt found the book."

He holds out his hand as if to say, *After you, Gemma.* I'm grateful that I am able to turn my back because I'm worried he'll read my expression and clue in to the entire scene that just happened in my head. He has the tendency to do that. Figure me out when I'm still unsure of my own thoughts.

When we exit the book maze, Aunt Livi is in fact standing next to the cash counter with a large, brown leather book cradled in her hands.

"I was skimming this in between customers today, and I think it has exactly what you need."

I join her at the counter, where she sets the book down in front of me. *Practical Magic: A Complete Guide for the Modern Mystic* is clearly not a self-help book. Its pages are yellowed with age, and the writing looks handwritten, as if the book was once a journal. At the top of the open page, written in loopy blue letters, are the words *Love Cleanse*.

"Is that a recipe?" Kiersten's boobs press against my back as she leans forward to get a closer look, her strawberry-blond hair falling on my shoulder.

"*To cut the cord of the one who has wronged you,*" she reads, "*follow these simple steps*—oh, hell no." Kiersten pushes the book away. "I'm already getting bad vibes from that thing. I've watched enough Harry Potter movies to know nothing good ever comes from reading aloud from a creepy old book."

"Oh, come on," Aunt Livi chides, "it's just for fun."

The floorboards creak as Dax crosses the room to join us. He reaches for the book, rubbing its aging yellow pages between the tips of his thumb and index finger, the comforting scent of his soap filling my nose.

"What do you think, Dax? If things go sideways, are you up for hiding a body tonight? I think it's worth the risk to rid Stuart from my life."

Dax's eyes skim the page. "I knew there was a reason I keep a shovel in my trunk."

Aunt Livi takes Dax's comment as consent and rips the book from my hands, barking orders to the three of us.

She sends Kiersten off in search of her old knitting bag, since this cord-cutting spell is not entirely metaphorical, and orders a reluctant Dax back up to the apartment kitchen to seek out chicken feet.

"Gemma, love," she says to me. "Fetch me a candle."

I search the cramped drawer under the cash register where she stores anything that doesn't have a proper place in her store, then hold up the two best options.

"I would have thought you'd have a better stash of creepy candles, but it looks like you only have a birthday candle or one of those battery-powered ones you stick in the window at Christmas."

Her brow furrows as her eyes flick from my hands to the scrawled directions on the page in front of her. "We need an actual fire."

I close the junk drawer with my hip. "Birthday candle it is."

"Daxon," she calls out loudly. "Where are we at with the chicken feet?"

Dax comes down the stairs a moment later, holding a red-topped Tupperware container. "I have secured jerk chicken thighs. Not exactly what you asked for, but the best we're gonna get tonight."

She takes the container from his hands and sets it down on the cash counter in front of her before beckoning me to take a seat at the barstool she keeps for customers who come to chitchat.

Kiersten emerges from Aunt Livi's back office with a ball of hot-pink yarn, which she hands to Aunt Livi as she reads aloud from the book.

"Once lovers, now enemies,
Soon to be strangers with some memories,
This love cleanse will rid you of your woes."

Aunt Livi pauses for a moment, but her eyes continue to skim the page as if she's reading silently to herself. This is the point where I'm usually rolling my eyes with Kiersten, but I find myself waiting on edge for her to continue.

She clears her throat.

"But if you wish to wipe away,
The memories of the very day,
A choice was made,
A path was taken,
Another lifetime long forsaken.
Light the wick,
Curse the day,
Cut the cord,
Send away,
The one that wronged you,
under waning gibbous
But be forewarned—"

Aunt Livi pauses, then licks her thumb and rubs the page in front of her with a soft grunt.

"Uh . . . you gonna tell us what comes next?" Kiersten tries to peek over her shoulder at the book, but Livi's oversized cardigan blocks the way. "Or are we just gonna ignore that whole cryptic-warning part?"

Aunt Livi squints at the book, moving so close that her nose almost touches the paper.

"There appears to be some sort of stain on the directions." She sniffs. "I suspect salsa. But don't fret." She sets it on the counter with a bang. "I think I've got it."

Reaching for the small yellow pad she keeps next to an old

rotary phone, my aunt tears off a blank sheet, then plucks a blue Bic from a mug of mismatched pens and pencils, handing both the paper and pen to me.

"Write Stuart's name down."

It's a command, and my blood alcohol level has me complying with little argument.

Aunt Livi picks up the sparkly white birthday candle and produces a lighter from her pocket. A tiny yellow flame ignites the wick, and she holds the candle out in front of her. "Now picture the night you met Stuart. Imagine him in that bar. Think about the moment you decided to see him again."

The dancing yellow flame combined with Aunt Livi's soothing voice is mesmerizing. I envision Stuart's face. His expensive gray suit, intense blue eyes, and the way he made me feel like everything in my life was going to work out fine.

"Now," Aunt Livi continues, "imagine walking away."

I picture myself leaving that crowded bar and getting into a cab alone. "Have a nice life, Stuart," I whisper. "I don't think I was ever meant to be a part of it."

When I open my eyes, the candle has already begun to melt, dripping tiny balls of waxy teardrops.

"Next," my aunt instructs. "Hold the paper with his name up to the flame."

Lifting my offering to the burning candle, I watch as the flames skitter across the surface, only letting go once the heat reaches my fingertips. The paper falls to the counter, and we all watch as the yellow sheet turns to ash and the flames move to burn the linoleum beneath.

"Oh, for the love of god." Kiersten pours the remaining margarita from her glass onto the now-singed counter, extinguishing the fire and leaving a black smudge in its place. "The fact that I am the only functioning adult in this room right now is scaring me a little."

Aunt Livi, seemingly unperturbed by her damaged countertop, ignores her and blows out the candle. "Now we need the cord."

Dax hands her the ball of pink yarn. She pulls scissors from the junk drawer and cuts off a piece that's roughly the length from her elbow to her fingertips. Pulling my hands into prayer position, she deftly wraps the yarn around both my wrists, tying them together with a tight knot.

"I'd be throwing out the S and M jokes right about now, Aunt Livi," I say. "If I wasn't afraid you'd maim me, or worse, tell me a story I'd never be able to unhear."

She pats the top of my head. "You're not quite ready for my stories there, poodle." She turns to Dax. "What's the next step, Daxon? The writing is too small. I can't make it out without my glasses."

Dax pulls the book toward him and squints down at the pages.

"The final step, do not be remiss,
Is to seal your fate with a kiss."

He looks over at me, his eyes a darker shade of green than I ever remember seeing. "I think it says we need a kiss."

Kiersten once again snorts. "A kiss, eh? Over to you, big boy. I knew we invited you tonight for a reason."

My cheeks immediately flush, which I blame on the booze, not the fact that Dax looks like he wishes he was anywhere but here.

"You don't have to . . ." I attempt to wriggle out of the binding my aunt has somehow expertly tied, knowing that, as uncomfortable as this is for me, it's got to be worse for Dax.

"I'm sure Dax doesn't mind." Aunt Livi practically shoves him into my lap. "It's all for a bit of fun."

I look into Dax's green eyes and think I see the reflection of the birthday candle flame, which is silly, since we extinguished it minutes ago.

"You're sure you're okay with this?" he asks.

"Are *you* sure?" I fire back.

The only answer I get is Kierst holding her margarita glass up to my lips. "Need a little liquid courage there, Gems?"

I drink, despite knowing that more tequila and kissing Dax are both terrible ideas. That this—all of this—is so bizarre that I'm going to kick myself when I wake up in the morning.

"It's fine," I tell her, then turn to Dax. "We'll make it fast."

I close my eyes, the obvious step one of any kiss—coerced or not. It provides the added benefit of no longer seeing Kiersten in the background making humping motions with her hips. And although all I can see is blackness, I can sense Dax only inches away.

It's just a silly kiss. The fluttering happening in my belly is only because it's been a while since my lips have touched anyone's but Stuart's.

I lick them and try to remember the last time I brushed my teeth.

But what if Kiersten was right this afternoon? What if this kiss leads to a second? And then I'm waking up in the morning next to him. And then one day, it's Dax telling me *It's not me, it's you.* There isn't a margarita in the world that could help me after that.

"No!" My eyes fly open and see Dax's closed ones only inches away.

Dax opens one eye, then the other.

"I think . . ." I search my brain for the right words. Ones that convey it's not him. It's the consequences.

"I really need to pee."

I get up, ignoring the odd look in Dax's eyes. Ignoring the fact that my hands are still tied. Ignoring Kiersten, leaning on the counter, muttering to herself, "What the hell were we supposed to do with the chicken?"

Chapter 3

I'VE HIT THAT stage of drunk where I could be easily persuaded to go to bed or dance until dawn. It's a toss-up.

However, after I spend twenty minutes too long in the bathroom, Aunt Livi makes the decision for me. She buttons me into my trench coat, finds my purse and the keys with my Dr. Snuggles keychain, and makes Dax promise—twice—that he'll get me home safely.

And he does.

He walks me right to my condo door and waits patiently while I attempt to slip my keys into the lock and open it.

My alarm beeps as the door swings open. We both know there's zero probability I'll punch in the password correctly and a far more likely chance that the alarm company gets called. He gently moves me aside and punches in my passcode, Dr. Snuggles's birthday, then stands in the doorway watching as I stumble into my living room, flop onto the couch, hit the cushions with a little too much force, and subsequently bounce off and roll onto the floor.

Fuck, I love my carpet. It was an obscenely expensive Crate & Barrel purchase, but it feels like it's made of velvet. I run my arms and legs over the soft fabric until Dax looms above me, holding out his hands.

"Come on, Gems. We need to get a little more water into you before you pass out." I let him pull me to my feet and lead me to my open-concept kitchen. The white marble countertops shine under the pot lights.

I also love my condo. It's not huge, but it's beautiful. Light-gray broad-board hardwood floors complement the concrete walls. The north one is made almost entirely of glass, with an unobstructed view of Hamilton Harbor. A winding wrought-iron staircase leads to a loft with a low platform bed and a non-walk-in closet, which will now be considerably roomier seeing that Stuart, the asshole, picked up all of his stuff.

We never decided to cohabitate, Stuart and I. Although he stayed at my place every weekend, he was never keen on committing permanently to the hour commute to his banking job in Toronto. I, on the other hand, didn't want to lose proximity to my aunt and sister. In hindsight, it may have been a relationship red flag. Like somehow, deep down, I knew the end was inevitable, and that's why I needed a backup plan. A safety net. Assurance that if everything went to shit, I'd still be okay.

"Here, drink up." Dax hands me a glass of cold water. "It will make for a better morning."

I take a small sip followed by a long gulp. "Margaritas were a terrible idea. I have, like, ten straight hours of meetings tomorrow."

Dax takes a second glass from my cupboard and fills it for himself. "Well, you could call in sick and hang with me. We could Uber Eats breakfast sandwiches and watch Netflix all day?"

That's exactly what I want to do, but I can't. My job as a hair-and-body products buyer at Canada's largest drugstore chain is surprisingly cutthroat considering I spend a large portion of my life anticipating whether Canadians are going to prefer smelling like lavender or ocean breezes next spring.

"I need a decent close to this quarter. Marley from finance is going on maternity leave next month, and if I want a shot at her job, I need to keep reminding them how good I'd be at it."

"I thought you said Marley's job was the worst."

It totally is. Finance is a slog meant for the soulless. "It has a nice paycheck. And I like nice paychecks." Not to mention the comfort that comes with having a little extra padding in the bank.

Dax takes my now-empty glass from my hand, opens my fridge, and pulls out my Brita for a refill. He shuts the door and stares at a Kijiji printout picture of an English bulldog puppy. "Who's this?"

I remove the magnet from the picture and cradle it in my hands. "That's Buster."

Dax lifts a curious eyebrow.

"Stuart and I were talking about getting a puppy. I wanted to give him a people name like Justin or Bradley, but Stuart said that was ridiculous. So we settled on Buster."

The sadness returns. I'm too drunk to figure out if I'm mourning Stuart or the dog. Either way, the feeling builds in my stomach until it fills my entire chest. I'm a fish tank with a crack. The fragile glass is fighting the pressure of the water, holding on as the crack grows and spreads, threatening to burst at any moment.

I tip my head back and gulp down my water. A last-ditch attempt to wash away all of the emotions inside me. With the last drop gone, I slam the empty glass down on the countertop. But instead of the typical *ping* of glass on marble, the sound we hear is more of a crunch.

"Ew!" I hold up the empty glass and the quarter-sized dark smudge on the bottom of it. "What the hell is that?"

Dax takes the glass from my hand and studies it. "Looks like a little spider." He takes a paper towel from the roll, wipes away the carnage, and hands it back to me. "What's wrong?"

My chest feels heavy, and my eyes are filling with tears as waves of remorse roll over me. My internal fish tank shatters.

"I murdered him," I sob. "I did. He was just crawling along minding his own business, and I snuffed the life right out of him."

"It was just a spider, Gems."

He doesn't understand. That spider did nothing wrong. He was just hanging out, trying to put one hairy leg in front of the other, and he got his life demolished. "Yeah, but he probably had a wife." A terrible thought occurs to me. "Oh my god, what if he had, like, little baby spiders?"

Dax takes the glass from my hand again. "Gems, I think you're really drunk."

"I know." I look down at my naked legs. "Where are my pants?"

Dax takes me by the shoulder and steers me toward my swirly staircase. "You left them at Livi's. We tried, but you insisted you never wanted to wear pants again."

Then I remember. "Oh yeah, right, pants are the worst."

Dax's hand is on my back as I stumble up the steps. When I look back, I laugh at the sight of his intentionally turned head, doing its best to avoid my underpanted ass. When we reach my room, I swan-dive onto my bed, rolling over to the side. I watch him watching me.

"You should take yours off too, join the movement, Dax." I kick my liberated legs to illustrate my point.

Dax stands by the stairs, looking uncomfortable. "I don't think that would be a very good idea."

I wiggle until I'm sitting up on my elbows. "Why the hell not?"

"Because . . ." He hesitates. "It just wouldn't."

I flip onto my back. "Suit yourself, no-pants party for one."

I attempt what can most accurately be described as a waterless backstroke until my words seep through the tequila and sink in.

Oh god. . . .

Oh god. . . .

"Oh god."

I roll my head back toward Dax. "I'm going to die alone, aren't I?"

He comes to the end of my bed and sits down. "What are you talking about?"

This breakup with Stuart is an omen.

"I am going to be having a one-person no-pants party for the rest of my life."

The tears return. Rolling and tumbling down my cheeks as I envision a lifetime of tiny closets and Lean Cuisine dinners for one.

"What if Stuart was my person? My one shot at a decent relationship and I fucked it up! Like I hit my peak, and now it's all downhill."

Dax reaches out his thumb and wipes a tear from my cheek. "Stuart was not your person."

"How do you know that?"

"I know." His voice is so firm. Assured. "Stuart was not the guy."

"You have to say that because you're my best friend."

"No." He looks up at me with a look I cannot decipher. "It's because I'm your best friend that I *shouldn't* say that."

Something is off between us. It's like there's some invisible tension, and it's weird and thick like honey. It makes it hard to think. So I default to feeling. Giving in to that big ball of ache that formed in my gut when Stuart gently explained that he'd fallen out of love. The tears multiply. Long gone are the cute movie-screen trickles, replaced with big black mascara-filled drops.

"Hey, hey, hey. Don't cry." The pad of Dax's thumb catches a falling tear, wiping it away.

"I'm trying my best over here, but tequila makes me really, really sad. Can you, like, tell me a joke or something?"

Dax thinks for a moment. "What about a story? It's about the night we first met."

I am about to remind him that the night we met is the same night that I met Stuart. The very person I'm not supposed to be thinking about right now. But Dax nudges me with his hip until I move over enough so he can fit his full ass on my bed, and by the time I remember to tell him to stop—he's already started.

"I was having a pretty shitty day. I was still living in my mom's basement, and she was making it clear that she wanted to move up north and having her adult son still living at home was cramping her style. And I was still looking for someone to invest in my business so I could finally get it off the ground. And I got dragged out to a birthday party for a guy I didn't even like. I was miserable. And about ready to head home when I saw this girl at the bar, and somehow I knew that if I talked to her, she'd change my life.

"So . . . ." he continues. "I did. And turned out she was one of the funniest people I've ever met."

"You *are* talking about me, right?"

He picks up my spare pillow and knocks me with it. "Yes. I'm talking about you. You made an impression."

His comment is followed by a moment of silence that stretches into two, prompting me to end it.

"Then we became friends and you learned the error of your ways?"

He opens his mouth as if he's about to say something, then stops and instead brushes a sweaty strand from my forehead and tucks it behind my ear. "I can say that after four years hanging out with you, Gems, there's no doubt in my mind that you're the real deal. If there's a flaw in you, I can't find it."

Dax doesn't do empty compliments. If anything, his love language is affection in the form of well-meaning teasing. So this story, this moment, feels different. "Thank you for saying that." I reach up and scratch his chin. "Who knew that under all these scruffles was a closet sweetheart."

He takes my hand and squeezes. "Yeah, well, I'm banking on you not remembering half of this in the morning."

His fingers linger, cupping my hand. Warm and strong. They fill my head with fleeting thoughts. Musings only allowed on lonely late nights or after too much tequila. I open my mouth, wondering what will spill out, and am half-surprised that what does come is laughter. Hysterical sob-laughs that make my stomach hurt until I clutch my knees to my chest and force myself to draw deep breaths.

"I think that's my cue to leave." Dax gets up, but before he can go, I grab his hand.

"Tuck me in?"

He pauses for a beat, but then peels back the corner of my covers and waits until I crawl under to pull them back over me.

"And a hug?" I open my arms. Again he hesitates before leaning forward and letting me wrap my arms around him.

I breathe him in. "You always smell good. Like soap but spicy."

He tries to pull back, but my grip is strong for my intoxication level.

"Uh . . . thank you."

"I love you, Dax," I whisper into his ear.

"I think that's Jose Cuervo talking."

I let go so I can look at him. "No, it's true. You are my best friend. And the best guy. And the best ever."

"That's a lot of bests."

It is. And I mean every one. "I don't know what I'd ever do without you."

"You'd spend significantly more time wandering the streets of Hamilton without pants."

"It's good that we never screwed things up between us, right?" I ask him, once again thinking about what Kiersten said this afternoon.

His forehead crinkles. "What do you mean?"

"I mean sex. It's good that it never happened."

He looks away before bringing his gaze slowly back. "Have you thought a lot about this?"

No. Or maybe? I mean, yes. What I mean is that I haven't *not* thought about it. But what I know for sure, deep down in my bones, is that I don't want to live in a world where he's not in my life.

"You're my best friend. If we had sex, everything could change. I don't want that." I reach for his hand, but he moves it.

"You're right. It would."

I extend my arms for another hug, but Dax stands up, then abruptly walks to the top of the stairs. As he flicks the light off, I call out to him, "Good night, Daxon McGuire."

He turns, hand on the banister, weight shifting from heel to toe as if he's deciding something.

"I wish that . . ." He doesn't finish the thought.

"You wish what?" I suddenly need to hear what he has to say.

Frowning, he bows his head. "Never mind. Night, Gems."

I hear him descend the stairs. The *clank, clank, clank* as he gets farther and farther away. In a moment, he'll be gone—I panic.

"Wait!"

I scramble to my feet, flip on the light, and peer down the staircase just as Dax reaches the bottom. "Don't go!"

"It's late, Gems. We both should get to bed."

"You can't go yet." He can't. Because Stuart. Because he never did finish that last thought. Because . . .

"Do you need something else?" he asks.

An excuse. A reason for him to stay.

"We never finished the spell."

I descend the stairs with a composure and grace I didn't know was in me.

"I know I stopped it before, but I really think we should complete it. Start tomorrow with a new leaf, right?"

His eyes flick to the door, but he nods. "If that's what you want."

I don't have the birthday candle. Or the yarn, or even the chicken. "Maybe we just try picking up where we left off?"

There's no need to explain which step that was.

Dax nods and steps toward me as I squeeze my eyes shut and wait.

This is a bad idea. This is a terrible idea. This is the worst idea I have ever had and—

Dax's lips are on mine.

It's a simple kiss. No tongue and he lingers for only a moment, but it's nothing like I expected. His lips are velvet soft, and I catch a whiff of mint as he presses them to mine, and I am overcome with this strange sense that I've remembered something I didn't know I'd forgotten.

"How's the heart?" he whispers, his hands still cupping my chin.

I don't know. It's tired. It's drunk. It's worried everything is going to change.

"Still a little broken, I think."

Dax doesn't say a word. And even though my eyes are closed,

I can sense that he's still close. The solid, steady presence that's been an anchor for the past four years of my life.

"Get some rest. I'll call you in the morning."

I feel him step away. When I finally open my eyes, Dax is already halfway across the room, reaching for my front door.

I'm left standing in my kitchen, wondering if I'm going to wake up tomorrow morning and regret all of it.

Chapter 4

EVEN BEFORE I open my eyes, I know that something is off.

It's not the throbbing pain that stretches between my temples or the way my stomach churns unless I lay absolutely still. It's the smell—AXE body spray and bacon—that alerts me to the fact that I am not in my own bed.

I crack open one eye, followed by the other. Sunlight streams in from a big bay window, illuminating a room that looks sparsely furnished on purpose. My naked butt is sprawled in the center of a California king covered in a cotton sheet so soft I estimate it took at least a thousand Egyptian threads to make it. It's raining. No—someone is showering.

Despite my sour stomach, I manage to turn my head in the direction of the sound. It's coming from behind a closed door. Most likely a bathroom. I deduce this just in time to hear the distinct sound of a shower being turned off. Then, with every available brain cell, I piece together the sounds of a shower door opening and closing. A towel being rubbed vigorously over a body. Then a lock being flipped, and a door handle turning. *Oh fuck.*

He emerges from a cloud of steam, like a cheesy sitcom fantasy scene. And I swear to god, I've never seen him before in my life.

"Oh hey, good. You're up." He rubs his still-wet black hair in a lazy way that conveys he's not surprised to see me in his bed.

I assume this is his bed, as it is very much not mine.

What the hell happened last night?

I have a very fuzzy memory of diving into my bed. Then stumbling back downstairs. Then kissing Dax. Then nothing.

Holy hell, I kissed Dax.

I need to unpack that memory. Somewhere safe. When I'm able to really assess the carnage of that particular grenade on our friendship. Right now, I have more pressing problems. Like, this man is not Dax. And I have no idea where I am.

I take a second look at my surroundings. There's a city outside the window. An early-morning sun peeking up over the horizon. And, yes, a semi-naked man at the end of the bed.

What did you do, Gemma?

My best guess is that I must have gone out, hit up a bar, and gone home with a stranger.

"I'm making breakfast," the stranger says. "I know bacon is not your thing, but you don't normally spend the night, so I wasn't prepared."

I'd be insulted that this rando has clearly mixed me up with another of his one-night-stands if I wasn't still attempting to piece together what the hell I got up to last night.

And looking for the nearest exit.

And my pants.

And freaking the fuck out.

"That's okay," I respond like things are completely fine. "I am not hungry." Just very confused and wondering what I'm gonna do next.

My stranger tosses the hand towel he was using on his hair onto the end of the bed and proceeds to open and close his dresser drawers, pulling out a pair of red boxer briefs and black dress socks.

My head is throbbing. My tongue feels like cheap velvet in my mouth. Although I really should be continuing to panic, or planning my escape, or something else much more logical, I'm waylaid as Horny Gemma takes over and instead, I pause to check the man out.

At least in my very inebriated state last night, I had the good sense to pick up a specimen.

His body is well muscled but lean in the right places. Great arms. Great abs. And judging from the curve of the white towel tied around his waist, great ass.

"You interested in some action before work?" He smirks, having caught me staring.

Before I have a chance to answer, he drops his towel.

And *oh! Ohhhhh* . . . My eyes drop low. He's only half-hard and yet already pretty impressive.

He moves toward the bed, taking my ogling as acceptance of his invitation.

"I can't." I spring from the mattress with surprising agility, grabbing the very tiny hand towel in a pitiful attempt to cover up. "I . . . um . . . have a big meeting this morning and really need to get going." It's not entirely a lie, but it's the least of my worries at this moment.

"You sure? Believe it or not, I can be quick."

I skim the room frantically, looking for my clothes, and spy them neatly folded on a chair. "Very sure." I pull on my favorite jeans and a sweater that I swear went missing three months ago. My panties are nowhere to be found, but at this moment, I'm willing to accept them as collateral damage for getting out of here as soon as possible. I lunge for the door, still buttoning up my pants as I move, but as I reach the threshold, the panic in my brain recedes enough for a little common sense to kick in.

"So last night—did we use protection?"

I'm using my boardroom business voice here because as much as I am mortified, my bodily health is at stake.

His eyebrows pull low. "Uh . . . we didn't have sex. You were pretty drunk when you got here and just wanted to cuddle."

Relief floods my body for the briefest of moments. "But I woke up naked!"

My stranger shrugs. "You have a thing for my sheets. You told me they feel like a thousand tiny angel kisses on your skin. You got here. You stripped down, jumped into my bed, and proceeded to do what looked like snow angels until you passed out. It was kinda cute, actually."

I am once again filled with a whole new type of mortification because he has just described Drunk Gemma with such perfect clarity that I can envision exactly how things went down.

"Well, okay, then." I am at a loss for words. I am not, nor have I ever been, a one-night-stand kind of girl. It's not that I have anything against them. I just get caught up in all the potential consequences. Pregnancy. STIs. Awkward morning-after ghosting. Speaking of . . .

"So, uh . . . thanks for letting me sleep here. And you have a very nice penis, but I really have to be going."

I don't give him a chance to reply. I grab my purse and fly down the hallway to his condo door. I'm halfway to the elevator before I have the last button of my jeans done up. It's only when I press the *L* on the elevator panel that I realize I have absolutely no idea where I am.

I ride the elevator down, then tumble through the lobby out into the bright morning sun. It takes a whole minute before I'm able to orient myself. The blue waves of Lake Ontario glitter in front of me, gently bobbing the slew of sailboats parked in the marina. I can even see the balcony of my condo on the other side of the bay.

Needing time and fresh morning air to sort out my brain, I opt to walk home. My purse bangs rhythmically against my leg as I strain my memory for any more clues as to what happened last night, yet I come up with a whole lot of nothing.

I need a shower. And some coconut water. And Aunt Livi's special peppermint essential oil blend that somehow feels like it possesses the magical ability to erase poor life choices.

By the time I reach the front door to my building, I've calmed down a little. However, as I pull out my keys, I realize Drunk Gemma did a lot more last night besides picking up some random man.

You have got to be kidding me.

The keys in my hand aren't mine. Wait, the Dr. Snuggles keychain is. But I'm missing the fob for my front door and my condo key and have somehow acquired two metal keys I've never seen before.

How does this even happen? There's no logical explanation. But Drunk Gemma did a lot of stupid things last night. If I ever needed a reason to quit drinking altogether, this was it.

I press the intercom buzzer and wait until a "How can I help you, miss?" crackles from the other side.

"Hey, Hammond," I reply. "It's Gemma Wilde here. I'm having a bit of an issue with my keys this morning. Any way you can let me in?" The front door buzzes, and I'm able to push it open, but when I step into the lobby, it's not Hammond, my usual concierge, behind the desk. It's Eddie, the concierge who was fired over a year ago after Stuart kept catching him watching Leafs games on his phone and complained to building management.

"Excuse me, miss. I didn't quite catch your name. Who are you visiting?"

I know it's been a whole year since he's worked here, but Eddie and I used to be buddies. We'd chat about the weather or last night's game. He'd spill all the tea about my neighbors, and I'd bake him extra granola every time I made a batch. I'm a little insulted that I've been so easily forgotten.

"I'm not visiting," I clarify. "It's me, Gemma Wilde. Unit 804. There's been a mix-up with my keys and . . . well . . . I don't have them. Any chance you can let me up?"

Eddie crosses his milky-white forearms, leaning back in his black office chair so far that I'm worried he might topple over. "Listen, lady, you and I both know you don't live in 804. I don't know what the hell you're selling, but I can tell you the residents here don't want it."

I'm starting to feel less bad about Stuart getting this guy fired. "Listen, Eddie. I know you've been gone awhile, and there's probably been a few new tenants since you left, but I am the owner of number 804, and I can prove it."

I pull my license from my wallet and thrust it at him with such enthusiasm that it feels like it wouldn't be out of place to add a *ha*. He squints at it for a moment before his hand subtly reaches for the cellphone attached to his hip.

"I don't wanna call the cops this early in the morning, so I'm gonna ask you once, nicely, to please leave."

Heat floods my body, and I become acutely aware that I'm clenching my jaw and a few seconds away from losing the last of my bananas. I have half a mind to tell him to go right ahead and call the cops, but as I open my wallet to shove my license back inside, my eye catches the address listed beneath my name.

What the actual fuck? It doesn't say I live in this building. It lists a Hamilton address. But it's a street I don't recognize. *What is going on? Am I a victim of identity fraud?* I was passed out cold in Mr. Big's bed for god knows how long. *Could he have done this?* Creating a brand-new license with a completely different address feels like it's a very involved yet unnecessary step for identity theft, but what the hell do I know?

I'm suddenly struck by the urge to call Stuart. Practical, sensible, logical Stuart, who always seems to know what to do in every situation.

But I can't.

We're done.

Merlot has been thrown. Relationship has taken a permanent vacation.

And even if I wanted to, calling Stuart would be a lot more difficult than anticipated because as I pull my phone from my purse, one very quick glimpse tells me with certainty that the phone in my hand isn't my nearly new iPhone. It's sparkly, white, and a Samsung. Most importantly, again, not mine.

Where the fuck is my phone, and who the hell does this one belong to? Did I pick up the wrong purse?

The bag in my hand is a simple black Matt & Nat. Definitely mix-up-able. However, I know it's the same one Kiersten bought me last year for Christmas because it has a small purple stain inside from that time I threw a bottle of nail polish in the pocket, and it wasn't completely closed. Yet, there's also a small bottle of hand cream I know I don't own and a pair of earrings I've never seen before. It's mine, but it's not mine.

I draw three deep breaths. Because it's the only coping mechanism I am currently equipped to execute at the moment. Even though I'm significantly more pissed at Past Gemma for her questionable life choices, the increase in oxygen intake has enabled me to focus.

On to plan B.

Dax.

We may have locked lips last night. But I was drunk, and he is Dax. If I pretend like nothing happened, he will too.

He owns All the Other Kicks, a custom sneaker shop on James Street about a block and a half north of my aunt's bookshop. It doesn't open until ten on Tuesdays, but he is usually in by eight-thirty, poking around doing whatever Dax does when he's alone.

I address Eddie with the renewed confidence of a woman who is sure of her own address. "I have some things to sort out, but I will be back."

He murmurs a not-so-convinced *mmm-hmm* as I exit the building, head held high, feet thankful I didn't opt for heels last night as I make the trek to James Street on foot.

Downtown Hamilton has undergone a bit of an extreme makeover over the last few years. Pawnshops and Money Marts have given way to artisanal cheese boutiques and legal cannabis dispensaries as Toronto's hipsters—priced out of the big city—make their way west.

Although hipster-adjacent, Dax was born and raised in the Hammer. Weekends of his youth were spent outside the Jackson Square theater back when you could see a flick on their Two-Toonie-Tuesday. He hung out on James Street long before it was cool, coloring his sister's hand-me-down, generic-brand sneakers with Sharpies from the Dollarama, dreaming about opening up his custom sneaker shop one day.

"Hey, Dax. It's me." I knock on the back door of his store and call his name simultaneously. When he doesn't answer, I try the knob and find it unlocked, which is fortunate, as Dax's spare key is in a very realistic-looking hide-a-key that takes me twenty minutes to locate more often than not.

"Dax," I call again as I cross the threshold. "It's Gemma. Not a murderer. Or a ghost."

I've let myself into Daxon's place a hundred times before. But Dax is convinced the building is haunted, and I don't want to freak him out, coming in unannounced and making creepy creaking sounds on his floorboards.

I walk through to the front of the store, already brightly lit from the morning sun, and take a seat behind the counter to wait, knowing Dax will be along eventually.

His space is long and narrow. A mix of old and new with a bit of wild thrown in, just like Dax. The far wall is half white shiplap and half red brick with perfect rows of wooden pedestal shelves, each holding up a pair of Dax's custom-designed sneakers. His art. His soul. Little pieces of Dax you can take home for the average price of three hundred Canadian dollars.

Whether it's the sun or the fact that I'm sitting down and finally in a safe space, the adrenaline in my blood starts to slow, leaving behind the hangover I woke up with. My head is thumping like a techno jam, which is not appreciated by my stomach, which is still all sloshy and queasy. My chances of puking are at a low but notable 30 percent. I rest my head on the countertop and close my eyes. Not sure if I drift off for a few moments or just zone out, but I'm all of a sudden brought back to reality by the very distinct feeling of a presence in the room.

"That better be you, Daxon. Or else I'm going to have to take back all that shit I gave you about this place being haunted." I don't open my eyes or lift my head, blaming the hangover but also not wanting to risk seeing an actual ghost.

If he's there, he doesn't say a word. However, the floorboards creak, but by the time I look up, whoever or whatever was standing there is gone.

Okay, nope. I am not in the mood to fuck around with the paranormal right now. I have bigger problems to deal with. I reach for my purse, which has fallen to the floor, and when I stand, my eyes catch the edge of a shadow.

I spin around. The second adrenaline rush of the morning floods my veins.

Dax stands in the doorway of his office, braced like he's ready to fight with a shoehorn clutched in his fist.

My taut body relaxes at the sight of my flesh-and-blood BFF. "Easy there, drama queen. Put the weapon down."

But he doesn't.

He stares at me, his eyes unusually cold. "What are you doing in my store?"

Chapter 5

"WELL, GOOD MORNING to you too," I chide. "What's with the hostile greeting? Your neighbors playing EDM all night again?"

I study Dax, who does, in fact, have dark bags under his eyes.

He doesn't answer. He stares. Fair point. It's almost nine on a Tuesday. I'm normally at work, not loitering behind his front counter. I'm not surprised he's looking dazed and confused about my unexpected visit.

"I'm having a crisis," I explain. "I need someone to tell me I'm not hallucinating."

Dax lowers his weapon-wielding arm, albeit slowly. "Do you need help?"

"Yes. That's why I'm here. I think I'm at the center of some weird conspiracy. People are trying to steal my identity."

My confession makes my heart race. This entire morning has been weird. My body feels jittery and off, and I'm starting to suspect it isn't just the morning-after effects of Livi's margaritas.

Dax steps toward me, placing his shoehorn weapon on the counter between us. "Are you hurt?"

I contemplate his question. "Physically, no. Emotionally . . . I

don't know if I'd use the word *hurt,* more like disoriented." Pan-
icked. Confused.

"Have you ever had one of those days where you wake up, and
everything just goes wrong from the second you step out of bed?"
I ask him.

At this, his eyebrows lift, and he looks more relaxed than the
moment before. "Actually, yes, I can relate to that."

"Okay, I'm having one of those days. Except things aren't bad,
they're just weird. And I desperately need to be told that I'm not
losing my fucking mind. And I know this sounds like a stupid
question, but humor me. Where do I live?"

I wait for him to answer. There was a very clear *Over to you, Dax*
on the end of that question. But his face is back to that half-
confused, half-concerned look he had earlier.

Finally, he opens his mouth. "I don't know the right way to
answer that question, but I know someone who can help. She
works at St. Joe's. Awesome to talk to, and if you give me five
minutes, I can call her."

"Are you talking about Jen?"

Dax steps away as if my very normal question has tripped his
weirdo alarm. "You know my sister?"

I resist the urge to roll my eyes. "Of course I know your sister.
Petite brunette. Great sense of style. Gorgeous legs. Every time I
see them, I seriously consider getting back into running. And funnily enough, I actually bumped into her last week at the pharmacy. She was shopping with your mom, who, I guess, was down
for the weekend visiting."

"You know my mom?" He's reaching for the shoehorn again,
but before he can grab it, I pick it up and throw it.

Dax looks at me, then the shoehorn, then back to me, as if he's
trying to confirm that I actually threw it.

"Focus, Dax. It's like you're as confused as I am this morning. Have you not had coffee?" *Come to think of it, I haven't had any either.* "Maybe we should pause this conversation until I can make a run. Tall, dark roast? Or is it a grande kind of morning?"

Dax's eyes flick from the wall to the door to the counter to me. "You know my coffee order."

This time, I do roll my eyes. "Of course I do. I've watched you order at least ten thousand times."

Dax takes a very obvious step away from me. "Listen, why don't I make us coffee? You sit here, and I'll be right back."

He gestures at his stool. My hungover brain welcomes the idea that he wants me to sit down again. I work on massaging my temples while he heads toward the stockroom in the back, pulling his phone from his hip.

Not in our entire four years of friendship has Dax ever offered to make our coffee. His entire philosophy around coffee is that it's not a beverage; it's an experience. And part of that experience is having someone else make it. He's acting weird. And because my morning has been completely bizarre and my inner radar is telling me something is afoot, I slip from my stool and tiptoe across the floor until I'm outside the stockroom, pressing my ear to the door like I'm Nancy fucking Drew.

"I've never met her before, Jen. Although she looks familiar. I think she works at that new place down the street."

He's on the phone. Talking about someone. I still don't get why he's calling his sister.

"I came downstairs, and she was sitting behind the counter. Not stealing anything. Just hanging out."

Wait. Is he talking about me now?

"She knows shit about me," Dax continues. "She knew that you run. Even my coffee order. I think she might be stalking me. I think she needs help."

He *is* talking about me. *What the actual hell?*

My throat instantly goes dry. And the low odds I gave earlier about upchucking on Dax's floor skyrocket as my stomach completes a double back tuck.

Something is wrong.

Something is very, very wrong.

It's like I went to bed last night in my normal life and woke up this morning to a completely new one. Unless, of course, I'm still dreaming? I pinch the skin of my arm just enough to feel a slight sting. Nope. I'm definitely awake. *Have I been in some sort of coma for years and only just woken up?* I pull the not-my-iPhone from my purse. The date reads precisely as it should, Tuesday, July 19. Plus, the coma doesn't explain Mr. Big, or my license, or the fact that my best friend is acting like he has no idea who the hell I am.

My pulse that was racing moments ago now feels as if it's beating at supersonic speed. I attempt the three deep breaths that somewhat helped earlier this morning. They do nothing but make my head woozy. *Think, Gemma. Think! You are a smart, capable woman.* There has to be a logical explanation for all of this.

My head is pounding so badly and I swear my stomach acids are starting a slow pilgrimage up my esophagus. I retreat to Dax's stool, letting my head fall into my hands as my elbows hit the countertop.

I can't think like this. I've got nothing.

Out of theories, I do what I always do when facts and science don't hold the answers I'm looking for: turn to the internet. However, before I can type "causes of temporary amnesia" into Google, the phone in my hands starts to vibrate. Aunt Livi's name flashes across the screen beside the words *incoming call.*

Okay, bizarro day, let's see what twist you're going to throw at me now.

Pressing the phone to my ear, I brace myself. "Hello."

"Oh hi, poodle." Aunt Livi's voice is its usual even timbre. "I'm so glad you're okay."

"Why wouldn't I be okay?"

"Well, Mr. Zogaib called me this morning to tell me your store is still locked up tight. He said he saw at least three different customers try the door and leave. He was worried something happened to you."

I lift my head from my hands and gaze around Dax's store. My vision is slightly blurred. It could be the way my eyeballs were pressing into my palms just now. Or maybe something is medically wrong with me. *Oh god! What if it's a tumor?*

"What store are we referring to," I ask, "and why would I be opening it?"

Aunt Livi pauses. The only reason I know she's still there is because I can hear her raspy breathing. "Your store, sweetheart, Wilde Beauty."

At the name Wilde Beauty, my heart does this thing where it completely stalls for a good three seconds, then beats like crazy as if catching up. What Aunt Livi's saying is impossible.

Now I know I must be dreaming.

I pinch my arm for a second time. It stings so badly that there's definitely going to be a purple bruise there in four to six hours, but I need to be absolutely sure I'm awake.

Years ago, when I was in university getting my business degree, I took a course where I had to create a business plan. *Wilde Beauty* was the name of the clean beauty, health, and lifestyle boutique I dreamed about owning one day. My plan was to open it up, build a strong brand and supply chain, and then expand. My very own clean beauty empire. This was long before I got the reality check that adulting involves paying off student loans and doing my own taxes. I never told anyone that name. Ever. Even when I submitted the assignment, I chickened out and called it Hamilton Health and Wellness.

This new fact is like a neon warning sign surrounded by flashing lightbulbs. There's something seriously wrong with the universe.

"Why don't you come by for supper tonight," Aunt Livi continues, oblivious to my inner dilemma. "Your sister is coming by to pick up a book I got in the donation bin this week. We could even make margaritas."

Aunt Livi's words make something in the back of my brain click. My sister. Margaritas. The book.

No. Nooooooooooo.

It can't be it.

I am not Bill Murray. Or Doctor Who. Or whatever the name was of Rachel McAdams's character in *The Time Traveler's Wife*.

My life is not a romantic comedy. It's . . . well, it's my life. Shit like this doesn't happen to me.

It doesn't happen, period.

"Uh . . . hey there."

I jump a good two feet in the air, let out a very loud *gahhhh*, and drop my phone onto the polished concrete floor. Picking it up, I stare up at Dax, who stands in the doorway holding two steaming mugs.

"Sorry to startle you. Just wondering how you take your coffee?"

My sweet Dax. He's staring at me with his big green saucer eyes and this crinkle in his forehead that only appears when he's concerned about something. Like when he finds a baby bird flung from its nest or reads about natural disasters in the news.

That look, that crinkle, is aimed right at me. I'm the broken baby bird.

"You don't know who I am, do you?" I'm trying very hard to keep the panic from my voice, but all of the potential causes I'm coming up with for his sudden bout of Gemma-related amnesia are not reassuring.

"Do *you* know who you are?" His voice is so deep and so kind that for a moment, I strongly consider diving into his arms, laying my head against his chest, and being that broken baby bird. But I can't. I need to figure out what the hell is going on.

"The name Gemma doesn't mean anything to you?"

Dax doesn't blink. There isn't even the teeniest tiniest flicker of recognition on his face.

"Gemma Wilde." I try again. "Wilde with an *e*."

He lifts his head. "Like the store down the street?"

"No! Actually . . . yes, I guess that *is* my store. But that wasn't—"

Then it hits me. A possibility. A perfectly logical explanation for everything. And I cling to the idea like it's a life raft. "Did Kiersten put you up to this? Because if she did, it's way too fucked-up to be funny, and I need you to end this horrible trick now. Right now, Dax."

So much for not sounding hysterical.

My nerves are so on edge that I feel like I could easily lift a Toyota Prius or collapse into a heap of ugly tears. It has to be a trick. It has to.

I stare down Dax as if the sheer will of my beliefs will make him open his mouth and confess everything.

He sets the two mugs down on the counter and pulls out his phone again. "Is there someone I can call for you? A family member?"

I need to fix this. Whatever we've done. I need to talk to my aunt and put everything back.

"Thanks for making coffee. I appreciate it more than you realize. But I need to go."

———

I WANDER DOWN James Street like I'm a character in a post-apocalyptic drama who's just emerged from a bomb shelter: staggering, dazed, not entirely sure if the world around her is real or a hallucination brought on by one too many canned kidney bean dinners.

The thing that's tripping me up the most is that everything is so ordinary. James Street is busy with its normal Tuesday morning pedestrian traffic. Little old ladies with their wire shopping carts on their way to the Jackson Square market. Tight-panted hipsters heading home after an all-night house party. Bleary-eyed parents pushing strollers. Lazy twentysomethings who refuse to buy a coffee maker when there's a perfectly good coffee shop nearby.

Typically, I fall into that last category. I share Dax's philosophy that coffee tastes better when someone else makes it, which is why, despite not being entirely sure if I'm going through a delusional episode, I join the line at Brewski's.

Coffee is never a bad idea.

"What can I get for you?"

Staring at me are two light-brown eyes belonging to the dark-haired, man-bunned barista.

"Oh hey, Gemma," he says. "Grande oat latte, right?"

"You know who I am?" It comes out in a kind of creepy whisper, but the barista, whose name I am almost certain is Snake, doesn't seem to notice.

"Uh, yeah. It's Gemma with a *G*. I remember because this one time I wrote it with a *J* and you said, *Actually, it's Gemma with a G,* so that's what I call you in my head every time I go to write on your cup."

This isn't weird. Well, it *is* weird, but for all the right reasons. I do order my coffee here pretty much every morning. And Snake is usually the one who serves it to me. This part of my life is exactly as it should be.

"I also wrote your name down in my phone after we made out that night. I figure if a woman is willing to put her tongue in your mouth, you should probably remember her name forever. I'm just a gentleman like that."

"I'm sorry, what?" In addition to being potentially delusional, apparently I also have broken ears. I must have heard him wrong. Because that did not happen. There always has been and forever will be an entire Brewski's countertop between Snake's tongue and my mouth.

"We made out?"

"Yeah." He smiles as he nods. "Last New Year's. Hooper invited you to his party. I think he was secretly hoping the two of you would bang. But then midnight came, and we were both doing Jäger shots out in the garage, and I said, *Wanna make out?* and you were like, *What the hell?* and kissed me. I'm kinda hurt that you don't remember that."

First off, who the hell is Hooper? Second, I don't remember because I was skiing in Sun Peaks last New Year's with Stuart and his family. I wasn't even in Hamilton, and I sure as hell wasn't in a garage making out with my barista.

"Listen." I brace my hands on the countertop and paste on the most perfectly normal, definitely-not-having-a-meltdown smile I can muster. "I'm having a rough morning. Can you add an extra espresso shot to my drink? I think I need it."

"Drink's on me, Gemma with a *G*." He winks and clicks his fingers at me.

Before I can protest, I'm ousted from the cash line by a pointy-elbowed toddler-mom, and Snake is moving on to his next customer.

Free coffee in hand, I take a seat at my favorite table by the window and refuse to let myself think about my dilemma until I've made it three-quarters of the way through it. By that time, the double shot hits my bloodstream. I'm feeling slightly more focused and ready to tackle the facts.

Last night we performed a spell. Or a cleanse. Or a ritual sacrifice involving jerk chicken and possibly my reality. This morning I woke up, and it's as if I've lived the last four years of my life without Stuart. That part doesn't seem too awful. Except in erasing Stuart, I've somehow extracted Dax from my life, which is an utter and total catastrophe.

I pinch myself one last time. Mostly because I have no other ideas to confirm that what I think is happening is actually happening.

Our spell caused a rift in the universe. We created a hot tub time machine without an actual hot tub.

I still can't believe it. I'm, like, 84 percent of the way there. The other sixteen thinks there might be a possibility that I have suffered some sort of emotional block brought on by the breakup with Stuart. Except, as much as I hate that my sister was completely right, I'm no longer that emotionally torn up that Stuart and I are over. But if that is the case, there is only one person who will tell me straight up, without any attempt to sugarcoat things.

The phone rings twice before she answers.

"Hey. Hold on for a second. The little one just pulled a knife from the dishwasher, and I'm not entirely sure if she intends to use it as a weapon."

A full minute and a half passes before Kiersten's voice comes back on the line.

"All good. What's up? Are we debriefing *The Bachelor* from last night? Because I passed out halfway and still need to watch the ending."

Excellent start. Kiersten is still Kiersten.

"I am going to ask you some questions," I tell her. "I need you to humor me and answer them and not ask why or get weirded out. Okay?"

"Sounds ominous, but I'm in."

I rack my brain for the right place to start. "Did we hang out last night?"

There's background noise that sounds like her kids yelling. Then the soft click of a door closing, followed by notable silence. "No. You were supposed to be going out to some new bar downtown with a couple of your friends. Didn't that happen?"

I have no idea. However, it fits with the timeline and why another Gemma was doing naked snow angels in the wee hours of the morning.

"Question two: Do the names Daxon McGuire and Stuart Holliston mean anything to you?"

Another long pause before she answers. "Is one of them that guy you sleep with sometimes? Except I thought his name was Connor or possibly Salvatore."

"Those are very different names, and no, Stuart and Dax are both guys I know very well. You sure you don't know them?"

She sighs on the other end. "I don't think so. You date a lot of guys, Gems. It's hard to keep track."

No, I don't. Or maybe now I do?

One last shot before I accept my fate.

"On a scale of one to ten, how solid is my grasp on reality?"

There's a very distinctive snort, and I can practically hear my sister rolling her eyes. "Normally a strong eight and a half, but you've lost a few points with this weird line of questioning. What's going on with you?"

I'm now 97 percent sure I've accidentally altered history.

"Are you busy this morning? I'm having a bit of a personal dilemma. Can you meet me at Aunt Livi's in an hour?"

"Yeah . . ." My sister's voice trails off. "Yeah. Trent is off today. I can see if he can stay here with the baby."

There's a noticeable pause on her end of the line. "You're okay, though, right? You're not about to tell me you're dying? Or pregnant?"

Both of those would be easier to explain.

"I'm fine. But just come with an open mind."

Chapter 6

"EXPLAIN THIS ONE more time for the mama who was up all night with a sleep-regressed two-year-old. You come from a parallel universe?"

My sister gives me the exact look you'd expect after dealing out such a bizarre story.

"Yes," I reply. "Or maybe it's an alternate timeline. I'm not exactly an expert on these things."

After I called Kiersten, I came straight over to Aunt Livi's and told her my story. She listened intently, responded with nothing but an *Oh, well, isn't that interesting*, then busied herself making coffee until Kiersten showed up.

Whether it's because of the familiar musty book smell of Aunt Livi's apartment or the fact that it looks exactly as it should, my heart rate has come down to a much healthier level, the adrenaline has stopped pumping through my veins, and my stomach has slid back down my throat to its proper place above my gut.

I've recalled the events of this morning twice now with an eerie calmness and consumed three cups of coffee (although for the last two, I suspect Aunt Livi has been slipping me decaf), and still I get the sense that neither my sister nor my aunt believes me.

"And just to be clear." My sister is using her toddler-mom voice on me. "In your timeline, you were dating a guy named Stuart, who broke up with you, so you cursed him and wound up here?"

I shrug, completely unsure of how to make the truth any more plausible.

Kiersten exchanges a look with my aunt before turning her attention back to me. "Any chance that in your universe, I'm married to Chris Pine?"

She leans in as she asks and sniffs my breath, not even trying to be discreet. I resist the urge to respond with a few unladylike words because I need my sister to believe me.

"I haven't been drinking." I push her away. "You're married to Trent. You have three beautiful kids and are a giant pain in the ass, albeit a happy one."

I turn to my Aunt Livi, who is sitting on the edge of the sofa. The little black book where she keeps all her important phone numbers is clutched in her hands. My spidey senses guess she's contemplating calling her GP. "You're the same too," I tell her. "The shop. This apartment. Everything is exactly as it is in my timeline, except—" A weird thought occurs to me. "Come!"

I don't wait for Kiersten or my aunt to agree before exiting the apartment and taking the stairs down to the bookshop. It's mostly empty except for my aunt's part-time employee, Barb, who throws me a friendly wave before returning to unpacking a cardboard box of what looks like healing crystals.

I push aside the barstool and run my hands along the linoleum countertop, feeling a swoop in my stomach at its near-perfect condition. "It's gone."

"What's gone?" Kiersten's boobs are pressed against my back. It's so eerily like last night that I get a shiver down my spine with the déjà vu.

"There was a mark." I rub my fingers over the unblemished surface. "We burned the countertop with the spell."

"Ohhhh, a spell." Kierst turns to my aunt. "This one has your name all over it. Did you give her those weird mushrooms again? I warned you they were probably laced with something. No wonder she's hallucinating."

My throat lets out a frustrated warble. "I can hear you and I'm not hallucinating. I'm telling you something is going on. We did that spell. Or that cleanse. Or whatever you want to call it. Now Dax, who is my best friend, doesn't know who I am."

Aunt Livi's head snaps up. "Daxon McGuire?"

His name from her lips shoots my heart into my ribs like a cannonball.

"You know Dax?"

She nods. "He's part of the James Street Small Business Association. You know, that group I've been trying to get you to join for months? To network more for your store?"

I don't. It's so weird. This store that up until now has only existed in the wildest depths of my imagination is suddenly a real thing that is apparently just flung into casual conversations. And yet other parts of my life, like Kiersten, or this bookstore, are so achingly familiar. It's like trying to put together one big jigsaw puzzle with the picture facing down.

Kiersten flips around so her back rests against the counter. "Okay, fine. I'll humor you. So we all came over to Livi's. I'm gonna go ahead and assume drinking was involved and then we performed—what did you call it earlier—a *love cleanse*?"

I draw a deep breath and repeat my explanation.

"Aunt Livi found a book in the donation bin. It looked old and creepy. But Aunt Livi thought it would be fun. Believe it or not, the other you totally predicted weird shit was going to happen, but we went ahead and did it anyway."

Kiersten snorts. "That's the first believable thing you've said since I got here." She holds her palm up to my forehead. "And you're sure you haven't had a fever or anything?"

I swat her hand away. "For the last time, no."

"I know that book." Aunt Livi claps her hands in excitement. "I showed it to you yesterday." She looks at me, her eyes big and round. "Well, not you-you, the other you."

My stomach flutters with hope. "Is it brown leather with blue loopy writing? Something like *Modern Magic for Practical People*?"

Aunt Livi nods. "That exact one. I thought it could help you find a nice, steady boyfriend. Not erase one."

This is good. If we have the book, then maybe there's something in it to turn everything back to the way it was. At the very least, it will provide some evidence that I'm not making all of this up.

"Well, where is it?" My eyes search the bookshelves covering almost every wall of the store.

"I'm not sure," she answers. "I gave it to you while you were at Wilde Beauty. Maybe it's still there?"

We head back to the apartment to grab our shoes and are out the door in less than a minute, walking the three blocks to the store.

When its white-brick storefront comes into view, my breath catches in my throat, and my pace slows to a halt because it's exactly how I dreamed it would be. Possibly even better.

Like most retail establishments on this busy downtown street, Wilde Beauty is narrow and long. At a closer glance, the bricks are, in fact, red, but have been painted a creamy white, which is a stylish but stark contrast to the shiny black door and painted sill of the big storefront window. Above, the word *Wilde* is spelled out in simple iron block letters with *Beauty* written below in a dainty gold script. Although the lights are all still out, I can see the arrangement of clean, all-natural beauty products displayed on mismatched wooden tables and crates. It's simple. It's perfect. Exactly like I envisioned.

Tears prick at the edges of my eyes because although I've never wanted children, I feel like I've just given birth.

"Yo. Marty McFly. We need the keys." My sister holds up her palms in a gesture easily interpreted as *Let's move things along here.* I pull the corgi keychain from my purse, insert one of the metal mystery keys, then, after it doesn't fit, try the second. It slides in, buttery smooth.

There's a beeping as I push open the door as a small alarm panel on the wall starts to go berserk. I instinctively type in 05-03-2015, Dr. Snuggles's birthday. It seems to do the trick, as the beeping is silenced.

"Good guess?" My sister's narrowed eyes are rightfully skeptical.

I shrug. "Apparently, this timeline's Gemma and I have a lot in common."

She holds her palm to my head again. I swat it away and move past her.

I know I should be looking for the book, but my holistic-loving heart cannot help but take in every tiny detail of the store. The products lining the walls find that delicate balance between truly beneficial ingredients and a price point that makes them accessible. I inch my way along the pine board floors, too afraid to touch anything out of fear that it might burst this beautiful bubble. Twice, I catch myself letting out an audible, very Aunt Livi–like "Oh my."

"You worked your ass off to open this place almost six months ago." My sister appears at my side with a smile on her face that I'd describe as proud. "I guess you don't own Wilde Beauty in your timeline?"

I shake my head because the answer is the exact opposite of Wilde Beauty. "I'm a senior buyer at Eaton's Drug Mart."

She raises an eyebrow.

"The pay is amazing," I explain, "but it definitely doesn't feel like this." I allow myself the luxury of running my fingers over a smooth aluminum shelf, then opening one of the tiny jars marked *sample* and rubbing a lemon-scented balm into my hands.

"Gemma, sweetheart," Aunt Livi calls. "If you were *you*, where do you think you'd put the book? I've looked around and haven't had any luck."

Right. The book. The entire reason we're here. I scan the walls and the cash-out counter, trying to figure out where Other Me may have put it. Everything is so different, I have no clue where to start.

"Honestly, I have no idea."

My aunt nods, then braces her hands on her hips.

"I guess we divide and conquer. Gems, you take the office, Kiersten the storeroom, and I'll check out the bathroom."

Although my store is adorable and quaint, it's not very big at all. Five solid minutes gives us the confidence to say the book is not here.

"I guess we'll try your house next," Aunt Livi suggests.

I nod, but as I do, I catch a flicker of movement outside. Adrenaline floods my veins even before I register the familiar broad shoulders and brown wavy hair of the tall pedestrian crossing the street—heading directly for my front door.

"We need to hide."

My hulked-up adrenaline-fueled body grabs Aunt Livi by the arm, then dives at Kiersten, bringing the three of us down in a tangle of arms and legs behind the cash counter.

"What the actual fuck, Gems." Kiersten kicks me until I roll off her. She hauls herself into a seated position next to my aunt, throwing me a dirty look.

"I don't want him knowing we're in here," I shoot back in a fierce whisper.

"Who?"

The answer to her question is a sharp knock on the front door followed by a "Hello, anyone home?" in a very male, very familiar voice.

"Dax is out there." I gesture wildly at the door. "We had a little bit of a run-in this morning. There's a strong possibility he thinks I require medical attention."

Before I can stop her, Kiersten's on her hands and knees, crawling to the end of the counter.

"Get back here, you jerk," I whisper-yell. "Don't let him see you."

"He's not going to see me." She waves me off. "I just want to see what all the drama is about."

To her benefit, when she peeks around the corner, it's slow and stealthy. That is, until she whips back around and says in a voice that is definitely not quiet, "Well, helloooooo, Dax. Your hallucination is hot, Gems."

Heat flushes my face for no good reason. "He's not hot. He's Dax."

"Seriously." My sister goes in for another look. "He's hipstery, but not too weird. And great arms. I've always been an arm girl."

"Stop being creepy." I shove her with my foot, but it does not deter her from stealing another look.

"There is nothing creepy about appreciating," she counters as she turns back around to face me. "You can see the man's chest muscles through his T-shirt."

"So now you're a chest girl too?"

She shrugs. "I'm simply acknowledging every fine thing your man has got going on. You've got to admit, he's a total babe."

I did think Dax was attractive the first time we met. We were standing beside each other at a local dive bar called The Prince and Pauper. It was crowded as usual and impossible to get a drink. The bartender slid a Guinness down the bar in our direction, and our hands collided as we both reached for the pint. There may have been tingles.

Dax's gentlemanly instincts kicked in, and he offered the beer to me. The feminist in me insisted it should go to the more Irish of the two of us, thinking my strawberry-blond hair and English surname gave me the upper hand. Until Dax pushed up the sleeve of his henley, revealing a sleeve of tattoos, including the McGuire family crest. *I dink I wen dis one,* he said in a perfect Irish accent that riled up the butterflies in my stomach. Kierst isn't the only Wilde that appreciates a forearm.

But then one of Stuart's friends spilled a drink down Dax's back. He went home to change, and by the time he returned, Stuart had me smitten. Dax became an acquaintance I'd run into at parties, then a part of a bigger friend group until we both realized we spent most of our time together, talking only to each other, and decided to cut everyone else out and become ride-or-dies. His Hemsworthiness became a moot point.

"Fine," I admit to my sister. "He's attractive, but we're not like that. Our relationship is purely platonic."

Kierst thinks for a moment. "And your boyfriend was totally fine with you hanging out with a facially gifted lumbersexual?"

Stuart was . . . neutral. He didn't understand the appeal of Dax. He was also so confident and assured that I don't think it ever occurred to him to be threatened by Dax.

"I never gave Stuart a reason to be worried."

She narrows her eyes. "You mean you've never once . . ." She looks over at Aunt Livi, who is busy looking for something inside her purse, then thrusts her hips suggestively.

"No!" I say loud enough for Aunt Livi to look up.

"Come on." My sister is not letting this topic die. "I can practically count his abs from here. That's hot. At least tell me you've kissed him."

My cheeks flush.

"Aha!" Kiersten pokes me hard in the chest with her finger. "I knew it!"

"It's not like that."

It was a whim? A mistake? Either way, it sure as hell wasn't what Kiersten is thinking.

We sit behind the counter for another five minutes. It's probably four too many, but I'm paranoid. This whole Dax-not-knowing-me thing has thrown me for a loop, and I need some time to figure out a plan before I see him again.

"Kierst—" I nudge her with the toe of my shoe. "Can you check again and make sure he's gone?"

My sister doesn't immediately move. I can almost see the wheels turning in her head, as if she's trying to decide if she will use this opportunity to blackmail more info out of me or surrender to the fact that it's her sisterly duty to have my back in times of dire need.

Dire need emerges the winner, and she crawls over to the corner, takes another peek, then jumps to her feet. "Coast is clear."

"Oh, good." Aunt Livi stands and brushes imaginary dirt from her palazzo pants. "So should we try your house next, poodle?"

My house.

The mystery location written on the front of my Ontario driver's license.

We walk back to the front of the bookshop, where we pile into Kiersten's souped-up white Dodge minivan—even though Aunt

Livi insists the distance from my store to my house is walkable, and I make the commute daily.

It's a quick five minutes before we pull up in front of a two-story beige-brick house. Like most in this Hamilton neighborhood, it looks like it was built in the 1940s, sits steps from the sidewalk, and is tightly fitted in between neighbors on either side. It's not my condo on the water, but it's cute.

I take the front steps in a single leap, then seek out the final mystery key from my purse.

"Not that door, sweetie," Aunt Livi calls from the sidewalk. "You use the one around the back."

I follow Kiersten and my aunt along a narrow sidewalk and through a chain-link gate to a small but neat yard. The two of them straddle a narrow staircase and wait.

I stare at the cracked cement steps leading down. My stomach drops like a stone. "I live in the basement?"

Both of them nod.

Sure enough, my second mystery key slips easily enough into the lock. However, I need to duck my head as I push open the door and step into what looks like a compact kitchen. Then, with an easy quarter turn, I take in the living room, bedroom, and even bathroom with one brief sweep of the eyes.

It's quaint. And it's terrible. My heart and head are at war, taking in a space that is obviously lovingly decorated in my specific Scandinavian-inspired taste with the low ceilings, lack of walls, and dim lighting.

Tears prick my eyes once again. Unlike at my store, they are not tears of awe and joy.

"I willingly moved here? It smells like chicken soup."

Kiersten gives my shoulder a sympathetic squeeze. "We think it's from your neighbor upstairs. At least, we hope it is. And yes, you did. Signed the lease the same month you opened the store."

I guess a storefront, even in Hamilton, isn't exactly cheap.

Decisions were made. Priorities were set.

At some point, after not choosing Stuart, Other Me must have made a choice to live in this damp, dark basement to launch her store.

"I found it!" Aunt Livi calls from the opposite side of the room, interrupting my little pity party.

She stands next to a small white IKEA desk with several unrecognizable books on top, save for the big brown leather book that gathered us here today.

It takes her three whole steps to join Kiersten and me in the kitchen. The three of us crowd around my very tiny counter, the book open between us so we can all see the pages.

"Dang it," Aunt Livi curses. "I didn't bring my reading glasses."

"Well, I didn't bring a flashlight." Kiersten nudges me with her elbow. "This place is a tomb, Gems. You really should invest in some floor lamps."

I'd argue with her if I didn't agree.

We decide it's best to take the book back to my aunt's apartment, where there's natural lighting and an ample supply of coffee.

The ride back feels twice as long as the ride there as the anticipation builds in my stomach. It doesn't ease until we're finally back above the bookshop, sharing the three-seater sofa with the book cracked open to the page with the spell that brought me here.

"*A love cleanse,*" Kiersten muses out loud. "Kind of fitting considering you and your love for everything crunchy granola, eh?"

I ignore her comment, too preoccupied with finding my answer.

My aunt flips through several pages, scanning the words with the speed of someone who spends most of her day reading. "I can't seem to find anything here about how to reverse it."

My stomach sinks. "So I'm fucked?"

Aunt Livi shoots me a disappointed look.

Kiersten kicks her feet up onto the coffee table. "I'm starting to feel a little bit insulted here. Why are you so desperate to ditch us? I might be biased, but I think our reality is pretty solid."

Kiersten's the person I would have thought would understand my urge to get back to the life I know. But I guess a small part of me understands her point. Aside from Dax and my terrible basement apartment, at first glance, there seems to be nothing wrong with this reality per se. It's just different.

But back in my other life, I had a carefully cultivated plan. One with a nice thick security blanket that kept me warm, fed, and a functional level of anxious. Yes, Stuart ripped a giant hole in said plan, but I'm a woman with contingencies. My terrible job came with retirement savings. I invested wisely with my condo. The predictable, uncomplicated vision I had for the next few years of my life should remain relatively intact, just with Stuart's head cut out of the picture—metaphorically, of course.

"I don't know what this reality's Gemma is like, but I do not go with the flow," I tell them. "I like plans. Ideally, well-thought-through ones. Where I know where I'm sleeping at night, and there is a minimal chance my life will go sideways."

My sister and my aunt exchange a look, and before I realize it, their arms are around me, forming a Gemma sandwich.

"I get it," my sister says softly into my hair. "You and I got the same raw deal here too, kiddo. We haven't seen mom since 2017. Dad sends a Christmas card every year, but it goes to an address Trent and I moved from before we even had kids."

So our parents are the same as they are back home: chronically absent and the reason my therapist holidays every winter in the Bahamas.

"It's not you. It's me." I cringe at the phrase. "I'm just freaking out at the idea that I might never get home."

"Let's not fret quite yet." Aunt Livi pulls the book from the coffee table to her lap. "Maybe we just need to think. You performed this cleanse and ended up here. What if we repeat the exact same thing, but instead of wishing you never had a relationship with Stuart, you wish that you did?"

I almost object because I do *not* want to wish that, and it feels too simple. But I have nothing better to suggest. "What do we have to lose?"

I pause and wait for Kierst to voice an objection. My gut tells me she's still far from convinced that I've managed to cause a rift in time.

Surprisingly, she shrugs. "Tell me what you need me to do."

Aunt Livi jumps to her feet with the same level of enthusiasm she had last night. "Gemma, you take the book and read out the list of ingredients."

The next five minutes are another eerie déjà vu. And my lack of tequila goggles makes the whole experience far less whimsical.

Still, we locate everything we had the first time we attempted to throw this spell down, including the white birthday candle, the hot-pink knitting wool, and even the leftover jerk chicken.

"So what exactly do we do with all this crap?" Kiersten pries open the Tupperware container of chicken and smells it while I consult the book. The events of last night are still a little muddled in my brain.

"We light the candle," I explain, "and then we tie my hands, and then we . . ." *Oh no. Oh no. Oh no, no, noooo.*

"What?" Aunt Livi and Kiersten say simultaneously.

"We don't have everything." My head drops to my hands as I chastise myself for being such a—excuse my language, Aunt Livi—fucking idiot.

"What? What do we need?" Kiersten grabs the book.

I watch as her eyes skim the directions to the very last thing on the list.

"The final step, do not be remiss,
Is to seal your fate with a kiss."

"Dax," I answer before she has a chance to ask.

"But he doesn't—" I can see, in her eyes, the precise moment she puts it all together. "Oh man . . . you are so fudged."

I drop my head to my hands again and moan. "Can't I find some guy at a bar to kiss? According to Kierst, I am very good at that."

My aunt flips through the pages. "This is not my particular area of expertise, but I think you'd have to re-create the original conditions as precisely as possible. Spells like these can be finicky."

I am fudged.

"The good news is," my aunt pipes in again, "you've got a whole month to figure it out."

I look up, confused, because I haven't the faintest idea what she's talking about.

"The moon." She pushes the book toward me. "It says right here, *Send away the one that wronged you under waning gibbous.* Waning gibbous. That's the phase of the moon just after the full. This makes perfect sense, as it's the optimal moon for any sort of cleansing or closure activity. But I'm afraid yesterday was the final night. The next one isn't for a month."

Kiersten's finger traces the spell until it lands on the spot just above the salsa stain, where it states, very clearly, exactly what my aunt just said.

"So even if we weren't missing lover boy, we can't do it today."

I stare down at the last line and read it twice as the adrenaline from the morning drains into a cool pool of dread in my stomach.

I'm stuck here for a month. And if I can't find a way to get Dax to kiss me, I could be stuck here indefinitely.

Aunt Livi points to the Tupperware in front of us. "If we're not using it for the spell, will anyone object if I heat up the chicken?"

Chapter 7

"So, Aunt Livi, what are we watching tonight?" I settle into my aunt's couch, resting my feet on the coffee table, reaching for her ancient converter.

She checks her watch before easing herself out of her La-Z-Boy. "I think I'm about ready to turn in for the evening. You're welcome to my couch for as long as you like, but I have a very steamy romance on my nightstand that I'm itching to get to. Darn it . . ." She looks toward her kitchen. "I hope I'm not out of double-A batteries."

There is no shame on her face. Not the smallest hint of flush to her cheeks. However, mine flare what I'm sure is a fire engine red. "Well, good luck with that. And I changed my mind. I think I'm gonna go."

We walk to the apartment door, where I grab my purse, avoiding her eyes. She holds her arms out for a hug. I crouch enough to lay my head on her ample bosom—a comfort move I've done since I was a kid, when sleepovers at her house became an almost everyday occurrence.

"Remember that great love and great achievements involve great risk," she murmurs into my hair before I pull away, puzzled.

"What's with the cryptic message?"

She cups my cheek with her wrinkled hand. "Just something I read on the tag of my morning tea, poodle. Send me a message when you get home. Let an old doll know you got in safe, okay?"

She places a kiss on my forehead before opening her door and letting me out.

I take my time walking home. I stop by the window of Wilde Beauty to gaze in awe at the manifestation of my dream, then head to my dark and potentially mouse-infested apartment—essentially a basic girl's nightmare.

It's just as I remember it. No better, no worse. And I last a whole seven minutes before I grow restless and decide that although I have almost a month until the moon is good to go, I don't want to wait that long to get Dax back into my life.

He may not know me, but I know him, and I know there's only one place Daxon McGuire hangs out on a Tuesday night.

THE GRAND VICTORIA Lawn Bowling and Curling Club is not known as a hot spot for nightlife in the city. But the lighting is dim, and they have twelve-dollar domestic pitchers on tap and a retired radio DJ who sets up a plastic folding table in the corner and plays hits from his iPhone.

I push open the doors and breathe in the scent of artificial ice and thirty-five-cent chicken wings. The same thing I've done every Tuesday from October until the end of May for the last three years of my life.

The club looks the same as I imagine it did sixty years ago. Paneled walls. A long narrow bar and a scattering of tables and chairs, all the same shade of light pinewood.

A big glass window opens to the curling rink, where eight teams look to be playing their tenth and final ends, after which they'll make their way to the bar for pints and socializing, the entire point of the sport for most curlers.

It doesn't take long to spot Dax. A special seashell in the Tuesday night recreational league, Dax doesn't come for the beer. The man loves to curl, which is evident as I gaze at him hovered just above the ice, spending two minutes too long assessing his next shot.

I never thought I'd grow up to be a below-average curler in a recreational curling league. However, a few years ago, my job at Eaton's Drug Mart had this annual health challenge where everyone was supposed to take on a new activity. I have the coordination of a newborn deer on ice. There's a good reason why I spin instead of cycling outdoors (the safety of my fellow Hamiltonians is at stake). Dax heard about my dilemma and suggested we join the most ridiculous sport we could come up with. It came down to curling and bobsledding, but the latter is ridiculously expensive and requires much more stamina than one would think.

So we joined the Tuesday night curling league. Dax revealed he's an ice shark who enjoys crushing senior citizens. I discovered I enjoy participating in Canada's third-favorite winter pastime more than I ever imagined.

"Great caboose on that one, eh?"

A gray-haired woman pokes me with her elbow, her eyes locked on Dax as he crouches in an attempt to better see the angle of his line.

"If I was fifty years younger, I'd be all over that. Hell, twenty years younger, and I'd probably at least see if he was in the market for a paramour."

She chuckles. It's a deep smoker's laugh and is immediately followed by an obvious up-and-down.

"You're not half-bad either. I'd introduce myself if I were you. Take it from an old bat; the good ones get snatched up quickly."

I get a second elbow poke. My companion continues to laugh until another elderly woman emerges from the locker room, and the pair leave, laughing together.

My gaze drifts back to the ice, where Dax is still contemplating his shot but standing now. Whether it's that horny woman's words still lingering like smoke in the air or the fact that I'm still orienting myself in this strange new world, I take a moment to check him out. *Really* check him out.

Dax looks exactly the same. He's wearing his "curling uniform," black sweatpants that sit low on his hips and cling to a butt that I guess—objectively—most women would consider attractive. His faded black henley hugs him in all the places that make it evident that he still makes good use of the YMCA membership he's had since he was sixteen.

His lips are pressed into a firm line, and his dark brows are pulled low as he examines the angles of the rocks. An earnest expression highlights the sharp angles of his face and strong jaw only half-hidden by his signature dark stubble.

As much as I love to rip into Dax when he gets all serious about his shots, I secretly love how much he loves to curl. I love the way I can always tell that he's rehearsed his pregame pep talks and the way he wraps me in the biggest, warmest bear hugs any time I do anything that even remotely resembles a well-executed curling skill. And although I complain about having to drag my ass off the couch every single Tuesday to a cold, damp arena, I wish I was out there with him tonight.

Who is out there with him tonight?

With me off the roster, there's an open vice-skip position on the Ice Ice Babies.

My eyes scan the length of the sheet. On the ice is Dougie, who is Dax's cousin, and Dougie's husband, Brandon. But it's unclear who their fourth is until she slides over to Dax like a

South Asian Tessa Virtue and crouches beside him, whispering something in his ear that makes him laugh. They bump fists, then complete this complicated handshake that makes my blood bubble under my skin because since when does Dax do weird bro-like handshakes? We never had one.

Sunny Khatri. In my timeline, she plays for the Hammer Curls. She's arguably the best curler in the entire league. She's also painfully beautiful with her long, glossy black hair and big brown baby-deer eyes. I've caught my Dax admiring more than her curling form on more than one occasion. In my world, they're rivals. Here, they look to be friends. Close friends.

This could be a complication.

I turn away from the window to gather my thoughts and pull together some sort of a game plan.

Tonight needs to go well. Not only do I have to recover from a less-than-stellar first impression this morning, but I also have to start our friendship over from scratch. Usually, when I meet someone new, there's no pressure. If we click—we click. If we don't—well, then I say a polite *thank you, next* and move on with my life. But if I screw this up with Dax, I won't be able to get back to my reality, which means I will lose the person who knows me best in the world. Even holding the idea of that happening in my head for a single moment makes my stomach feel like someone's wringing it out like a dishcloth.

I need booze. Something to steady my nerves. Clearly not having learned a lesson from our margarita party last night, I make my way to the bar. Sliding onto a maroon cracked-leather barstool, I greet the bartender, Larry, with my sexy wink that Dax has informed me, on more than one occasion, is not the least bit sexy.

"Evening, Lawrence." I nod at the television mounted to the wall behind him. "Your Jays are looking pretty decent this year.

It's just a shame Joe Nintendo broke his toe. Won't be rounding the bases like he did last year." I rest my chin between my two hands and wait for Larry to argue with me. It's our shtick. We do it every Tuesday night. I say something about sports that's completely ignorant or entirely made up. He gets all riled and red, arguing with me until he realizes I'm joking. Then he pulls his bar towel from his back pocket and pretends to swat me with it. I run away, yelling, *Free beer!* He puts it on my Visa card at the end of the night.

However, this Larry just squints at me and scratches his balding head.

Right. I'm still in curse country. And since I'm not friends with Dax, I don't frequent the Grand Victoria's bar, so this poor guy doesn't know who I am.

"Uh, yeah," he finally says. "Looking like it's going to be an interesting season. What can I get for ya?"

There's no need to think hard about this answer.

"Pitcher of Hurry Hard, please and thank you." It's what Dax and I drink every week. We split a pitcher of beer and a Rock On party platter. Dax eats the wings. I get the potato wedges. We order two dipping sauces for the mozzarella sticks because we both refuse to share. And although Dax in this timeline doesn't know me, it's never a bad idea to approach someone with free beer. I figure I can use it as a peace offering.

With the pitcher in one hand and a stack of glasses in the other, I turn in time to see a group of players exit the ice. Half of them head to the changing rooms to shower or change or grab belongings from lockers. The rest head straight for the bar.

Dax skips the shower and heads straight to our usual table, next to the window but far enough from the DJ table that you can hold a conversation. I intercept him just as he's about to sit down.

"It's you." His eyes widen as they meet mine. "What are you doing here?"

My stomach instantly fills with a hundred fluttering yet very confused butterflies. Fluttering because I haven't had my beer yet, and I'm nervous. Confused because this is Dax I'm talking to, and there's no reason to be nervous. I should be good at this by now.

He doesn't sit. But he grips the back of the chair with enough force that his knuckles turn white. I wonder if he's considering throwing it in my path and seeking out the nearest exit. After this morning, I don't blame him.

"I am not stalking you, I swear. I came for the cheap hot wings and to check out the league because I'm thinking of joining. And then I saw you out there on the ice and I wanted to apologize. I think we may have gotten off on the wrong foot. I'm Gemma." Setting the beer down, I thrust my hand toward him and wait. He shakes it because Daxon McGuire is a true gentleman, even in the face of a potentially unstable female.

"I owe you an explanation." I take a seat on one of the benches, completely uninvited. After a moment of deliberation, Dax takes the chair across from me.

Grabbing a glass from the stack, I pour myself a drink, taking the time to conduct one last mental run-through of my story.

Kiersten, Aunt Livi, and I all agreed that it was probably best for me not to tell Dax the whole parallel universe story, seeing as my mission is to get him to sign up for a lifelong friendship. Instead, I've concocted a string of excuses that are close enough to the truth that I'll remember them and normal enough that they'll make me appear quirky—or at least that's the plan.

"I was having a bit of a rough time this morning." I dive right in. "My boyfriend broke up with me, and my best friend . . .

well—to shorten a very long story—I thought something terrible was happening with him. So when I wandered into your store, I wasn't thinking straight. And then it seemed like a safe place to let all my pent-up angst out, so I did. Then I got embarrassed. But I'm good now, and I want to thank you for your kindness."

I stop talking. Or yammering. Or whatever you'd call the jumble of semi-sensical words pouring from my mouth.

Dax stares back at me for a solid moment before he gives a sharp, curt nod. "All good. I get it. We all have days where we need to scream into the void. I'm just glad to see you're okay."

He moves to stand, as the conversation is over, and I'm good, so he's good.

"So yeah," I say, a little too loud for an indoor setting. "If you ever need me to return the favor, I'm happy to. We could grab drinks. Or if you ever need a safe place to let out your pent-up angst, you could come to my place. It's a basement. But the walls are pretty thick. Great for angsting."

Dax raises a brow. "You want me to come to your basement where no one can hear me scream?"

Shit. That sounded way less creepy in my head. This is not going well.

I push the stack of glasses toward him. "Can I offer you a beer?"

Dax eyes my cups and the beer pitcher on the table before shaking his head. "Thanks, but I'm not a fan of lagers. I'm gonna grab something else from the bar, but you have a great night, Gemma."

He smiles at me before he gets up, but it's stiff and forced—no teeth. It's the smile he gives tollbooth operators and those people who go door-to-door selling internet packages. Our conversation is over.

I'm a little stunned. Shell-shocked. Also, in what universe does Dax not like Hurry Hard? Splitting a pitcher of beer after curling is our thing. We do it every Tuesday, which makes me suspect that this is less about the beer and more about the person offering it.

On my walk over here, I pictured many ways this night could go. Envisioned awkwardness, maybe even a little groveling on my end, but at the end of every one of my fantasies, Dax and I became friends. He'd find me funny and charming. Recognize our souls are kindred spirits. We would end our evening both knowing we'd stumbled upon a friendship that was really special. Not once did I ever picture him rejecting my friendship. And frankly, that hollow, aching hole in my chest feels a hell of a lot worse than it did when I broke up with Stuart.

Abandoned and alone, I contemplate my next move with limited options. Aunt Livi is in bed. Kiersten's probably watching reality television or doing god knows what with Trent, and although I live by the philosophy that abandoning a nearly full pitcher is a mortal sin, I have too much pride to sit here by myself and drink it.

I stand and shoot one last longing look in the direction of the bar, where Dax is chatting with Larry, before gathering my purse and heading for the door.

"Gemma Wilde, what the hell are you doing here?" a voice booms behind me, and I turn to face the broad grin and open arms of Dax's cousin Dougie. There's no mistaking the invitation for a hug, and I fall into it, letting his white hairy arms pull me tight to his chest, where he's all lemons and mint and comfort. I hold on for what is probably too long. But with the wound from Dax's rejection still painful and fresh, it feels wonderful to be known.

"What are you doing here?" he asks again. "Not that I'm complaining. I guess I've never really seen you out in the wild. Brandon"—he turns, calling to his husband—"you remember Gemma, she owns Wilde Beauty."

Brandon extends his hand for a very firm handshake. It provides zero clues about our relationship in this life, as I swear you could know Brandon for fifty years and he'd still greet you with stiff British formality.

"Ah yes." He releases my hand. "The woman whose mortgage we are likely paying with the amount you spend on skincare."

He runs his hand down Dougie's arm with a level of affection reserved for only his husband. "We were just about to grab a pint. Would you care to join us, Gemma?"

I gesture to the pitcher left abandoned on the table. "I bought that, and you are welcome to it."

Brandon may be formal, but one can buy his heart with free beer. For the second time, I take the same seat at our regular Tuesday night table. This time, my companions accept my friendship beer with a *thank you* and cheers.

"So you came here tonight to lure handsome men with beer." Dougie winks as he takes a sip.

His statement isn't far from the truth, although not in the way he thinks.

"I actually came to check out the curling," I lie. "I used to play in a league, and I've been finding myself missing it lately." Not a lie at all.

Dougie twists around in his seat to face the bar. "Dax!" he yells. "Get your ass over here."

Dax turns at his name, his eyes flicking from Dougie to me. He grabs his beer stein from the bar, gives an air-cheers to Lawrence, then makes his way slowly to our table.

"Dax, this is Gemma." Dougie points his beer at me.

"We've met," Dax says as he slides into the seat next to Dougie, who shoots him back a look because there's now three of them on their side of the table to my one.

"Gemma owns that skincare store down the street from you. It's funny. I've been thinking for a while that the two of you should meet. You've got a lot in common. Both young. Unattached. Not to mention Gemma is looking to join a curling team." Dougie shoots me a not-so-subtle wink. "I know we're often short a player when Sunny gets called in to work. I thought you'd maybe want Gemma's number. Give her a call sometime, eh?"

It's very apparent what Dougie is trying to do here. The slight raise to his eyebrows. The way his arm nudges at Dax's ribs. And even though Dougie just confirmed Dax is single, I have zero desire to make *Gexon* a thing. But I also can't help but feel offended by the way Dax shifts uncomfortably in his seat, as if it's the last thing he wants to happen as well.

I rack my brain for a new topic of conversation. Something unabashedly Gemma-ish I can say that will immediately click with Dax. Identify me as one of his people.

Then she appears.

Like an apparition at the end of the table. Smelling of cocoa butter and confidence.

"What's up, team? Why are you all sitting in a row like weirdos?" Her attention turns to me. "Oh hey. We haven't met. I'm Sunny."

She slides onto the seat beside me and extends a graceful hand. Her skin is smooth and soft. Her smile is wide and genuine and so naturally beautiful that I freeze for a half second in awe. Until she turns it to Dax, and he smiles right back, and my insides curdle.

Dax has these intense green eyes. They're this beautiful emerald shade that I was sure was fake until one night, when we were very drunk, he let me poke his eyeball to prove he wasn't wearing contacts. So I've confirmed they're genuine. And mesmerizing, especially when he gives his undivided attention. It's like the whole world melts away, and you feel like you're the most interesting person he's ever come across. Those eyes have talked me into road trips, drinking kombucha, and asking my boss for a raise I deserved. They've talked me out of buying Crocs, getting bangs, and many moments of self-doubt. Dax's undivided attention is a powerful drug.

He's giving it to Sunny right now.

"It's nice to meet you." I extend my arm for a shake, selfishly drawing her attention from Dax's magic eyes to me as I repeat the whole *I am Gemma, and I'm here to curl* spiel.

"Gemma should give her number to Sunny," Dax says more to Dougie than to me. "She's the one who is always looking for a sub."

I'm sure there's a practical, logistic reason for Dax's rationale. Still, it feels like he's reached into my chest, pulled out my heart, and left it lying on the table next to my rejected friendship beer.

Sunny, however, hands me her phone. "Gemma, that would be amazing. I always feel like such an ass when I have to cancel and don't have anyone to replace me."

"Well, I'm more than happy to replace you." I smile sweetly as I reluctantly plug in my digits.

"Sunny's a two-time Canadian junior curling champion." Dougie brags on her behalf. "Do you think you can compete?"

He winks at me. It's supposed to be a joke. And yet that little quip needles its way straight to my heart, hitting me where I'm most vulnerable. Can I compete?

"I'm more of a warm body on the ice who knows slightly more than the fundamentals," I admit. "But I have a good sweeping arm and am easily cajoled into buying the first round."

"Hear, hear." Dougie raises his glass of beer and cheers his husband. As he sets his glass down, I catch Dax's eye for the briefest moment, noting the slight curl to his lips. Progress?

"You toss a few samples my way before we play, and I'm willing to overlook any shortcomings on the ice, my friend." This time Dougie's cheers is aimed at me. I clink his glass, feeling Sunny's eyes on me again.

"Samples? Are you a chef, Gemma?" she asks.

I shake my head. "No. I own a store. We focus on clean skin and beauty products. It's just down the street from Dax's."

There's a swell of pride in my chest. This is something Dax and I have in common that he likely doesn't share with Sunny.

"Do you own Wilde Beauty?" Sunny's eyes grow wide as I nod. "I have been dying to go in there. Work just keeps me so busy. I can never find the time. That place looks so beautiful."

Her tone feels 100 percent genuine. No sarcasm. No envy. None of the ugly green feelings that are currently bubbling in the pit of my stomach.

"And what do you do, Sunny?" I ask because it's the polite thing to say next.

She breaks into yet another blinding smile. "I work over at McMaster."

"Sunny's a cardiothoracic surgeon," Dax adds, although he doesn't brag as Dougie did earlier. He says it more appreciatively.

McMaster. The children's hospital. Could this woman get any more perfect?

"Yeah, between work and curling and volunteering at the animal shelter, I don't get a whole lot of time to shop." She squeezes my arm again. "But I'd really love to visit your store. I will make some time to come see you, Gemma."

In this moment, I get it. The appeal of Sunny Khatri. Why Dax wants her as a friend. Hell, I'm beginning to think *I* want her as a friend.

The phone on the table in front of her vibrates. She picks it up, swipes and types, and then holds it out for us to see. "I swear to god I say the word *work*, and it sends out some sort of bat signal. Unfortunately, I need to go in. I'm gonna try and see if I can get an Uber. It was lovely meeting you, Gemma."

If I were a good person, I'd be disappointed for her that the night was cut short. But I'm not. I'm too happy that this might mean I get some more time with Dax without the shinier, newer model sitting next to me for immediate comparison.

However, Dax also gets to his feet. "I can give you a ride. It's late."

It takes every single shred of my self-control not to shout out, *No! Stay here. Hang out with me.*

I watch him clap both Brandon and his cousin on the back and throw a friendly wave in my direction. "It was nice to see you again, Gemma."

He turns to follow Sunny, who is headed for the door, but stops when Larry intercepts him with his appetizer platter.

He takes the plate from Larry's hands and returns to our table, and for the briefest of moments, my heart fills with the hope that maybe he's changed his mind and decided to stay.

"Any chance you're hungry?" he asks me. "Dougie and Brandon won't eat carbs, but I swear this place makes the best mozzarella sticks in town."

I manage a nod.

He sets the plate in front of me, then jogs to catch up to Sunny, disappearing with her out the door.

I stare down at the wings and wedges and four brown blobs of cheese on my plate, garnished with a lone leaf of limp romaine lettuce. The only consolation is the single side of marinara sauce.

I need a drink. Not to cope with my problems with alcohol, but to wash down the bitter disappointment climbing up my throat. And the cheese.

However, Dougie and Brandon have drained the last drop from the pitcher. I excuse myself to the bar, checking out the line of taps for possibly the first time in my life. I've never ordered anything but Hurry Hard at the club. I thought it was Dax's favorite. But when I really think about it, it's actually not that great of a beer, and since I'm on my own tonight, I figure I might as well order what I want.

"One Guinness, please," I tell Larry. He gives me a leery look but grabs a glass and pulls the tap without argument. Larry is a good bartender, and Guinness is a pain in the ass to serve due to the two-part pour. Knowing it will be a minute or two before my beer is ready, I excuse myself to the ladies room.

I don't need to pee. I only need a moment to splash a little water on my face. I collect myself and stare at the mirror to ensure I'm still me. It's not a given anymore.

Two gray eyes stare back from the reflection. They look the same as they always have. Maybe a little tired. Dimensional travel will do that to a girl.

When I return to the bar, I feel a little more composed. I catch Larry's eye. He takes the perfectly poured Guinness from the base of the tap and slides it down the bar top toward me.

Larry might be a solid bartender, but he's not so great of a curler. He overshoots, and the beer slides past me. I reach for it but bump hands with another patron doing the same.

"Sorry." We both say it at the same time before I register the emerald eyes staring back at me, and my fingers start to tingle.

"You're stealing my beer now." His words are curt, but his tone is playful.

"I thought you left." My gaze takes a quick trip around the bar and confirms that Sunny isn't here.

He nods toward the front door. "There was a cab in the parking lot waiting. The person who called it didn't show or something. Sunny insisted that she take it and I come back inside."

I make a mental note to take back any negative thoughts I may have been emanating out into the universe about the woman.

"Well, it appears we are both Guinness drinkers. I was certain Larry was sending this to me."

Dax looks at Larry, who is too engaged in an animated conversation with two bar patrons to identify the beer's proper owner.

"Why don't you take it." Dax nudges the glass toward me. "You've had a rough day."

"I'm fine," I insist, and then an idea strikes. It's mixed with a memory. Twirled and swirled together in such a way that I can almost see exactly how the next two minutes are going to play out.

"What about this?" I propose. "The beer should go to the one of us that's more Irish. It's a Guinness. That's practically universal law."

Dax smiles that same slow, easy half smile he gave me the first time I suggested this little wager. In another life.

His fingers tease the cuff of his henley, lifting it slowly, revealing the flesh of his forearm like a slow striptease, but before he reaches the patch of skin where I would bet my life the McGuire family crest is, he looks up. His eyes meet mine and—*poof*. It happens. The rest of the bar dissolves around us.

"Ah . . ." he drawls in his soft Irish brogue. "I'm afraid you've made a terrible decision. You see . . ."

He tugs his shirt. My fingers reach for his skin to trace the outline of the knight on horseback. My heart knows this is how we start. We'll be planning road trips by Friday.

"Sorry to interrupt. . . ."

Fuck.

Sunny stands just behind Dax with at least the sense to look like she's intruded on something.

"So sorry, guys. Turns out the women who called for the cab were smoking around the corner of the building." She holds up her phone. "The closest Uber is twenty minutes away, and they really need me at work. Any chance . . ." She glances from Dax to the front door.

He stands, pulls down his sleeve, and slides the Guinness in front of me in a single fluid motion.

"Looks like the universe wants you to have this beer. See you around, Gemma."

For a second time, I watch him leave without me, wondering what kind of fucked-up universe I've walked into.

Chapter 8

"Dax has a girlfriend? Doesn't that kind of fudge up your plans?"

My sister is hands-free in her minivan. She's driving my nephew, Riley, to school and my nieces, Lucy and Jan, to daycare while talking me through this fudging crisis.

"I don't think she's his girlfriend," I clarify. "I've dealt with girlfriends before. They stick around for three months tops before Dax finds some lame reason why he's not into them. No, this is worse. I think she's his best friend." The words leave a terrible taste in my mouth, one that I'm attempting to rinse away with my second *Gemma with a G* oat latte of the morning.

"Well, that's good, then," Kiersten says, not getting it at all.

I guess in the grand scheme of the plan, it's good. It's a lot easier to kiss an unattached Dax than a happily-in-love one, but truth be told, it feels like Dax is cheating on me. It's irrational, I know. Dax didn't meet me in this timeline until yesterday. But the idea that he could find another *me* feels like a karate chop straight to the throat because I don't think I'd ever be able to find another Dax. And part of me wonders if maybe he's gotten an upgrade.

"So if he doesn't have a girlfriend, when are you going to see him again? Make your moves? Seduce him with the famous Wilde sister charm? Wait! Hold your answer for just a second."

There's indistinguishable white noise on Kiersten's side of the line, followed by the sound of a car door opening and closing and my sister's distant voice yelling, "Have a great day, sweetheart." Then there's a second or two of shuffling and an under-the-breath curse word before Kiersten's voice comes through clearly. "Okay, she's gone. You can dish. How terrible is this woman? Feel free to swear and use awful language. My car is child-free."

I blow out a long breath. I wish I could vent right now. Call Sunny all sorts of terrible names to make the nagging ache at the back of my chest go away. But something tells me it wouldn't help.

"Honestly, Kierst, she's lovely. So nice. So smart. She's a legitimately good curler."

"Well, you're smart. And you're also beautiful. Having seen you fail at multiple sports, I'm going to guess you're a pretty terrible curler. Still, you always look awkwardly adorable when you're bad at things. It's endearing."

I don't know if I'm caught off guard by her statements or if it's just taking me a second to process, but I don't answer her right away.

"Hey," she says. "You're quiet. Are you still there?"

I nod, even though it's stupid because she can't even see me. "Yeah. I think I just really needed to hear that."

"Yeah, well, the sisterly bond transcends dimensions." Her voice softens. "He obviously means a lot to you, so I don't want to see you fuck it up."

I don't want to fuck it up either.

"Okay. I will figure out a way to talk to him. And then come up with some sort of diabolical plan to get him to kiss me. If you have any brilliant ideas, please send them my way."

There's a *click, click, click* of Kiersten's turn signal. It reminds me of a clock. As if the universe is sending a sign that time's a-wastin'.

"You say this guy is your best friend," Kiersten says. "You must know all sorts of things about him. Exploit that. Be the Gemma you know he likes."

That's exactly what I've been doing, and it hasn't exactly been working.

"And if that doesn't snag him, show him your tits. He'll kiss you for sure."

My sister hangs up the phone. I'm not entirely sure if she does it on purpose. She rarely goes through the formality of goodbyes but also often mistakes the radio button for the hang-up one.

I chuck my phone in my purse and walk to the door of Wilde Beauty, where I flip the CLOSED sign to OPEN.

It seems weird to operate this place, seeing as it sort of appeared out of thin air. But I figure it gives me a low-risk way to try out what is essentially my dream job. Skincare is my jam. I know a hell of a lot about it, as I've been buying drugstore skincare for Eaton's Drug Mart for years. Plus, I have a good business head on my shoulders. Running Wilde Beauty should be a cinch.

Narrator: It was not a cinch.

At a quarter to ten, exactly forty-four minutes into my new adventure, a customer enters my shop. Middle-aged white woman, gray shirt, cropped hair.

Her eyes immediately set upon me and narrow. "I'd like to speak to a manager."

My store is eighty square feet. I don't know where she thinks I'd be hiding my managerial staff. She scowls when I tell her, "I'd be happy to help you out."

She produces a bottle of moisturizer. "I don't like the smell of this. I'm here to return it."

I know the brand immediately. It's from a fragrance-free line. So, kind of weird. But okay.

"Not a problem," I tell her. "I can offer you an exchange or refund. Whatever works best."

She marches over to the display of the same line of products, picks up a bottle identical to the unacceptable one in my hands, then promptly stomps over to my counter, where she slams it down. I can already sense that I will be calling Kiersten immediately following this interaction.

"Hi, um." I hold up the returned bottle in my hands. "The product you just picked out is the same one you wanted to return."

She stares at me like I'm stupid for stating this fact. "Yes, and?"

Deep breath. "Well, if your reason for the return is that you don't care for the smell, this new one isn't going to smell any different."

The roll of her eyes is so exaggerated that I worry her eyeballs will get stuck.

"Well, maybe there's something wrong with the one I bought. It has probably gone bad."

I have a jar of this very same cream in a shoebox under the sink in the other timeline. I use it whenever I run out of my favorite stuff. It's my backup cream and is easily two years old. It smells just fine.

I unscrew the top of the lid. "Let's see what is going on here."

Ah. Well, there's a problem, all right. Just not the problem she described.

"This jar is almost empty." I hold it out to her in case there's been some sort of mistake.

She folds her arms across her chest. "So?"

I summon my best customer service voice and try to form kind words, but what comes out is more of a "You can't return an empty jar."

She glares at me. "You're telling me you don't stand by your products. I even have a receipt." She tosses a white sheet of paper on the counter.

A brief glance down has me biting my lip to both stifle my laughter and prevent the string of profanities running through my head from making their way out of my mouth.

"You didn't even buy the cream here." The receipt is an email from one of those huge online retailers.

She scoffs. "That shouldn't matter. You sell this product. You should stand behind it."

I count to ten and then politely tell her to leave. She responds by threatening to ruin me with a bad Tripadvisor review. I tell her no one under forty uses Tripadvisor and to go right ahead.

It's barely ten, and I'm already done with this day.

My next set of customers comes about fifteen minutes later in the form of three teenage girls. They wear matching blue V-neck sweaters and blue-and-gray kilts. I ask if they need help, but they completely ignore me until finally, one breaks away from the pack and comes over to my counter.

"Wow, you are so pretty. You need to tell me what you use on your skin."

Now, I don't normally think of myself as a vain person, but after spending a night with Sunny, my confidence is in need of a boost. I take my new friend through my skincare routine, showing her the products, even letting her sample a couple. I'm sure I've made a sale, but when I ask her if she'd like to purchase anything, she smiles with a "No thanks," then turns and leaves with her two friends out my front door. It isn't until I'm back behind my counter that I even notice something is missing. The cleanser I showed her when she complimented my pores has vanished. As have a toner, two lip gloss tubes, and a pot of hand cream.

"Those little bitches." Or am I the bitch? I was duped. Lulled into a false sense of security with shameless compliments. My sole consolation is that those fuckers made off with the almost-empty jar of stink cream.

Now I'm really done with this day.

Tears brim my eyes, and when they threaten to fall, I squeeze my eyes shut until the feeling subsides. When I open them again, he appears like an apparition. Walking briskly down the sidewalk past my window, tall dark roast from Brewski's in hand.

"Dax." I only whisper the word, but it's as if it reaches him anyway. He turns and raises his hand in a wave, and our eyes meet through my front window. I wave back, sending him subliminal messages with my eyes. *Dax, if there is any part of you that recognizes how great we are together, give me a sign.* He smiles. My heart fills like a helium balloon.

Because that right there is a genuine Daxon McGuire smile.

Chapter 9

THE TERRIBLE, HORRIBLE, no good, very bad day ends with nervous energy and a strong desire to avoid spending any length of time in my dark and dreary apartment. The sizable pile of well-loved runners in my bedroom closet hints that I don't own a Peloton in this reality (who even am I?) and instead get my exercise from a good old-fashioned run. After questioning Other Gemma's life goals for a few moments, I accept my fate and strap on a pair of Nikes.

By the time I reach the end of my street, I miss Cody's motivational quotes. And watching Olivia's perfect abs. And even Miss Calibrated, the high-five creep. Mostly, I miss knowing the exact resistance and cadence I need to burn my 405-calorie workout goal.

However, the soothing pitter-patter of my sneakers on the pavement is almost as good as therapy. By the second long loop around the lakeshore, the cool night air hits my sweat-soaked skin, and I stop stressing about the clusterfuck that is my life. There's nothing quite like a runner's high.

There's also nothing quite like the hanger that rears its ugly head exactly thirty minutes after I get home.

I open the fridge with a beastly snarl paired with high hopes that my love of clean beauty products translates to clean eating. But other than a box of baking soda and my half-filled Brita water filter, my fridge is completely bare. As are the cupboards.

My shower, however, is occupied by a tiny black spider. I name him Frank. He absolves me for accidentally squishing his cousin and we make an agreement that if I vacate the apartment for forty-five minutes, he'll skitter off back to his web and save us both the trauma of attempted murder by Kleenex.

I throw on my salt-and-pepper Roots sweatpants, pull my sweaty hair into a bun, and grab my old faded pink Abercrombie hoodie.

I love this sweatshirt. It is aggressively pink and incredibly comfortable. Yet, I gave it away in my timeline because Stuart said it reminded him of Pepto-Bismol.

Well, fuck you, Stuart. I slip it on with a smile, grab my phone, and google nearby grocery stores.

In my old life, I mostly shopped at the market downtown, held every Saturday in Jackson Square. Or had my groceries delivered, as my high-paying job came with demanding hours that allowed little time for browsing the aisles. Occasionally, I would shop at Giovanni's No Frills over on Main—until two years ago, when Dax and I had a minor incident in aisle five, resulting in a lifetime ban.

We had come from one of our curling games. There had been a few more postgame pitchers than usual. I'll admit we were a little bit tipsy, at that happy level of drunk where everything made us giggle.

We needed ketchup, chips, and white milk (which may sound gross in theory but will change your life). Our cart was empty otherwise, so I told Dax to get in (or maybe he got in on his own). Either way, it ended with me attempting to push him down the aisle at full speed.

All I remember is Dax yelling, *Beware of rogue bananas.* And then seeing an abandoned, half-eaten one on the aisle floor. I didn't slip on it (that would have been far too cliché), but in my attempt to avoid stepping on it, I took a sharp turn, causing Dax and the cart to crash into the paper towel display. It toppled everywhere. The assistant store manager, Manny Paletta, came running. Dax named it a top-five moment in his life. We were told to never, ever step foot inside No Frills again. In all fairness, it was a fitting punishment.

I haven't thought about setting foot inside since.

Until now.

Because it occurs to me, as I head out into the late-July evening, that in this life, Dax and Gemma—dynamic duo—does not yet exist. Therefore, neither does the ban.

A fortuitous loophole.

My rule-loving heart still palpitates as I walk through the automatic front doors. It keeps its off-tempo rhythm until I reach aisle five and the rows of no-name potato chips and off-brand pop.

The aisle is empty, save for a stack of President's Choice diet colas in its center.

I breathe a soft sigh of relief.

"Is there anything I can help you with, miss?" I recognize the male voice behind me immediately.

Manny Paletta.

Supposedly he's the nephew of Giovanni Paletta. As in the Giovanni of Giovanni's No Frills. Although it's possible Dax made that fact up to fuck with me.

He looks the same as in my timeline. Gangly body. Full mop of dark curly hair. A fresh face that makes it look like he's still a year away from high school graduation. Eyes that indicate he's seen a lot more life.

"Are you looking for something in particular?" Manny asks again.

"No?" I answer, assessing him assessing me. I'm curious if our enmity transcends space and time.

It appears it does not, yet I'm tempted to test the waters.

"Where do you keep the paper towels?" I ask him.

He points to a display a whole five feet away. "See that pyramid of paper towels?"

"Yes."

"That's where we keep the paper towels."

He turns and leaves me completely unattended. I know I'm in the clear.

A small ache blooms in my chest as I stare at the perfectly piled stack of knockoff Bounty. Another tiny memory that makes me miss Dax more.

"You ever get the urge to dive straight into that thing?"

At first, I think he's a hallucination brought on by multiverse travel and hunger.

But he's real. Dax in the flesh. Standing with his arms crossed. Staring at the scene of one of our best friendship moments.

"I can tell you, on good authority, it's not a good idea if you plan on shopping here in the future."

Then it occurs to me. Dax is a bit of a health nut. He insists on shopping at this overpriced organic store over on Locke. "What are you doing here? You don't shop here."

Dax looks around the store. "I don't?"

Shit. I need to stop letting words come out of my mouth before I've had the chance to filter them. "What I meant is that I've never seen you shopping here before."

Dax gives me a curious stare. "Well, I can say on good authority that I have been shopping here pretty regularly for the last few years. I am almost on a first-name basis with the assistant store manager."

Manny walks by, eyeing Dax and me and the paper towel display as if he can sense we're talking about him.

"Ah, right. Manny," I tell Dax. "Giovanni's nephew."

Dax raises his eyebrows, impressed. "That's a fun fact. I will file it away for a rainy day."

There's an awkward pause in our conversation that draws out for a while, leaving me searching for the right words to say next. It is a twist of fate that we're both here. Although I might have preferred nonfluorescent lighting and to have put on more presentable pants, my body craves Dax. Not in a sexy way, but the kind that I want to go home with him. Curl up on his tiny two-seater couch, steal his favorite big fuzzy Hudson's Bay blanket, and watch reality television until our eyeballs start to ache.

I eye his basket. "Those look like great bananas. Ripe, but not so ripe that you'll be forced to make banana bread tomorrow."

Dax nods. "That's the hope."

There should be a thousand conversation starters on the tip of my tongue. I've never, ever had problems talking to Dax. But the only thought that seems to surface is to comment on the plumpness of his plums. At least I have the self-awareness to know that that's fucking weird and not at all in line with the fun-loving friend I'm trying to portray.

So I stand there. Awkwardly. Mouth shut. Staring creepily at his fruit until he makes a wide turn with his cart to get past mine. "Have a good night, Gemma."

"I guess I'll see you around," I say to the back of his head.

Jeeeeeesssssuuuusss. Okay. Deep breaths. Round three with Dax has gone slightly better than round one, about on par with my performance at the curling club. At this rate, it will take me another four years before we're friends. Maybe Kiersten was right. Not the showing-Dax-my-tits part. But maybe I should change my tactics. There are only so many opportunities to have Dax practically falling into my lap.

I finish my shopping and head for the checkout counter, where I'm grateful Other Gemma also uses the same debit card pin she picked out when she was thirteen.

By the time I get outside my arms are burning, and the yellow plastic bags are cutting my palms, a painful reminder never to shop when I'm hungry. I start down Main toward my basement, but a passing car catches my attention. An old Toyota Avalon— I swear for a moment that it's Dax's old car. The one he nearly drove to rust before he finally gave it up and got his Jeep. I turn to get a better look. My body makes the rotation, but my flip-flop does not. My foot slips right off the side of my shoe, and instead of dropping my groceries and saving my face like a rational human, I try to save my bananas from bruising.

My knee hits the pavement with a hard thud. It slows my fall but not enough to counter the momentum that thrusts my torso forward, connecting my chin with the curb.

"Ahhhh," I cry, abandoning my groceries two seconds too late.

Woman down.

I'm wounded.

I'm . . .

I roll to my back like an injured turtle, pressing my palm to my chin, which is stinging like a motherfucker. It's unclear if I'm dealing with a minor flesh wound or something that requires medical attention until I remove my hand and determine that although there is a notable amount of blood, it's probably not ER worthy.

It is, however, serious enough to justify retiring my Pepto-

Bismol sweatshirt from any future public appearances. I pull its cuff over my hand and press on my wound as the entirety of my chest aches with a heavy, hollow feeling.

I want to go home. Not my basement home. To my condo and my old life.

And although my common sense fully acknowledges that a slip and fall could have easily happened to anyone, my temporal lobe blames Other Gemma. Her lack of a car. Her tightly managed budget that only allows for the necessities of frill-less groceries.

I'm pulling myself from my puddle of self-pity and into a seated position when a car drives up beside me, and its familiar grumbling engine and chipped red paint calm the thunderstorm inside my chest.

The driver's side door of the Avalon opens and slams, and mere moments later, Daxon McGuire is kneeling beside me, asking in a worried tone, "Are you okay, Gemma?"

His hand slides under my chin, tipping it up toward him, cradling my face as if it is his firstborn's.

"Can I take a look? Do you mind?" His fingers cover mine, and he waits until I nod before he carefully moves my hand from my chin.

"Oh shit." He winces at my wound and then returns my hand to my face.

"Hold tight for just a sec. I'll be right back."

He runs to his trunk and pops it open. I'm blocked from seeing what exactly he's doing until I hear a slam, and he returns with a white piece of cloth in his hand.

"Here." He hands it to me. "Use this. It's clean. I promise."

I recognize the soft cotton fabric immediately. It's Dax's favorite shirt. Well . . . one of his three favorite shirts. He got them in a three-pack two years ago at a Boxing Day sale at The Bay. They feel like butter, have the perfect level of V (not too much chest), and are the right length to fit his long torso yet slim enough to pull tight in all the right places. He loves those shirts far more than any human should love a piece of clothing.

He wore the first of the three so often that it had holes and was so thin you could see his nipples. His mother got so fed up with him wearing it that when she came to visit, she offered to do his laundry and had an "accident" with the bleach (or so Dax tells the story). Shirt number two suffered a run-in with a bratwurst at a Jays game. No bleach could stand up to the bright-yellow mustard stain. Dax cried when he threw it out.

If the same things happened in this timeline, the shirt in my hands is the last one. Dax's final perfect shirt, and he's giving it to me.

"You're really bleeding." He takes the shirt from my stunned hands and presses it to my chin before I can tell him I'm not worth the sacrifice.

It stings. Oh fuck, it stings. But the tears in my eyes are not ones of pain.

"You didn't even hesitate." I fight back a swelling lump of gratitude in my throat.

His other hand cups the back of my head, his fingers checking for bumps. "Do you think you need to go to the hospital?"

I shake my head. "Just home to an ice pack and a Band-Aid and maybe a shot of tequila, but that's more to soothe the ego bruise."

He smiles. "That sounds like a solid plan. Think you can stand?"

I wait until my heart steadies to a pace where it feels like it's not going to give out at any moment, then let him help me to my feet.

He gathers the can of tomatoes, the bruise-free bananas, and the rest of the scattered groceries into my bags. When he's done, he brushes a few stray hairs from my forehead and once again repeats the chin lift and assesses.

I get the emerald stare. It's all mine. And I soak it up like a neglected house plant.

Yes. Fine. He's probably checking to make sure my pupils are still dilating, but staring into his eyes feels like home.

"You're sure you're okay?" His voice is so calm and steady. It's everything I need right now. But all at once, the weight of the day hits me like a sucker punch, and my lower lip begins to tremble. I can feel tears brimming my eyes at a rate too fast for me to blink away.

His hand finds my shoulder and squeezes, and before he can pull away, I melt into him, pressing my head to his chest, not caring whether he thinks it's weird or not.

He smells the same. Exactly like my Dax. Irish Spring soap. The faintest hint of cologne. And when I begin to worry that I've overstepped his gesture of chivalry, his arms wrap around me, and he holds me close, firm, yet light enough that I know it's my call on how long our embrace lasts.

And as odd as it is—the bleeding, the oat milk and eggs puddling at my feet—I need this. To be held. To feel safe. To know that Dax will always have my back when my world implodes. So I stay, tucked into the little nook between his arm and his chest, greedily breathing him in. Bathing in this feeling I've been missing.

"You're a good guy, Daxon McGuire." My voice is muffled against his chest. And as I pull away to look at him, his arms stay wrapped around me, and it makes me think.

I'm very much in the proximity of his mouth. It's possible that if I pressed up onto my toes, my lips could easily meet his. Aunt Livi was pretty adamant about performing the cleanse in the proper order, but would it be so terrible if I kissed him now and banked it for later? Instead of waiting for the moon to be right to make my wish and my chicken dinner sacrifice?

"You look like you're thinking pretty hard about something." Dax lets go of my shoulders, though his hands pause on either side of me as if he's half expecting I'll tip over.

"It's nothing," I lie. "Just happy I didn't bruise my bananas."

"Wouldn't want to be forced to make premature banana bread."

He's making fun of me.

But his smile is playful, that is, until he removes his perfect shirt from my face and gives my cut another once-over.

"The bleeding has slowed but not stopped. It's more of a scrape than a cut, so I don't think you need stitches." His eyes meet mine. "Do you have any Band-Aids at home?"

"Your guess is as good as mine."

His gaze flicks to his car. "Pretty sure I have a stash. Why don't I give you a ride?"

I nod as he reaches for the passenger door and holds it open like a valet. In any timeline, I imagine Dax is always a gentleman.

Once he's in his own seat, he leans across the console, pops open the glove compartment, and digs until he pulls out a strip of Band-Aids.

"I wasn't sure if I still had these." He holds the strip between his teeth, then yanks one off with a quick jerk of his head.

"Aren't you the Boy Scout."

He pulls the Band-Aid from the packaging, letting the little white papers fall to his lap. "I didn't make it to Scouts. I quit after Beavers, so no promises."

He tilts back my chin and applies the Band-Aid with the softest press of his fingers. Satisfied, he reaches for a second Band-Aid. I watch him—he's absorbed in careful concentration, brows pulled low, biting on his lip. God, I've missed him. This comfortable ease between us. It's only been forty-eight hours, but they were long hours, and the ones where he didn't know me felt empty and wrong.

"You thinking about bananas again?" Dax looks up briefly from his work to smirk at me.

"Nope. Just thinking about a friend. You remind me of him."

Dax looks up. "Ah, so he's incredibly handsome."

"Some would say."

Dax sits back in his seat and gives my face a satisfied nod.

"I think you're all patched up."

My hand finds my chin, and as my fingers skim over the covered surface, they encounter a lot more Band-Aid than anticipated.

I flip down the overhead passenger mirror and fight back a snort. The wound that required a single Band-Aid is now covered with four.

"I told you I wasn't making any promises." He feeds his key into the ignition, and the engine rises to life.

"Where can I take you?" he asks.

"Oh, I live over on . . ."

Shit.

I can't remember my address.

It's either Catherine or Mary. Definitely a girl's name. How the hell am I going to explain to Dax that I don't know where I live?

"Take King to Victoria, left on Cannon. I'll tell you where to turn."

Dax pulls the car out into traffic, and we travel down King in silence, hitting green lights all the way. The lights from the streetlamps temporarily illuminate his features, highlighting his strong jaw.

I'm not sure if it's the lighting or if the last five minutes have scarred me in ways I can't begin to unpack, but Dax looks different. Older? Wiser too, maybe? It's like that goofy guy I met four years ago in a bar has slowly been replaced piece by piece with this quietly confident man. And for some reason, I failed to notice it happening.

If I'm having an epiphany, it's halted when I recognize the scraggly maple on the upcoming corner. "Left!" I point to what is, in fact, Catherine Street.

Dax makes a quick turn.

"It's the white house up on the right."

He pulls up in front and cuts the engine.

"Well, thank you for the ride. And the rescue. And the patch-up." I rub my bandage-covered chin.

"Do you need help getting to your door?" Dax nods at the darkened house behind me.

I shake my head. "It's pretty much a straight shot. Only one sharp turn, but you can see it coming. I think I'll be okay."

He moves from his seat, around the car, and to my door so quickly that I have barely undone my seatbelt before he's holding my door open. He offers his hand, helping me and my groceries out onto the sidewalk, and we stand, facing each other, both with the same uncertain posture as if neither of us is sure of what comes next.

Dax clears his throat. "Maybe I should give you my number. So you can text me and let me know you got in okay."

I know his number by heart, but this is the progress I've been waiting for.

I pull my phone from my purse and enter his digits as he says them, then send a text to him with the message, *thanks again. Gemma.*

As I place my phone back into my purse, the strap slips from my shoulder. Dax moves like a flash, catching it before it falls to the sidewalk.

"Thanks," I tell him as he carefully places the strap back on my shoulder, noticing how warm his fingers are even through the heat of my sweatshirt.

It fills me with this urge to dive into his arms again. To feel safe. To feel like me. But he removes his fingers before I do anything stupid.

"You good?" he asks.

"Great," I answer honestly. "Really great."

I keep to my promise and make it all the way to my basement without any serious injuries.

I unload my groceries and get ready to take what is thankfully a now spider-free shower, but before I start the water, my phone vibrates on the counter.

It's a text.

From him.

A link to a recipe for banana bread and the words *just in case*.

Who knows. With everything that's happened, maybe I will get wild tonight and make it. New world. New me. Right?

Chapter 10

WHAT YOU THINK you become.

What you imagine you create.

Tell the universe what you want.

Trust that it will gift you with all that you need.

The text flashes across my screen as I'm slipping my keys into the lock at Wilde Beauty. I fling my purse onto the front counter while simultaneously kicking the door closed with my foot and responding to my aunt's cryptic message.

More advice from your tea leaves?

She responds back immediately, almost as if anticipating my skepticism.

Krystal my yoga teacher said it this morning during Savasana. Although I suspect she was misquoting Buddha. Either way, I think it's a good mantra for your day. Tell the universe what you want. It may surprise you.

What I want is a grande oat milk latte. And to have Dax back in my life. And to not completely screw up my store, like I did yesterday, as I'm not entirely sure how dimensional time travel works. On the off chance there is another Gemma out there, I don't want to completely fuck things up for her when I go back and she returns. So although I'd normally roll my eyes at my aunt's suggestion to manifest what I want to happen, today, I'm willing to try it.

"Hello there, you," I say out loud to no one in particular. "I'm Gemma Wilde. And I'm a little new at this manifesting thing, so bear with me. Um . . ."

I look around my store, which appears to be plucked straight from my imagination. Stuff I only dared to dream about in my old life.

Logically, I should be over the moon right now. I am living the manifestation of my dream. But yesterday's fleeting few moments with Dax have me longing for a life where nights like that were the norm and not the exception.

"I want my best friend back." I speak my heart to a table of cleansers and toners.

Other than the morning sunbeams streaming through my front window, hitting the glass jar of crystal-handled jade rollers and causing tiny rainbows to splay across my ceiling, nothing particularly otherworldly happens. However, my chest feels a little lighter, and it makes me wonder if Aunt Livi is onto something.

"Also, please banish anyone who thinks yelling at me is cool or who feeds their self-worth by posting negative Yelp reviews. And please just send the angry old ladies up the street."

I may not exactly be manifesting, but getting out all of these worries and fears I've been holding in since I stepped foot in Wilde Beauty is cathartic.

"While you're at it, I wouldn't mind a little wrath aimed at anyone who tries to distract me with shameless compliments while stealing my stuff. Curse them with flaky skin and cystic acne."

"Remind me to stay on your good side," says a voice behind me.

I wheel around, clutching my heart, which has momentarily lodged itself between my ribs. "You scared the shit out of me."

Dax leans on my doorframe, seemingly at ease. "Just stopped by to see how the face is healing."

My fingers instinctively stroke my now Band-Aid-free chin. "Face is recovering. Ego is still a little bruised. How long were you standing there?"

He responds with a single lifted eyebrow. "Long enough to have a few questions."

I don't know how to explain this without looking ridiculous. "I was . . ." *Wishing? Hoping? Complaining?* "I was manifesting."

"Oh yeah?" His mouth curls into a smile. "How is it working out for you?"

Fair question. I have no idea. "I think I might have been doing it wrong. I was trying to aim for good things and instead spiraled a little and started listing a bunch of thoughts that confirm entrepreneurship is probably a terrible career choice for me."

He breaks into an even wider grin, as if something I've said is amusing. "I hate to tell you, but I think it's a little late for that. And . . ." He makes a show of glancing around the store. "I think you might be better at it than you think."

It might be the words or the way he says it. Either way, Dax's comment creeps under my skin. And for a moment, I look around Wilde Beauty with wide, new eyes.

Other Gemma really knows what the fuck she's doing. The carefully curated products. The tiny touches. Even the minty-lemon smell of Wilde Beauty is exactly how I think a clean beauty store should smell. But the thing I admire most about Other Gemma is that she had the guts to actually try.

For a whole half second, I'm jealous. *Why her? Why not me?* We share the same DNA, right?

But then my eyes land on the display of hand creams. The one missing a couple of jars from yesterday's teenage crime spree. And I'm painfully reminded that cosmetics are the most stolen retail item in North America. A fun little tidbit I picked up in my old job. However, big-box retailers, like my former employer, have resources to cover shrinkage. An organized high school crime ring could sink a small store like Wilde Beauty.

"I don't know how you do it," I say accidentally out loud to Dax, who has been worrying about this stuff for years. "There's just so much that can go wrong," I clarify.

There's a longer-than-normal beat before Dax answers. "You're right. Owning a place like this isn't easy on the heart."

I look around again, weighing the loveliness of Wilde Beauty against the boulder that has taken up residence in my gut since I first walked into this place. "I don't know if it's worth it. . . ."

"Well . . ." Dax pushes open the door to my store, holding out his hand to me. "As the treasurer of the James Street Small Business Association, I feel as though it's my sworn duty to tell you about all the cool things that come with the deal. If you have a few minutes, I'll show you the best one."

It takes me a full block before I realize where he's taking me. And when he pushes open the door, and the smell of roasting coffee beans floods my senses, I wonder if the high is my body anticipating the caffeine buzz or the fact that maybe . . . just maybe, Aunt Livi's idea worked and I manifested this moment.

Brewski's has always been our spot.

"So the best part of owning a store is coffee?" I ask as he steps into the line and motions for me to take the spot in front of him.

"And being the boss. Opening up a few minutes late because caffeine always takes priority."

This fact I agree with. My workday mornings in my other life are usually so filled with meetings that my coffee gets cold before I can finish it.

"Good coffee is a perk. But I'm still not sold on the rest of it."

Dax thinks for a moment. "If you're not won over by the coffee, I might be in trouble. The only other perks I've got left are complete artistic license over your work and being the one who benefits from the long hours, instead of some suit in a corner office. Plus, no one ever argues when you show up in shorts."

I snort at that last one, but Dax makes a point. There is something satisfying about knowing that when the grind is long and hard, you're doing it for yourself. But it's not the hard work that freaks me out.

"I get what you are saying, but what I'm having a hard time wrapping my brain around are the what-ifs. Like what if I wake up tomorrow, and something bad that's completely out of my control happens, like a flood or a hurricane or, please don't hate me for saying it, another pandemic. Not only could I lose Wilde Beauty, but I could lose everything else. My savings. My ability to make rent." *My security.*

"You're right." Dax slowly nods. "It can feel heavy at times. It's just . . ." He runs his hands through his hair. "All of the very best things in my life have come when I've said *fuck it* and listened to that feeling in my gut that tells me *this is right.* It doesn't always make sense at the time, but I have to think that sometimes it's worth taking a leap of faith.

The smile on his face makes the heaviness inside me dissolve. Dax has always loved owning Kicks. It's his baby. His soul. And part of me wants what he has. The ability to ignore the what-ifs and focus on only the what could be's.

The coffee line moves, shifting us up so we're the next ones in line.

The woman in front of us has a stroller the size of a small Buick, so when she spins it around, I have to take a quick step back. The action throws me off balance, and I worry I'm going to fall until I feel Dax's fingers on my hips steadying me.

"Thanks," I tell him, suddenly aware that the line logistics are leaving nothing more than a small span of air between our two bodies. It's a feeling that intensifies as he leans forward, bending so his mouth is level with my ear, close enough that I can smell his morning shower still lingering on his skin.

"You know I'm going to judge you on your coffee order."

He's joking. Well, maybe 10 percent serious. But it makes me stop and consider. Why not try something different? I've been ordering the same drink since I was sixteen. Maybe the Gemma who has sexy one-night-stands and isn't afraid to start her own store orders something wild.

Snake appears at the counter. "Hey, Gemma, want your usual this morning?"

"Actually, no." *Fuck it. I'm listening to my gut.* "I'm going to take a wild leap and order an oat milk Americano misto."

Snake doesn't comment on my drink order other than to tell me I owe him seven dollars and fifty-three cents.

Dax, however, gives me a funny smile. "Make it two."

"What is your usual?" he asks as we wait for our coffee.

"Oat milk latte."

Dax's eyes flick to the barista making my drink, then to me. "Isn't that the same as a misto but with more milk?"

I shrug. "I'm not ready to jump off a cliff here. Baby leaps."

We get our coffees at the same time. And because Brewski's is busy and we both still have stores that need opening, we head for the door and out onto the sidewalk. I remove the lid from my cup and blow on it a little before taking my first sip.

Dax watches me. "What's the verdict?"

It's good. A little different from what I'm used to, but it's still nutty and smooth, and I can taste the coffee a little more. "Pretty delicious baby step."

Dax takes a small sip of his own drink, winces, then takes a second, longer one.

"You don't strike me as a misto kind of guy." I instantly feel better getting the words off my chest.

"Oh, I'm not," he replies matter-of-factly. "This is an attempt to understand you better, get into the head of Gemma Wilde."

"And what do you think?"

He takes yet another sip, holding the coffee in his mouth for a moment before swallowing. "It's a bit of a shock at first sip, but after a couple, it kind of grows on you."

"Are you talking about me or the coffee?"

Dax looks over at me and grins. "Let's go with the coffee." He stops walking, and his gaze drifts to something across the street.

"I've actually got to stop in at the bank." He points at the TD. "But if your manifesting doesn't work out and you need to go with plan B, let me know. I'm always good for a coffee."

"Thank you for this." I hold up my coffee but mean far more than that.

"Anytime, Gemma Wilde." Dax cheers our cups and turns to walk back across James Street.

I walk back to Wilde Beauty, feeling at ease in this new life for the very first time. We're nowhere near the Dax and Gemma we used to be, but it feels like we've planted a seed that, with enough time, could blossom into the type of friendship we once had. Or at least I can hope.

When I get back to Wilde Beauty, two young moms with babies in those koala-pouch things are waiting by my door. I apologize profusely for opening late. They hold up their very large Brewski's cups. We bond over our shared love of caffeine.

I recommend a few products to help with dark under-eye circles. They purchase what I suggest, plus a few more things. We share a few laughs before they leave.

Next comes a middle-aged woman with a textbook Karen haircut. I brace for an inevitable berating.

But she's lovely and kind. She's a little clueless about skincare but seems happy to listen while I preach the benefits of vitamin C. When it's time to pay, she hands over her Visa with a smile, and I get this urge to try something new. Take a risk. Be the Gemma who drinks oat Americanos and doesn't clench her jaw when there isn't a clear plan.

"Would you be interested in joining our newsletter?"

Karen, whose name, ironically, is actually Karen, pauses before she asks, "Is it about products and stuff?"

This newsletter came to me on a whim. I have no clear plan. But I do have tons of ideas. "Yes. But also tips and advice and information about events we're hosting at the store."

Because apparently I'm hosting events now. *Since when?*

"That sounds wonderful. Sign me up."

I open a note on my phone and take down her contact info. The idea of a newsletter makes me smile. And that smile sticks for the rest of my very busy day until it's time to lock my doors and cash out for the night.

By seven o'clock, I've added five more names to my newsletter list.

As I swipe my note app closed, I see a message from my aunt. It's only a kiss emoji from her morning message that I must have missed. However, I pause and read her words again.

What you think you become. What you imagine you create. Tell the universe what you want. Trust that it will gift you with all that you need.

Okay, universe. Today was a good one. No one yelled or stole.

I managed to avoid any crippling thoughts of doom. You did a decent job at delivering on what I want. Now tell me what I need.

My phone buzzes with a text from an unknown number.

Hi, Gemma, it's Sunny. We have a bonspiel Saturday night, and I've been scheduled to work. Any chance you can sub in for me??

A Saturday night hanging out with Dax? Touché, universe, touché.

Love to. Let the guys know I'll be there.

Chapter 11

I PLAY THREE of the greatest games in the history of curling. It's probably more like three above-average games in a very mediocre recreational league, but it feels momentous. My hits—hit. My curls—curl. I have zero trouble finding the button, which I announce multiple times, each one getting heavier on the innuendo. We make it to the finals. Then we win. Absolutely crush Janice Simmertowski and her team, Curl Power. Which results in at least six rounds of celebration, all involving beer.

It's happening again. That thing where one minute my beer glass is empty and the next it's full, and I lose count—because fractions—and can't even blame my sister. It's 100 percent Dougie. He keeps filling my glass, then Dax's glass, and then mine again. At some point during my very heated argument with Dax about whether mountain lions are the same animals as cougars, Dougie disappears with Brandon.

It isn't until the bartender Lawrence announces last call and I look up at the clock, which says twelve forty-five, that I realize they're not coming back.

"Those jerks cut and ran," I say to Dax as he tries to hand his credit card to Lawrence, who refuses it.

"The good news is they paid the tab first." Dax places his card back in his wallet, pushes back his chair, and holds out his hand.

I take it and appreciate its warm stability as I get to my feet and find out the world has gotten a little spinny. Dax keeps hold of me until we push open the Victoria's doors and step into the parking lot, where Dax's old Toyota Avalon is one of two cars left.

"We should probably walk," he says.

"Definitely should not drive."

Dax is probably as drunk as I am. Also, I don't quite trust my dinner to stay down while riding in the back of an Uber.

We start walking in the direction of my place, which is the exact opposite direction of Dax's. Still, I only realize this fact after two entire blocks have passed.

"Hey, you don't need to walk me home. I can manage on my own."

The moment the words leave my mouth, I trip over the teeniest, tiniest crack in the sidewalk, pitching me sideways, straight into Dax's chest. His hard chest. And his muscular arms hold me tight until my feet once again find steady ground.

"I'm walking you home." His voice is firm. Authoritative. And I like it far more than I should.

"I'm out of your way," I insist again. "If you walk me home, you're going to have to walk twice as far to get—"

Oh shit.

Even in my intoxicated state, I realize I've yet again spewed out a fact I shouldn't know.

Dax, however, doesn't seem to notice. "Stop arguing with me," he says, "I love walking. You don't get an ass like this one without at least ten thousand steps a day." He scoots ahead of me with an exaggerated waggle of his peach butt, then stops and looks over his shoulder. "I saw you checking it out earlier."

"I was not."

I totally was.

The first time was an accident. He was talking to another team. I didn't even realize it was him when I ogled. The second time, he was crouching, and what can I say? He loves his tight pants, and he has a great ass. He knows it. I know it. I just don't usually admit to it.

He begins to walk backward with cocky confidence fueled by a pitcher and a half of beer. "You're telling me you weren't checking me out? Even when I was doing this?" He turns and drops into a deep curling lunge like he's just thrown a rock. It pulls his already-tight black jeans even tighter, and if I wasn't staring at his ass before, I absolutely am now.

"Or maybe this." He starts to thrust, which he definitely did not do on the ice tonight. And though I know he's trying to be funny, I find it very sexual, which has me thinking of Dax doing all kinds of other sexual thrusting motions, to which my body is reacting with tingles.

In very private places.

Places that should absolutely not be tingling in response to my BFF.

"I deny everything," I say, highly suspecting my flushed cheeks are indicating otherwise.

Dax comes out of his lunge and throws up his hands as if he's giving up. "Fine. Deny it all you want. But you should probably know I was checking yours out."

I don't know what to say.

What I want to do is ask *why*? But that question has a strong probability of leading to an answer I'm not 100 percent ready to deal with at this moment. Me. Dax. All the consequences that come if we take another step. Instead, I walk on.

"Good," I call over my shoulder. "Glad we straightened all of that out. Let's go."

We make it half a block before either one of us attempts to start a conversation.

It's Dax who does it. While we're stopped at a crosswalk, standing so close that I can smell the sandalwood-and-vanilla hand lotion they put in the bathrooms at the Victoria.

"Tell me something," he asks, less like a question and more like a command.

"What do you want to know?"

He thinks for a moment. "Something personal. Favorite color? Pet peeve? Have you ever been in love?"

The crosswalk signal switches from the little red hand to the white walking person.

"Mint green, people who use the word *whilst,* and I thought I was once, but the longer I think about it and the better perspective I get, I'm learning I wasn't even close. What about you?" I poke him in the arm. "You can't throw out a question like that and not expect it back."

He grabs my poking finger and holds it. "Banana yellow. Lines of any nature. And no, I've never come close."

I think the Dax in my timeline might answer this question the exact same way. Funnily enough, it's not one either of us has asked before.

"Standards too high?" I guess.

He shrugs. "That could be it. I keep telling myself I'm just a late bloomer."

My response is a hiccup. It's not even a cute hiccup. It's a loud and borderline obnoxious one, and it's followed by two more in rapid succession.

"You are drunk," he says to me, laughing.

"I am very drunk, and you're still holding my finger."

We both look down and stare at his hand, which has somehow weaved its way through all five of my fingers.

"People make bad decisions when they're drunk."

He probably means it as a joke. A throwaway statement. But he's right. My track record in the intoxicated-life-choices department isn't exactly stellar. Case in point: agreeing to an ancient ritual that managed to flip my entire life upside down.

"And now you look like you're thinking about something again." Dax squeezes the hand he's yet to let go of.

"Just recalling my last bad drunk decision."

Dax finally drops my hand but doesn't step away. "Did you kill a man?"

I don't know if it's the raspy timbre of his voice or the way his eyes lock on mine and don't look away, or maybe it's just some invisible signal he's giving off. Still, I get this feeling that Dax wants me at this moment.

And I . . . I don't know how I feel. The tiny part of my brain not bogged down with beer is screaming, *Think about the consequences.* The rest of me has been lulled into a dreamy haze by the deepness of his voice and the smell of the damn lotion. Every cell of my body feels like it's tuned to the highest frequency.

I stop walking.

To catch my breath. Or steady my mind. Or stop my body from vibrating. I don't know.

He stops too, then takes his time walking back until his toes are inches from mine, and I can feel the heat of his breath, and he can probably hear the beat of my heart, which is launching itself against my rib cage.

"You about to confess to murder there, Gems?"

He's calling me Gems. Yet it feels so different in that damn voice.

I look up. "If I did, would you help me hide the body?"

His smile spreads slowly. "That's a big commitment. Do you think we're there yet emotionally?"

I shake my head. "Probably not."

He leans in, and for a second, I think he's about to kiss me. Instead, he whispers, "I'd help you ditch the car."

I could turn my head and kiss him.

He's lingering.

I know it. And although all along, my plan has been to get him to kiss me, it's not supposed to be here or now, yet I still want it to happen.

Whether he reads my hesitation or not, he backs off. My head clears, and I realize how close we were to doing something irreversible.

I start walking before either one of us changes their mind.

It takes a full block before my heart stops beating like a sledgehammer and a second block before I rationalize that the almost-kiss was entirely in my head. Maybe. Probably. No. Definitely in my head.

By the time I'm feeling somewhat normal again, we're walking up Catherine Street, and I can see my house.

"Thank you for walking me home. This is me." I point at the front porch, which is completely dark.

Dax gives the house an assessing look. "I remember. Seems like a nice place."

I shrug. "Frank and I like it."

His eyes cloud. "Who's Frank?"

"My spider. We share a shower. I live in the basement. My entrance is around the back."

Dax eyes my yard. "Right. Down that creepy dark pathway."

"It's not creepy," I say defensively. Then I give it a second look. "I guess it's a little creepy."

He nods and settles into an awkward silence that stretches longer than a beat. "Text me when you get inside," he finally says.

"I can do that."

Again, he points to the path. "I'd walk you, but . . ." His voice trails off.

"But what?"

Now I want to know what he's thinking.

It takes so long for him to answer that I almost think he isn't going to.

"You told me earlier you make terrible decisions when you're drunk, so it's probably better that I stay out here on this sidewalk, and we leave it at that."

There are many ways I could take that statement. And the most obvious one has dangerous implications.

"Goodnight, Daxon McGuire."

"Goodnight, Gemma McGuire."

"It's Gemma Wilde, you drunk."

He shrugs, smiling. "Slip of the tongue."

I turn and leave before I change my mind and do something stupid. When I get to the gate, he calls out, "Hey, Gemma, care to make one bad decision tonight?"

I turn, ready to agree to whatever he suggests.

"Always."

"Friday. Dougie and Brandon are having a party. You should come."

I nod. "I'll let Frank know not to wait up."

Chapter 12

I HAVE BEEN to enough Dougie-and-Brandon parties in my timeline to suspect I'm walking into a frat-boy-style kegger with fancier cups.

The text message that flashes across my home screen on Wednesday confirms this theory.

Dax: Hey there hot stuff!!! Party on Friday is hero/villain-themed. Come dressed to kill. Handcuffs encouraged (seven kissy-face emojis).

It's immediately followed up with a second message.

Dax: In case it wasn't clear. Dougie stole my phone, but looking forward to friday . . . hot stuff (single winking emoji).

Last year, in my timeline, Dougie and Brandon held a hero/villain party. I invited Stuart, but he wasn't into crowded places and held strong opinions on wearing costumes past middle school, so I skipped our standing Friday night date and instead went with Dax. We spent two full weeks scouring the thrift shops on James Street until we found replica costumes of Batman and Robin of the Adam West era. They looked just homemade enough to be amazing. We were the hit of the party.

For some reason, I can't let the memory of that night go. And although I don't have weeks to source the perfect pieces for my costume, I manage to find a pair of beige tights and a red sweater vest and to borrow a yellow cape and black mask from my nephew Riley. Not amazing, but good enough to do Burt Ward justice.

The party is only a twenty-minute walk from my basement address. I can hear Beyoncé blasting before I reach Dougie and Brandon's block. Already there are costume-clad partygoers on the lawn with fancy rose-gold-trimmed plastic cups in hand, playing what looks to be croquet.

The music is so bumping that I can feel the bass reverberate in my chest as I climb the steps to the porch and push open the brightly painted blue door. It opens into Dougie and Brandon's living room and dining room, both of which are packed with sweaty bodies clad in a rainbow array of vividly colored spandex.

My gaze pans the crowd, looking for a familiar face. A very particular familiar face. But instead of finding Dax, I spot Sunny, standing alone in the corner, bopping her shoulders off-time to the music, completely unaware that she's being ogled by half of the Y chromosomes in the room.

She's dressed as Wonder Woman. A DC version that skips the skimpy bodysuit, favoring more modest blue leggings. However, Sunny is all legs, and butt, and boobs. All of which look incredible in spandex and make me very aware that on top of my tights, I'm wearing a pair of cotton Hanes green underpants.

As she weaves through the crowd toward me, black curls bouncing behind her, I reassess that it's not just the Y chromosomes who are guilty of openly ogling and count myself among the guilty.

"I'm so glad you're here." She wraps her arms around me, pulling me into her incredible boobs. "I was standing in the corner feeling awkward because Dougie and Brandon are busy, and I don't know anyone else at this party."

I dwell on the idea that someone who looks like Sunny could ever feel awkward before moving on to processing the second part of her statement. "So Dax isn't here yet?"

She shrugs, then stands on her toes to see over the crowd in the living room. "I haven't seen him, but I only got here about twenty minutes ago."

For a moment, I panic, thinking maybe he made other plans tonight, until I turn and spot him, head above the crowd, working his way through the busy living room toward us. His green eyes catch mine, and as tempted as I am to hold his gaze, my eyes travel south of their own accord.

He's wearing gray pantyhose.

They hug his legs like a second skin. Every muscle, every nook, every curve. And despite my heightened awareness that he's watching me watching him, I home in on a particular curve and find that I am equally delighted and disappointed to see it covered by a pair of matching Hanes black underpants.

I tear my eyes back to his face just in time for him to raise his hand.

"Robin."

I meet him for a high five that, to my delight and surprise, turns into a side hug.

His eyes have a glazed sheen, and his breath smells like the faintest hint of scotch, but here, in the little crook of his armpit, all I can think is *this*. This is exactly what I've been missing. For a whole second, he's my Dax.

"Did the two of you plan this?" Sunny points at our coincidentally coordinated outfits as Dax releases me and repeats the high-five-side-hug with her.

"Not at all." Dax doesn't try to hide the up-and-down he gives my body. "Guess it's just great minds."

Sunny produces a phone from somewhere under her spandex

and snaps a candid photo. She flips the screen, showing it to us. "Well, the two of you look fabulous."

We do. Smiling. Eyes locked on each other. Zero shits given that we look utterly ridiculous. That picture could have been taken in my timeline.

"Your hands are empty, ladies. Let's put some drinks in them." Dax holds out his arms to shepherd us toward the kitchen area, but Sunny steps outside his span.

"Sorry, guys, I can't. I'm on call tonight, but you go ahead."

Dax offers me his elbow. "Shall we?"

I reach for him, my blood humming with the anticipation that I'm getting exactly what I want tonight, time with Dax, alone. However, my head can't help feeling a little guilty, abandoning Sunny at this party.

"Are you sure you don't want to come along for the ride?"

She shakes her head. "No thanks. I just spotted a friend from the hospital. I'll catch up with the two of you later?"

I swear I see her wink as Dax drops his arm and instead places his hand on the small of my back. We navigate the sweaty bodies, finally making it to the kitchen at the back of the house. There's a literal keg set up in the corner next to a rowdy game of flip cup happening on the kitchen table.

Dax fills a fancy rose-gold cup with beer, hands it to me, and then proceeds to fill a second.

"Not drinking Guinness tonight?" I ask between sips.

He holds his beer glass up to the light. "I was actually drinking scotch before you got here, and you can't play flip cup with scotch. I mean, I guess you can, but then you wind up passing out behind Dougie's couch and scaring the shit out of him when you reappear the next morning while he's watching Sportsnet—not that I'm speaking from experience."

"You want to play flip cup?"

Dax has never been a flip cup guy. In fact, we usually spend Dougie and Brandon's parties together on the couch, making fun of Dougie's friends who use flip cup as an excuse to get their dates wasted.

"I was going to suggest *we* play flip cup." He holds his beer out for a cheers.

There's a look to Dax that I can't quite decipher. Not to mention that I have no idea where his head is at, wanting to play this game. But I cheers him back with an enthusiastic "Let's do this," deciding that my objective tonight is to show him that I'm easygoing, fun Gemma. And tonight, easygoing, fun Gemma plays flip cup.

When the next game starts, we take our places at the table. It's five on five. The opposing team is made up of guys who used to play rugby with Dougie back in the day.

On our team is a set of twins, Miranda and Mariah, who are dating two of the rugby players and claim they've never played flip cup before in their lives. We also have Brandon's younger brother Peter, Dax, then me in the anchor position.

My guess is we won't be crushing the competition.

We sing the obligatory *olé* to kick off the game, then get a run of what I'll deem beginner's luck, as both twins drink, then flip their cups on the first try. We have a stellar lead on the rugby boys until Peter gets too excited and flips his cup so hard that it completes two full rotations, hits the table, bounces right off, and rolls underneath. By the time he recovers it and flips, our opponents are on their last player, with both Dax and me yet to go.

But our luck continues.

Our opponent, Jessie, whose name I glean from the aggressive chanting of his rugby bros, seems to have the yips. He can't get his cup to flip. And although he's lightning fast with his attempts, nothing sticks.

On our side of the table, however, Dax flips his on the very first shot, and all of a sudden, we're all tied up.

It's just me. The only person standing between loss and sweet victory, and although it's situations like these that make me hate being the anchor, I manage to down my drink in a single gulp.

I place my cup on the table and focus on giving it just the slightest of flicks. It completes a textbook ninety-degree rotation and lands on the table with a *thwack*.

My hands shoot up into a *V,* and all of a sudden, my feet leave the floor as I'm scooped up into the biggest, tightest bear hug and spun around in circles.

The ceiling swirls above me. My flip-cup beer hits my bloodstream, combining with my euphoric high from our win.

Things are perfect.

Exactly as they're supposed to be.

I've won in more ways than one.

But then Dax stops and lets me down slowly. My thoughts shift to how hard his body feels as it's pressed to mine.

And how I can smell him.

All scotch and sweat and pheromones. And although I should be thrilled that I've finally received the Dax McGuire bear hug my body has been craving, now all I can think is that his eyes are such a beautiful shade of green. And that our faces are unnaturally close right now. And how everything about this moment is borderline dangerous.

No. Wait. This isn't how things go.

Dax and I do not have sexy moments like this. We high-five. We make asshole remarks under our breath. We do not get mesmerized by each other's eyes and the flecks of forest green we never noticed despite four long years of deep friendship involving ample eye contact.

"We should check on Sunny." I end the eye business, completely chickening out on whatever is happening.

Dax takes a step back, putting much more pheromone-free air between us.

"She texted me while you were flipping. She got called in to the hospital and had to leave."

"Oh," is the best reply I can come back with.

Okay. This is fine. It's just me and Dax. Dax and me. We've done this more times than we can count. NBD. Nothing to get worked up about—

"Hey, Dax—" a male voice calls.

Oh, thank god.

I welcome the sight of yet another one of Dougie's rugby dudes.

"We have a bit of a situation outside." He inclines his head toward the back door.

"Do we need to find Dougie?" Dax asks.

"It *is* Dougie."

We follow Rugby Guy to the yard, where there's a wooden ladder perched up against the roof of the detached garage and a plus-size Spider-Man sitting on top of it with his head between his hands.

"Why the hell did he go up there?" Dax asks, echoing my thoughts.

Rugby Guy shrugs. "We thought it would make a cool photo for his Instagram. Dougie forgot to mention he was terrified of heights. He was fine going up, just freaked the fuck out when it was time to come down."

Dax's eyes meet mine for a long moment before he grabs the rungs of the ladder and climbs up onto the roof. He pulls himself to a seat next to Dougie, who is huddled in a ball, shaking like a leaf.

"Come on, Dougie," Dax coaxes. "It's not that high up. Even if you do fall, odds are you'll be fine."

Dougie visibly shudders. Obviously that wasn't the pep talk he wanted to hear. It's followed by a screech so high the neighbor's dog starts to bark.

I climb the ladder before I can think of a reason not to. It feels a lot higher up as I settle in next to Dougie and eye the grass below.

"Hey, buddy." I rub slow circles around his back. "I know you're feeling pretty terrified right now, but Dax and I are here to make sure you get down safe. Okay?"

Dougie nods.

"So," I continue, "when you're ready, I want you to look up, but when you do, I want you to look at my face. Right into my eyes. Nowhere else, okay?"

Again Dougie nods.

It's a full five minutes before there's any more movement. Eventually, Dougie lifts his head, and when he does, he looks directly into my eyes, just as I've asked.

"You feeling okay?"

He nods, although he's sweating so badly that it looks as if he's been sitting out here in the rain.

"I want you to very slowly extend your legs and roll onto your belly. Then Dax is going to guide one of your feet to the ladder. We won't let you go, and we will be with you the entire time."

Dougie closes his eyes and keeps them shut. And just when I think we're back to square one, he follows my directions perfectly. Left foot. Right foot. Belly wiggle to the ladder.

Dax guides his feet to the rungs, just like I promised. A few shaky breaths later, Spider-Man is once again earthbound, and the city, or at least tonight's party, is saved.

"Nicely done." Dax reaches his fist out for a bump. Next to the bear hug, it's the highest form of Dax-praise.

"My sister has three kids," I explain. "I also specialize in negotiating bedtimes and making eating broccoli look cool."

I expect him to mount the ladder or make some sort of *after you* gesture. Instead, he stretches out his legs, folds his arms behind his head, and lies back on the roof, gazing skyward.

I don't know if it's the cool evening air mixing with the heat from the roof or the way the patio lights below sort of blur in the twilight, making everything feel surreal, but it feels like a perfect moment. As if the universe got one right.

I stretch out beside him in a matching pose. Two peas. Exactly as we're meant to be. We watch the sky slowly grow darker, completely at ease with the silence, until the pinks and blues of the summer sky give way to darkness and a million twinkling lights cover the heavens like a blanket.

"I love it when you can see all the stars," Dax says, more to the sky than to me.

He's right. The night sky is so clear that you can see the Milky Way, the Big Dipper, and Cassiopeia. A bit of a phenomenon for the city. Something that marks this night as special.

"When I was a kid, I used to think each star was its own world, almost exactly like ours." Dax glances over at me before returning his gaze to the sky. "Except one thing was different. Like, in one world, everyone wore their shoes on their hands or ate pancakes for dinner and pot roast for breakfast. The idea was a bit out there, but I was convinced I knew the secret of the universe."

"I don't think it's odd at all." I tilt my head toward Dax at the exact moment he turns his face to mine. Our eyes do that thing again where they lock, and neither one of us looks away. And there's definitely something between us. Weird energy or a charge.

I think I like it. I definitely don't hate it. It's just different. Something I need to get used to.

But then he buzzes.

Not Dax.

His phone is tucked into his Hanes underpants. And he's so close that I can feel the vibrations along the roof.

He slides his phone out and swipes it open.

"Sunny." He flips the screen to face me. "She made it to the hospital safely."

I stopped stressing about Sunny and Dax sometime between my first beer and the flip cup game, but now I'm back to wondering if it's something I should be worried about.

"You two seem really close?" is the least jealous way I can think of to ask, *So what's the story between the two of you?*

Dax resumes his stretched-out position. "I wouldn't say close. Sunny's great and all, but we don't hang out all that much outside of curling. She's a lot tighter with Brandon."

Sweet relief floods my body. I needed to hear that. I know, new timeline, new rules. But deep down, a part of me hopes that my connection with Dax is special. That it somehow transcends time and space. That there's some weird little unbreakable thread that connects our two souls.

"I'm not dating her if that's what you're asking. I'm not dating anyone right now."

Heat rushes into my face. "No. Um . . . that wasn't what I was asking at all, I'm—" I'm mortified. "I thought she might be your best friend."

There's a beat of silence between us. Awkward silence this time. Finally, Dax clears his throat. "Any best friends in your life?"

There isn't an easy way to answer this.

"I had a best friend for a long time."

"Feels like there might be a *but* at the end of that sentence."

Is there ever.

"But he and I . . . I don't know. I guess our relationship changed."

Dax rolls his head to face me. "Who fell in love with who?"

Wait. No. He's got it all wrong.

"Neither of us fell in love. Why would you think that? We both just changed."

Dax pushes up, propping his upper body up with his forearms. "I don't know, Gemma. I've had a few close female friends over the years, and it's always ended the same way. One falls for the other, and we try the couple thing, or the friendship sort of fades out when the one in love finally realizes it's always going to be . . . unrequited."

"You're wrong."

He is.

And I hate the fact that I can't give my best evidence to the contrary.

His eyes narrow a little. "And you never thought of this guy as more than a friend?"

It's such a complex question. Maybe? Briefly. Right in the beginning. But then Stuart happened, and things between us changed. Besides, that's not the point.

"Nope. Thoughts were always platonic."

It's the truth, but it feels wrong as I say it. However, Dax rolls onto his back again. The argument's been won. The silence is back, and it's comfortable again. And just when I think we're back to the place we were meant to be, he draws a deep breath. "Well, then I guess he was the one who was in love with you."

Chapter 13

THE WATER STAIN on the ceiling above my bed looks like the *Mona Lisa*. Same chilled-out attitude. Same relaxed smile. Like her biggest burden is deciding what she's going to eat for lunch that day, not figuring out whether her best friend in the entire world has been secretly in love with her for the last four years of her life.

To say that I've been thinking about Dax's revelation on the roof last night is an understatement. I've been obsessing. His lazy, laid-back smile infiltrated my dreams all night. Making me question his motives. My motives. And every decision I've made for the last four years.

Eventually, I summon the energy to roll out of bed, throw on a presentable pair of sweatpants, and head out into the way-too-bright-for-this-early-on-a-Saturday-morning sun.

There is no debate between tequila or doughnuts this morning as I walk down James Street. Mostly because the liquor store doesn't open until ten and I'm mildly hungover from last night's party.

"Half a dozen fritters, please," I tell the cashier at Nana's, then, after an uncharacteristic moment of spontaneity, rethink my order. "Actually, on second thought, make that half a dozen of whatever you recommend."

I have no idea what has gotten into me. Maybe my sister has rubbed off on me after all these years, or maybe there is something in this reality that has knocked me off-kilter.

After I pay for my doughnuts, I head over to meet my aunt at her bookshop. She had a huge donation this week from the estate of a former customer. She asked Kierst and me if we could come over and help her weed through and catalog the new books. Since I have a part-time employee who helps out at Wilde Beauty on Saturdays and my sister's kids swim at the YMCA, we agreed to meet my aunt at the ungodly hour of eight.

"Morning." I push open the front door to my aunt's apartment and find both my aunt and sister already sitting on the floor with a stack of books between them and a tray of Brewski's coffees still in the recycled paper tray.

"You read my mind." I nod at the cup with my name on it. "I only had time for one stop and chose doughnuts, secretly hoping you'd get my telepathic messages. I'm in desperate need of caffeine."

Kiersten takes the doughnut box from my hands and pops open the lid. "Aunt Livi texted and said you were doing doughnuts, so I was in charge of coffee."

I look over at my aunt for an explanation because I haven't talked to her since the day before yesterday and then, there was zero mention of bringing anything. However, she appears to be reading the inside cover of one of the donation books, too engrossed in the task to offer an explanation, and I frankly don't care enough to interrogate her. Instead, I stretch out my legs in front of me and lean my throbbing head back against the couch.

"You're looking a little rough there, Gemmie, late night?" Kierst reaches over and smooths back the frizzy temple hairs that have escaped my half-assed attempt at a ponytail.

My night wasn't late. It was only midnight when I got home. But after Dax casually dropped the suggestion that my best friend might be harboring secret non-platonic feelings, I couldn't stop thinking about it. Ironically, we stayed outside talking about anything and everything except that until we got cold and headed inside. Not ten minutes later, Dougie attempted to climb back up for a reenactment of *Spider-Man: No Way Home*. It took three attempts to get him down and Brandon asked Dax if he would stay on Dougie duty for the rest of the evening. Dax agreed and I went home to my apartment and my spider and all my convoluted feelings.

I take a long sip of coffee before attempting to rationalize the dark-purple circles under my eyes.

"Was at a party. But then I got home and I couldn't sleep."

"What's up?" my sister asks, concerned.

"Some serious internal conflict," my aunt pipes in before I get the chance to answer her.

"What did you say?" I ask my aunt, who appears to still be reading the same book as before.

She looks up at my question and blinks twice. "Internal conflict. The theme of this book." She holds up the paperback. It has a handsome duke-like man on horseback, showing a single nipple. "This book could be an excellent option for my next book club meeting." She writes something down in the notebook in front of her, then sets the paper back down on a pile.

I turn my attention back to Kiersten, who hands me the box of doughnuts with the explicit instructions to "eat one, then spill."

I pick up a pink-frosted round one and bite. The summer strawberries explode in my mouth. I can taste happiness. "Oh my god, this is incredible," I moan, before finishing the rest in three bites. As I lick the remaining frosting from my fingers, I think about the best way to broach the next topic.

"Do you believe men and women can be friends?"

Kierst grabs her coffee from the tray and moves up to a more comfortable seat on the couch. "Yes," she replies, then removes the lid and blows. "I married Trent because he was my best friend. It just happens to be a bonus that he's an animal in the sack."

"Gross." I grab a pillow from the couch and whack her with it. The pillow narrowly misses hitting her coffee, which earns me a glare because while Dax sees his coffee as an almost religious experience, my sister considers hers a drug that enables her to function.

"There are things that, as your sister, I do not need to know. But my question was not about being married to your best friend. I'm wondering if you believe that a man and woman can be true, platonic friends, without sex stuff ever entering the picture."

"Of course I think it's possible," Kiersten says. "Why do you ask?"

I think back to the rooftop conversation. "Last night Dax said something that implied the Dax in my timeline might be in love with me."

I expect a wisecrack back. Or some sort of rib about how not every guy who wants to hang out with me is secretly in love with me. Instead, she sets down her coffee and looks at me thoughtfully.

"Well, do you think he is?"

"No," I answer before my brain has a chance to process that the real answer might be *maybe*.

"He's never said anything," I clarify. "Never implied that he has any other feelings aside from friendship. The night before I wound up here, I was very drunk. And not wearing pants. And I'm pretty sure I told him I loved him and then kissed him and he just left. Poof. Took off. Zero moves made from his end."

Kiersten narrows her eyes. "You don't think that had to do with the drunk part?"

She's not getting it.

"He dates other people. He was probably going to have sex with this hot, sexy vet before all"—I wave my hand emphatically around the room—"this happened."

Kiersten raises a skeptical eyebrow as she lifts the lid to the doughnut box. "And you're not in love with him?"

"She is."

Again, Aunt Livi answers before I get a chance to.

"I'm not," I say to both her and Kiersten.

"You're not what, poodle?" My aunt looks at me with wide, innocent eyes.

"I'm not in love with Dax. He's not in love with me. No one is in love with anyone else."

Aunt Livi nods her head in agreement. "Of course, sweetheart. We're not doubting you."

I throw up my arms. "Well, why did you just say I was?"

Aunt Livi squishes her eyebrows together. "I must have been talking to the books. It happens sometimes. Ignore the old bat. I'm probably going senile."

My aunt is far from senile.

"I have known you for twenty-eight years, Gems." My sister injects herself back into the conversation. "And I've never once seen you talk about someone the way you do this Dax guy. You are either trying to figure out how to see him again or talking about the last time you saw him. All signs are pointing to smitten. But what I can't figure out is why you've never dated this guy in your timeline. You guys like all the same things, and he's dreamy. I'm failing to see the problem."

"He's my best friend. I don't think of him like that."

"Yes. You've said that. But there must have been a point when he wasn't yet your best friend. You're telling me you never considered . . ."

I don't know if the rest of the sentence is *dating him* or *fucking him*. Either way, the answer is, "It's complicated."

She pulls a second doughnut from the box. "Explain away. I've got time."

I'm sure she does. And I'm sure when I tell her all of it, she'll understand. The problem is that I don't quite know where to start.

"I guess I never got the chance to think about Dax as anything but my friend."

Kierst opens her mouth, which is filled with doughnut, and says something that sounds like, "I'm not following."

I rack my brain for the best way to summarize the last four years. "Well, I met Dax the same night I met Stu. Dax also got my number and asked if I wanted to hit up a new bar the following weekend with him and some of his friends. I said yes because I liked Dax, but our meetup ended up being pushed out a week because of some reason I can't even remember, and then I had a stupid work thing the week after that and had to cancel. By the time we did hang out, I had already gone on, like, seven dates with Stuart. We were basically in a relationship."

"But it wasn't a good relationship?" Kierst asks.

There's far more to it than that. "It was in the beginning. Stuart, as much as it pains me to say it, is a pretty great guy. He's smart and reads a lot. We used to stay up late on the weekends drinking wine and talking about the dumpster fire that is our world. It was a lot of fun at first. I liked him. It's possible I even loved him at some point. But then things slipped from great to good, then eventually into fine territory. I found myself dreading our predictable Friday night dates and wishing that, instead of hanging in and talking all the time, we could go out and try something new. Nothing terrible ever happened between us. We just . . ."

"Suffered from the boiled frog effect?" my aunt pipes in.

That's it. There isn't enough coffee in my system this morning to let that comment slide.

"Are you going to sit there all day saying random, weird things?"

Aunt Livi sets her book down on the stack in front of her and looks up. "No. I'm referring to your conundrum. It's like boiling a frog."

I exchange a look with Kiersten, who is sporting the same blank expression I imagine is on my face. "Yeah, you're gonna have to explain this one," I say.

My aunt rolls her eyes as if she's disappointed that I'm not following her logic. "Have you ever tried to boil a frog?"

Another look with Kiersten.

"No," I answer for both of us. "And I'm hoping that you haven't either."

Aunt Livi shakes her head. "Of course not. But if I were to heat up a pot of water and try to put a frog in, it would immediately jump out."

"I would say that of most living organisms," Kiersten mutters under her breath.

"Well, if you put a frog in cold water, then heat it up slowly, the changes are so subtle that the frog doesn't notice until it eventually boils to death."

"This is a disturbing analogy," Kierst says.

My aunt nods in agreement. "Yes, I regretted telling it about halfway through, but the sentiment remains."

"Okay, fine. Your relationship suffered a slow, painful death. But let's get back to McDreamy. Sure, the timing never worked out before. It happens. But now the universe has done some weird-ass magic mojo shit and given you a do-over. Why not try now? At least take him for a test drive."

Kiersten doesn't get it. It's not that I don't see Dax as boyfriend material. I do. But I got a taste the other day of what my life would be like if Dax wasn't in it. It was arguably the worst twelve hours of my life, far worse than breaking up with Stuart, so I have no desire to feel that way again. If Dax and I were to hook up and then break up, we would never be able to go back to the way things were. I once had a sex dream about him and swore there was a weird tension between us for the better part of a month. If something happens between us here, how can I go home and not think about it? How will it not irrevocably impact the good thing we've got? It's that idea that makes me build a wall in my head—a mental friend zone, if you will—with Dax on one side and my heart on the other.

"Are you going to get that?" My aunt nods at my silent iPhone.

"Get wha—" Before I can complete my sentence, my screen lights up with a message.

It's from Dax.

It's a picture of Dougie crouched on the roof of his garage in his Spider-Man suit. Likely taken moments before he realized he was so far off the ground. Then a message.

Sorry I bailed last night. Spider-Man refused to retire the tights until 4 am. Want to try again? Drinks? Friday?

"Message from Dax?" my sister asks.

I lock my screen and set it on the table. "Maybe."

She shakes her head, her smile stupid and smug. "You're smiling like an idiot. You like him." She takes a very long drink of her coffee. "And as soon as you admit that to yourself, the less sexually frustrated you'll be. You can bang all the random big dicks you want, but nothing is as good as sex with your best friend. Think about how well Dax knows your mind. That will translate into how well he knows your body. Orgasms for days, my friend. For days."

Chapter 14

My week drags on at a glacial pace. And with a clear, beer-free head, I'm not entirely sure if Dax has asked me on a date for Friday night or if we're simply hanging out. Two colleagues. Entrepreneurs in the James Street Small Business Association.

It's not like me to obsess over a guy. To be fair, I spent four years dating Stuart, who was as predictable as the number two setting on my BLACK+DECKER toaster. He called me every morning to provide a full weather forecast and make recommendations on my outerwear and texted me when he got home from work to give me a quick debrief on his day and wish me sweet dreams. I never once second-guessed our relationship. Mind you, I didn't exactly see our breakup coming, but that's another issue for another day.

Today my issue is Dax.

And our date or non-date this evening.

And how I know we should keep things platonic. Yet, I still take over forty-five minutes to pick out a pair of black jeans, boots, and a simple white camisole trimmed in lace, telling myself it's because I'm trying to present a certain image to my customers, not because Dax once said lace on a woman is his kryptonite.

My phone rings while I'm on my walk to work. My heart picks up a few notches until I see the name on my screen.

"Hey, Aunt Livi."

She doesn't answer back immediately, but I can hear the sound of her voice somewhere off in the background, and it sounds like she's talking to a customer.

"Oh hi, sweetheart, just wanted to check in. Mr. Zogaib called to say you're not quite open yet, and I wanted to make sure you didn't go back to your other dimension or anything."

I'm simultaneously impressed that she managed to make that statement with such nonchalance and slightly annoyed that my next-door neighbor feels he has to tattle every time I'm a few minutes late.

It's only nine-fifteen, and I needed a few extra minutes to blow out my hair.

"Everything is great. I'm almost at the store and sticking around this dimension for at least a couple of weeks."

I wave to Mr. Zogaib as I pass his flower shop, then unlock the door to my store with my aunt still on the line.

"Have you talked to your sister this week?" Aunt Livi asks.

"Not since Saturday. I've been busy." And avoiding her. Although Kiersten would typically be my go-to when it comes to analyzing important things like whether Dax has asked me on a date, I already know her opinion, and I am not mentally ready to see the smugness on her face when I admit she might be right.

"Well, maybe give her a call later," my aunt says. "I think she's a little stressed lately."

I snort-laugh, which ironically is a classic Kiersten move. "Kierst is Superwoman. She's the perfect wife. Amazing mom. Would probably be PTA president if she had a filter or wasn't such an asshole. I'm a hot mess on a good day. What would she ever need from me?"

"That's a good question . . ." She clears her throat but doesn't speak. It's her tell when she's worried about something, though I'm not entirely sure if it's Kiersten causing the angst or if she's agreeing with the state of my life.

"I'll call her later," I promise.

"Thank you, poodle. I worry about her." And although she doesn't say it, I can hear in her voice the *And I worry about you too.*

I end the call with a promise to call her back tomorrow, flip the sign to OPEN AND AWESOME from its previous state of CLOSED BUT STILL AWESOME, and immediately greet my first customer: Mr. Zogaib's elderly mother. She has a thing for my lemon-scented hand cream.

The small blessing in my day is that my store is busy. I don't get a single chance to scroll on my phone or stress about Dax because every time I ring through a customer order, a new one appears. So at ten after seven, when the little bell chimes as my front door opens, I'm caught off guard to see Dax standing there in a pair of tight-fitting black jeans and a white button-down shirt tailored perfectly to showcase the lean lines of his body.

Oh shit. This is definitely a date.

Dax never wears a button-down. He has three types of tops in his wardrobe that he chooses from based on the temperature outside: henleys for cool weather, T-shirts for when it's warm, and tank tops for when there's little chance of running into me, as I tend to be vocal about my feelings about tank tops on grown men.

I have never seen Dax in a button-down, and that scares me. It feels like I'm stepping into uncharted waters, unaware if anything below the surface bites. Undecided as to whether I want it to.

"You look nice," I manage to croak out.

His eyes, I notice, are lingering on the laced V of my camisole. "That was my opening line. You ready to go?"

My store is a mess. I haven't done any of my closing paper-work nor looked to see if my hair has any weird baby curls around the temples from running around all day—but I nod. "Yup, just let me grab my purse." Future Gemma can deal with all of this tomorrow.

We're headed to Hess Village, which is less of a village and more of an intersection of two cobblestone streets, lined mostly with pubs and bars at the west end of Hamilton's downtown core. It's a solid twenty-minute walk from James Street, but the night air is warm, and I have nervous energy to burn and best friends in dress shirts to analyze, so we opt to walk and save our hard-earned retail dollars for an Uber ride home later.

"How was the day?" I kick off the conversation, hating myself for asking such a lame question, but the button-down has thrown me so badly that I'm second-guessing everything.

Dax shrugs, running his fingers through his wavy hair, sending a whiff of his ocean-scented shampoo in my direction.

"It wasn't as busy as I wanted it to be." He sighs. "I don't know if foot traffic is down or this just isn't the year for custom sneakers, but it hasn't been a great month. What about you?"

Now I'm not quite sure that I want to tell him that although I've only briefly glanced at Other Gemma's forecast, my guess is that I've doubled my sales for the month. Instead, I go with an honest, "I had some very chatty customers today. It felt like I barely blinked before you showed up on my doorstep."

Hess Village is bumping when we arrive, packed with a mix of the work crowd, still in their business casual, celebrating the end of another week, and the tight-jeaned, crop-topped party crowd, getting an early start to the weekend.

"What vibe are we going for tonight?" Dax points to one of the busy pubs. "The Pauper? Or the Duck?"

The Prince and Pauper is a brightly lit pub. It's busy and loud, with live music and a street-facing patio that's already packed.

The Laughing Duck is far more low-key. Dim lighting, spaced-out tables. Quiet. Romantic. Coltrane in the background.

"Let's hit the Pauper. I'm in the mood for a cold beer." And I'm panicking. The dress shirt has tripped me up. There's an entire yarn ball of feelings rolling around inside me, and they're way too tangled to figure out at this moment.

I don't miss the brief look of disappointment that flashes across Dax's face before he nods and replies, "Cool." He leads the way to the patio, where the hostess tells us there's a twenty-minute waitlist for a seat, but inside is a free-for-all. If we can find an empty table, it's ours.

We head in and find that the indoor seating is almost as full as the outdoor. No empty tables, not even seats at the bar. I can practically sense Dax wanting to say, *Why don't we head to the Duck?*

In sheer panic mode, I scan the room, hoping to chance across someone looking like they might be getting ready to leave. Instead, I spot two people making perfect eye contact and waving at me.

I have absolutely no idea who they are.

"Friends of yours?" Dax leans in, and I'm temporarily distracted by his warm breath on my neck, suddenly acutely aware of our proximity.

"Uh . . . I think so?" I squint my eyes, looking for further clues or clarity to their identities and finding nothing. "And it looks like they have room to spare."

"Do you want to join them or try somewhere else?"

Before I can answer him, a bachelorette party woos by. The last pink-boa-wearer underestimates the room she needs to squeeze through. As she passes, she stumbles a little, jostling me and knocking my back into Dax's front. I'm briefly acquainted with the fit muscles of Dax's chest and the warmth from his hands as he steadies my hips.

"You okay?" he asks, turning my shoulders so I'm facing him.

"No permanent damage."

The space between us is mere inches. We're so close that I catch the faintest hint of mint. Whether it's from gum or a toothbrush, all I can think is, *That's kissing breath*. And then, *Is Dax planning on kissing me?*

Oh shit.

My heart is booming so hard that I worry it's going to dislodge itself. I press my hands to my chest just to hold it in.

I think I want him to kiss me.

I mean, that's been my plan all along. But Aunt Livi was pretty insistent that we keep the proper order of the cleanse. Not to mention it may also ruin four solid years of beautiful friendship. The smart thing would be to get off this train to heartbreak before it leaves the station. Yet, I'm still running my tongue over my teeth, kicking myself for not taking a few moments to make a minimal effort earlier to freshen up.

"What are you thinking?" Dax's deep voice pulls me out of my thoughts.

I debate my answer until it dawns on me that his question is about the table.

"Let's stay here." I chicken out, using a voice an octave higher than normal. "Haven't seen those guys in ages." Or ever.

"Okay," says Dax's mouth, but his eyes betray him. And I get a weird twisting in my stomach because even though this plan was my call, I think I'm disappointed too.

"Shall we?" Dax holds out his arm, allowing me to lead the way. I don't miss that as I pass, he places his fingers ever so lightly on the small of my back.

I weave us through the crowd until we reach the table, too preoccupied with the heat from his hand and the way it permeates through the cotton of my camisole to figure out how the hell I'm going to navigate introductions.

If I had any doubts that the eye contact and invitation to sit were meant for me, they are erased as we approach the table, and the woman sitting there jumps to her feet, holding her arms out for a hug.

"Oh my gosh, Gemma, it is so great to see you!"

I hold out my hands and meet her embrace, looking from her to the man with her as we squeeze. She is petite and Asian, with a short black bob and a stylish leather jacket. The man is white and exceptionally tall, with sandy-colored hair and a plain blue polo shirt.

I am 100 percent sure I've not met either of these people in my life.

But in *this* life, we are on hugging terms.

"This is Dax." I try the age-old trick of introducing the person whose name you know first, hoping the unidentified parties will follow by introducing themselves. It works. As they shake Dax's hand, she introduces herself as Lux, he as Leo.

"So, how do you know Gemma?" Dax asks, and I'm as eager to hear the answer as he is.

"The three of us used to sail together down at the harbor," Lux explains. "Leo and Gemma took lessons on Mondays, Gemma and I took lessons on Wednesdays. She thought the two of us would hit it off, and she introduced us."

Leo puts his arm around Lux's shoulders and pulls her tight to his chest. She looks up at him in this adoring way. You can practically see the cartoon hearts floating between them.

"We sort of lost touch with you after classes ended," Lux explains. "But we're so happy we ran into you because . . ." She thrusts out her left hand. There's a gorgeous emerald on her ring finger. It's almost as big as her smile. "We're getting married in August. You obviously need to be there, Gemma. You too, Dax."

I squeal because they're engaged, and it's so obvious it's true love. It's a tiny bit overwhelming. Hearing about this life I've lived but wasn't present for.

I remember wanting to take sailing lessons years ago. It was right before I graduated with my degree. I was at the edge of adulthood and thinking *new world, new me,* and maybe it was time to take a baby step outside of my comfort zone. Sailing seemed like a doable leap. But then I met Stuart. He wasn't a fan of the water, so I never ended up pursuing it. There have been a few points when I've regretted not signing up for those classes over the years. And sitting here recalling memories Other Gemma lived with Lux and Leo, I am regretting that choice even more now.

"We should celebrate our reunion." Leo gets up from his seat. "Let me buy a round." He heads to the bar and returns several minutes later with a round of drinks.

"So . . ." Lux points at Dax and me. "How did the two of you meet?"

My stomach clenches in panic because the absolute last thing I want tonight is to relive our disastrous first meeting. But before I can form a nice way of explaining that I had a meltdown in Dax's store, he presses his knee to mine, a silent exchange that says, *I got you, don't worry,* as he smiles back at Lux. "Our stores are down the street from each other. We kept running into each other."

Lux nods and moves on to another topic. I'm only half listening, too focused on the heat from Dax's leg pressed to mine and the familiar feeling in my chest of knowing, no matter what, that this man will always have my back.

"Tell me . . ." The sudden heightened pitch of Lux's voice draws me back into the conversation. "How long have the two of you been dating?"

My cheeks flare. "We're just friends," I answer automatically.

"Oh, I didn't realize." Lux's cheeks flush a pretty shade of red. "You guys seem so . . . I just assumed—Leo is always telling me I love to jump to conclusions."

Her eyes shift to my shoulder. It's only then that I realize Dax's arm is resting lightly on the back of my chair. Sometime between our leaving my store and now, he's rolled up his sleeves, exposing a few inches of his muscular forearms. He lets go of my seat, dropping his hand to his side as if the back of my chair has suddenly turned hot. I immediately notice it's missing.

The moment of awkwardness dissipates as, once again, the conversation shifts to James Street and reviewing all of the new restaurants that have popped up over the last year.

The next hour is filled with more talking. More laughter. More memories of this life I don't remember living.

I can see how Other Gemma instantly bonded with both Lux and Leo. I completely understand why she—I—thought they made the perfect match.

Lux launches into another sailing story about a time we almost capsized our boat on the lake.

Dax tilts his head close to mine. "Are you having a good time?" His low whisper is only loud enough for me to hear.

"I really am," I whisper back.

He smiles. "I can tell. You look happy. And very beautiful."

The last part seems to startle him as much as it does me. As if he didn't mean to say it out loud. But now that he has, it hangs there between us. A declaration. An offer of *what if?*

And I'm tempted.

Tempted to scooch my hand two inches to the left and rest it on his thigh. To feel the hard muscle underneath with the possibility that if I play things right later tonight, I could touch a whole lot more. I won't deny that the idea feels right. That even though we're a perfect fit as friends, we could be as good as something more if only I'd let myself try.

But then my brain takes charge.

It reminds me of my friendship with Dax and everything I'd risk losing. Relationships go wrong far more often than they go right. People change. Grow apart. There are a million ways for a relationship to die. Dax and I work as friends. Satisfaction guaranteed. You don't screw around with perfection. Unless you're willing to risk damaging something that can never be put back together, and frankly, I'm not willing.

"Hey, guys. What's up. Fuck, it's packed in here."

A new body intrudes on our conversation. He's tall, handsome, and wearing a suit. He oozes that Brooks Brothers vibe that tends to surpass my head but appease my panties.

"Elliott, hey." Lux hugs the stranger and then motions for him to take a seat.

Another round of drinks is ordered. Introductions occur.

Newcomer Elliott manages a hedge fund. He's a friend of Lux's older brother, here in Hamilton to visit a friend.

Lux notes me as "her old sailing friend Gemma" and Dax as "Gemma's good friend Dax." At the *F* word, Elliott slips a noticeable glance at the lace trim of my camisole. Whether Dax notices or it's mere coincidence, he stiffens beside me.

Our conversation slips easily back into that familiar friendly rhythm, although this time, I find myself distracted and staring at our new friend. Not because Elliott is so conventionally attractive (you could chisel *David* with that jawline), but because I swear I know him but can't place how. That is, until he catches me staring and winks, and it clicks.

He looks exactly like Stuart.

Well, not exactly. Where Stuart is light-eyed and blond, this guy is dark and possibly dangerous. But they give off the same energy. That cocky confidence that says, *I know what I want out of life, and I'm going to do whatever it takes to get it.*

And from the way his thigh presses into mine and how he leans in just a little too close to ask if I could use another drink, I get the sense that I may have just been added to the want list.

"So, what do you do?" His voice booms loud, but his eyes make it clear that the question is directed at me and only me.

I almost tell him that I'm a buyer for Eaton's Drug Mart but catch myself right as I open my mouth. "I own a beauty supply store over on James." The words come out rather proudly. "So does Dax. Well, not beauty, but sneakers. You should totally check it out."

Elliott's eyes shift past me momentarily to where Dax is sitting staring into his beer stein. Elliott's eyes drop to Dax's sneaker-clad feet, then rise back up again.

"I don't think I've stepped into a shoe store in years," Elliott exclaims. "Can't seem to find the time. I buy everything online these days. Gotta think it's been a shit couple of years to be in retail, eh, man?"

Dax, I notice, forces a smile. "Can't say it's been easy."

There's an awkward beat before Elliott turns his attention back to his beer. And although I want to continue—to gush about Dax's incredible talent—Dax seems as eager to talk about his work as Elliott is to listen, so I let the conversation shift to a new topic: travel.

Lux and Leo are going to Iceland for their honeymoon. Hiking. Geysers. They're doing the whole deal, and it sounds exciting and wonderful and romantic.

"Ever been to Iceland?" Lux asks both Dax and me.

I shake my head. "I've never been to Europe." Or at least I think that's the case. Stuart was too busy with work to travel. Kierst had little kids she needed to be home for. I was terrified of going anywhere on my own. Travel to foreign destinations was limited to Friday nights watching *House Hunters International*.

But here, now, listening to Lux and Leo talk about whale-watching and soaking in the Blue Lagoon, I let myself dream a little about seeing the world. Argentina. Croatia. My bucket list is growing exponentially by the minute. And as I picture myself seeing every place, I imagine Dax there beside me.

"I've got a good buddy who has a place in the South of France." Elliott startles me out of my daydream. "He rents the place out to friends. Right near the beach in Saint-Tropez. I can hook you up if you want."

Dax and me in the South of France. "Oh my god, that would be great." My dream morphs to include crystal-blue waters, wine, and picnics in the sun until it's brought abruptly to an end by the screech of a chair as Dax stands.

"Anyone need anything while I'm up?"

I still have three-quarters of my beer, as do the rest of my friends. With no takers, Dax nods and heads toward the men's room. I get a weird vibe as he walks off. Nothing specific triggers it (the man is allowed to pee), but as he disappears into the crowd, I have a strange sense that something is off with him.

However, Lux distracts me, diving into a story about her and Leo's last trip to Mexico. It quickly shifts to inside jokes that make the two of them laugh and look at each other as if they were completely alone at the table.

I'm watching them, feeling a little envious or homesick or just plain old jealous, when Elliott leans in. "I know you're here with your friend, but we should hang out later."

His words send a prickle up my back with déjà vu.

Elliott is not Stuart—we've established that. But the lean and his words remind me of the night Stuart and I first met.

Rewind to a few weeks ago, when I was margarita-drunk and hurting. I wished I could teleport back to the night I met Stuart and do everything differently. To get in a cab and go home alone. In a weird, twisted way, it feels like I'm getting to fulfill that wish.

"Thanks, but I'm good."

Elliott shrugs, looking far from forlorn. "It was worth a shot. At least give me some details about your store. My buddy's girl-friend loves that shit. I'll tell her to check it out."

"Give me your phone," I say to Elliott, who hands me an iPhone I swear isn't even available yet. I open his contacts and plug in Wilde Beauty's address, website, and store phone number.

As I hand it back, I get this weird pain in my chest and an overwhelming feeling that something is wrong. I look up and see Dax across the bar watching me.

Our eyes lock and hold for a beat before he breaks contact to look at Elliott, then the door.

Dax and I have always shared a weird telepathy. The ability to communicate entire thoughts with the raise of an eyebrow or roll of the eyes. Although this particular Dax is still technically a stranger, I have no trouble piecing together what he thinks he just saw.

No. Wait! Noooooooo. I fight the urge to yell out, *This isn't what it looks like.*

And when Dax turns toward the door, it's as if the entire bar freezes, and I'm teleported back to four years ago. Because it was here, in this very same bar, that I met Daxon McGuire.

It started with the Guinness mix-up, then moved on to charm-ing banter. I was far from smitten but definitely intrigued. Dax was exactly like me back then. Trying to find investors to start up Kicks and as uncertain about his future as he was about what he was having for dinner that evening. A man without a plan.

Then drinks were spilled.

And up walked Stuart.

After some run-of-the-mill flirty chitchat, he asked me, "Where do you imagine your life in ten years, Gemma?"

I didn't have a good answer. But he did.

"Anyone can make a five-year plan. I can tell you where I will be in ten years and exactly how I will get there."

He was speaking my love language.

A vice-president position at Godrich and Dundas. A semi-detached house in Cabbagetown. A dog—preferably a golden-doodle.

I'd lived most of my life with lots of uncertainty—I fell hard, craving the safety of a stable relationship.

So I screwed up. I chose the wrong guy.

Or maybe he was the right guy at the time, but here, tonight, sitting in this bar, things are different. I am different.

This is my second chance. To be with Dax. Not just as friends. More. So much more.

But everything is going wrong. Spiraling in the wrong direction.

Even as he takes his seat, I can tell things between us have shifted.

His knee is no longer pressing against mine. And he's moved his chair ever so slightly away, leaving a cavernous space between us.

The hand that once rested on the back of my seat now clutches his beer and refuses to budge no matter how much I will it to return.

All night, Dax was telling me without telling me that he was into me, and I ignored it.

What else have I ignored these last four years?

"We should probably get going." Lux gets to her feet. Our last round of beer is now empty glasses.

She hugs me and whispers into my ear. "Let's stay in touch. I don't want to let another year go by without seeing you again." I squeeze her back because I don't want that to happen either. I want many, many more nights exactly like this one.

"I should head out too." Dax doesn't quite look at me as he says it.

"I'm ready," I tell him, ignoring the *I* that wasn't a *we*.

Oblivious, Elliott hugs Lux, then holds up his phone to me. "Maybe I'll see you around."

I turn to Dax to—I don't know, explain? But he's purposely looking past me to the door.

I have a sinking feeling that I've screwed everything up before it's even started.

We weave our way back to the exit. His hand is noticeably missing from my back. Like I was his before, and now I'm not so sure.

We part with Lux and Leo on the street. They head south. We walk north to a blue Ford Focus and a driver named Ahmed, who blares Tiesto so loud that neither of us says a word until he pulls up in front of my house.

"I had a good time tonight," I say because I'm not sure of where to even start.

"Me too," he replies.

"Do you want to come inside?"

He thinks about it for a second. I can see it in his eyes, but then he opens his mouth. "I think it's better if I head home."

"Okay," says my voice. *What the hell?* says my head. This isn't how it's supposed to go now. I've realized it. *I've figured it out, Dax. I'm supposed to be with you.* Except all I say is, "We should do this again sometime."

He nods, then opens his door and helps me out.

I wait for him to open his arms, to pull me into a hug like he has done every single night we've ever hung out together, but his hands stay gripped on the open door of the waiting Uber.

"Text me when you get inside." He nods at the darkened side path. "Let me know you're okay."

I'm not okay. But I nod and walk toward the house, closing the gate behind me, pulling my keys from my purse, opening the door, then locking it with a quiet click. I pull my phone out and stare.

My head is so messy. I'm still reeling from the idea that I want to be with Dax. But if I tell him how I feel—especially after the disastrous end to our evening—there's a strong possibility he won't feel the same.

It's a risk.

And I have never been good at taking them.

My hands hover over the keys.

Home Safe

I don't hit send. Because as much as I don't want to risk losing Dax, I'm also worried that if I don't say something tonight, tomorrow will be too late. I may wake up and rationalize all of these feelings away, or, worse, he may wake up and realize I'm not worth the trouble.

I delete my last message and type, *I think I might have screwed up tonight. I want to be more than your friend.*

Send.

The whoosh of the message is followed immediately by a *knock, knock, knock* on my back door. The sound pulls my breath from my lungs.

Shaky baby-deer legs take me to the door.

I flip the lock. My insides are a storm of anxiety and hope that collide to form a cool rain of relief as I take him in, standing there, phone in hand, reading.

He looks up. "I didn't like the way we ended things tonight."

I step back to let him in, but he stays rooted on my doormat.

"I saw you with that guy, and I got jealous, and then I think I overreacted because you and I have never talked about . . ." He holds up his phone. "I think we need to talk."

My heart is beating so hard that I can feel it in my throat. "Want to come in?"

He ducks his head and steps into my kitchen. The light from the tiny lamp next to my door leaves most of his face in shadows.

He holds up his phone again. "Did you mean this?"

I nod. "It's arguably the bluntest and most honest text message I've ever sent."

"You're going to have to elaborate for me a little," he says softly. "I'm suffering from a bit of emotional whiplash tonight."

I take a deep breath and push away all of the excuses that have kept me from saying this to Dax before now.

"I think you and I might be very good together."

He swallows. "Why am I sensing a *but* on the end of that sentence?"

Because there is one. A big one. I think it's what's always held me back from even considering the idea of Dax and me before.

"What if we don't work out? What if we wake up one morning and one of us decides that they aren't happy? I don't think we'll ever be able to go back to being friends."

This time it's Dax who takes a shaky breath. "I don't know about you, but to me, we've never just been friends. I don't know quite how to describe it, but we click. And I think things will go really good before they go bad—if they ever go bad. So you're right. If we do this, it's going to go one of two ways."

I feel like I'm standing on a cliff. My toes are curled over the edge, and I want so badly to jump, but I can't see what's at the bottom.

"Could you be?" I ask him. "If we stop this here. Could you be only my friend?"

Dax closes his eyes, and for a very long moment, I'm worried he's going to say no. Finally, he opens them. "Yes, I can. But to be very transparent, I don't want to."

"I don't want to either." The words leave my mouth, and they are so achingly true that I hold out my arms, close my eyes, and I jump.

Chapter 15

HE REACHES FOR me at the same time I reach for him. My hands find his face. His hands find my waist, and our lips crash somewhere in the middle.

Half of me expected this kiss to be soft and sweet, like Dax. The other half was expecting something otherworldly, like the night at my condo where the whole room fell away for a moment.

This kiss is something entirely different. It's hungry, and it's heated. As if days, weeks, or even years of unsaid words and dormant feelings are exploding. Full-blown warfare of lips and tongues and groping hands making up for lost time.

My fingers curl around the hair at the nape of his neck as he backs me against the kitchen countertop. His mouth traces a line of kisses from my jaw to my collarbone, then back to my mouth again.

My hands itch to touch him, to explore the hard planes of his chest, to find the places where he's ticklish or that make him draw breath a little quicker. At the same time, I want to memorize how his hands feel on my skin, the confident way they travel down my back and cup my ass as if he already knows how I like to be touched. He squeezes. I laugh because Dax McGuire just touched my ass. He squeezes again. This time both of us laugh, and we have to pause our kitchen make-out to catch our breaths.

My entire body begs for more—more touching, more stroking, more tongue—while my mind works out how we can do with less: less clothing, less waiting.

We should get naked.

Our telepathy works its magic once again. Dax slides his hands up under my shirt, kissing my neck while his thumbs graze the skin below my bra. He presses his hips into mine, and I can feel him hard and thick beneath his jeans.

We should definitely get naked.

I grab a handful of his shirt with one fist and slide my other hand underneath, feeling the warmth of his skin and the firmness of his stomach. I've seen Dax shirtless too many times to count, but never with the idea in my head that I could touch him or even taste him. And with the thought of *How does Dax McGuire taste?* I run my tongue along the nape of his neck, then playfully nip on his earlobe.

"What was that?" he asks between kisses.

"I'm not really sure."

"Do it again." His voice is so low and husky. I like this. Commanding, sexy, knows-what-he-wants Dax. This time when I do it, he's the one moaning and pressing his hips to mine. Pressing his erection exactly where I'm aching.

For a moment, my brain dwells on the meaning of this moment. I think I'm about to have sex with Dax. And although I've thought about doing a million things with Dax, sex didn't really enter the realm of possibility until tonight. I haven't mentally prepared for it, and because now I'm certain Dax and I have telepathic powers, he stops mid-kiss.

"Are you still into this, Gems?"

My body votes a clear yes to this question, and my heart is on board as well, but my brain is still asking questions like *What does this mean?* And *Have we thought through all of the implications?* And *Do I even have condoms?*

Screw my brain.

"Yes. Absolutely yes. We should take our shirts off. I am definitely a fan of where this is going." I pull his face toward me, and as his tongue brushes mine, it's so, so good. Almost as if that very brief pause had me forgetting how well Dax kisses. How perfectly we fit together. And how all signs point to the idea that we're about to shed our clothing and—*holy shit, I'm about to have sex with my best friend.*

Dax breaks our kiss and pulls away.

"Why are you stopping?" I ask him. "This is the part where we take our clothes off. It's literally the best part."

But Dax shoves his hands into the pockets of his jeans. Like they have minds of their own, and he's trying to contain them.

"I can't believe I'm saying this. I can't believe I'm even thinking this, but what if we hit pause on this—just for tonight?" He scrubs his hand down his face. The lines of his forehead suggest that what he's saying and what he's thinking may not be one and the same.

"We should both go to bed," he continues. "Separately. And then tomorrow, I will call you, and we will make a date to see each other. Hopefully, do all of this again and maybe other things that I can't really think too much about right now while I'm trying to convince myself that going home tonight is the best plan."

"Why?" I nearly scream in sexual frustration.

"Because I like you, Gemma. And I think that a lot of things happened tonight, and I want to be sure this is what you want."

"This is what I want." Okay, now I am yelling at him.

"Fuck." He draws the word out. "I want it too. But please. Agree with me here before I change my mind. Tomorrow. We can go on a date. I will take you somewhere nice. If you still want to, we can—"

"Oh, I will want to."

Dax squeezes his eyes shut, looking pained. "I am going to regret this the moment I walk out of here. I know it, but I'm going to go."

He runs the tips of his fingers down my arms until they reach my hands, which he holds, pulling me to him. He leans in and places the sweetest, softest, feathery-light kiss on my lips, and it drives me wild because I know it's the last one I'm going to get tonight.

"You good with this plan?" he asks as he pulls away.

"No, but you're probably right. I hate being responsible."

He laughs and pulls me into a hug, which turns into a long hug that I end up breaking because if Dax sticks around here any longer, there's a strong chance I may start begging for sex. Instead, I walk him to the door. He takes the steps two at a time and pauses at the top to wave.

"Goodnight, Dax McGuire," I call to him.

"Goodnight, Gemma McGuire," he calls back.

"Slip of the tongue?"

He shrugs and smiles. "Something like that."

SATURDAY MORNING FINDS me on Kiersten's doorstep at 7:36 with two oat lattes, a dozen Nana's doughnuts, and a heavy heart.

After Dax left, I got into bed and started thinking. Which led to analyzing. Which led to making new plans and questioning all of my life decisions.

"Oh god. What happened?" Kierst is a bit of a mess. There's a mysterious green stain on the shoulder of her white sweater, and her hair is half falling out of her bun and I suspect it's not intentional. She hoists Lucy onto her hip as Riley ducks under her arm and heads for the minivan in the driveway.

"Nothing happened," I lie.

Kiersten doesn't say anything but raises a single eyebrow as she pulls her front door closed behind her and hands me the car seat with Jan.

I help her load the kids into their various seating contraptions, then seat myself in the passenger side.

We drop baby Jan at Kiersten's mother-in-law's and Lucy at her swimming lesson and are on our way to drop off her oldest, Riley, at a friend's house when I grow impatient and crack.

"Would it be so terrible if I didn't go home?"

My sister eyes me, then checks her rearview mirror. I suspect it's less about watching the traffic and more about wanting to make sure her eleven-year-old is as engrossed in his handheld video game as the beeping and bopping from the back seat suggest.

"Are you talking about living at Aunt Livi's or, like, the whole parallel universe thing?"

Now it's me checking the mirror and confirming there's no eavesdropping. "The latter."

Kiersten doesn't say any actual words. But she does *huh*.

I wait a full three seconds before poking her hard between her ribs.

"Ow. Sorry, I was thinking. . . ."

"About?"

"About how I was sort of hoping you'd come to your senses and admit you were making all that parallel universe shit up, but I guess you're still sticking with your story."

I glare at her. "Kierst, I'm telling the truth."

"Yeah, yeah, I know." She shrugs and drives a full block and a half before she continues. "Well, from a personal perspective, I'm all for you staying here, as I've had a small but meaningful existential crisis trying to figure out if I cease to exist if you go back to your world or whatever. But I'm curious, what has you changing your mind?"

I feel my cheeks heat. "I went out with Dax last night, and we . . ." I don't finish the sentence. I don't need to. She pulls the car over to the side of the road and hits the brakes so hard that I test the effectiveness of my seatbelt.

"You had sex! How was it? I need details. Don't feel like you need to skip over things because I'm your sister."

"Kiersten!" I point at her rearview mirror. She turns around to look at Riley, who is still engrossed in playing video games in the back seat.

She turns back to me, rolls her eyes, and waves him off as if it's a non-issue. "He's in grade six. He knows more about sex than I do, and we talk about it openly." She raises her voice. "Isn't that right, Ry? Sex is beautiful and not at all shameful when it's between consenting individuals who fully understand the consequences."

Riley doesn't even look up. "You're disgusting."

Kiersten shrugs. "See."

"We didn't have sex," I clarify. Kiersten again gives me the skeptical eyebrow.

"We didn't have sex," I repeat louder so Riley can hear, then lower my voice. "We just made out a little."

Kiersten eyes me for a long moment. "Must've been one hell of a make-out."

"It was."

Kiersten rolls her eyes with an exaggerated scoff, but then she drops all the drama, and her face gets all big-sister serious. "So, all jokes aside, you're actually thinking of giving up on your whole plan?"

I let myself dwell on the consequences of that statement for a whole second.

"Kind of."

She shakes her head. "He must be one hell of a guy."

He is. And although I've known that fact for a long time now, it feels like I've woken up and seen Dax with a completely new set of eyes.

We pull up at a red-brick bungalow, and Riley jumps out. I catch an eye roll fueled by middle school angst that flares my face an even deeper shade of red, and I pray that I'm not the topic of his future therapy sessions.

My sister stays pretty silent until we turn onto Discovery Drive, which leads to the waterfront. I can see her eyeing me and opening her mouth like she's about to talk, then shutting it like she's changed her mind at the last second. She pulls into a spot across the street from the lakeshore path we plan on walking. Before she can get out whatever speech she's spent the last five minutes composing in her head, I preempt her.

"It's not just Dax. It's everything."

She takes off her seatbelt. "Define *everything* for me."

I don't even need to think. "I am starting to love my store. It's so pretty, and it smells so good. Not to mention I've run the numbers, and I significantly underestimated how many Hamiltonians are into clean beauty. It's the best job, and I'm getting paid to be there."

She nods. "Okay, I'm following, and if you don't own Wilde in your timeline, it means poor Other Kiersten is paying for facial moisturizer. I can get behind this reason. Are there more?"

The rest of it I can't quite put a finger on.

"I just wake up so happy. I caught myself skipping yesterday, Kierst. You and I both know we Wildes do not skip."

She thinks before saying, "Well, I'm happy you're happy."

I can see in her eyes that there's a caveat to that statement. "But?"

"But I want you to hold off on making a final decision for a bit."

I don't say anything, but my face must reveal that I am far from in love with her statement.

She reaches for my hand and squeezes. "Everything is shiny and happy and wonderful when all you're doing is fucking. But eventually, you get tired of banging like bunnies and reality checks in."

"Kiersten!"

She waves me off. "Just humor me and make sure it's absolutely what you want. Rash decisions can lead to hasty weddings and suddenly you wake up one morning with three kids and you don't know who you are."

A silence settles over the van.

"Um, are we still talking about me here?"

My sister blinks twice, then shakes her head. "Of course we are. But that reminds me. Can you babysit tomorrow night? I'm in a bit of a bind. Trent's away fishing for the weekend and my usual sitter has a night class."

I know without checking that my calendar is free. "Moms Gone Wild night?"

"You haven't partied until you've partied with the PTA," she replies with perfect deadpan.

"Yeah. Sure. Your kids are into movies, right? *Saw III* is new on Netflix."

She glares at me.

"That was a joke. You're not the only comedian in the family."

Her scowl deepens. "Yes, but the difference is that I'm actually funny."

Our conversation pauses as a group of women in bright-colored lululemon gear passes our car on the way to the path.

"Are we gonna do this?" I nod at the women, who are walking twice as fast as Kierst and I get up to on a good day.

Kierst eyes the doughnut box. "If you don't go home, it won't accidentally cause a rift in the universe or anything, right?"

I have to think for a moment.

"I'm honestly not entirely sure?"

She swears under her breath, leaving me lost in this conversation.

"What's wrong?"

She picks up the box of doughnuts. "I was going to skip the walk and eat this entire box, and now I can't."

I am not even kind of following. "Why not?"

"Well, if you're sticking around, I'll have to live with the consequences. Sugar goes right to my ass."

We compromise and each eat one full doughnut, then split a second one with the promise that we'll walk an additional kilometer than the five we have planned.

We stop after three.

Blaming the ominous-looking thunderclouds rolling in from the east and the grande oat lattes that accompanied this morning's doughnuts, we pile back into the minivan and drive to my place so we can pee.

"Dibs on the bathroom," I call as we pull up to the sidewalk.

Kiersten hits the locks as I try to open my door. "Bathroom etiquette always defers to the person who has squeezed the most humans out of their vajay."

I manually flip the lock and push the door open. "If I run, you won't be able to catch me without peeing yourself."

I race up the walkway and through the gate and get ready to

leap the steps before I'm forced to skid to a stop to avoid the obstacle in my path.

I hear Kiersten's huffing breaths before she turns the corner, also stopping to stare. "I take it all back. Stay here. Marry that man. Lock him down. You've found yourself a keeper."

It's only a small mason jar filled with wildflowers. And judging by the heather, honeysuckle, and cornflowers—the same variety that grows down near the water—the flowers are handpicked. But I know for a fact that Daxon McGuire has never, ever in his thirty-one years sent a woman flowers, except for my Aunt Livi last year when she was in the hospital getting her hip replaced. He made a huge deal when he brought her the also-handpicked bouquet, telling her that his mom was a gardener who taught him the meaning of every flower and that the act of giving them wasn't to be tossed around lightly. Aunt Livi got anemones, buttercups, and irises for protection, humility, and wisdom.

I reach for my phone and search. According to Google and the *Farmers' Almanac,* Dax has sent me *admiration, devoted affection,* and *be gentle with me.*

"Trent gave me flowers once." My sister picks up the jar and inhales deeply. "He was still wooing me. Showed up for a date with a grocery store bouquet, and I fell head over heels in love." She hands me the jar. "This year, for our eleventh wedding anniversary, he bought me a steam mop. Believe me when I say, enjoy this while it lasts."

I take the flowers inside and set them on the counter. With the flowers and the late-morning sun streaming in through the window, it almost looks cheery in my little space. Kiersten remembers her quest for the bathroom, giving me a few precious moments to read the note carefully tucked between two stems.

It's written on notebook paper in blue Bic pen ink and Dax's nearly illegible handwriting.

This is me attempting to do things right. Pick you up at seven—Dax.

Holy shit. I grip the counter as my legs momentarily forget how to function. My stomach feels like it's ballooned up into my chest. Like it's filled with happiness and hope. I've never, ever felt this way in my entire life.

A few moments later, the bathroom door opens, and a relieved-looking Kiersten emerges.

"So, where's he taking you on this big date tonight?"

I hold up my hands. "I have absolutely no idea."

She grabs her purse from where she threw it on the counter and pulls something from her wallet.

"Beautiful, sweet boy, isn't he?" It's a picture of Riley. His school photo from last year.

She reaches into her purse again and presses something into my palm. "I don't care how sexy he looks in those tight jeans of his. Never trust the pullout method."

Chapter 16

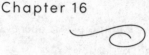

THERE'S A SOFT knock on my door at exactly 6:58. It stirs the swarm of butterflies that have taken up residence in my stomach. I open it to find Dax, standing in a pair of black jeans and a different white button-down shirt with the sleeves rolled up just enough to expose the bottom of his tattoo on his inner left arm—a clock face. I used to think it was edgy, but now it's an ironic reminder that I'm up against my own ticking clock.

"You look beautiful." Dax ducks his head and steps into my kitchen, where I have to hold myself back from pouncing. I'm almost afraid to kiss him because kissing will lead to groping, groping to grinding, then, before we know it, we'll be naked on the linoleum floor, and that's not what tonight is about. Instead, I press up onto my toes and kiss his stubbled cheek. He smells exactly like he's supposed to—Irish Spring soap and the faintest trace of aftershave.

"So, what's the plan for tonight?" I ask.

Even though he's been texting me questions all day, Dax has been vague about what exactly we're doing on our big date, although this Dax now knows my favorite cheese, chilling-out album, and shoe size: a dainty seven.

"I packed us a picnic," he says. "Thought we could hang out at the harbor. Eat cheese. Watch the sunset. Does that work for you?"

When Stuart took me on our first date, it was at a restaurant in Toronto's Ossington neighborhood where he knew the chef. The food was delicious, but the vibe was pretentious. I both loved it and felt completely out of place. The beach with Dax feels comfortable. Like slipping into a pair of perfectly worn-in shoes.

Speaking of shoes. "Why did you need my shoe size then?"

Dax opens my door and holds out his arm, waiting for me to exit ahead of him. "That was to throw you off. I wanted our date to have an air of mystery."

Strangely, it does. Surprises from a man I thought I knew everything about.

We take Dax's car to Bayfront Park on the lake. I love Bayfront because 90 percent of it is waterlocked, so it's only accessible on foot.

We park the car near the marina, grab the basket from the trunk, and walk the small paved trail that cuts through the center.

Bayfront is a pretty chill and serene spot in the city. Aside from the trail, the park's other features include a grassy area in the middle and a small strip of beach on the west side.

It's a bit of a hike to get from the car to the sand, but since it's a cooler August evening, we arrive and find the beach deserted. Though I'm not normally a fan of PDA (both watching and participating), with the beach empty and Dax looking all fancy and handsome in his button-down, I'm more than willing to make an exception should the opportunity present itself.

"I brought a blanket." Dax lifts the basket slightly. "Want to hang out here? Or there's a gazebo just back there." He points to the grassy area, where there's a small, covered, modern-looking gazebo.

"Beach sounds great to me."

We find a spot in the sand near some large rocks that provide shelter against the breeze that has picked up since we arrived. Dax lays out one of his mom's quilts (I smile because I know he's amassed quite a collection since she started taking classes at the community center), then pulls a bottle of white wine, a French-style baguette, an assortment of olives, hummus, and a large wheel of Camembert from his basket.

"Did I do okay?" He holds up the cheese.

"You've found my weakness. There's very little I won't do for a soft cheese."

The Dax in my timeline would not have let me get away with a comment like that. He'd demand clarifications with implied innuendo. We'd be talking about sex without talking about sex in that safe, third-party way that never implied that the two of us could actually have it.

Even with this Dax, I can see him holding back. It's in the way he bites his lip and avoids my eyes as he asks, "Would you like some?"

I'm in a weird place. Because part of me misses that ease that comes with four years of friendship. How we can communicate entire thoughts with a glance or an eyebrow raise. But these last two weeks, I've seen a whole new side of Dax. I love him because I've always loved him, but I'm also falling for him at the exact same time—if that makes any sense.

"You seem to be thinking awfully hard about the cheese." He holds out a small plate with two pieces of Camembert, some baguette, and what I hope is red pepper jelly.

"Just got lost in my head for a second. But everything is good. Everything is great, actually."

He reaches into the basket and pulls out two wineglasses, offering one to me.

"And now we're getting drunk." I take the glass from his hand. "My kind of evening."

Dax screws open the bottle and fills my glass. "Not quite drunk. I was going for buzzed enough to make some questionable decisions but sober enough to know we're making them."

He's definitely talking about sex. I know I've been thinking about sex since he showed up this evening looking all sexy and adorable. I've for sure been thinking about sex since our hot little kitchen make-out, where I was both ready and willing to let him have his way on my countertop. However, as we sit here now, the thought hits me. *Do I really want to have sex with Dax?*

I've never been one to put a whole lot of meaningful weight into the act of sexual intercourse. This timeline's Gemma seems to have also embraced this principle. However, unlike her, it's been four whole years since I considered doing the deed with anyone other than Stuart. Still, my rules haven't changed: be safe, be fully into it, but it doesn't have to be some big meaningful gesture. Sex can be just sex.

But with Dax, it's different. For one, it will mean something. The sex will be more than sex. And on top of that, if I do go back to my reality, I will never be able to forget that we did it. I won't be able to unsee Dax's penis.

Oh god, if we have sex, I'm going to see Dax's penis.

"You are really thinking hard about something." Dax looks at me, concerned.

Somehow I don't think he wants to hear that I'm contemplating the future ramifications of seeing his dick.

"Those clouds." I point to the darkening puffs of gray gathering out on the water. "They're looking a little ominous."

Dax follows my gaze and sighs. "I think you're right. I was hoping they'd hold off for an hour, but it's not looking good."

And as if the sky was waiting for that perfect cue, it lets out a slow, low rumble.

"Shit," Dax says. "Probably not a great idea to be out in the open on this beach, eh?"

"Probably not—" My answer is cut off by a crack of thunder so loud it sounds as if the sky above us is tearing open. I look up in time to see thousands of big, thick raindrops make their way toward earth.

"Make a run for it?" Dax asks.

I look around frantically and point. "Gazebo?"

Dax whips his head around and reaches for my hand, his other still holding the wine bottle.

We get to our feet and start to run, but I stop when we're half-way there. "The cheese!"

Dax drops my hand and passes me the wine bottle. "Here." He reels around and sprints back toward the blanket.

But he doesn't just grab the cheese.

His arms reach for the four corners of the picnic blanket. Gathering them together, he sweeps it over his shoulder like a sack, then grabs the basket with his other hand and runs back to meet me. We make it all the way to the gazebo before the next boom of thunder cracks above us.

I'm soaked down to my underpants. Dax is so wet he's got raindrops dripping off the end of his nose. He sets the blanket down in the middle of the gazebo. Our poor little picnic— decimated by rain.

"Thank you for saving the cheese." I manage a straight face.

Dax holds up the half-wrapped wheel, also soaked.

The rain is sputtering all around us.

"I'm sorry our picnic was ruined," he says, and I can tell by the way his chest deflates and his shoulders drop that he means every word.

"I think this is even better." I sink down onto the soaking-wet blanket beside him. "We're in a gazebo, in the middle of a rainstorm. This is one of my top three romantic fantasies."

Dax raises a skeptical eyebrow. "Is that right? What are the other two?"

"Meeting a handsome stranger at a masquerade ball. And the lift from *Dirty Dancing*. We can try that one later once we finish the wine. Make it a two-outta-three kind of night."

Dax smiles, relaxing a little. "I had a whole plan."

"Tell me about it."

Dax looks back wistfully at our picnic. "We were going to eat, maybe drive up the mountain and look at the city lights, and then head to my place for more wine."

"Where we'd have hot sex on a bearskin rug in front of a fire? Because that's a solid number four on my list."

Dax laughs. "My rug is from IKEA, and my fireplace isn't functional."

"I have a very good imagination."

Dax looks around the gazebo. The rain falls like a curtain around us and makes a soft pitter-patter sound on the roof.

"This is pretty romantic." I inch a little closer, bringing my hands to his chest. "And your shirt is kind of see-through."

His eyes drop to my chest. "So is yours."

He brings his index finger to my chin and tips my head up ever so slightly so that I'm looking up at him as he places the softest, most chaste kiss on my lips. The effect it has on my body is not chaste. Quite the opposite. It sends a blazing heat from my mouth all the way to the tips of my toes.

I kiss him again, but this time, I wrap my arms around his neck and pull his body tight to mine. Our tongues intertwine, and he lets go of a low little growl that comes right from his chest, and it has me wondering if it would be so terrible to shed all of our clothes and have sex right here. The cement floor doesn't bode well for comfort, but with the rain flowing down around us, turning everything outside of our little bubble into one big gray blur, it's pretty idyllic.

"You're shivering." He runs the pads of his fingers down my arms, giving me goosebumps.

"I'm usually a fair-weather maker-outer. Not used to the elements."

Dax pulls me in tight, bringing me closer to the heat of his chest.

"So I'm at a disadvantage already. Guess I better up my game if I'm going to make this night memorable."

He brings his mouth to mine. A slow, soft press that deepens as his tongue parts my lips. For a moment I forget everything. The rain. The cold. Every kiss that came before this one. As if none of it matters but him and me and this moment.

When he finally pulls away, I feel the loss immediately. I mourn it and the feeling sends an involuntary shudder down my spine.

"Okay, your teeth are chattering now. I'd take off this wet T-shirt and give it to you, but I don't think it would help."

"Oh, it would definitely help."

He pulls me back to his chest again. Into that little nook below his chin where I fit just perfectly. Like he was made for me. And he runs his hands down my arm. Faster this time. "What do you say we make a run for the car?"

The friction brings enough heat to make me admit that I'm freezing. Part of me wants to suck it up. To stay in this perfect romantic bubble where there's no ticking clock. The other part is very aware that Dax's T-shirt is no longer leaving anything to the imagination. And the faster we get out of here, the faster we can get out of these wet clothes.

"You grab the basket. I'll hold the cheese."

Dax dumps all of our drenched picnic gear back into the basket, then reaches for my hand.

"We go on three?"

I nod, eyeing the rain still pouring down in sheets.

"One." Dax squeezes my hand. "Two." He weaves our fingers together. "Three."

We race straight through the grass to the parking lot. By the time we reach the car, I'm so drenched that it pains me to get inside.

Dax's Toyota may be getting on in years, but it's meticulously clean. He holds the door open with a pace and ease that ignores the rain teeming around us. I ease my way in, trying hard to touch as little of the seat as possible as Dax runs around to the driver's side and climbs in beside me.

"I'm sorry, I'm squishy and wet." There's a literal pool of water at my feet.

He reaches over and brushes a stray strand of hair from my forehead. "I'm sorry our night went to shit."

"Picnic may have gone a little south, but the night is savable. I'm still having a lot of fun."

"Me too." Dax leans across the center console, and I'm treated to another chaste kiss. *Oh, dear lord.* If these sweet little pecks are driving me this wild, I'm going to be in trouble later on.

Reaching into his jeans, he pulls out his keys and inserts them into the ignition, but when he turns, all that happens is the dreaded *run-na-nun-ah* sound.

He tries a second time, then a third, and when still nothing happens, he coaxes the engine with a "Come on, baby," gently rubbing the leather dash.

For a moment, I'm convinced it's going to work. If Dax rubbed me like that and whispered those sweet words, I'd be turned on in an instant. But nothing happens.

"Shit." He leans his head against the leather steering wheel, squeezing his eyes shut.

"I always thought Toyota Avalons were immortal, but I guess everything has its breaking point."

Dax doesn't laugh. Doesn't even smile. And I swear I hear him whisper, *"This is the last thing I need right now."*

I reach up and squeeze his shoulder. It's the same comforting gesture he gave to me the night of the grocery store rescue.

Dax rolls his head toward me, his temple still on the wheel. He reaches across the console, grabs my hand, and laces our fingers together.

"Any chance you have CAA?" I ask.

Dax lets out a long sigh. "I did until about a month ago when I let it lapse." He lifts his head and reaches into his back pocket, pulling out a phone. "I'll text Dougie. He's got a guy who hopefully won't hose me."

Ten minutes and two phone calls later, we have a tow on its way to get us.

"Sorry again, Gemma, I really—"

"Hey." I hold a finger playfully up to his lips. "Enough apologizing already. You can't control the weather or when your car will die. And if you could, I would have a much bigger problem I would need your help to tackle. I wasn't lying earlier when I said I was having fun. And I still am. I like hanging out with you."

Dax brings his hand to my cheek, then brings his forehead to mine, so they're touching. "Where on your list is making out in a car?"

I debate how honest I should be here. "Somewhere north of fifty, as cars were like eighty percent of my high school make-out experience. But I am still very much up for it if you're offering."

Dax leans in for another kiss, and because I expect it to be sweet like its predecessor, I'm happily surprised when his hand slides into my hair and his tongue parts my lips with an urgency that tells me he's as eager as I am to pick things up from where we left them yesterday.

I kiss him back. Matching his intensity, then leveling up. He may want this, but I've been waiting far longer.

His hands move from the back of my head to my waist and pull me into his lap. They stroke my back, my hair, my neck as we kiss over and over. I can feel him growing hard beneath me, and all I want to do is reach my hand down and unbuckle his pants, but my back is jammed up against the steering wheel, which is making the logistics impossible.

"You're thinking about something again," Dax murmurs between kisses.

"I'm trying to figure out how I can take off your pants. Toyota Avalons were not made with make-outs in mind."

"Don't underestimate my baby. She's got a few tricks left in her." Dax reaches down, and there's a loud crack as the seat springs back, taking both of us with it.

"That did not go as smoothly as it did in my head."

"Maybe not, but now at least I can do this." The added room allows me to wedge one knee in between Dax and the center console and swing the other over to straddle him.

We pick up exactly where we left off with the feverish kissing, but this position allows Dax the ability to run his hands up my bare legs, under my sundress, and to my ass, which he squeezes playfully.

"I thought the plan was to take off your pants." I grind my hips into him, rubbing against the bulge in his jeans.

"That was your plan." His finger hooks around the waistband of my thong. "I had a slightly different one." He pulls back, eyebrows raised. "Yes?"

I'm not entirely clear what he's proposing, but it doesn't matter. "Yes." I'm a *yes* to anything that involves my panties and his hands.

He slides his finger along the waistband, heading toward the space between my legs, but before it reaches anywhere interesting, it reverses, making its way back toward my ass. It makes a second trip, then a third, and I'm so turned on from the feel of his fingers on my skin that I'm practically vibrating before his hand makes one last trip to just below my hip bone, then follows the edge of my thong down, down, down until he reaches the spot where I'm aching.

His finger slides between my folds, and he starts to rub with the perfect amount of pressure.

"You are so wet." His breath is hot on my neck, and his voice is so low and growly I swear it makes me even wetter. Then his whole hand slides inside my underwear. His thumb begins to circle my clit as his finger lingers at my entrance.

"Keep going?" he asks in that voice.

"Oh my god, yes," I manage to get out while all my concentration is centered around how good his thumb feels and how badly I want to shift my hips and ride his hand. Instead, I wait as he slowly pushes in one finger and pumps it until it's slick. He adds a second finger while his other thumb finds my nipple. I'm torn between two tantalizing sensations, both caused by Dax's talented fingers. When he adds his mouth on my neck, it almost becomes too much. I'm lost in a haze. A sea of fingers and thumbs and tongues. All swirling and twirling in time. But then he nips at my collarbone, and although it's just a playful bite, the slight sting to my skin drives me over the top. The sensation between my legs explodes like a confetti cannon, sending ripples of pleasure through my body. My mind slides into that well-orgasmed haze where everything is perfect, wonderful, and right. And I stay there, all happy and floaty, until I see the lights of nirvana in the distance.

Except nirvana is a late-model white Ford pickup with the words *Benny's Tow and Go* stenciled in blue on the side.

Chapter 17

"OH SHIT!" DAX says as the headlights of the tow truck hit his rearview mirror. He pulls me into his chest, wrapping his arms around me as if it will shield what we've done from the tow truck driver, who probably can't see anything yet. "You okay, Gems?"

I manage a nod, enjoying the feeling of being nuzzled to his neck. "A lot better than okay."

His quiet laugh shakes his chest. "I really hate to cut this short, but—"

There's the same cracking sound as our seat jolts back into the upright position. He plants a soft kiss on the top of my head before he lifts my hips up and over the console, back into my own seat.

"Why don't you hang here for a minute while I deal with this guy?"

Dax gets out of the car and goes to talk to the tow truck driver, who looks exactly how I pictured Benny of Benny's Tow and Go: white male, round belly, a full head of light-brown hair, and a goatee to match. I can't hear what he says to Dax, but it's pretty easy to follow the nodding as they talk, then the frowning as they pop the hood of the car and poke around. I'm not at all surprised when Benny closes the hood, retreats to his truck, and maneuvers it so it's directly in front of the Avalon.

Dax comes to my side of the car and opens the door. "Benny's gonna tow the car back to his shop. We can ride up front with him." He reaches out his hand and helps me from my seat. The moment our fingers touch again, I feel a spark. It may be entirely in my head. Or the fact that my body is still coming down from what those fingers did only minutes ago. Either way, our evening is far from over if I have any say. This interlude with Benny and the tow truck is just an intermission.

Once the Avalon is secured to the back of the truck, Benny opens his passenger door. "Sorry, kids, only one passenger seat. You'll have to make do." I suck back a smile because Benny just called us kids despite being maybe five years older than Dax, and I am not the least bit upset about this arrangement.

Dax gets into the cab first, then offers me a hand. We quickly determine that our two sets of hips will not fit in the seat side by side, so the best arrangement is me on Dax's lap. The seatbelt doesn't quite reach around our two bodies, so as Benny starts the engine and the truck rumbles to life, Dax winds his arms around my waist, once again pulling me into his chest.

My god, I love his smell. The soap. The cologne with a little sweat and sex. I'd lick his neck if Benny weren't two feet away. And because the Dax and Gemma telepathy continues to be a thing, Dax's thumb finds the cutout of my sundress. He slowly strokes the tiny triangle of bare skin, back and forth. It's the smallest movement, but it drives me wild and has me thinking of his fingers on the hem of my underwear not so long ago.

I shift my hips, mostly because all my lower regions are getting all riled up again, and when I do, I notice that I'm not the only one in this truck who is turned on.

Dax is hard. Really hard. Like, metal-rod-topped-with-denim

hard. And with the way I'm positioned in his lap, if said denim was removed, we'd be halfway to sex right now. The current situation, although clothed, is still rather pleasant. I shift my hips slowly back and forth, providing a delightful amount of friction exactly where I need it. It feels good. Damn good. So good that if I'm not careful, I'm going to come on Benny's front seat, and with the way the pressure is building below, I doubt I could be discreet.

Dax's thumb pauses, and his arms squeeze me tightly, limiting my ability to maneuver my hips. Dax dips his head and nudges me with his nose so he can whisper in my ear, "You're killing me right now, you know that, right?"

The heat from his breath makes the little hairs on the back of my neck stand on end. I'm so turned on that I can't think rationally. Half of my brain thinks it's an excellent idea to undo his pants right now just so I can stroke him, Benny be damned.

The tow truck takes a sharp left, pulling into the back parking lot of a garage and sabotaging all of my plans.

"I just need to go in through the side and open the garage door, then I'll be back to take care of ya," Benny says, completely oblivious to what is happening on his passenger seat. When Benny disappears out of view, Dax lifts me off his lap and onto the seat as he slides out and walks uncomfortably away from the truck, shaking one leg and then the other.

"Where are you going?" I call after him, knowing exactly what he's trying to do.

He turns and gives me a stern glare as he points to the situation in his pants. "I need to get this under control before I'm arrested for being a pervert."

Dax makes a long loop of the parking lot. By the time Benny opens the garage door, Dax and his pants look normal again.

"I got some good news," Benny says to Dax. "Called a buddy

in the east end, and he has the part you need. We can get it done this week. But I'm gonna need to charge you for the part now. We can settle on the rest later."

Dax's face drops as his hands move to his back pocket. He looks over at me, then back to Benny. "Yeah. Not a problem. I'm just gonna need to figure something out. I left my credit card at home."

There's an easy solution to this problem. "We can use mine." I open my purse and root through it for my wallet.

"No," Dax says, a little more forcefully than I expect. "No. You do not have to do that, Gemma. I got it. I just . . ." He pulls his phone from his other pocket. "I'm gonna call you an Uber. I hate doing this again, but I think we need to cut our night short. This is gonna take a while to deal with."

The sinking in my stomach is trumped only by the state of confusion in my head. There's an easy and logical solution to this problem that allows us to get out of here quickly and on to the sex. But as my eyes find Dax's and see the same crushing disappointment on his face, my thoughts are clear enough to recognize that this Dax still doesn't know me that well. I can see how it would be awkward to ask your date to help fix your car. We're still a long way away from that level of closeness.

"Okay," I say reluctantly. "And please don't worry about the Uber. I'm going to walk home."

Dax is not the only one who needs to walk off that tow ride.

"Are you sure?" Dax holds up his phone to show me a map with several tiny car graphics circling the nearby streets.

I nod, and he holds his arms out for one last hug.

"Text me when you get home, okay?" he says into my hair.

"You got it. Call me when you get home?"

He lingers as if he's considering going in for a kiss, but then looks over at Benny, who is still waiting, and lets go.

"I'll make this up to you, I promise."

Chapter 18

He CALLS.

Well, technically FaceTimes.

As soon as he gets home from Benny's, he crawls into bed—or at least I imagine it this way. When his face pops onto my screen, all I can focus on is the curve of his bicep as he lazily cradles the back of his head in his palm and the crispness of his white pillow—a stark contrast to the dark stubble on his face. Something about that combo makes me squeeze my thighs together and remember the conversation not too long ago with Kierst, where she insisted a night with Dax would end with a morning of whisker-burned thighs.

We talk for a little while. Then he says good night, and I attempt to self-serve with my Lady Pro 3000. The effort is lacking. I go to bed disappointed. And wake up in the morning with sex on the brain.

As if I'm not struggling enough, he sends a text while I'm walking into Wilde.

Morning beautiful.

Hope you have a good day.

The *ping* of the second text hits me in the chest and zings all the way down to my clitoris, giving me shivers in a way my Lady Pro couldn't. I'm like Pavlov's dog. Phone pinging. Lady parts zinging. I even have to put the phone in my desk drawer because Kiersten starts to send me a play-by-play about some sort of brawl at Riley's soccer game. Even though I know the texts are from her, the pings have me thinking about the types of things one definitely should not be thinking about while talking to a sixty-three-year-old grandmother of five about her skincare routine.

Then it comes. The text I am waiting for. Though it isn't from Dax; it's Sunny again.

Hate to drop this on you at the last minute but any chance you can sub for me tonight? I can't believe I'm saying this but I have a date. Totally fine if you can't.

I don't even ask her about the guy, or girl for that matter. My libido's too riled up to think of anything but that now I am definitely going to see Dax tonight, which leads me to wonder if we'll pick up where we left off—after the game, of course.

He texts not long after Sunny.

Heard you're filling in tonight. Been thinking about you all day. Got a meeting at the bank, but I'll meet you at the game. Can't wait to see you.

I melt into a puddle of goo on the floor.

After I re-form, I manage to finish my workday with minimal sex fantasies and get myself to the bus stop to make it to the game. The bus, however, has not prioritized my sex life. It comes late, so I am late, only making it onto the ice with seconds to spare. There's not enough time to talk to Dax alone and confirm the things I would like to confirm: like the odds I'll be seeing his penis later.

I'm horny. Like, teenage-boy horny. It's just that Dax looks so good. He's wearing the same thing he always wears, but the black sweatpants are maybe sitting a little lower than normal. And every time he reaches up for a high five, I can see that little dip below his hip bone, and it's driving me feral.

Dax loves to throw the high fives, and I have to physically restrain myself from sliding up to him and dragging my tongue along that thin strip of skin and biting. Since when am I a biter? If I had ever attempted to bite Stuart, he would have sent me the contact info for his therapist, followed by articles about uncovering my childhood traumas.

Uh, gross. I don't want to think about Stuart at all right now.

Not while I have sweatpanted Dax in my line of sight. Crouching. And stretching. And exposing just the tiniest trail of belly hair just below his navel.

I have that song in my head. That clichéd one with no words that everyone knows means sex. It's playing over and over like a porno soundtrack. Dax bends down to assess his shot. Bow-chicka-wow-wow. Dax leans over to sweep the ice. Bow-chicka-wow-wow. Dax stands there doing absolutely nothing but suddenly looks up. Even though there is a good hundred feet of ice between us, my insides burn like they're on fire. Bow chic—

"Gemma . . . Gemma!"

I think it takes Dougie three tries to get my attention. And he's either a lot more perceptive than I've ever given him credit for, or the expression on my face is so thirsty that half this arena can figure out there's an elaborate sex fantasy going on in my head.

"Need your eyes over here." He winks.

Right. The game.

I slide over to him for "thinking time," the thirty-eight minutes allotted each game for strategizing your next shot. Normally Dougie uses the time to make jokes or plan which appetizers he's going to order after we finish, but tonight, he wants my advice.

"What do you think there?" He points his broom at the other end of the sheet. Our opponents have a rock in the ring, but ours is farther back and closer to the button. "Set a guard? Or see if I can sneak one in behind?"

I'm not that skilled at curling on a good day. Layer on the fact that my head isn't even remotely in this game, and I'm basically useless. To illustrate that fact, just as Dougie asks his question, Dax slides past me to confer with Dougie, and his fingers graze my hip bone. In the grand scheme of Dax and Gemma touches, it's nothing. Yet, the brush of his fingers sends tiny tendrils of want through my bloodstream, where they spread and settle into the farthest crevices of my body until I'm completely consumed.

"You ready?" The gravelly tone of Dax's voice pulls me out of my sex trance. I almost shout back a *hell yes* until I realize that Dougie is crouching in the hack, ready to throw his rock, and Dax's question is if I'm okay to sweep.

"I'm good," I tell him while simultaneously trying to force any non-curling thoughts from my head.

Dougie slides into a lunge, letting go of his stone with a delicate turn of his wrist. The rock glides toward us. Dax bends over, his forearms taut, ready to sweep.

My defenses hold for exactly fourteen seconds.

The first dirty little thought creeps back in as I grasp my broom with an assured and confident grip. My hand-job grip. Then the back-and-forth of the broom on the ice becomes rhythmic. A quick, firm stroke that has me thinking of other things I'd like to stroke, which then leads to wondering what exactly I will find when I finally get to take off Dax's pants.

I have to close my eyes so that I'm not tempted to look at the curled tendril of dark hair that falls across Dax's forehead as he sweeps. Or check out the curve of his sweatpants below his beltline, which bulges every time he leans on his broom and his pants pull taut. Or think about how good he smells when he's a little sweaty. Like right now, as he's working the broom, biting his bottom lip in concentration as the muscles in his back contract and flex.

Oh fuck. Now I'm picturing it.

Dax naked.

Fingers, lips, and tongues. Caressing, stroking, licking, and bit-ing. My eyes fly open in an attempt to halt the steamy narrative in my head, and I search the arena for something else to look at. Something safe that won't have me thinking about dicks, or Dax, or sex. I settle on a game happening two sheets away. An elderly man with a beer belly is stretching the limits of his wine-colored lululemon shirt as he dips into an impressively agile lunge. Yes. He's safe.

Or maybe not.

"Hurry hard," yells Red Spandex. He's talking to his sweepers, but the chant becomes my mantra.

Hurry hard.

Hurry hard.

Hard.

Harder.

Harder.

Harder.

Hard—

Dax looks over at me, as if I'm emitting pheromones that sig-nify that I'm seconds away from having a curling-induced orgasm right here on the ice. His fingers flex against his broom. *Oh god, those fingers* and all the magical wonders they are capable of. I'm mentally calculating the size of the supply closet and the odds of Larry doing his nightly check of the locker rooms if Dax and I were to slip away, while also simultaneously staring at the second hand of the black-and-white analog clock hanging above the gallery windows, secretly wondering if, in addition to parallel-universe travel, I've also been gifted the ability to manipulate time. I have not. If anything, the clock seems to move slower. *Tick. Tick. Tick.* I'm waiting for the *boom*.

I am the boom.

No. The boom is the clashing of Dougie's rock against our opponent's. Hard and fast, it slams the stone toward the outer ring, then spins in a slow twirl off in the opposite direction. Dougie has completely messed up his shot. Or maybe this was the new plan, and I missed it.

"Sweep," Dougie yells at me as Dax and I part to tend our respective rocks. I brush my broom back and forth, pouring all my pent-up angst into the motion until the rock clears the house.

When I compose myself enough to look up, Dax is sliding his way back to our end of the ice, and my seventy-year-old opponent is watching me, eyebrows raised.

"Looking a little flushed there, honey." She makes a point of looking at Dax, then back at me before winking. It's a *go get 'em tiger* kind of a wink, and I want to tell her *I would if I could.*

"Had to put my back into that one." I bring my hand to my hip as if that makes the lie believable.

"I'd save a little for later if I were you." She glides past me, and her gaze flicks to the scoreboard.

It continues to be a nail-biter of a game.

We end up tied four-all at the tenth and final end, with one rock left to throw.

Mine.

Old Gemma would be freaking the fuck out right now.

But this Gemma can't tear her eyes from Dax as she glides back to our end of the ice.

He's talking to Dougie. But as I approach, Dougie slides off and heads down to the other end to help call the next shot.

Dax moves to meet me at the hack, and the part of me that has yet to be fully taken over by hormones expects a pep talk.

Dax absolutely hates to lose and takes curling far more seriously than one should ever take a sport that's dominated by senior citizens. I'm prepared for explicit instructions on how and where he wants me to put my rock, but as he slows to a stop in front of me, he lands just a little too close. His eyes slide over my body as if he's mentally deciding in what order he intends to remove my clothes later tonight.

"Hey."

It's just one word. But the way that he says it has me absolutely certain that the next ones out of his mouth are not going to be about curling.

"I was thinking, after the game. We could maybe head back to my pla—"

"Yes," I answer before he finishes, and he smiles. The sex-face gives me away again.

"You look really good tonight," he says.

I'm wearing leggings and a massive hoodie because the arena is freaking cold. Still, Dax's eyes are on the tiny patch of collarbone where my neckline is a bit stretched out, and the way his eyes linger makes me wonder if tomorrow morning I'm going to need to wear a turtleneck.

There's an impatient clearing of the throat from Brandon, who is quietly waiting for us to cease the eye-fucking and throw the last rock. It's not the worst idea. The quicker the game is over, the faster we get out of here. Dax turns and glides over to where Brandon is waiting to sweep.

"Hey," I call after him, pointing at the rock at my feet. "You didn't tell me what you want me to throw."

He shrugs, looking unfussed. "Whatever's gonna get us out of here the fastest."

THE CURLING GODS look favorably on me.

I throw my rock a tad bit heavy. However, my aim is dead-on.

It takes out two of our opponent's rocks and one of our own, but it holds on to the outer edge of the circles.

I believe the correct curling term is a *biter*.

How fitting.

It earns us a point. Which means we win.

The crowd goes wild. Or at least Dougie and Dax do, and I'm swept into a burly-man group hug.

Dougie makes us stay for a postgame beer (which we drink in record time).

Buzzed from the beer and the sweet taste of victory, we decide to walk back to Dax's place since his car is still in the shop. I also suspect that Dax is worried that if we're confined to an Uber's back seat, I might try to take his pants off.

He has every right to be afraid.

His postgame shower made the ends of his hair curl, leaving it a little wild. And his shirt clings to him in all the right places, leaving enough to my imagination that I flip-flop from picturing him naked to feeling like I need to feel his hands on me immediately or I'm going to crawl right out of my skin.

Dax, however, is not as feral. He grabs my hand as we walk along the near-empty street, lacing his fingers through mine. And that act makes my heart swell. I can read Dax like a book; I note his side-eye toward me, his smile when he knows he's been caught looking.

"What?" he asks.

"I think you like me."

"What makes you say that?"

"You're holding my hand, for one."

He looks down at our entwined fingers. "What if I'm making sure you don't wander out into traffic? I think with you, it's not out of the realm of possibility."

"Okay." I shrug. "We can go with that one if you want."

Dax stops mid-walk, and because I don't expect it, I keep going until he tugs my arm, causing me to fall back into his chest, where he catches me in a hug.

I look up, and his eyes are so dark that I can see the reflection of the streetlights. He moves his arms up my back until he cups the back of my head. He tips it back and lays a slow, lingering kiss on my lips that steals my breath away.

"You might be right. I might like you a little."

He kisses me again as if he likes me a lot.

Our make-out acts like dynamite to a dam. Once we start, we can't stop. It takes us upward of twenty minutes to make it half a block. We don't make it more than six feet at a time before one of us pulls the other into an embrace, and then it's all lips and hands and tongues until one of us pulls away with a *We should keep going.*

Make out, walk, repeat. Make out, walk, repeat. Until finally, Dax pulls away.

"I'm another two blocks. As much as I'm enjoying every single second of this, I'd really like to get you back to my place at some point tonight."

"Ah yes, the bearskin rug. Well, what do you say we make a run for it?"

Dax eyes me like he thinks I'm not going to do it. I take off in a sprint, as fast as my sandals will allow. It's half a block before his long legs catch up, and he once again grabs me by the hand and doesn't let go until we reach the front door of his three-story walk-up.

We make out in his front lobby. He presses me against the wall, leaning his hard body into mine. He nibbles and licks and kisses my neck from my jawbone to my shoulder while his hands grip my ass and pull my hips to his. He's so hard. I'm so turned on, and, apparently, we're also both loud, which is why his elderly neighbor is standing in her doorway, giving the pair of us a dirty but completely understandable look.

"Apologies." Dax tips the brim of a hat he's not actually wearing. He grabs my hand, and we take the steps two at a time until we reach the third floor. I'm pulling his shirt from his jeans as he fits his key into the lock. I've got it completely out by the time he opens the door and flips on the lights.

My only objective is to get Dax naked, but I pause in shock at the sight of his apartment.

I've been to my Dax's apartment easily a hundred times. It's the same one in this timeline. A spacious one-bedroom with parquet floors and a kitchen that hasn't been updated since the late seventies. But this place looks so different.

I always joked that Dax's place was decorated to look like it walked off the pages of a Crate & Barrel catalog. In my timeline, he has a tan leather sofa that he agonized about for a full six months before buying. He's so in love with his carpet that he refuses to let me drink red wine in his living room.

This room is meticulously neat, like the one in my world. But the couch is faded and worn, as if he bought it secondhand. The furniture, although tasteful, shows the scars of many years of scratches and dents and cups left without coasters. Dax's big screen is nowhere to be found. His carefully curated art is missing from the walls. The room looks half-empty.

"It's not much, but it's home."

I flip my attention back to Dax, who is watching me take everything in.

"It's great," I lie, knowing my poker face is shit and that Dax can see through my words. I want to explain that there's nothing wrong with his place at all. It's just different from what I was expecting. But I can already tell from the way he's avoiding my eyes that I've screwed up and offended him.

"Hey." I cross the room and wrap my arms around his waist. "I'm like a cat. It takes me a minute to get oriented in a new environment. Your place is great. Most importantly, you have a couch that looks big enough to make out on."

I reach for Dax's belt, pull the end through his pant loops, then use the fact that it's still on his waist to pull him over to the couch. With a light push, he falls back and sinks onto the cushions. I straddle him, knees on either side, and abandon his belt for the buttons of his dress shirt, only getting distracted when he reaches up and brings my face to his.

We have done a lot of kissing tonight. From sweet pecks to horny, hungry ones, we've pretty much covered the bases. However, this kiss is slow and deep and lacks the urgency of our earlier ones. It's as if it melts away the room around us, leaving only Dax and me alone in our own little universe.

At some point, my hands remember how to function and manage to finally resume their quest to remove his shirt. With Dax now top-naked, I'm able to run my hands over his smooth skin, his chest, his arms, parts of Dax I've never explored before.

He pulls my dress up over my head, undoes my bra with an impressive single hand, slides the straps off my shoulders, then shoots it like a slingshot across his living room. I laugh as it lands on top of his lampshade, then gasp as he takes a nipple into his mouth, his hands finding the ticklish spot below my ribs.

It all feels so good. The kissing. The ease we have together. I wonder for the millionth time why we haven't been doing this all along. Not this Dax and me, but *my* Dax. Was I so obsessed with Stuart that I failed to see what was in front of me? I don't remember ever feeling this way about Stuart. Like I'm on the edge of a cliff and about to fall and 100 percent okay with it.

"You're thinking awfully hard again."

He's abandoned my breast to nuzzle my chest, just below my chin.

"Only sexy thoughts in this head. Trying to figure out how I can get your pants off. I think it's next to impossible in this position."

"Well, I have a solution for that." He lifts me by the hips, flips me over, and lays me down on the couch. I am treated to the most delicious view as he stands, undoes his belt, and sheds his pants to a puddle on the floor.

His boxers are navy with tiny white polka dots all over them, but I am far more interested in the erection they are failing to contain. He moves toward me, his hands reaching for my panties.

"Nope." I hold up a single finger. "Yours first. I am way too excited to see what's going on under there. Boxers off. Now."

Dax hesitates for only a second before reaching for his waistband and removing his last layer.

"Holy shit!" I clap my hand over my mouth, mostly to prevent any drool from escaping, but *holy shit* is the correct phrase to use here. Dax's penis is glorious. Thick, hard. It's the Christmas present I never knew I wanted. I picture it in a bow. It would need a very big bow. "Where the hell have you been hiding that thing? I mean, your pants are all pretty tight."

Dax raises an eyebrow. Then he makes a second attempt to reach and remove my panties, but I squirm away.

"Seriously, Dax, your penis is glorious."

"Gemma." He looks up at me, his expression feigning annoyance as two locks of dark waves fall in front of his eyes. "I'm trying to get you naked over here."

I brush the strands away and take his head into my hands. "I know. Sorry. That was just an unexpected surprise." I brush my lips against his. He kisses me back, and I can feel the muscles in his back relax a little. We make out again, this time with only my lacy pink thong keeping us from both being completely naked.

Dax's hand finds my breast at the same time his mouth meets mine, and I abandon all other plans. Part of me wants to stay like this for hours, kissing, stroking, touching, teasing. The other part of me still has the image of his penis burned into my head and can think of nothing but *I need that thing inside me.* Especially because every time Dax moves, I can feel it hard and ready between my legs.

"I very much want to remove these." Dax's finger slides beneath the elastic of my underwear. "However, you stopped me before, and I want to make sure you're okay with me taking them off."

"I am very much okay with you taking them off. My hesitation earlier was wanting to enjoy the moment while you took off yours."

Dax lifts his head. His smile is all wolfish and sexy. "Then I won't hear any complaints if I take my time." He doesn't wait for an answer but travels down the length of my body, stopping every few inches to kiss or lick until he reaches the elastic waistband. Then he moves to my left hip, dragging his hot breath over my skin as he takes his sweet time kissing his way across.

"You're killing me, you know that?" I throw back the same phrase he used last night.

He ignores me and keeps kissing. "We are going to be at this for a while. No need to rush things." And just to prove a point, he drags his tongue all the way back to the left and starts over.

All-night, slow, hot sex with Dax is exactly what I want. I am fully signing up for this activity. But I also desperately want my panties off and to be reacquainted with his talented fingers, so much so that my hips lift from the couch in anticipation.

Dax laughs. "I can take a hint when I see one." He hooks his fingers under the waistband and shimmies my panties off in one quick motion. Then flings them across the room, where they join my bra on the lampshade.

"Nice shot."

Dax bends down and plants a quick kiss on my lips. "I'm a talented guy." And to back that thought up, his fingers once again find my aching clit. It's better than I remember, the feeling of his fingers and the swirls of pleasure they elicit from my body.

I moan into his mouth. He responds with another soundless laugh as he dips a finger into the wetness between my legs. He circles my entrance. "Again?"

No actual answer from my end, just another moan and my best efforts at an *uh-huh*. He pushes in one finger. And as he starts to pump, he scrapes his stubbled cheek down my chest to my breast. When his lips find my nipple and suck, the sensation drives my hips from the couch. "Holy fuck."

"Good?" he asks.

"Better than good." I don't have a word for this feeling. It's pleasure and satisfaction and aching all wrapped up into one intense sensation emanating from my clit, and my breast, and everywhere in between. I'm so close to orgasm that it's almost embarrassing. A guy lasting a minute would be shameful. For once, there's a double standard where we women come out on top.

By sheer will, I hold on for another minute until the sensation builds to a point where my body can no longer contain it. And the feeling explodes like a shaken bottle of champagne. But instead of a *pop*, I let go of a satisfied *ahhhh* as my body fills with that delicious rush.

Dax slows his strokes but remains inside me as my floating body returns to earth.

Chapter 19

I'M A LIMP noodle. A post-orgasm, well-sexed noodle who can barely find the energy to lift my hand to Dax's cheek as he again brings his lips to mine.

"We should do that a lot more often," I tell him.

"You'll get no objections from me."

"Speaking of you." The sight of Dax's erection gives me a second wind. I reach to stroke him, but he stands before I have the chance to.

"We are far from done, Daxon B."

He leans over. "I agree. But I think we could use a little more room for this next part."

With that, he scoops me into his arms and lifts me from the couch. We're the cover of a grocery store romance paperback, only way more naked. He carries me to his room, not bothering with the light, and sets me down on his neatly made bed.

"Round two?" I reach for him again. His penis is so hard and thick. As I stroke him, I'm torn between wanting him in my mouth or between my legs. He makes the call when he reaches for his nightstand, pulls out a condom, and holds it up.

"Just making sure you want to do this tonight."

I point at his penis. "I am not leaving here until I do that to-night. Ideally twice."

He tears the wrapper with his teeth and rolls the condom on in a single motion. I get a brief sensation of butterflies as he climbs onto the bed in between my legs.

I think we passed the point of no return for our friendship hours ago. But this act somehow makes it official.

He dips just the tip into me, then swirls it around, making his cock wet and me wetter. So when he pushes in, it's in one long, smooth, gliding motion, and I'm lost again in that delicious stretch.

"It's even better than I hoped it would be."

He laughs at my words. A single *ha* with a chest heave. Then he drops his head, brings his lips to mine, and kisses me like he's been thinking about this moment all night.

When he finally breaks the kiss, his hips begin to move. Slow, even strokes that I can feel all the way up to my eyeballs.

I think I may be in love with his penis. There are many, many things about Dax that I enjoy. But at this very moment, they all seem to pale in comparison.

He picks up his speed, and the intensity builds between my legs. I don't remember the last time I orgasmed twice in one night. I don't know if I've ever orgasmed twice in one night. But just as I think I'm going to set a Gemma Wilde record, Dax stops, hovering mid-stroke above me.

"What's wrong?" I ask and attempt to move my hips.

He holds my hip firmly with one hand. "Hold on, I just need a second. I got a little carried away there."

I pause underneath him, my breath held and ready to burst from my chest before he lets out a long breath of his own.

"All good, but we might need a change in position. I'm not ready for this to be over yet." With that, he rolls onto his back, pulling me with him, reversing our positions so I'm now strad-dling him on top.

I start to move my hips ever so slightly, enjoying the way he fills me in a new way. His thumb finds my clit, and he matches my rhythm, stroking me as I ride him. Fuck, this feels so good. I throw my head back and get lost in the movement.

"You look so damn sexy when you do that."

I lean down to kiss him again, using the new angle to grind myself into him. When I lift my head, he catches one of my breasts in his mouth and sucks. And the sensation drives me over the cliff. I close my eyes, arch my back, and get lost in the tidal wave ripping over my body. Somewhere far off, I swear I hear Dax cry out too, but I'm too lost in the moment to be sure. When I finally come down, he's looking at me with the same satisfied smile I imagine is on my face.

"We're pretty good at that." I kiss him once more before roll-ing off to lie next to him. Dax gets up to dispose of the condom, then climbs back in bed beside me, pulling the sheet up and over us both.

He holds his arms open, and I tuck myself into the little nook between his neck and chest. I think I love this part too. Just lying here breathing, listening to the late-night street sounds of the city below.

I look up at Dax. His eyes are closed, but he has the sweetest smile on his face. It makes my chest swell. "Tell me something else," I whisper to him. "Something you've never told anyone. Even your best friends."

Dax peels one eye open, then the other, and brushes my hair from my neck, letting his fingers linger on my back.

"My deepest, darkest secret is that I love using Q-tips in my ears," he finally says. "I know they're supposed to be terrible for you, but I don't care. I do it at least twice a week. What about you?" He adjusts his arm, pressing me even closer. "What secrets have you been hiding?"

I don't need to think too hard about my answer. It's the one thing I've wanted to tell him since I figured everything out. "I'm from a parallel universe."

Dax kisses the top of my head. "Well, that explains a lot. What is your universe like? Do you eat pot roast for breakfast?"

I know he thinks I'm joking. I never intended for him to think otherwise, but it feels like a small weight has been lifted from my chest.

"My universe is the same as this one, except in mine, we're just best friends."

Dax lets out a long yawn. "Well, I think I like this universe better then. Don't you?"

If I had any reservations about staying here, they're gone. This place, with Dax, is so much better than I ever imagined. There's no reason why I have to leave. I'm happy here, I have my family, and I have Dax. My mind is made up.

"I do," I finally answer, but Dax doesn't hear. He's already fallen asleep.

Chapter 20

"SERIOUSLY, GEMS, WHAT the fuck?"

Kiersten is waiting on the stoop of my store, glaring at me and my morning latte.

"What?" I reach past her to fit my key into the front door. She steps aside to let me flip my sign to OPEN AND AWESOME, though I secretly hope that no one shows up for at least ten minutes or until I've had the chance to make a good dent in my coffee.

Kiersten follows me inside, still giving me laser-beam eyes that I swear I can feel boring into the back of my head.

"Where were you last night?" she asks. "I called you, like, ten times."

She is not exaggerating. I accidentally left my phone at home yesterday, and when I finally found it this morning, there were eleven missed calls and a long string of progressively angry text messages.

"I temporarily lost my phone," I explain. "What's the problem?"

Kierst folds her arms across her chest and glares at me. "Hello. You didn't show last night?"

I rack my brain for the significance. "Was I supposed to?"

"You promised me you'd babysit."

I have a vague recollection of agreeing to do this. But wasn't it for Sunday? Shit. Yesterday was Sunday.

"I'm sorry." My apology is genuine. "I got a little caught up in everything that's been happening lately, and I completely forgot."

"I was counting on you." The angry bump in her brow softens to an expression I'm not used to seeing on her. "I had a really important meeting last night, and I had to switch it up and do everything virtually, and it's hard to look professional when you have a two-year-old in the background and she's not wearing pants."

"A meeting? For what? You don't have a job."

The moment the words leave my mouth, I know I've fucked up big-time. If I was getting the laser eyes before, I am getting death rays now.

"I mean, besides raising your three beautiful children." I attempt to backtrack. "That's like having two jobs."

Kiersten continues to glare, then slowly reaches for my latte on the counter, lifts it to her lips, and takes a long, drawn-out sip.

Finally, she sets it down. "It's like having *three* jobs. And it doesn't matter what I was doing. It was important to me, and you bailed."

I know. And I hate that I've let her down.

"I'm sorry, Kierst. Really, I am. It was a jerk move. I am a terrible human. Can I make it up to you?"

She huffs loud enough to communicate she's still annoyed but shakes her head.

"You're not a terrible human, just an occasionally inconsiderate one, and it's fine." Her words suggest forgiveness, but I'm not entirely convinced.

She gives me an obvious up-and-down. "If you're going to stand me up, at least tell me you're well sexed. The fact that you're walking around like you rode a horse all weekend makes me think it was a good one?"

I open my mouth to tell her all of the wild and wonderful things that have happened since discovering my best friend has an incredible penis, but I'm momentarily halted when the bell above my front door chimes, and a new but familiar customer walks through.

"Sunny, hi."

She's dressed in yoga wear but looks like she's going to and not coming from class. Behind her is another woman, also looking like she's ready for sun salutations, but in an edgier version of Sunny's outfit, with her midriff bared, fabulous boobs proudly displayed, and leggings that look distressed on purpose.

"Oh, Gemma, this place is so lovely." Sunny holds out her arms and breathes in deeply. It's the same thing I've done almost every morning since waking up in this life.

"Three hundred square feet, am I right?" The woman behind Sunny steps forward. "Great natural light. Ambience is everything. Not too much product on display, so your shelves aren't cluttered, but customers can still self-serve. Definitely a must. What do you pull in on an average month? Two hundred? Three hundred? No, there's no way. Well, maybe during a peak period. The foot traffic is decent."

I'm not entirely sure if this woman is talking to herself or Sunny or me. Sunny makes a point of letting me see her roll her eyes as she grabs her friend by the shoulders and turns her to face me.

"Gemma, this is my dear friend Priya."

Priya holds out her hand and shakes mine with a firm pump. "I assume you lease? Do you store your inventory here? If so, how much? Or are your suppliers reliable enough that you can order on demand?"

Again, Priya doesn't wait for me to answer. Something on the far wall catches her eye, and she wanders off before I can ask why I'm being interrogated.

"She's an old friend of mine from medical school," Sunny answers, sensing my many questions. "Although she abandoned me after our first year."

Priya turns, jumping back into the conversation. "I wasn't destined to be a doctor. It took me a brutal year to figure out I'm grossed out by sick people and lack any sort of bedside manner, or at least Sunny thinks so."

If I was confused before, I'm even more confused now.

"Well, my brutally honest assessment of your skills gave you the push you needed to jump from the nest and follow your dreams, which is part of the reason we're here today, Gemma, other than that I've meant to stop by and haven't had a day off to do it."

Sunny turns her attention to Priya, who is now walking the length of my store in long, even strides as if she's measuring. I look to Kierst to see if she's following any better than I am. She meets my gaze with a subtle shrug.

I turn my attention back to Priya, who looks up, then walks purposefully back over to where Sunny and I are standing, pulling something from her purse.

"I would like to talk." She hands me a white business card. Her full name—Priya Bhavani—and the words *Spa Dérive,* along with an address, are scrawled on the front. I know the place. It's a bougie spa in downtown Toronto. I think there's even a second one in Oakville. Their shtick is that they are a European-style bathhouse, modernized for the millennial. A second glance at the card has me noting Priya's title: owner and CEO.

"Priya's opening three new spas over the next few years," Sunny explains. "She's visiting to check out this neighborhood as a possible location."

"And I'm looking for someone reliable with the same brand vibe to lease a small retail space in my spa. I have zero interest in all of this skincare crap—no offense, Gemma—but I need someone who obsesses over all of the details, and judging by this place, I think you'd be a good fit."

I hear her words.

They process.

I get the gist of what she's saying to me, yet I feel like I still need to clarify.

"You want me to help set up your retail space?"

She crosses her arms, pinning me with her frank brown eyes. "I want Wilde Beauty. This—" She waves her hand in an erratic circle. "I want *this* in my spas. Potentially. No official offer on the table yet, obviously. We still need to talk business. Are you free to come visit the Toronto office tomorrow?"

I nod because I am free, or at least I could close for the afternoon and be free. "I think I can make tomorrow happen," I tell her, still not entirely sure what I'm signing up to do.

"Excellent." She nods once curtly. "Now, you'll have to excuse us. I have a class in thirty minutes and I cannot stand being late." With that, she thrusts out her hand, we repeat the firm handshake business from earlier, and she turns on her heel, the door chiming behind her before I can fully absorb what has happened.

Sunny squeezes my arm. It pulls me from my stupor and reminds me that she and Kierst are still here, likely gauging my reaction.

"I know she's intense," Sunny says, "but she's probably the smartest person I've ever known. Take everything she said today as a compliment. I've accompanied her to a few of these meetings over the last year. Usually, she walks in, visibly gags, and immediately walks out. If you have any desire to franchise this place or expand, she's the one to do it with. You can trust me on that."

I manage a nod. Expand Wilde Beauty? I'm not entirely sure if the double-knotted state of my stomach is because I'm exhilarated or terrified.

Sometime during my mild panic attack, Sunny also leaves, although her exit is far less dramatic. She abandons me to a customer-free store with only my sister around to verify that the last ten minutes have actually happened.

"Holy shit, Gems." Kierst whacks me kind of hard in the chest. "I feel like we're in a movie. Like, when does something like that actually happen in real life? What are you going to do?"

This is a huge deal. Something I would have only admitted to wanting in my wildest dreams.

"I think I need to talk to Dax." I reach for my phone on the counter in front of me, but Kiersten moves like a ninja, slapping her hand on top of it first.

"No, Gemma. You need to go home tonight, pour yourself a glass of wine, possibly take a hot bath, and think about what *you* want."

I don't like her tone or the snippy emphasis on *you*. "Do you have a problem with him? Or are you still pissed off at me?"

"Neither. I barely know the guy, and I forgave you when I finished your latte. What I want is for you to figure out your own opinion first."

"Why?"

She opens her mouth to speak but pauses. It hangs there open with no sound coming out until she takes a deep breath that makes her nose hiss. "Because you're absolutely terrible at making life decisions, Gemma."

Okay. "I'm glad you held back to spare my feelings."

She shrugs, not arguing with me. "Deny it all you want, but every time you're faced with something big in your life, you start making lists of things that can go sideways instead of trusting in your own abilities to make things happen. Then you choose the boring safe route."

"I do not."

I don't.

I make plenty of risky decisions. Every single day. This morning I decided to bring back skinny jeans, all on my own. Besides, there's absolutely nothing wrong with wanting to overanalyze major, life-changing decisions. That's normal adult behavior.

Kierst's soft, open mom look is gone. Her arms are folded across her chest. She's not trying to hide the fact that she's annoyed.

"Humor me for a second. I've been thinking about you and this other timeline you are supposedly from, and I have a few theories kicking around in my head. I just want to see if one of them is right."

"Fine."

"You said you work for Eaton's Drug Mart? As a buyer, right?"

I have no idea where she's taking this. "Yes."

"And you love it?"

It's totally a trap. "I wouldn't say *love*. It's fine."

"Well, the Gemma I know would hate working for someone else. She's ambitious and smart, so I'm very curious to hear why you pursued that job."

She doesn't ask an actual question, but it's clear from the eyeballs she's giving me that it's now my turn to fill in the blanks. She will be sorely disappointed when she hears there was no big drama behind my decision. Yes, four years ago, I thought of starting Wilde Beauty. I had a little bit of money tucked away, a small inheritance from when Aunt Livi's older sister passed away. Then the job offer came along. I remember feeling uncertain about it. I only applied because one of Stuart's friends worked at the company and offered to put my résumé on the top of the pile. I interviewed for the experience, and it went well. Then I guess I decided it was a better idea at some point.

"I applied, I got the job, and I thought it would be a good investment in my future.".

Kierst raises her brows half an inch. "You thought it would be a good investment."

I think back again. That's exactly what happened. Stuart was so excited for me when the offer came in. We went to a fancy dinner in Toronto. He thought it was the right move for my future. They had a solid benefits package and a generous annual allotment for retirement savings. I wrote the acceptance email during our Uber ride home.

I look up. Kiersten's eyebrows are still doing their thing. Okay, fine. She might be onto something. Stuart may have slightly influenced me to accept the job, but it's not like it was a bad idea.

"Can I tell you the story of the night you decided to open Wilde Beauty?" Kiersten asks.

I nod, my curiosity greater than my desire to continue the argument.

"We were over at Aunt Livi's for margaritas. You had one too many and started spilling all your innermost secrets, one of which was Wilde Beauty. I could tell by the look on your face that you loved the idea. But in typical Gemma fashion, you were freaking the fuck out thinking of all the things that could go wrong. I know you, Gems. I appreciate that you like having all your ducks in a row and your future on solid ground. Lord knows our childhood wasn't exactly stable. But I could also see how much the idea of your own store excited you. All the things you could make it. Aunt Livi and I could tell you wanted to do it; you just needed a little bit of encouragement to make that leap of faith. So the next morning, I gave you my realtor's phone number. Aunt Livi gave you the names of her lawyer and account manager at the bank, but then you took the wheel from there. You made Wilde Beauty happen."

Kiersten's story sparks a new memory from the night in my timeline. When Stuart took me to dinner, I had two full flutes of champagne, and, just like the margaritas, they acted as a truth serum. I told Stuart about my dream to open my own store. It's not like he laughed at me or told me it was a terrible idea. He just pointed out all of the risks of owning your own business. Kierst is right. I hate not knowing how things will turn out. I check with Dax before starting a new series on Netflix to make sure I'll like the ending. I read romance books because I want the guarantee of a happily ever after. I'm low risk. I appreciate predictability.

Kiersten uncovers my phone and hands it to me. "Call Dax if you want. All I'm asking is that first, you take a moment to breathe and think about what you want. Then look around this store and remind yourself that you're the GOAT."

"The goat?"

Kierst rolls her eyes. "Riley says it all the time. It's a good thing."

Her phone chirps loudly in her purse. She pulls it out and looks at something on the screen.

"I gotta run to an appointment, but call me later so we can talk about this more, okay?"

As soon as she's out of sight, I pick up my phone to call Dax.

But unfortunately—or I guess fortunately—my door opens, and my store fills with patrons demanding skincare.

It's another busy day.

A blur of moisturizers and cleansers and SPF 50. The closest I get to telling Dax is a *Big news! Talk later?* text, to which he replies, *Can't wait to hear it.*

My feet ache by six o'clock, but my cheeks also hurt from smiling because the few spare moments I had in my day were divided between thinking about Dax and contemplating Priya's offer to make more little baby Wilde Beauties happen.

Despite my weary legs, I practically skip down the sidewalk to Dax's store.

All the Other Kicks is still brightly lit when I reach Dax's block, making me wonder if he's got some straggling customers.

I reach for the front door but pause at the sound of voices inside. Angry. Male. Arguing. One is most definitely Dax. I'm torn between feeling like I'm eavesdropping, standing there on his front stoop, and not wanting to barge in and interrupt something I shouldn't. My debate is cut short when the door flies open, and the unidentified male storms out, nearly body-checking me onto the sidewalk.

"So sorry, miss." He grabs me by the shoulders to steady me, or maybe him—either way, he keeps both our bodies firmly rooted on the ground.

"I think the store has closed up for the day," he says. "You might need to come back another time."

With that, he steps around me and takes off down the sidewalk. I rack my brain to place his face. He's middle-aged and white, with light-brown hair that's thinning on top and a nondescript white button-down covering a pronounced beer belly. I swear I've seen him before but cannot place where.

Ignoring his warning, I step inside. The main area of the store is still lit but empty.

"Hey, Dax?"

He appears from the back office almost immediately, that worried crinkle between his eyebrows visible even from where I'm standing.

"Hey. What's up?" I ask. "That sounded intense."

Dax's eyes flick to the street. "You heard that?"

It might be the lighting, but I swear he's paled a shade.

"Not really. Just shouting. Then I nearly got run over by that guy on his way out. What's going on?"

Dax runs both his hands through his hair, then drops them with a frustrated groan. "Honestly, it's nothing. He's my landlord. We've been arguing about a few things for a while now. I missed a payment on my insurance. Total accident. I meant to pay it, but the month got away from me. Anyway, they reached out to him, and now he's pissed about it. Not a big deal. I'm working through it."

Ned. Dax's landlord. Now I can place his face. We met at Dax's Christmas party last year, although he was dressed as Santa and a hell of a lot jollier than he was just now. Could have been the holiday eggnog.

There's a weird edge to Dax's voice, and my spidey senses wonder if there's something else going on.

"So, what's up?" Dax asks, interrupting my overanalysis. "You said you had big news."

Right. The whole reason I came over here. I push away all the weird thoughts and instead let out all the wildly excited ones I've been suppressing all day. "The most incredible thing happened to me this morning. Have you ever met Sunny's friend Priya?"

Dax shakes his head. "Name doesn't ring a bell, but maybe I just don't remember her."

"Oh, you would remember her, trust me. Anyway, she came by to visit my store today, and she owns a bunch of spa locations. And she wants to talk to me about leasing some space to Wilde Beauty. As in me, putting a bunch of Wildes into her spas. Isn't that amazing?"

Dax's muscles pull taut. A quick stiffening, lasting no longer than a pulse. Something I would have missed if I hadn't been momentarily distracted by his gray henley and the way it hugs his chest so perfectly.

"Yes. Amazing. Sounds like a great opportunity." He opens his arms and pulls me into his chest for a classic Daxon McGuire bear hug. It's exactly the right reaction, and yet it feels off.

"Are you okay?" I ask, pulling back.

His brow crinkles, and I swear it's even deeper than it was when I first came in. "Of course I'm okay. Why wouldn't I be okay?" He leans down and places a tender kiss on my forehead. "It's great news. I'm pumped for you."

His voice is back to normal, and the little crinkle smooths out. It makes me wonder if maybe I imagined the angst. Invented drama where it doesn't exist because I'm still not used to our new relationship dynamics.

"So tomorrow," I continue. "Come play hooky with me. We can take the train to Toronto. Visit the spa. Do lunch. Maybe even shop a little. We can make a whole day of it."

The stiffening thing happens again. I'm definitely not imagining it this time.

"I don't think I can, Gemma. I need to be here."

He doesn't offer any further explanation, and although he's perfectly within his rights to turn me down, it bothers me more than it should.

My Dax would have dropped everything without a second thought. His next question would have been, *What time do we leave?* He immediately would have fought me on where we were going to eat lunch and reminded me not to wear my pinchy shoes that look cute but always end up killing my feet by noon.

"Please, Dax." My voice comes out slightly whinier than I intended. "This is a huge deal. I need moral support. The opportunity could be life-changing, and Priya kind of scares the shit out of me. I need you."

He releases me and steps away. His hands take another stressed-out run through his hair. "I don't think I can make it work. Trust me when I say I wish I could. But I'm sure you'll be amazing."

I don't get it. My Dax ditches work all the time for shit that's way less of a deal than this. He once closed up shop four hours early to stand with me in the rain outside FirstOntario Centre to buy scalped Taylor Swift tickets because I promised him a slab of day-old Roma pizza left over from my lunch.

"Come on, Dax, it's just one day. If you can't get someone to cover, can you close up shop? I'm sure your customers will understand."

"No, I can't." His voice snaps. "And I really hate to do this, but I need to run. I've got a couple of appointments tonight, and I can't be late."

He takes me by the hand and leads me to the front door. He's gentle, but there's a very clear *Gemma, get out* tone to his actions.

I'm not going to beg him to stay or offer to accompany him to whatever appointment he has after six on a Monday. It's clear I've crossed some line or pressed an invisible button that I shouldn't have.

"I'll text you later, okay?" His tone softens a little. I get a brief hand squeeze before he opens the door and waits for me to exit.

I make my way back out to the street, noting the sound of the metal lock flipping behind me.

Standing on the sidewalk in the twilight, I'm not sure if I should feel pissed at Dax for ousting me so abruptly or be asking his forgiveness for a relationship crime I've somehow unknowingly committed.

Confused, I walk home to Catherine Street, to my basement,

with my bed and my spider and all my messy feelings. It's probably for the best that I'm in for an early night anyway. I need to prep for my meeting with Priya.

Even though I've technically only been running Wilde Beauty for a few weeks, I do know a lot about the retail industry thanks to four long, soul-sucking years at Eaton's Drug Mart. However, with Wilde, everything is different. First off, it's mine, and I say that with the possessive confidence of a regency duke claiming his virginal soon-to-be bride.

Four times the number of Wildes would mean four times the profit and, therefore, four times the number of cute shoes in my closet.

On the other hand, it will be significantly more staff to manage, which means an exponential number of ways everything can go wrong. My brain ignores all the positives and instead imagines every possible scenario where things could go sideways. Fire, flood, famine. A bad review that goes viral. I start to spiral down into a deep, dark hole of *this is a bad idea*, even though I know in my gut that it's a great one.

It's the part where I normally call Dax. The part where he tells me to get out of my head and reassures me by reminding me of all the fabulous things I've done in my life. He holds my metaphorical hand until I calm the fuck down and can see straight again. I need his opinions. My itchy fingers reach for my phone. Just one little text to ask him if he thinks I'm making a mistake. If I'm steering the SS *Gemma* in the right direction.

But I hesitate. Because he's acting weird. Because things are different here. And I still have Kiersten's words from this morning lingering in my head.

She picks up the phone on the fourth ring.

"I am capable of making risky decisions." I say it before she has a chance to get out anything but a "Hello."

There's the sound of a deep sigh on Kiersten's end of the line, and I can hear the muffled shuffle as she adjusts the phone to her ear.

"I know you are. And I'm sorry if I came off sounding a little harsh earlier. I had a long talk with my therapist afterward, and she told me I was an asshole."

"Did she actually say asshole?"

"No. She used far more expensive words, but the sentiment was there."

This is how Kierst and I work. No timeline can change that. Even when we fight, it only takes a phone call and a half apology to put things right. And even though we're good now, I feel the need to explain to her why even though I know something like Dérive is probably good for me, looking into the future and seeing a giant gaping black hole of infinite possibility is terrifying. I need reassurance. Whether it's her or Dax or someone else doing it. I don't like to stare into an unknown abyss alone.

"Do you remember when I was little, and I watched *Little Women*, like, every single day for a year?"

I can hear the light laugh in Kiersten's breath. "I still can't watch that movie."

"I liked knowing the end," I admit. "Even the part when Beth died. I was okay with it because I saw it coming, and I could mentally prepare for it."

"I get it, Gems," she says. "I really do, but the predictable path is boring. And you miss out on the chance to try some really incredible things."

"You make sense in theory. I don't know. I think that's why I always turn to you and Dax. If both of you agree with me, then it can't be a bad idea."

"You're not wrong. However, I think there are some scenarios where the only answer is to trust your own gut. You're a smart cookie. You make good decisions."

"I guess."

"So, are you going to see that woman about the spa tomorrow?"

"I think I should. I'm interested in hearing what Priya has to say. Wanna come and be my cheering section? I will pay in doughnuts and undying devotion."

"I think this is one you need to do on your own." There's a long pause on Kiersten's end of the line. "But I'm really proud of you, Gems," she continues. "Whatever you decide, I know it's going to be incredible."

I hang up the phone with a lighter heart and a stomach filled with amped-up butterflies. Tomorrow is the first day of the rest of my life.

Or this life, at least.

By the time I turn out my bedside lamp, I feel ready to take on whatever tomorrow brings. And as I lay there in the darkness, staring up at either a mark on the ceiling I've never noticed or Frank's new girlfriend, I think there's only one thing that would make all of this more perfect.

My phone buzzes. It's strangely on cue, and as I stare down at the text, it feels like the universe is sending me a message.

Dax: Hey. Sorry about earlier. Things are a little up in the air for me right now, but I'm really excited to hear how tomorrow goes. I'm sure you'll kill it. xo

Chapter 21

By NINE THE next morning, the excited fluttering butterflies have morphed into a swarm of pissed-off bees. I've gone from being cautiously optimistic about my meeting to pacing my apartment chanting, *"What the hell am I doing?"*

It's too early in the morning for a shot of tequila to steady my nerves. Three cups of coffee have not exactly helped the situation. My hands are jittery, my heart is palpitating, and my meeting isn't until eleven-thirty.

I've reviewed the train schedule three times. The nine-thirty GO train will get me downtown with plenty of extra time, even if there are train delays. The Hamilton GO station is a quick three-minute walk from my place. There isn't a whole lot that can go wrong in a few short blocks, but as soon as I think that thought, I worry that I've now jinxed myself and decide to be safe rather than sorry and leave extra early.

I'm putting on my non-pinchy, comfortable shoes when there is a knock on my front door.

My first thought is Dax.

He came after all.

Our psychic bond must have strengthened with all the sex

we've been having. Dax always knows when I'm freaking the fuck out and is here to back me up.

However, when I fling open my door, it's not my tight-panted, sexy friend-turned-lover, but my middle-aged aunt in a floral-patterned jumpsuit, holding a hot-pink lunch sack and a tray of coffees from Brewski's.

"Aunt Livi, what are you doing here?"

She holds up the bag and turns the tray so the large steaming cup with my name on it is facing me. "This one is chamomile. I figured you'd be hopped up on caffeine already. And I packed you a lunch. If anything, it will give you something to do on the train other than fret."

I take both items from her hands and then pull her tiny body into a hug. "Thank you. I needed this." I squeeze her tighter. "And this as well." I release her and take a sip of the hot tea.

She nods curtly and smooths the hug wrinkles out of my blouse with her hands. "I talked to your sister last night. We're both very proud of you. Why don't you grab your purse? I'll walk you to the train."

The walk to the station takes five minutes instead of three at Aunt Livi's flower-smelling pace. Still, by ten after nine, I have my ticket in hand with the train platform a mere step away. I settle onto a wrought-iron bench next to my aunt to wait.

It feels like I'm back in elementary school, waiting for the school bus to arrive on my first day. Uncertain what will unfold. Unsure if I want to smile or throw up.

I slip my phone from my purse and discreetly check it for messages.

"Are you checking the time or something else?" Aunt Livi's eyes stay on the train platform as she asks.

"I was hoping for a message from Dax," I answer honestly. "We left things a little weird yesterday. I asked him to come with me today, but he couldn't. I think we're good now, but I'm not exactly sure."

Aunt Livi doesn't say a word, but I watch her eyes follow the green-and-white GO train slowly chugging its way into the station.

Finally, she turns to me. "I know you think you know everything about Daxon. But you have to remember that in this life, he has spent four years on a slightly different path. There's a lot of life that can happen in four years." She leans over and places a kiss on my cheek, then stands and holds out her arms, completely ignoring the fact that she just dropped a weirdly cryptic message. "Knock 'em dead today, kid."

I hug her again, trying to absorb some of her confidence in me. I point to the waiting train. "I'm going to go get a seat."

I grab my purse, and when I stand, Aunt Livi is holding out another coffee cup.

"If I drink that one too, I'm going to pee my pants."

She presses it into my hand anyway. "Then sit near the bathroom, poodle."

I take the cup because I learned long ago not to disobey my aunt. However, I can tell by the smell and the slosh of the black liquid onto the lid as I walk that it's coffee. A bit counterintuitive to the chamomile.

I find my track and walk to the very back of the platform. I've never lost the childhood thrill of riding in the caboose. GO trains have two levels, and I choose a compartment on the lower one. I find a seat by the window and settle in. A female voice comes over the PA system announcing that the train will depart in two minutes and arrive in Toronto on time. I check my phone one last time for a message. There's nothing.

The PA system repeats the message in French, and the doors *ding* and then close. The train pulls slowly away from the station, and my heart sinks in my chest at roughly the same speed. Maybe I've watched too many romantic movies in my life, or, as Aunt Livi said, maybe I'm clinging to a different Dax who doesn't exist in this world. Still, a part of me hoped to see him running down the platform. A last-minute change of heart.

My phone vibrates. My heart slingshots upward toward my throat until I pull it out and see the 1-800 number. Just a scam call. Not Dax. I need to calm down and focus on my meeting. Aunt Livi's right. Dax and I are different here. We're not yet morally obligated to support each other in the big moments.

I lean my head back against the seat. The one upside of this trip is that I have the whole train car to myself. No annoying house music blasting from someone's earbuds. Or weird smells from an on-the-go breakfast. Or worst of all, a non-commuter who has yet to learn the first rule of the GO train: Don't make unsolicited conversation with strangers.

No sooner do I think it than I hear the familiar *thump-de-thump* of heavy feet coming down the stairs.

Way to go, Gemma. Have you not learned your lesson? The universe lies waiting to fuck with you at any moment.

Shoes appear in my line of sight first. White Nikes with a thin strip of brown leather above the sole and a matte black Swoosh.

Custom Nikes.

As the shoes come farther down the steps, the next thing I see is a pair of black jeans. Jeans that leave nothing to the imagination.

He smiles when he sees me.

And suddenly, I know. We are the same here. The universe could make us live a thousand different lifetimes, and we'll always find a way to be there for each other.

"You came."

He doesn't get the chance to answer because the moment he sits down next to me, my lips are upon his. Screw my feelings on

PDA. This is an emergency. I kiss him, long and hard, until I'm out of breath and need to break for air.

"I managed to sort things out." He plants a slow, soft kiss on my lips.

"You got someone to cover the store?"

He swallows. "Nah. I closed up shop. You were right. One day won't make much of a difference."

He glances at my extra coffee. Before I can explain why I have two cups, it hits me.

This coffee wasn't meant for me.

Aunt Livi, sometimes I wonder about you.

"Need some caffeine?" I hand him the untouched cup. "I have a strong suspicion this is dark roast."

Dax raises an eyebrow but doesn't argue as he takes it from my hand.

"This is going to be so much fun. We haven't been to Toronto together in ages."

Dax takes a long sip of coffee, then closes his eyes and lets out a satisfied exhale. "Pretty sure we've never been to Toronto together. Must be thinking of your other boyfriend."

My heart bangs so hard that I worry there's damage. I can't even focus on my screw-up because unless my ears have temporarily malfunctioned, Dax just dropped the *b*-word.

"Yup. I just did that," Dax says as if reading my mind. "Didn't exactly plan on calling it out this early, but now that it's out there, I have zero regrets. I like you, Gemma. I have no intention or desire to date anyone else, and I hope you also think we're headed in that direction, or this might be a long and awkward train ride."

I know Dax well enough to know that the bout of humor at the end is my out. My chance to dodge the question, make a joke of my own, and put an end to this impromptu relationship talk.

"I am all in, Daxon B. I have been for a while."

He lets go of a breath, the relief suddenly easy to see on his face. His jaw drops open as if he wants to say something more, but instead, he shakes his head and lifts his eyebrows.

"A while, eh? It was the night we went curling, all the lunging. It totally won you over."

I shrug. "Something like that."

The rest of the train ride passes in one big happy blur. I almost forget about Priya and the meeting until we pull into Exhibition Station, and it dawns on me that today is about securing my future in more ways than one.

My heart kicks up a notch with every step we take into Liberty Village, following the little blue dots on my Google Maps app until we reach the converted lumber-factory-turned-day-spa. It's a large, red-brick building with four huge front windows with painted black grills. Simple yet chic, the exterior lives up to the *Toronto Life* accolades naming it the best chill-out spot in the city.

"Do you want me to come in with you?" Dax nods at the two massive black doors.

"Yes. But I suspect it might be frowned upon to show up for a business meeting with my boyfriend."

Dax smiles at my first use of the word.

"Well, then I'll go grab a drink and wait." He points to a small distillery and bar across the street. "Come and find me when you're done."

My nerves flare, sending a cold panic through my chest. And as if Dax can tell, he reaches out and squeezes my hand. "She'll be lucky to get you, Gemma. Think of today as your chance to find out if she's worthy of your time—not the other way around." He tugs me toward him and envelops me in another hug, holding me firmly to his chest as if he can sense that my knees have suddenly gone a little wobbly, and I need a quick moment when I don't have to carry the weight of it all.

"Okay," I say into his chest. "I think I'm good now."

He places a quick kiss on my forehead and waits on the sidewalk as I climb the steps and push open the doors.

The moment I step inside, my nose fills with the scent of eucalyptus and something else that I'd call *Summer Rainstorm* or *Sun-Dried Linen*. It doesn't matter because I'm hit with a familiar feeling of nostalgia, even though I know I've never set foot inside these doors in this life or any other.

It feels like Wilde Beauty. It's hard to describe. Dérive and Wilde are very different; still, I can sense all the tiny little touches that have gone into the place. The relaxing acoustic guitar pop cover that floats through the sound system. The mellow color palette of taupes and browns. Even the staff's uniforms, comfortable yoga wear that looks pulled together and stylish. I may have met Priya only briefly, but I already feel like I know her.

I give my name to the receptionist and am escorted into a glass-enclosed office at exactly eleven-thirty.

"Gemma, welcome." Priya walks from behind her desk and extends her hand.

I'm prepared for her firm shake this time, and I return it with one of my own.

"Sit." She points to a cream leather chair. "Let's talk about what the two of us can do together."

We spend the next two hours talking about Wilde. The products we carry, why we carry them, and the type of experience I want my customers to have. Priya listens to me. Asks me all sorts of questions that set off a flurry of ideas in my head. I feel smart. And excited about the future of Wilde Beauty and everything it could be. It's the future I dreamed about late at night in bed when I'd close my eyes and allow myself a few moments of what-if. Dreaming without letting my rational brain take over with realities.

"We still have a lot of details to work through before we start to formalize anything, but I want to be up-front about the level of investment from your end. What I'm envisioning is that I'd own or lease the primary space. You'd sublease from me based on the square footage of the store. Inventory would be all you. Staffing is obviously also your responsibility." Priya's tone is nonchalant, but her words feel like a tidal wave.

"As you can imagine, the financial commitment is fairly significant. Am I correct in assuming you'd need a loan? I have solid relationships with my financiers. If we get to the point that we want to make a deal, I'd be happy to arrange an introduction. They're very familiar with my business, and their terms are fair. However, you'd be under no obligation to use them." She slides a piece of paper across the desk. It's not like in the movies where there's a single obscene number written on a paper. There are several, and it takes me a minute and a double take to find the particular one I'd be responsible for.

"I'll give you a minute to look it over." Priya leaves me alone in her office. It's possible she noted my sweaty forehead and shallow breaths and deduced that I was moments away from a heart attack. Or maybe it's just her business practice. Either way, I'm grateful to be alone so I can vocalize the single thought playing on repeat in my head.

"You have got to be shitting me."

It's a lot of money. Money I don't have. The kind of money I only think about when I go to buy milk at the corner store and see the weekly Lotto 6/49 numbers at the cashier counter.

Why the hell did she ever think I'd be able to come up with this type of cash?

I read the paper again, giving my brain time to process the entire plan. Priya wants to open three new spas over the next seven years. That means three more Wilde Beauties, each with its own lease. I could probably come up with the money for one if I ate nothing but ramen and learned to make my own coffee. But three! That's an astronomical amount of money.

Priya returns. She brings me a cool glass of cucumber-and-mint-infused water as she dives back into some proposed next steps. I'm fairly certain I only process half of it.

"Take all the time you need to think this over, Gemma," she says, handing me a full binder of information. "I'll be in touch next week to see where you're at."

Somehow I move my body up from my seat, out of her office, and back to the front lobby. It feels like I've just been in an accident. I'm in shock. It's as if my head has become detached from my body, and the two are operating separately from each other. It's a small miracle that I can open the front door and step outside.

Dax sits at the bottom of the steps, eyes closed, face turned up to the sun. I don't think I make a noise, but his eyes open, and he turns toward where I'm still lingering by the door.

"Hey, how'd it go?" he asks.

I don't answer. But the warmth in his eyes wills my feet down the steps, where I melt down next to him.

"You look a little out of it there, Gems." He brushes the hair from my neck, then his fingers make massaging circles into the muscles I only realize now are so tense they feel like boulders.

"Just give me a sec. My entire life is flashing before my eyes. I'm hoping it gets to the part where I see your giant penis for the first time, so at least the whole experience will have a silver lining."

Dax laughs. "Meeting go that well?"

I draw three long, cleansing breaths before opening my eyes and looking at him. "It started off so great. Priya is so smart. I could see her vision perfectly and how well Wilde Beauty would fit into her space. I get why she's excited about the idea. But then we started talking about the money. And then, all of a sudden, I was envisioning all of these terrible scenarios. One of which was me standing out on the street with Frank in a little glass jar and me wearing nothing but a barrel with these straps on the shoulders, which is stupid, I know, because why would the bank try to repossess my ratty old Abercrombie sweatshirt? They'd for sure let me keep my clothes, right?"

Dax's arm comes behind my back. He sucks me into that little nook under his armpit that always has this magical ability to make me feel safe. I stay there for what feels like hours as the adrenaline in my bloodstream slowly starts to dissipate.

"I think I'm okay now," I whisper, and he releases me.

"I brought you these." He reaches to the step below and produces a to-go cup that I assume is coffee and a brown paper bag with grease spots seeping through. I open it and find a frosted vanilla doughnut covered in coconut flakes.

"It might not be a Nana's doughnut, but Google said they're pretty good."

"Thank you," I say, my mouth already half-full of baked deliciousness.

"I've learned Gemma Wilde isn't her best self when her blood sugar is low." He laughs, but he's definitely not wrong.

"You ready to tell me more or do you need to finish your coffee first?"

I hold up a finger as I guzzle half of the oat latte. Each sip makes me feel that much better.

"It was a really good meeting, right up until the end." I attempt to explain it all again. "I knew it would be a lot of money, but seeing the numbers on paper really triggered a reaction. I think I could get the loan. But if things didn't work out, I'd be completely screwed, and I'd have nothing, and that thought is totally terrifying."

Dax doesn't respond right away. He lifts my coffee to my lips and waits until I finish the entire thing. "You're right. It's terrifying. Working your ass off for something and seeing it not work out kills you a little inside. But do you know what happens next?"

I shake my head, and little coconut flakes fall into my lap.

Dax brushes the remaining ones from my lips with his thumb. "You get up the next morning, and you start working on a new plan. And yes, the world sucks for a while until you figure the next thing out, but you will figure it out, Gemma. You're a smart woman." His thumb moves upward on my face and wipes a single tear I didn't realize had fallen.

"I think the doughnut and the compliments are helping," I say.

Dax pulls my forehead to his lips and plants a soft kiss. "Tell me something," he says. "How are you going to feel five years from now if you don't at least try to see if you can do this?"

I think about his question. The advantage I have here is that up until a few weeks ago, I'd spent night after night wondering if I would have been able to make Wilde Beauty a success if only I'd had the guts to try.

"I think I'd regret not at least seeing if it was possible. I just wish I had some sort of guarantee it would all work out."

Dax gets to his feet. "I can't promise you everything will work out. But what I can tell you is that you're smart and you're driven and incredibly talented, and you have everything you need to make this thing happen."

"Yeah, except a giant bank loan."

Dax holds out his hand. I place my palm in his and let him pull me to my feet. "You're right," I say to him. "About all of it. You're very good at this. If you ever get sick of running Kicks, you should consider becoming a therapist."

Dax laces his fingers through mine. "I'll keep that in mind for the future."

We start walking in the direction of Queen Street. "And since you are so smart," I tell him, "I'll let you pick where we have lunch."

Dax thinks for a moment. "Pho?"

"I think you meant to say *sushi*."

We settle on Indian from a tiny little family-run place wedged between a ramen noodle shop and a podiatrist's office. By the time I'm through my paneer tikka, I'm feeling better, and I have a plan to set up a call with my bank on Monday and then with Priya's investors to determine my best financing options. It may not end up working out, but I'm going to try.

We leave the restaurant, bellies a little too full and hands clasped together, taking the long route back to the train station so we can window-shop all of the little independent stores along Queen. My heart feels a little lighter and more hopeful with every step until the door to one of the stores opens. We have to stop to let a mother and her stroller out, followed by a man who is so achingly familiar that my heart momentarily stops beating in my chest.

He's wearing a navy-blue Tom Ford suit.

The jacket rides up as he reaches down to lift the stroller over the single front step. He looks directly at me as he straightens, and it feels like a kick straight to the shins. It stings because it isn't Eric. Or Aiden. Or Elliott. Or whatever the hell that doppelgänger's name was at the Prince and Pauper that night.

It's the real thing.

Stuart Holliston in the flesh.

The mother with the stroller beside him fusses with the baby, then searches for something in her bag. Stuart takes the stroller's handles and starts to steer it around Dax and me. It takes a full moment for me to realize that Stuart and this woman are together.

I guess if he hasn't been dating me for the past four years in this reality, it means he's been free and clear to find someone else. Apparently, Stuart's someone else is curvy, stunning, and happy, judging by the way she lovingly pops a pacifier into the infant's mouth, then takes Stuart's arm with the kind of practiced affection I don't think I ever gave him.

Kids were a sore spot in our relationship. Possibly even the weakened support beam that led to our collapse. He wanted. I didn't. I was too unsure of what a good parent looked like to be confident enough that I'd make a good one myself, so it feels weird—almost like I've been betrayed—to see him so natural in the role of doting dad.

Our eyes lock as they pass. He holds my gaze for longer than a second, and I think part of me expects him to stop. To acknowledge me and the four years we spent together. But he continues on his way as if I'm simply a stranger, not the least bit affected.

I can't say the same thing for me.

"Friend of yours?" Dax asks, reminding me that he's here, watching me have a mild meltdown about my ex-boyfriend.

"Was," I answer honestly. "In another life."

I'm acutely aware of the way Dax's eyes shift over my shoulder, presumably to where Stuart is still walking down the sidewalk.

"Do you want to tell me about him?"

Oh god, is that ever a question.

I take Dax's hand, and we walk a few blocks to the south end of Trinity Bellwoods Park, finding an empty bench under a tree next to a pickup Ultimate Frisbee game. Dax takes the seat beside me and waits.

"I feel like I just got a glimpse of what my future could have been," I tell him.

He nods as if what I'm saying isn't completely wild. "Is it a life you want?"

"No." There's no hesitation in my reaction. None at all.

"Even the guy?" There's a vulnerability in Dax's voice.

"Especially the guy." I shift my body to face Dax, tucking my leg under my knee and scooting close so I can attempt to explain how my reaction wasn't about wanting Stuart at all. It was just shock. And it was my brain making that final click into place, sorting through my changing feelings about Dax.

"I think he may have been one of those decisions you were talking about earlier. Where my heart knew it wasn't right but my head overruled with practical reasons why I should stay in that relationship. And I need to explain something to you. It might not make complete sense, but I need you to roll with it."

Dax nods.

"I want you, Dax. Every day it becomes even more clear to me how stupid I've been. I am better when I am with you. That whole meltdown I had before lunch, where I looked into my future and freaked the fuck out, and then you Master Yoda'd me into realizing what I really want? I need that in my life. I need you in my life. You are good for me, and I'm hoping I can be as good for you."

Dax's hand cups the side of my face. He doesn't say a word, but he pulls me toward him, and our foreheads meet for a few moments before my lips meet his for a long kiss.

I realize two things.

This very moment, here, might be the happiest of my entire life.

And in my other one, it never would have happened.

Chapter 22

I SLEEP THROUGH most of the train ride home with my head on Dax's shoulder, content with the world around me.

Dax walks me home from the station. We have a quick sidewalk make-out before he heads off to curling. Sunny, Dougie, and Brandon are all available to play this evening. My substitutional services are not needed, so I head over to Aunt Livi's place to hang out.

Although her bookstore is closed for the day, there's a group of about ten women gathered in a circle, matching paperbacks in their laps, each holding a lit candle. Weird for normal people. Not so weird for Aunt Livi.

Not wanting to interrupt, I gesture to Aunt Livi that I will let myself upstairs. She hands her candle to a heavyset woman with wild curls and meets me at the entrance to the back hallway.

"You had a good day with Daxon, I see." Her tone is more comment than question, and although I'm tempted to ask how she knew he'd turn up, I know her well enough to know that even if I ask, I won't get a straight answer.

"We had the best day." I'm still high on the memories. "It feels like my life is finally falling into place. I don't really know how to explain it."

My perfect mood is temporarily marred as Aunt Livi's eyes shift to something behind me and her face clouds for the briefest of moments.

"I love that for you, poodle. But maybe you should head upstairs. And be quick about it."

She shoos me off. Actually, to be more accurate, she shoves me off—down the dark hallway that leads to the stairs up to her store-top apartment. I ignore the weird vibes of our parting and follow her command until I'm halfway down the hallway and the bathroom door flings open and someone steps out.

"I'm so sorry, dear, pardon me."

Her face isn't familiar, but she looks like most women in my aunt's book clubs: in her fifties, wild curly hair, lots of jewelry, smells like a mix of sage and roses, although the rose part could be the lingering scent of my aunt's bathroom hand soap.

"No worries at all." I step aside to let her pass, but as she moves by me, she halts mid-step. Turning, she grabs me by the wrists and looks straight into my eyes, pinning me to the wall with her intense stare. I get the strange sensation she's looking for my soul.

"You don't belong here." Her words feel like arrows piercing my chest, and even though I don't think she intends them to be an insult, they feel like one.

"I'm Livi's niece. I'm not part of the book club. I'm just heading up to her apartment."

I move to leave, but she doesn't let go of my wrists. She steps in even closer, studying my face. "That's not what I meant. You're not *from* here. You don't belong."

She lets go of my hands and steps away. There's enough room between us to escape now. To slip away from her and her eerily intense stare and retreat to Aunt Livi's apartment, where I can ease my feelings with pinot grigio and the stash of mint chip Aunt Livi keeps in her freezer for emergencies, but I'm rooted to the spot.

"What exactly do you mean?"

She reaches for my hand, turning it over. She opens my palm and runs her index finger from my wrist to the tip of my middle finger. "Your aura is off. It's not of this world. You don't fit here. This is not where you're supposed to be."

I snatch my hand away, suddenly defensive. "Why would you say that?"

She tilts her head to the side, grabs a fistful of what I think is air from above my head, opens her palm, and studies it. "You've changed things."

I resist the urge to roll my eyes. Yes, of course I've changed things. That was the whole point. I wanted to change my life to one that never had Stuart in it.

"What's wrong with changing things if it's for the better?"

She studies me, squinting her eyes, tutting softly to herself. "What may be better for one may not be better for all. We are all tiny threads in a greater tapestry. If you pull one, you may risk undoing everything."

The words *what the actual fuck* are on the tip of my tongue, but I suck them back as we're interrupted by another middle-aged woman. This one is short and a little round in the middle, with light-blond curly hair and big glasses. Far less judgy eyes. "Are you ladies waiting for the restroom?"

I shake my head.

"You go right ahead, Rosaline." My mysterious companion waves her in. "God knows with the amount of tea I've been drinking, I'll need it again by the time you're done."

This time, I do take the opportunity to exit. I climb the back stairs two at a time and don't breathe until I'm in Aunt Livi's apartment with the door closed behind me. That was weird, right? Three weeks ago, I wouldn't have thought twice about that conversation. I'd make some sort of joke in my head about the contents of her tea and move on with my life, but now I'm not sure. There's a weird gnawing in the pit of my stomach. I'm rattled. And I really need to talk to someone.

Kiersten's phone goes to voicemail, but she calls me back two minutes later as I am pulling the emergency ice cream from the freezer and scooping myself the sizable bowl needed to cope with hearing that my life choices might be dooming the entire universe.

"How'd things go today?" she asks. "You going to become a millionaire business mogul and support your sister and her ridiculous family?"

Oh yeah, Priya's meeting. I almost forgot.

"Meeting was great. It might be a decade or two until I'm rolling in it, but I promise to put you up in a nice retirement home."

Kiersten snorts. "I'll take it."

"Are you busy right now?" I ask her. "I'm over at Aunt Livi's, and I need some moral support."

Kiersten lets go of a long breath. "Problems with lover boy?"

"No. Actually, things with him are really great. It's my other problem. I'm worried I might be causing a permanent rift in the space-time continuum."

There's the muffled sound of Kiersten's voice on the other end, as if she's covered the phone with her hand and is talking to someone. "Give me thirty minutes. I need to make sure Riley finishes his math homework, then I'll be over. Are we coping with booze or sugar tonight, and do I need to stop at the store on my way?"

I stare down at Aunt Livi's near-empty ice cream container.

"Sugar. And yeah, maybe pick up a tub or two of ice cream." It may take more than one bowl until I feel okay about potentially destroying the universe.

BY THE TIME Kiersten makes it over, Aunt Livi has wrapped up her book club. The two of them enter the apartment together. I suspect they may have been conversing outside, judging by the minute-long gap between the thumping on the stairs and them actually opening the door. The likely theme: Has Gemma slid through time again, and do we need to seek out some professional help?

Kierst plops a new pint of mint chip on the counter. They both scoop their bowls before settling into their usual spots, Aunt Livi in her armchair, Kiersten on the fainting couch. I give them a few bites of untainted chocolate-mint joy before launching into the recap of my potentially paranormal encounter downstairs. When I'm done, I look up. Aunt Livi looks stressed, with deep lines etching her forehead. Kiersten looks like there's a sarcastic comment on the tip of her tongue, waiting patiently for its turn.

"What do you think?" I ask Aunt Livi specifically.

She exchanges a look with Kiersten before drawing a deep breath. "It sounds like you were speaking with Miranda. She's new to our book club but very well read when it comes to historicals."

I love my aunt and how she judges a person's credibility by their reading tastes.

"Does she seem to know what she's talking about? Should I be worried about causing a catastrophic event here?"

Aunt Livi thinks for a beat. "I think if the universe were on the verge of imploding, we'd probably get a sign or two first. That's usually how these things work, I think."

She glances down at her tea, and her worry lines deepen.

"What?" An uncomfortable feeling settles in my stomach. "Do you see a message in your tea leaves?"

She reaches into her cup and pulls something out. "Hmm . . . looks like a Cool Ranch Dorito. Wonder how that happened."

Kiersten chokes on her mint chip. Several coughs and a firm slap on the back from me later, she recovers enough to speak. "I think you're stressing about nothing, Gems. No offense to you, Aunt Livi, but your book club gals can be a little eccentric, not to mention that more often than not, they are hiding whiskey in their teacups."

Aunt Livi shrugs. "I take no offense to either of those things."

Kiersten turns to me. "I think you're freaking out because you've got some big things happening in your life, and you're worried you're going to lose them. I hate to say it, but that's a peak Gemma move."

She's not wrong. Even though I hate to hear it.

"But weren't you the sister who only a few days ago was telling me I needed to slow down and not make any rash decisions? I distinctly remember you telling me that I should think about the consequences of my actions."

Kiersten flops her feet to the floor and pushes herself into a seated position with a grunt. "That was me getting all big sister on you. I wanted to make sure you were giving yourself time to think. Make sure that a relationship with Dax is what you want. I have never, this entire time, thought you were seriously going to alter our entire existence. I love ya, Gems, but you're not that important. Free will and all."

Her words make sense to my rational brain. My stomach, however, feels like I swallowed a brick.

"You're absolutely sure I'm not screwing up reality? Like a butterfly effect thing?"

She shakes her head. "I'm sure. It's fine. Look, I'm happy. You're happy. Dax—judging purely based on all the sex you've been having lately—is probably very happy. Aunt Livi," she calls to my aunt, who looks up.

"Yes?"

"Are you thriving?"

"Oh, I'm doing great over here, girls."

Kiersten holds up her arms as if she's just presented irrefutable proof. "See, we're all great. The universe is just fine. Stop stressing about it. Nothing's going to happen."

Kiersten walks to the kitchen. In her opinion, the argument is over. Aunt Livi buries herself in a book, but every once in a while, I catch her staring at me with narrowed eyes. There's also a growing feeling of unease in my gut. It churns, and it burns. It could be heartburn or possibly guilt. Or maybe it's just Kiersten's words still lingering in my thoughts because it's universal knowledge that the moment you say *Nothing's going to happen,* something happens. And it's not good. Call it Murphy's Law, or karma, or getting smug about the fact that your life feels perfect. I suspect my gut pain is me waiting for the other shoe to drop.

At 11:03, just as I'm getting ready to leave Aunt Livi's, my phone rings. It's a text from Brandon.

The other shoe drops. A custom Nike.

Dax has had an accident.

Chapter 23

I BREAK OUT in a cool sweat as I imagine a car wreck or Dax getting hit by a bus or sucked under the Zamboni. There's enough adrenaline in my veins that I could run halfway to his place, or the hospital, or, god forbid, the accident site if this text is immediate. So when the three dots appear, signaling that Brandon is writing more, I hold my breath. It takes him so goddamn long to write that I almost have an accident of my own.

He laughed too hard while eating a potato wedge. Got one lodged in his windpipe. Dougie had to do the Heimlich, and Dax thinks he's cracked one of his ribs. He's getting an x-ray at urgent care but otherwise good.

Sweet relief floods my senses. I don't know if it's a reaction to the chemicals raging through my body or the absurdity of the story, but my knees collapse underneath me, and I melt into Aunt Livi's carpet in hysterical laughter.

"Dude, were you spiking your ice cream without me?" Kiersten stares down at me like I've lost my mind.

I hand her my phone and watch as she reads Brandon's text.

"I'll admit it's a little bit funny but not the type of content that brings me to hysterical sobs. What is wrong with you?"

Sure enough, when I bring my fingers to my cheeks, they come away wet. I'm crying. I'm laughing. There are a thousand fucking feelings pouring from my body, and not all of them make sense.

"I don't know." I get to my feet. "I think I was waiting for something to happen that could be my fault, and when I got this message, I was certain that my actions somehow hurt Dax. To find out it was just a stupid potato wedge was such a relief. There's no way I could have caused that—"

Except there is.

Oh shit.

"She was right," I whisper.

"Who are we talking about now?" Kiersten asks.

"That woman from the book club. She said I've pulled a thread, and everything might unravel. It's unraveling, Kierst. I caused the accident."

Kiersten holds her palm to my head. I swat it away. "I'm serious. Dax, in my timeline, doesn't eat potato wedges on Tuesday nights. He eats wings. I get the wedges. This would have never, ever happened in my timeline. I did this."

Kiersten holds out her hand as if urging me to my feet. "It's not your fault. He's a grown-ass man who makes his own grown-ass decisions about his appetizers. None of this is on you." She extends her hand again, but I ignore it. I still need a moment.

Kiersten grabs her coat from the hook next to the door and puts it on. "Would it make you feel better if I took you to see him?"

I'm on my feet in seconds. "Thank you, Kiersten. I owe you like a million favors for this."

She pulls her keys from her purse and slings it over her shoulder. "Yeah, yeah, yeah. Put it on my tab."

———

THE DRIVE FROM Aunt Livi's to Hamilton General Hospital takes about six minutes for most people. Kiersten and her minivan make it in a cool four and a half. She pulls into the short-term parking and flicks the locks but doesn't cut the engine. "I love you, but I told the babysitter I'd be home by midnight, and if I'm not, she starts charging double time."

I pause, my hand on the handle. "How old is your babysitter?"

"Fifteen. I know. I wish I would have had that kind of audacity at that age. Call me tomorrow? Let me know everything is okay."

I nod as bravely as I can before walking through the glass sliding doors of the ER waiting room.

It's packed, and it takes me two loops around the broken bones, fevers, and other potato-wedge choking victims before I spot Brandon on an orange plastic chair, head dropped back as if asleep, with Dougie's husky frame curled up like a napping kitten beside him.

"Hey." I gently shake Brandon's shoulder. His eyes immediately fly open.

"Gemma. You're here. Sorry about that. Must have nodded off. It's been a bit of a day."

Dougie, still asleep, responds with a grunt.

"How's Dax? Where's Dax? Is everything okay?"

Brandon looks around the waiting room as if he's only now realized Dax is missing.

"He got called in for his X-ray." He checks his watch. "Maybe an hour ago. Sunny called in a favor before she left. I imagine he won't be too much longer."

There are no free seats on either side of them. It forces me to stand, towering awkwardly above them.

"Pardon me if this comes off sounding a bit brash, but there's no reason all three of us need to be here. Would you mind if I got this one home?" Brandon runs his hand affectionately down Dougie's back. "My darling really does need his beauty rest. Otherwise, he's a bit of a bear."

I nod. "Of course, by all means. I've got this. You guys go."

Dax showed up for me today. Spending the night in the ER is the least I can do.

It takes two gentle nudges and a hard shove to wake Dougie fully. It's another fifteen minutes before I'm settled in one of their leather-vinyl-covered seats, still warm from their bodies. The monotony of the room starts to get to me, as do the scrolling CNN news stories on the volumeless television mounted on the wall and the rhythmic scraping of the automatic sliding doors. Even the monotone announcements through the loudspeaker lull me into a state where I find my own head dropping back.

But then the doors slide open, and it's as if I can sense his presence before he even walks into the room.

His eyes scan the crowd for only a second before locking with mine. His dark hair is all mussed as if he's been sleeping. He's walking a little more gingerly compared with his usually confident stride, and his eyes have a glazy sheen. He's tired, but he's okay.

"Hey." I open my arms and then realize that a rib-crushing hug is the last thing he needs right now.

"What are you doing here, Gems?" The tone of his voice is tired but affectionate as he reaches out a hand, cups my chin, and holds it there while I press my cheek into his palm.

"Brandon told me what happened. I'm the reinforcements. Let's get you home."

He takes my hand, and we walk toward the exit doors.

"Mr. McGuire," a female voice calls from behind us. "Mr. McGuire!"

We turn simultaneously to see a middle-aged nurse in seafoam-green scrubs step through the sliding doors separating the ER and waiting room. "You left this on the counter." She hands Dax a piece of white paper. A prescription.

We step out into the night air, which is still a little chilly despite it being August.

"We should call an Uber." I pull out my phone, but Dax shakes his head. "It's okay. I can walk." He starts off in the direction of Barton Street.

"Daxon B. McGuire," I say in a voice that is sterner than I ever thought I was capable of, "you are not walking home with a broken rib. Come back here right now. Or else."

My empty threat is enough that he turns around, eyebrows raised.

"Or else what?"

"You and I know that even in your injured state, you could still take me, so I physically can't do anything, and I refuse to use sex as a weapon both on principle and because I fully intend to ride that beautiful penis again when you've recovered, so I'm asking you, as your newly minted girlfriend, to come back here and get in a cab with me."

He takes a single step closer. "I'm locked out of my Uber app."

I throw my hands up. "So? Mine is working. I'm calling one right now."

Dax mumbles something under his breath. It doesn't sound overly happy, but he reverses his steps and waits with me until a bright-orange Mazda pulls up in front of us.

Neither of us says a word as we cruise down Wellington until we pull up in front of the pharmacy and stop.

"What are we doing here?" Dax's eyes are rightfully skeptical.

I snatch the white sheet still clutched in his hand. "Getting you drugs. I have a plan to get you high and uncover all your secrets." Dax tries to take the paper back from my hands, but the quick motion causes him to gasp with pain to the point that I regret testing him.

"Shit. I'm so sorry. Are you okay?"

He nods, not looking okay at all. "It's fine, Gemma. I don't need anything."

I have no idea where this is coming from. Dax normally would consider prescription pain drugs to be a blessing and welcome the deep, delicious sleep they bring.

"Stop being silly. I'll go in. Just give me your insurance card."

Dax's face flares so red that I can see it even in the dim lighting. "Um . . . I had a small issue with my insurance provider. I'm between plans right now."

Shit. Still, it's Percocet. I can't see it costing more than fifty bucks. "No worries, I'll pay cash."

I reach for the car door handle, but Dax stops me. "Honestly, Gemma, I'm fine. Let's go."

Dax has never been good at letting anyone take care of him. I have never been good at backing down once I've set my mind to something. This back-and-forth will likely end with a twenty-minute passive-aggressive argument in front of the Rexall leading to an unnecessarily obscene Uber bill—unless I impose some tough love.

"You are hurt. I have a script for some very magical pills in my hand. I'm gonna go in. You can take off and leave me stranded, but I know you won't do that because no matter how pissed off I make you, you're never an asshole."

"Gemma—"

I fling the car door open, not letting him finish.

The pharmacist's name is Stan. We talk sports while he fills my prescription. I talk up my curling abilities to impress him, and I think it works because along with Dax's pills he hands me a Coffee Crisp from the candy bar rack "on the house."

As I expected, Dax and the Uber are waiting for me when I get out, although he doesn't say too much on the ride home.

There's no make-out in the corridor tonight. Only me following Dax up the stairs, half-worried that he's going to pass out from the pain and that I'm going to have to catch him.

I'm relieved when we reach the third floor and his door is in sight.

Dax reaches for his keys, and as he shifts his body, it gives me an unobstructed view of his door and the white piece of paper taped to it. I scan the twelve-point Times New Roman font, not quite registering that I'm invading Dax's privacy until I read the words that turn my blood cold.

In the movies, eviction notices are blunt and impersonal. Big block letters spell out with certainty that you're days away from being tossed into the street. Alexander Tsang, apartment manager, Cayley Court Apartments, appears to be a much gentler soul. He explains that Dax is three months behind on his rent, and if he doesn't settle his debt by the end of the month, they will have to ask him to seek other accommodations.

Whether it's the pain or the late hour, Dax doesn't notice the note until his key is in the door. His eyes immediately fly to me, and we exchange an unsaid conversation.

You saw that?

I did, and I'm sorry.

He pushes his door open and flips on the light. The apartment looks the same as it did the other night, although in the context of the last few hours, I start to see a pattern emerge that I completely missed before.

"Is everything okay?" I mean it in the context of his life, but Dax responds by ripping the notice from his door and crumpling the paper into a ball.

"That's a misunderstanding. I'll sort it out in the morning."

I know he's lying. It's the way he turns away so I can't see his face.

"You know you can tell me anything, Dax," I coax.

He lets out a frustrated groan, scrubbing his left hand down his face. "You can't wave a magic wand and fix my life, Gemma. This clusterfuck has been years in the making."

"But maybe I can—"

"You can't." His voice is sharp. "And I'm sorry if I sound ungrateful because you are amazing, and I appreciate you coming tonight, but what I need is for this day to be over and to go to bed. Alone."

His emphasis on that final word stabs a bolt of pain right through my chest.

I'm trying hard not to make this about me. He's hurt. It's late. Something is going on, and he's obviously upset about it. But I don't want to leave here unless I'm certain that he's okay. That *we're* okay.

"Let me get you your meds, at least." I reach for my purse and the white paper bag inside it. His fist slams down on the counter when he sees it, making him wince in pain so badly that he needs to grab the counter to steady himself. I try to grab for him, but he waves me off.

"Jesus Christ, Gemma."

"Just take the pills, Dax. Why won't you let me help you?"

Dax has always been more practical than stubborn. And with the pain lines etched into his forehead, I'm not surprised to see him reach for the pill bottle and pop two into his mouth.

"I'm going to bed," he says again. "Please call me when you get home and let me know you made it safely."

With that, he walks to his bedroom. A moment later, I can hear the sound of his sheets being pulled aside and him getting into bed.

I should go home. It's clear Dax wants to be alone. I should respect his need for space. However, my irrational brain is spinning wild scenarios. What if he wakes up for a glass of water and the pain makes him swoon, and he smacks his head on the counter? Or what if he has some adverse reaction to the drugs? What if something happens to my best friend and I'm not here to help?

I grab one of his mom's quilts from the back of his couch and settle down to make myself comfortable.

The brown fabric smells a little musty but is surprisingly comfortable as I scrunch a decorative throw pillow under my head and try to tune out the sounds of the city I'm no longer accustomed to in my scream-proof basement.

I close my eyes. My body is tired, but my brain keeps racing. What the hell is going on with Dax? The apartment. His old car. The fact that he shops at No Frills. Something has changed from my timeline to this one that has set his life off in a slightly different direction. And I have no idea what it is or how to fix it.

"Gems?" His scratchy voice has me immediately on my feet.

"Yeah."

"What are you doing?"

There's no point in lying now.

"I know you didn't hit your head, but I somehow convinced myself that you would slip into a coma in the middle of the night. It makes me feel better to be here."

There's a long pause on his side of the conversation.

"Come sleep with me?"

I love that he asks it like a question. His voice is shaky and uncertain. Full of vulnerability. Like I wouldn't dive under his covers at any form of an invitation just to sleep next to him.

His room is pitch-dark. I take my time peeling back the covers of his cotton bedsheets and slipping in beside him so as not to jostle the bed and cause him any more pain. His hand snakes under the blankets until it finds mine, and he laces our fingers.

"Sorry if I was a dick earlier. I've got some stuff going on. I'm happy you're here."

My lips find the stubble of his cheek. I want to ask, *What's happening? Explain everything to me. I'll understand, I promise.* But instead, I kiss him, whispering softly into the dark, "I'm here. I'm not going anywhere. We'll figure everything out in the morning."

Chapter 24

I WAKE TO a buzzing sound, then panic because I don't recognize the feel of the sheets or the crack in the plaster ceiling above me.

I'm not in my bed.

Oh shit, it's happened again.

Before I can bolt upright, warm fingers squeeze mine, and a wave of relief washes over me.

Dax.

I'm in his bed. Exactly where I'm meant to be.

"I think that's your phone." His voice reflects a short and painful night's sleep.

It's still dark, and it takes me a moment to locate my little white Samsung, flashing on the floor next to the nightstand.

"Hello?" I'm still half-asleep. My eyes are too heavy to open. The heat from Dax's body is too pleasant to even consider leaving this bed.

"Gemma?" My aunt's voice wakes me enough that I'm now coherent.

"What's up? What's going on?"

"Well . . ." There's a distinct hesitation in her speech. "Mr.

Zogaib just called me. . . ." She pauses again, and I roll my eyes beneath my closed eyelids.

"It's still dark outside. If Mr. Zogaib's mother needs moisturizer, she's gonna have to wait like the rest of the city."

"No—" Her voice takes on a new tone. One I can't quite place. "There's been a fire. We've been trying to get a hold of everyone, but . . ."

I don't hear the rest of her sentence. It's as if the world around me goes silent for a moment. Like time freezes, and the only thing that's allowed to move is my hammering heart.

"Wilde!" My body fills with adrenaline, and I sit up so quickly that the mattress shifts, and Dax lets out a soft groan beside me.

"Wilde is fine, sweetheart. No troubles on that block, but, um, is there any chance Daxon is with you right now?"

The vise around my heart wrenches another notch tighter. "What happened? What's wrong with Kicks?" As the words leave my mouth, Dax lifts his head so quickly that he grabs his side in pain.

"What's going on?" he asks.

"Aunt Livi," I say into the phone, pulling it from my ear. "Dax is right beside me. I'm putting you on speaker. Hold on, okay?"

The next minute is a blur. It feels like I'm watching a movie. Like the words *fire, quickly spread,* and *significant damage* all belong to someone else and not me. And they do, in a way. My store and my block escaped all harm, but Kicks and two others were collateral damage from a kitchen fire at the new Nashville-style chicken shop that opened only a week ago.

Dax takes it all in without saying a word. I swear he's a shade whiter, although it's hard to tell in the light of my phone.

"Do you want to go down there? See what the situation is?" I ask.

He nods, but he heard Aunt Livi as well as I did. *Significant damage. Firefighters are still working. We won't be allowed in for days.*

"Are you okay?" It's the world's stupidest question to ask. How can he be okay? I'm far from okay, and it's not my store, my dream that has turned into ash.

Dax doesn't say a word as he dresses, as we descend the stairs of his building, or as we get into the waiting cab.

We see the fire trucks and the smoke long before the block where All the Other Kicks comes into view.

"Fuck." He says it so softly under his breath that I almost miss it. We pull up, and the small span of space in between two fire trucks drains any hope still left in my heart. His storefront is black. The big beautiful glass window that once looked out onto James Street is now shattered into a million pieces, mixing with puddles of water and ash.

"It looks like the fire is out now." I point to the group of firefighters standing on the sidewalk, talking. Not clutching hoses. Or running into burning buildings. That's good news, if there can even be good news in this entire fucked-up situation.

When Dax doesn't answer, I turn to find him with his head between his hands, drawing deep breaths.

"Hey." I rub slow circles into his back. "I'm so sorry, Dax."

He continues the deep breaths. I make eye contact with the driver in the mirror and give him a silent nod that says, *No rush. Let him take all the time he needs.* At least five minutes pass before Dax raises his head.

"I'm so fucked, Gem."

I stare at the charred pit that was once his beautiful space. "I know this feels so shitty now, and it's gonna take some work to rebuild it. But I'll be here to help. And I'm sure Dougie and Brandon will too. We'll all—"

"No, we won't," he interrupts. "It's done. I'm done. This is the end of the road for Kicks."

His eyes look so resolute that it scares me. Dax is the guy who tells you not to stress. That life always turns out the way it's meant to be. In the worst of the worst moments, he's the one saying, *I bet one day we'll all look back and laugh at this fuckery.* He's an eternal optimist to the point that I've often wondered if anything can get under his chilled-out skin. But slumped in the back seat of this Ford Explorer, staring at his charred dreams, it looks like the last glimmer of hope has been snuffed from his body.

I press my lips to his temple. "Let's wait until we talk to your insurance adjuster. It may not be as bleak as you think."

Dax unclicks his seatbelt, opens his door, and steps out onto the street before I even realize what is happening. By the time I thank the driver and find my way to the pavement, he's halfway down the block, and I have to run to catch up.

"Dax! Wait up."

His pace slows, but he doesn't stop.

"Hey." I finally catch him. "Where are you going?"

He runs his hand through his hair and looks around like he's not entirely sure how he wound up where he is. "I have no idea. I had to get out of there. I couldn't look at it anymore."

Kicks was Dax's dream long before I knew him. I watched him turn it from a basement operation to a huge success. Seeing it in that state makes me want to vomit. I can't begin to imagine what Dax is feeling.

"Is there anything I can do? Anyone to call? I get that you don't want to deal with any of the insurance stuff now, but maybe I can, and it will help."

"There's no one to call." He starts walking away, much slower this time, and I follow. "I've been behind on my insurance payments for the last two months. I received notice last week that they're going to pull my policy for non-payment. I can't see a scenario where they'll have a change of heart, and even if they do, I'm so deeply in debt that it won't be enough to get things started again. I'm done, Gemma. It's over."

No.

None of this is right.

This isn't how things are supposed to be.

I've helped Dax do his taxes the last two years. I know Kicks is doing well.

"What happened?" I don't mean to say it out loud, but I do, and Dax looks up. It makes me feel the need to explain my question. "I thought Kicks was successful. I remember the lines down the street when you first opened."

Dax sits down on the edge of the sidewalk, stretching his legs out onto the road. He reaches out his hand for mine and pulls me gently down beside him.

"Things were great in the beginning. I thought I was finally getting somewhere. My sales were amazing. I was starting to get some great word of mouth. People were even coming from Toronto for my shoes. Then the pandemic happened, and everything went to shit. We had to close for so long that I didn't have the funds to get an online store up and running because I was still in debt from the opening. Everything snowballed from there. Even when we could open up again, I was too far underwater to catch my breath. The end was inevitable. It just happened a little quicker than expected."

Something is wrong. Aside from the terrible realization that I guilted my best friend into closing his already-struggling store yesterday, there's a second, even more sickening sensation creeping its way up my spine. This isn't how Dax's story unfolded in my timeline. I remember him opening, and the sneakers were practically flying off the shelves, just as he said. And yes, the pandemic happened in my timeline too. But he had *already* gotten his online store up and running before lockdown. This guy came in, Jeremy was his name, and he loved Dax's shoes so much that he wanted to open a second location in Toronto, but Dax wasn't interested in that. Instead, Jeremy offered to invest, and Dax set up his e-store. He had a warehouse just south of Barton and a small staff helping him to keep up with the demand.

Why didn't that happen here?

I retrace my steps through my memory, trying to figure out where everything went wrong.

The realization hits so hard that it knocks all the air from my lungs, and I have to brace against the sidewalk so I don't topple over.

Jeremy was a business colleague of Stuart's.

I met him at a party, and when he told me he was visiting Hamilton the following week, I mentioned a bunch of places he should hit up, including Dax's store.

If I never dated Stuart, I never went to that party, and the catalyst conversation never happened.

"Hey. Are you okay?" Dax's arm comes around my shoulders, and he pulls me into a side hug.

I'm not okay. Not at all. How can I tell Dax that I've ruined his life?

"I can fix this." I get to my feet. The book club woman was right. I have pulled a thread, and everything has unraveled, and it's left a giant gaping hole in my best friend's life.

Dax reaches for my hand again. "You can't fix this, Gemma. I love that you want to, but it's not your problem."

But it is. He just doesn't understand. I can put it all back. I just need to return to my timeline and set things back the way they were. Dax will get his store back, everything will be fine. It just means that I have to make sure I go back and—

I will lose what I have right now with Dax.

And I'll lose Wilde.

My knees turn to Jell-O, and my ass hits the pavement with a hard smack.

I can't breathe.

I can't think.

I've fucked up so hard that I can't find a way out. There isn't a way for this to end well. Either I stay here with a front-row seat to watch my best friend lose everything he's worked hard for, or I go home, and Dax goes back to being just my friend, and I'll have to live with the memory of what we could have been.

So much for unraveling the tapestry. I've soaked it in gasoline and lit a match, and now I'm watching everything burn.

"Gemma? What's up?"

He's not supposed to be comforting me. It should be the other way around.

"I'm okay. Just worried about you."

"You don't need to be. I'm already working on my new plan."

"You are?"

Dax nods. "Brandon's brother Peter manages an H&R Block. He's said a few times that if I ever got tired of the small business hustle, he'd take me on and train me as a full-time tax associate. I'll take it. I bet I can move into Dougie's basement for a while until I get on my feet. Still think you want to date a guy who lives in his cousin's basement?"

"Yes." I take his head between my hands and try to communicate via telepathy every single one of the million thoughts I've ever had about how I think he's the greatest human being on this planet. How I know with every cell in my body that he's the one for me, my perfect match. How I've fucked us up once, and now maybe twice, but in both those scenarios and any that may follow, I will always want him, always.

The words *Dax, I love you* are on the edge of my breath, ready to fall. But his phone begins to buzz, and before I can say everything that's left to be said, he's pressing it to his ear.

"Hey, Ma. Did Dougie call you? Yes, I know. . . . Everything's gone. . . . Everything."

My head is swimming. But it's not water in there. It's thick sludge, and it's preventing me from collecting my thoughts. Should I take him back to Aunt Livi's right now? Reverse the spell? Right this wrong immediately?

No, I can't. It won't work. Not yet anyway. I still have a few days before the moon is ready.

Should I just tell him about our life in some other universe and hope he understands? Would it save him some heartache if he knew I could fix this? One spell and we could put everything back. Do I want to put everything back?

Somewhere in the middle of my spiraling, Dax hangs up the phone. He holds out his hand and helps me to my feet, but before he can step away, I throw my arms around him.

I take in his smell. The way his body feels under my hands. The way I instantly feel safe and perfect and right. I'm memorizing everything. Cataloging all the little things I took for granted for four long years.

I feel him inhale, and I can hear the pain in his breath. It isn't until I pull away and his hand presses his ribs that I realize it was physical pain and not emotions.

"Shit!" My hand flies to my mouth. "I am so sorry, Dax. I forgot. With everything . . . I totally forgot."

"It's fine, Gemma, don't worry about it."

But I do.

It's the last straw.

The final bolt in the floodgates keeping everything in comes loose.

Hot tears stream down my cheeks, and my breath turns short and shallow. I know I shouldn't be crying. This isn't about me. I should be strong for Dax. But once I start, I can't stop. It's like a landslide.

"Hey, come on, don't cry." Two arms come around me and pull me into his chest. I stand there, frozen, unable to move, not wanting to hurt him any more than I already have.

"It's just a store, Gems," he says into my hair. "No one was hurt."

I pull away, cleaning my face with my sleeve. "That's the kind of stuff I'm supposed to be saying to you. I give you full permission to become the blubbering mess in this relationship right now. I can be the reassuring one. I got this."

He picks up my hand and tilts his head back in the direction of the fire. "I'm okay for now. But I may take you up on it later. Dougie just texted me. He's here. Your aunt is with him too. My sister is on the way. We should go talk to them."

We walk back to Dax's store. I'm still not prepared to see it so burned and broken. My stomach again twists at the gaping wound that once was Kicks.

At some point, Dax's hand is replaced with one that's leathered and steady and even more familiar.

"You hanging in there, poodle?" is whispered in my ear as I'm pulled into a lavender-scented hug.

"This is all my fault," I whisper, feeling a little better after finally letting the words out.

"Oh, honey, no." She holds my face between her hands, using her thumb to dry the tears that have made an encore performance.

"Sometimes bad things happen in life. And when there's nowhere solid to place the blame, we get stuck holding on to it. But there's nothing you could have done to prevent this. Nothing at all."

Sure, this fire might've been inevitable. Dax, in my timeline, might be staring at a big black hole that once held his dreams. There may be a thousand other timelines with a thousand other Daxes, each having the absolute worst day of their lives right now, but I have no way of knowing that, nor do I have the brainpower to process something so meta in this coffeeless disaster of a morning.

But there's one thing I do know.

Even if Kicks is a pile of ash in my timeline, Dax is a lot better off there than he is here. He will be able to rebuild. His dreams might suffer a minor setback, but they won't be crushed.

And there is something I can do about it.

"I NEED SOME tough love." I stand on Kiersten's front doorstep, two lattes in hand, smelling like a sad campfire.

She doesn't take the coffee. Or invite me in. Instead, she shakes her head. "I'm sorry, Gems, but I'm on my way out and can't talk right now. I'll call you later, okay?"

She turns around as if our conversation is over but leaves the front door ajar. I ignore her words and follow her back inside. She clearly hasn't heard about what happened yet.

Everything about Kiersten's house is the same as in my timeline. On her wall is the picture of a cow that Riley drew with a Sharpie when he was five. Kierst framed it instead of painting over it. Sitting on top of the television is the LIVE, LAUGH, LOVE sign that she got from Trent's mother for her first wedding anniversary. I would bet a million dollars it says "Cry, Drink, Fuck" on the back, written in the very same Sharpie as Riley's wall picture.

It also smells the same. Pancakes and coffee. If I close my eyes and clear my mind, I can almost pretend that I'm back in my own timeline. That I haven't fucked everything up.

"This is an emergency, and I need you to tell me what to do."

Again, she ignores me, hopping around on one heeled shoe as she searches through a pile of mismatched runners and rubber boots.

"Seriously, Gems. I have somewhere I need to be. I promise I will call you later, but right now, I've got to go."

She pulls her missing shoe from the pile and slides it on. Catching her reflection in the mirror, she ruffles her roots with her fingers and then grabs her car keys from the shelf next to the door, shoving them in her purse.

She's not getting it. I've unraveled the tapestry. I've fucked up the space-time continuum, and Dax is paying the price.

"There's been a fire." My voice wavers as I say it, but it doesn't have the desired effect. She reaches past me to open the door, ignoring that I'm having a third-degree meltdown in her front hall.

"I know," she calls over her shoulder. "Aunt Livi called me. It's awful, and I hope Dax is okay, but if I don't leave now, I'm going to be late."

Desperation floods my veins, and I launch myself after her, grabbing her arm. "Kiersten. I need you."

She wheels around, gripping both my shoulders. She stares hard and unwavering into my eyes.

"No, Gemma." The harshness of her tone feels like a slap. "You can't just show up on my doorstep and expect that I'm available to drop everything because you need to vent. I love you. I'm sorry this sucks. But you need to figure it out on your own or hold on 'til later because I can't right now."

She doesn't wait for my response. She marches out the front door and down the front walk to her driveway, not even stopping when I run out after her.

"But I brought coffee."

She looks up. I would say she's praying, but Kiersten is as atheist as they come.

"Get in the car."

She climbs into the driver's seat and starts the engine. I'm too stunned to move until she starts backing down the driveway, and I have to sprint to catch up, flinging open the passenger door just before she hits the street.

"What is wrong with you?" I yell as we speed down her street with my door still open.

"I told you. I have a meeting. We have exactly fourteen minutes before we get there, so start talking. Because you are not coming in there with me."

"Where are you going?"

I finally realize that she's wearing a suit. I have no memory of Kierst wearing anything that formal. Along with black heels and her hair nicely blown out. I think she's even wearing lipstick.

"I am pitching to a potential client." She says it like this is something normal she has said before.

"Pitching what? To whom? Who are you, and what have you done with my sister?"

The light in front of us turns yellow. Kiersten presses the gas and flicks her left blinker. The minivan takes the corner with surprising agility.

"I've decided to start my own marketing business," she says as we exit the intersection. "Nana's Doughnuts wants to rebrand. They're getting squeezed out by all of the hipster doughnut shops. They want a new look. A new name. Logo. Everything. I was supposed to meet with them the night you promised to babysit. I guess the virtual meeting wasn't as shitty as I thought because they liked my pitch. Now it's down to another independent consultant and me. And I really want to win this thing."

In this moment, I completely forget about Dax.

"That's amazing, Kierst," I say and truly mean it. "I had . . . no idea."

She shrugs, not looking at me. "Yeah, well . . . I have a marketing degree I've never actually used. I'm pretty smart. I've got some great ideas. But no one ever thinks that about me because I've spent the last fifteen years giving everything I have to everyone else—and I'm tired. I want, for once, to have something for me. And I think I'd be damn good at this."

I showed up on her doorstep to tell her how I ruined Dax's life. To detail out how my actions caused a ripple that got out of control. Because that is what I do.

I expected her to listen. To calm me down. To tell me exactly what I should do next, then tease me about it later. Because that is what she does.

It's how we've always worked.

But all along, I assumed she didn't mind.

"How long have you been thinking about starting a business?"

Kierst keeps her eyes on the busy weekday morning traffic. "For a while. But I decided to get off my ass and actually do something about it when Aunt Livi forced me to go to that weekend yoga retreat last fall. There was a part where we went around in a circle and had to talk about our hopes and dreams, and I realized that all of mine were for you and my kids. None were about me. And I decided I was going to do something about it."

I remember that retreat. It happened in my timeline as well. And when Kiersten came home, she was weird for a week and a half. I chalked it up to too much time with Aunt Livi. But now, I suspect the Kiersten in my timeline might be feeling the same way.

And I've been completely oblivious.

This time I can't even blame a glitch in the universe. I was too wrapped up in my drama with Stuart, my job, and my problems to even realize what my sister was going through.

We pull up in front of the doughnut shop, and Kierst gives herself one last look in the overhead mirror.

"Okay, spill it. Do you want to talk about the fire or your feelings? I have six minutes."

I shake my head, still rethinking everything. "You take them to prep. I think I'm gonna try this thing where I attempt to figure out my problems before I come crying to you."

Kierst eyes me as if she's waiting for a *ha* or a *but* or any other indication that I'm not completely serious. When it doesn't come, her eyes soften, and she reaches over the center console to squeeze my hand.

"I'm always going to be here for you, Gems."

I squeeze back. "And I'm gonna work on sending some of that support your way, starting now." I rub a tiny smudge of black mascara from her cheek. "You're going to be great. You were meant to do this."

She takes one last look in the mirror, then snaps it back in place. "You're right. I was. And whatever got into you just now, I think I like it."

I think I like it too.

She unbuckles her seatbelt and opens her door.

"Hey, Kierst," I call after her. "You're the GOAT."

She turns around and gives a sharp nod. "Fuck yeah I am."

Chapter 25

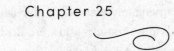

"So, what do you think? Home sweet home."

I set the last of Dax's boxes onto the concrete floor of Dougie and Brandon's basement. We spent the afternoon packing up Dax's apartment. Although I tried to keep up the optimism and perpetuate the lie that he's moving on to bigger and better, there's been a mournful energy to the day so far.

It doesn't help that Dougie and Brandon's basement isn't exactly an ideal bachelor pad. I secretly swear to myself to never, ever complain about my own murder basement ever again.

Where mine is fully finished with painted drywall and faux-hardwood floors, Dax's new place is a true basement, complete with cinderblock walls, exposed support beams, and the entirety of Frank's extended family.

"It's not glamorous, I know. But the guys are letting me stay here for free until I get on my feet. I'll have my own place again soon, I promise."

"I don't doubt that for a second." I wrap my arms around his neck, hating the look he's giving me right now. "This place has that rustic industrial vibe that's totally in right now. The low lighting gives you a broody look that I find very attractive. This place has all the makings of a sex cave."

This earns me a small smile.

"Is that right?"

I run my hands down the front of his chest. "I mean, I walked down these steps and immediately wanted to tear your clothes off. It might have been all those muscles you were flexing, lifting all of those boxes and everything, but I feel like this place has big sex energy."

His hands cup my face, and I expect a flirty kiss or a hungry kiss, something to go along with the tone of our banter. Instead, I get a long, deep, soulful one that I feel all the way to my core, along with the distinct impression that it means something to Dax.

"Thank you." He pulls me into his chest, and we stand there for what feels like hours but is probably only a handful of minutes. I could linger there happily for many more, but the sound of Dougie's not-so-delicate footsteps clunks down the stairs, followed by a grizzly-like clearing of the throat just as Dougie's head pops around the corner—hand readied to cover his eyes if needed.

"Okay, good," he says when he sees us still fully clothed. "Wasn't too sure what the two of you were up to down here. We should probably work out some sort of code. I just promised Brandon I'd make him bacon for brunch, and we keep it down here in the big freezer. But while I'm here, I thought I'd tell you both that Brandon and I are planning on throwing a party here on Saturday to welcome our new roommate. Real classy affair. I'm thinking either Tight and Bright or *Twilight*-themed. Mark it in your calendar."

I take out my phone to make a note of it in my calendar and

make sure I have the time this week to find the perfect costume.
However, when I flip to Saturday, two words stare back at me.

Waning gibbous.

My time is up. As of Saturday, the moon will be back in position, and I need to decide what the hell I'm going to do.

Stay or go.

Dax as lover or Dax as friend?

My dream or his.

"You okay there, Gems? You've gone a little white." I look up
to see that Dougie has retreated back upstairs, and I'm once
again alone with Dax.

"I have a question for you." My heart is sticking with its deaf-
ening *lub-dub, lub-dub.*

"Okay."

"Theoretically. If I could bring your store back, exactly as it
was before but even more successful, but it meant you and I had
to go back to being friends, would you want me to do it? Hypo-
thetically. Completely hypothetical."

Dax studies my face. "That seems like a very Don Corleone–
like question?"

"Who?"

He pulls me into his chest, laughing. "There it is."

"What?"

"Your tragic flaw. I knew you were too good to be true, Gemma
Wilde."

"You think that's my tragic flaw? Have you forgotten how we
met?"

He pulls back and plants a light kiss on my forehead, smiling
for the first time since stepping into this damp, dark, extremely
not-sex-cavish basement.

"Fair enough. And to answer your question, no. My store is a place, and you are a person. A very weird person sometimes, but I think that's why I love you."

My heart stops.

Completely.

It ceases to beat inside my chest until my brain catches up and processes his confession.

"You love me?"

He lets out a long breath as if his lungs were suffering from the same momentary malfunction as my heart.

"It wasn't supposed to slip out quite like that. I probably should have made it way more romantic, but yes. I do. I love you, Gemma."

He doesn't move toward me. Instead, he teeters on his toes as if he isn't entirely sure how this will go.

This is a big deal. A huge deal. Dax dated his last girlfriend for almost four months, and he never once uttered those perfect three words.

He loves me. And although I've suspected? Hoped? Sent intentions out into the universe that he hopefully feels the same overwhelming emotion that's overtaken any rational thought these last few weeks? It still feels wonderful to hear it out loud.

"I love you too, Daxon B. I have for a long time."

My confession is enough for Dax to take a step forward, although his arms stay glued to his sides. "You still gonna feel that way when I'm an associate tax professional?"

"Uh, especially when you are an associate tax professional. Taxes are hot."

He gives me a very unconvinced one eyebrow raise.

"I love men in practical chinos."

"Gemma."

"If you promise to do my taxes for me this year, I swear to god I'll drop down on my knees right now and give you a blow job."

"Gems." His tone is all laughs, but I've said the magic *b*-word. Now his eyes are all heat and sex. His hands finally find their way back to my body, resting lightly on my hips, the pads of his thumbs finding the bare strip of skin between my T-shirt and jeans. He leans in and presses three light kisses on my neck. One by my collarbone, one just below my jaw, and the last one just south of my ear. Then he runs his tongue to my earlobe and nips playfully. "We have seven more months until tax season."

It's all the invitation I need. We're in a sex cave, and I'm craving the feel of his body. My fingers seek out the drawstring to his jogging pants. He flicks open the button of my jeans with a single hand. Undergarments follow in the same coordinated, frenzied motion. We're bottom-half-naked in under a minute.

Efficiency.

I like it.

I think I'll enjoy fucking Dax the tax associate.

I push him back, only realizing after the fact that his ribs are likely still tender. He falls onto the bed with a small grimace as he hits the mattress. But as I climb on top, carefully straddling his waist with my knees, his face melts into a slow smile as his hands slide up my thighs and slip beneath the hem of my T-shirt. The rough skin of his calloused palms is a stark contrast to the softness of his fingertips, which tickle as they travel up my rib cage, sending a ripple of pleasure up my spine.

I doubt I'll ever get sick of him touching me like this. Or the way his smile widens when his thumbs brush the undersides of my breasts, or the way he looks at me, half-lidded and content, like he too could do this forever.

"Come here and kiss me already." Dax pulls my head to his for a kiss that starts off all sweet and slow but quickly shifts to heated and hungry until it is momentarily halted by the sound of raised voices arguing in the kitchen above us.

"I have a feeling . . ." Dax whispers as his eyes lift to the ceiling, "that they're debating whether they should invite us up for brunch, so . . ."

He gathers my shirt into his fist and pulls me down for another kiss. This one wastes no time. It is all tongue and want and efficiency. *Messages received, Daxon McGuire.* Time is of the essence.

He lifts my shirt up just enough to pull my bra downward and free my breasts. He takes my nipple into his mouth, which causes me to moan a little too loud, seeing as we're trying for covert sex here. Maybe if Dougie knew the incredible sensations Dax was creating with the swirl of his tongue, he'd leave us alone for the next hour. Or maybe the rest of the afternoon.

I can no longer worry about Dougie or anything besides Dax's talented mouth as it alternates between licking and sucking. Especially when the pad of his thumb seeks out my neglected breast, moving in teasing slow circles until both of my nipples are so hard they ache.

My hips start to move of their own volition, seeking out Dax's hard erection, raised and ready between my knees. As I rock, his shaft slips between my folds. I get lost in the rhythm, enjoying the friction every time his dick brushes against my clit.

"Be careful, Gems." Dax lifts his lips from my breast. "You're so wet. It feels fucking incredible, but I haven't put anything on."

I reach between my knees and stroke him, loving the fact that he's both long and thick. "Well, we should probably take care of that now, just in case I get too carried away."

Dax lifts me off his hips and flips me onto the mattress beside him, then rolls off the bed, reaching for his abandoned joggers and the wallet in their back pocket. He returns with a foil packet already between his teeth, but I notice how his eyes hit the ceiling above us, and he pauses for a moment before they come back to focus on me and my half-naked body. "Aw, fuck it." He tears the condom open and sheds the wrapper on the floor before crawling back into bed and lifting me back into the same position on top of him that I was in before he left.

"Please continue." He smiles as he lifts my shirt and turns his attention now to my other breast.

There's another creaking overhead, and we both freeze. My Dax telepathy is absolutely sure that both of us are sending simultaneous prayers to the gods of brunch to create some sort of diversion upstairs to buy us some more time. When the cooking sounds resume, I abandon my plans to tease Dax slowly and instead position myself above his cock.

"I'm skipping straight to the main event," I tell him as I lower myself, careful not to touch his ribs. He groans, but it's one of pleasure. Despite my bold claim, I go slow, easing him in, inch by inch. I pause for a moment, letting my body adjust, enjoying the feeling of being stretched and full and happy before building into a slow rock, enjoying how even the slightest of movements feels so incredible.

"Fuck, Gems—"

He doesn't finish his sentence. His hands, however, find my hips and squeeze, and I interpret his body language perfectly. *I want more. I want you. Make me come.*

I pick up my rhythm, dropping my hands to either side so I can angle my body forward and enjoy the added sensation of my clit rubbing against his pubic bone. I close my eyes and get lost for a moment in the delicious friction of grinding against him.

"I'm gonna need to stop watching you or else this will be over before I want it to." The husky tone of Dax's voice is another added layer to the thousands of pleasure points firing through my body.

"I thought we were trying to be quick?"

"Not that quick." He runs his left hand through my hair, then tugs me forward for another kiss. His other thumb finds my clit, and he circles it with the perfect amount of pressure as I continue my rock forward and back.

"You're going to make me come," I tell him. His only response is a low groan.

Our kissing gets wetter, messier, and more urgent. We both have the same finish line in mind, ecstasy in the form of a climax, ideally before it's too late.

I can feel it coming. My body is there, ready to fall, arms open, waiting to be pushed over the edge. But my mind is hesitating, wanting to cling to every single moment I have with him. Wanting to memorize every curve, every grunt, every moment in case this is the last time—

"Fuck, Gems, I want to do this forever, but . . ."

Dax lifts my hips, giving him the room to meet me with a quick, hard thrust. It's what I need to get out of my head. My body takes over as he thrusts deep into me with one last moan followed by a "Fuck, I'm coming."

I barely hear him. Because I'm there too. We fall together.

When my heart stops beating like a wildfire, I collapse beside him on the bed. He strokes my back as his lips plant a small kiss on my temple. The only sound in the basement is our heavy breathing until there's a creak above and the sound of footsteps on the stairs.

"Who's up for a little English breakfast?"

Chapter 26

"WHAT DO YOU think? Too tight? Or not tight enough?"

Dax draws back the curtain of the tiny changing room in the back of our local thrift store One More Time and stands in a pair of what I would describe as light-gray skinny jeans that leave nothing to the imagination—not that I need to imagine him anymore. However, I feel a bit of possessiveness over that above-average penis, as I'm sleeping with it regularly now. I have half a mind to beat my chest and grunt a primal *mine* at the cashier who can't keep her eyes off the beer-can-shaped bulge protruding from Dax's right leg.

"I'd go a size up there, big boy."

With my eyes now on his dick, Dax does one final turn in the mirror, then retreats to his dressing room, muttering "on to bigger and better," a fitting mantra and one I've used a lot this week as Dax has adjusted to his new digs and new life.

It's been a week, to put it kindly. As expected, things did not go well with Dax's insurance. His account is in arrears. There's not much he can fight them on, even if he could afford a lawyer. The power scales are tipped in the wrong direction.

Dax is also struggling with his new living situation.

Dougie and Brandon are welcoming and supportive. They're just both really set in their ways. Brandon likes to do his virtual CrossFit every morning at five-thirty. Normally, he does it in the basement, but he happily moved to the living room to accommodate Dax. However, that means Brandon's doing burpees above Dax's bed. It's like waking up to a violent thunderstorm every morning. But Dax feels terrible about sleeping in Brandon's usual burpee space, so he feels like he can't complain.

Then there's Brandon's regular bacon craving and Dougie's continual memory lapses and failure to stick to the secret knock when he's on a mission for the freezer. We've started to have sex with shirts on just in case Brandon gets hungry because we only have twelve thumps on the staircase before Dougie's head appears, asking us if we're hungry.

This shopping trip was an attempt to get Dax out of the house. We need costumes for tomorrow night's party. Dax needs something to take his mind off the fact that he has to go in for his orientation session in the morning to start training on Monday.

"I think I found the winner. How sexy am I in these?"

He draws back the curtain. If the last pair of pants were tight, these are painted on. They look like leggings. Dove gray, and I enjoy how they cling to every muscle and curve of his body.

"I'm sure we could find you a vest and a puffy shirt. You'd make a very dashing Prince Charming." The party theme Dougie and Brandon finally settled on, *Lovers in a Dangerous Time*, leaves lots of room for interpretation. I don't recall Cinderella's story being filled with danger, but I'm sure the prince carried a sword, and Cinderella's shoes were made of glass.

I leave Dax to scour the racks for anything that could work for the rest of his costume. As I search through piles of secondhand clothes, my mind turns to the same place it has gone whenever I have a moment to think: the invisible hourglass looming above me, with only a few grains of sand left before time runs out. To-morrow night the moon moves into *waning gibbous,* and I've yet to make a decision. Actually, that's a lie. I've made my decision several times over the last few days, but then changed my mind an equal number of times. Do I leave behind my glass slipper or turn around and run into the arms of my prince?

Maybe it's fitting that I go to the party as Cinderella. She too had a curfew. A ticking clock counting down until her dreams turned to dust. But even when she ran out of time, things worked out for Cinderella and Charming, right? Their love prevailed. In the end, their happily ever after was worth all the angst that led up to it. Maybe that's a sign? In the end, Dax and I will be fine. He might be a tax associate. It may take us some time to get on our feet, but we will be happy.

I find the perfect white shirt, as well as a purple velvet vest and a hat that's a bit more Pan than Charming but that I bring to Dax anyway. He disappears behind the curtain, then reappears a few moments later, looking like full thrift shop royalty.

"I think we have a winner, my prince."

Dax's eyes linger on his image in the mirror. He does a quarter turn one way, then the other. "I like it. Although I'm getting more Montague vibes. What do you think? Are we better suited as Romeo and Juliet? It's far more dangerous."

He does have a point. As soon as he says it, I see it. His outfit is all Romeo. Except that story is not the type of ending I'm aiming for. But Romeo and Juliet's issue wasn't a lack of love. It was logistics and preteen-level communication skills. Dax and I don't have any big secrets to hide unless, of course, you count the fact that I've somehow created a slip in time.

Conflicted, I return to the racks. It's time for me to find something equally amazing to stand beside Dax. I find two old prom dresses that, with the right costume jewelry, could transform me enough that I'll look the part once everyone has had a couple of beers. When I step out of the changing room, Dax is staring at his phone, looking like his dog just died. Or maybe like his life's work burned to ash, and the wound is still very fresh.

"What's wrong?"

He looks up at the sound of my voice, shoving his phone into his back pocket.

"Got my work schedule for the next week followed by a flash of what the next fifty years of my life are going to look like." He forces a smile, but his eyes give him away. He's miserable.

"It's my problem to adjust to, Gems." He tugs my arm so I fall against his chest, and he wraps me in a comforting hug that both of us need. "I'll be fine. There's only one thing you can do, and you're doing a pretty bang-up job of it."

"Oh yeah?" My face stays pressed to his chest because I'm not sure what I'll do if I meet his eyes right now.

"Yeah. You being here with me. That's all I need."

Chapter 27

EVEN BEFORE I open my eyes, I know that I'm not in my own bed.

You'd think I would have gotten used to it by now, seeing as waking up in beds that are not my own is apparently my thing now. This time, what sets me off is the blaring of "Fergalicious" somewhere far above me and the smell of men's cologne mixed with basement musk and the sound of water running. A shower.

I stretch my hand across the cotton sheet and find Dax's side of the bed still warm. I roll over and plant my face in his pillow, breathing in that perfect combination of cologne and soap and the lingering smells of sleeping Dax that I somehow find intoxicating. I could do this every morning. Forever. Wake up next to him.

I roll over and stare up at the ceiling just as the water turns off. There isn't exactly a bathroom in this basement. I guess the previous homeowners were told they could increase their property value by putting one in, so they installed a shower, sink, and toilet but never finished the floors or walled any of it in, so they just linger, open and exposed in the far corner of the basement.

Dougie and Brandon never needed it until now. It's a quirky

little feature of Dax's new bachelor pad that I find endearingly unconventional, though he finds it horrifying.

I lay for a bit, counting cobwebs, listening to Brandon's random thumping above, and expecting Dax to climb back into bed at any moment. Maybe even wake me with some morning penis. After a few more moments go by, I start to get restless and horny, so I wrap myself in his comforter and look around for him.

He's sitting so still that I almost miss him. He's in a suit I haven't seen him wear since his uncle died almost two years ago. Around his neck is a red tie that I'm pretty sure he picked up yesterday at the thrift shop. In his hands are a pair of black socks. He's staring at them with a look that is so forlorn it makes the spots between my ribs ache.

"Are you okay?" I ask.

He looks up, and his eyes find mine, and for a moment, it's like I can feel his emotions. The helplessness, the sorrow, the *Where did I go wrong?* The *What will happen now?* The *Is this how I'm going to begin my days for the rest of my life?*

However, Dax just smiles. "Got the first-day jitters."

We both know he's lying, and I'm lying when I say, "I'm sure it's going to be great."

We both keep up the faux-happy charade as we climb the stairs, join Brandon for breakfast, and walk to Dax's bus stop.

"Give all the other tax associates hell." I straighten his tie and give him one last kiss as the bus pulls up and opens its doors.

"I'll see you tonight at the party." He squeezes my hand as he boards the bus. I feel that squeeze all the way to my heart.

"THOSE DON'T LOOK like exercise clothes."

Kiersten eyes my jeans and gladiator sandals before her eyes settle on the giant box of Nana's doughnuts in my hand.

We're down by the bay in the parking lot next to the marina, getting ready for our regular Saturday morning walk along the lakeshore path.

"I'd argue that we don't really exercise when we walk," I counter. "It's more of a leisurely stroll."

Kiersten shrugs. "You make a good point." She lifts the lid of my doughnut box, revealing the assorted dozen. I hold my breath as she looks inside.

I debated buying the doughnuts. Kiersten has yet to tell me how her meeting went. I may have to boycott Nana's indefinitely. But I craved the comfort of sugar the moment I saw Dax making sad eyes at his socks this morning.

"So . . . any word about the job yet?"

Kiersten picks up a pink-frosted doughnut covered in white coconut flakes. "I didn't get it. They said it was close, but ultimately the other woman had more experience. I had a good, long, ugly cry about it last night, but I gave myself a little pep talk this morning, and now I'm feeling better. Someone will eventually give me a shot. I just need to keep trying. Right?" Her words are bright, but her voice cracks as she takes a heaving sigh.

Kierst has always been my person. The one I run to when my life falls to pieces. Now she's the one with big, sad raindrop tears staining her cheeks. The one who needs someone to tell her it's all gonna be okay.

I open my arms and pull her cheek to my boobs, letting her cry as I rub slow, soothing circles down her back.

"You're a natural at this." Her voice is muffled against my chest.

"Yeah, well, I learned from the best."

Her hands tighten around my waist as she draws a deep breath. "I know it's stupid to cry like this. It just felt serendipitous, you know? I know doughnuts, Gems. I would have been so perfect."

"You would have."

"I feel stupid saying it, but I need this." She pulls away and wipes her cheeks with the back of her hand. "It feels like I've put my life on hold for years. I've been taking care of everyone else for so long that I . . . forgot who I was. I thought starting my own business would make me feel like me again."

The tears return, and I rack my brain for something I can do to make it right.

"What if we rebranded Wilde Beauty?"

Kierst pulls a Kleenex from her pocket and attempts to wipe the black mascara smudges from her cheeks. "I appreciate what you're trying to do, but any changes I'd suggest would be downgrades. You made Wilde Beauty perfect the first time."

But that's the thing. *I* didn't actually do any of it. Yes, I've had ideas over the years, half-formed plans from the nights I let myself dream, but the Wilde Beauty we both know and love was Other Gemma's baby, not mine.

Kierst blinks until her tears clear, then takes a long, deep breath. "I thought Nana's would be the perfect training wheels. Nana is so sweet. I fucking love doughnuts. I figured if I could learn as I go, it would give me the street cred to try something less familiar. Now I don't know if I'll ever be able to do it. It's not like another Nana's will come along anytime soon."

Another Nana's won't.

But a Wilde Beauty could.

A Wilde Beauty whose owner still has a lot to learn about starting up a business. Who needs to take risks and know that even if she fucks up a little, she will still be okay.

In an instant, the answer to whether I should stay or go becomes clear. My head may want to stay, but my heart knows what I need to do. For Kierst. For Dax. For me.

"I'm gonna go home." I know it's the right thing to do the moment I say it.

Kiersten stares intently at her doughnut. "Like to your house or home-home?"

The look on my face must communicate my answer because she nods.

"Let's find a place to sit down."

We walk to a nearby bench that looks onto the waterfront just off the paved path. The sky is a light blue with big fluffy storybook clouds. There is no breeze, so the lake is calm enough to see to the bottom in the shallowest parts.

"What prompted this sudden change of heart?" She takes a bite of her doughnut and moans softly to herself. "Oh, Nana, I forgive you already."

I try to put into words what snapped in me just now. If I tell her she's one of the reasons I need to go back, she'll tell me that I'm being ridiculous. That she's fine and I shouldn't worry about her. So I focus on my second reason.

"In my world, Dax has everything he's ever wanted. Kicks is locally famous and successful. But more importantly, he has this look to him back home—I don't know how to describe it. It's like a fire in his eyes. But here, that fire's gone out. It's like he's lost. And I know you're going to tell me that it's not my fault, but I know I can fix things if I go back."

For him and for Kiersten.

Kierst pauses with her doughnut midway to her mouth. "You didn't mention all the parts about how happy you are here."

Yes, those parts. I can't deny that this is the happiest I've been in years. These last few weeks have been a weird kind of blessing. A chance to see all of the wrong turns I've made over the last four years and all of the things that could have been if only I'd trusted in my own abilities instead of taking the safe route.

"I am happy here. Really fucking happy. But you and I are the same back home. Same with Aunt Livi. And there's no reason why I couldn't have a Wilde Beauty in my other life. Right? I'm smart. I'm capable. I'm far from perfect, but I'm working on it. And sure, in my world, Priya will probably find someone else to partner with. But another Priya will come along, and if she doesn't, who's to say I can't go out and find my own Priya? I want to try. I'm going to go home, and I will work my ass off until I make Wilde Beauty happen."

"What about Dax?"

That's the question that's burning a hole in my stomach so bad that I can't even look at the box of doughnuts. "I don't know what's going to happen with him. Our relationship is different back home. There's a strong possibility he's dating a veterinarian's assistant."

"Do you think he wants more?"

Another question that I can't answer.

I think back to the last time I saw Dax in my old life. The whole event is still hazy in my head, but the one thing that's clear is the feeling I had. That catch in my chest that came with the idea that maybe, just maybe, Dax and I might be finally acknowledging that we were something more than friends.

I'm pretty sure I told him I loved him.

I'm also pretty sure he told me sex would change everything.

It's hard to separate out the feelings and the facts.

What I do know is that we kissed.

Then he left.

Although I don't want to admit it, isn't that my answer?

"I just don't think he's looking to change things between us."

"And yet you still want to go back?"

I nod, tears spilling down my cheeks. "I love him too much to stay."

Her arm comes around my shoulder, and she pulls me into a hug as my cute little tears morph into a full-blown ugly cry.

"It's gonna be okay, Gems. I have a feeling it's all gonna work out."

"You can't know that."

She releases me but tilts my face so I have nowhere to look but her eyes. "You're right. I can't. I do not possess any sort of psychic ability. You are the only one in the family to inherit the weird paranormal shit. Well, I have suspicions about Aunt Livi. She's been way too calm over the last few weeks. But let's park that for a moment. There is one thing I know well, and that's you. I've known you for twenty-eight years and loved you for most of them. You're smart and resourceful, and when you trust in yourself and what you want, you make it happen. Now, I can't promise you'll end up with Dax. But I've watched you find real love over these last few weeks, and I don't think you'll settle for any less than that. You're done with kissing Stuarts. And I hope it works out for you. This universe has thrown some fucked-up shit your way lately. In my opinion, it owes you a solid."

I dive back into the comfort of another Kiersten hug. "I love you, Kierst."

She pats the back of my head. "I love you too. Please pass this karma on to me in your other life."

"I will."

"And since we're still in this life, please pass me another doughnut."

Chapter 28

TONIGHT IS THE night. Time is up. It's the end of the road. We're in the bottom of the ninth. Elvis is putting on his blue suedes and preparing to leave the building.

I have a plan. Aunt Livi is away for the weekend at a book fair. Kiersten has assured me that Livi's fridge is stocked with chicken, there's a white candle on the counter, and pink yarn is ready and waiting. I'll have to invent on the spot a reason why Dax needs to bind my hands, but he hasn't balked at any of the other sex stuff I've suggested thus far in our relationship, so I'm confident I can make it happen.

But now comes the hard part. The part when I have to say goodbye to everything I've loved in this life, starting with my second-hardest farewell.

"You are beautiful and perfect, and fuck, you smell like a dream."

My store doesn't answer because it's a store, but a weird sense of calm washes over me. "This isn't goodbye," I whisper to a bottle of sea salt grapefruit body scrub, "this is until we meet again, and we will, I promise."

I take one last deep inhale, lock the door behind me, and head home to get ready for the party.

I never thought I'd ever get nostalgic about my creepy basement. But as I walk around my tiny apartment one last time, an uncomfortable ball forms in the back of my throat. Goodbye, tiny kitchen. Farewell, living-room-slash-dining-room-slash-bedroom.

I pull it together when it comes time to use the bathroom for the last time, that is, until I lay eyes on my eight-legged arachnid friend, dangling in the corner of my shower.

"Frank, you've been the best roommate I've ever had. I'm grateful we set aside our differences and coordinated our shower schedules. I hope you have a great life."

I'm very aware that things have gotten a bit ridiculous. When my eyes start to brim with tears, I take it as a sign that I need to rip off the proverbial Band-Aid and head to the party.

For a party I've been dreading, it starts off pretty great. I spot Sunny dressed as *Pretty Woman* Julia when I'm still half a block from the party. She runs full speed in her hooker heels. Her tight red dress doesn't hinder her in the least as she throws herself into my arms.

"Gemma! You're here. There's someone I want you to meet!"

Andre Cortez is a pediatric nurse. Turns out he and Sunny apparently made eyes at each other for a solid year and a half before Sunny got sick of waiting for him to make a move and asked him out for coffee the night she asked me to sub for her. My heart aches at the idea that I'm not going to see how this plays out, and I hope with every fiber of my being that Sunny gets the happily ever after she deserves.

The three of us walk into the house together. Like at the last party, the place is packed. However, Dax doesn't seek me out this time. I make polite chitchat with Andre, who is interesting and funny and makes the kind of eyes at Sunny that let you know he's got it bad. When Dax still doesn't appear, I seek him out, searching the living room, dining room, and kitchen before finally finding him in the backyard, sitting alone on a plastic Muskoka chair, staring at a potted fern.

He's not in costume. The same funeral suit from this morning is still on his body, the red tie loosened and askew. There's an empty scotch tumbler in his hands.

"There you are."

He looks up at the sound of my voice, and a wide, genuine Dax smile breaks across his face.

"Hey, Gems." He sets his glass down next to him and holds out his arms. I gladly accept the invitation to crawl into his lap.

"How'd the first day go?"

He hesitates before he answers. And because I know Dax, I know he only does that when he's choosing his words carefully. Not a good sign.

"It was exactly what I expected it to be. People were nice enough. Work was fine."

"But?"

He sighs and pulls me into his chest.

"I'm glad you're here."

It's a very distinct subject change, and I go with it. "I love me a good costume party."

"Oh yeah, I guess I should probably change. Although, maybe if I don't, Juliet will find another guy at this party, and things will work out better for both of them."

I know he means it as a joke. But I've drawn too many parallels between our costume choices and our situation tonight to find it funny.

"Hey." He presses the pad of his thumb to the crinkle between my eyebrows and rubs it as if he's erasing all my worries. "I was just kidding around. If you found another guy tonight, I honestly don't know how I'd handle it, but it wouldn't be good. When I said I'm glad you're here, I meant more than at this party. I'm glad you're in my life. This last week has been the fucking worst. I still can't think about my store for too long because I get so depressed. And it wasn't even the fire. My shit wasn't together long before that. I'm living in a basement. But the thing that makes me happy every time I think about it is seeing you. It would be an absolute fucking terrible time in my life right now if I didn't have you, Gems. I just hope I can get back to the guy that I used to be. I think you'd like him better."

I want to open my mouth and tell him that I know the guy he used to be, and I love that guy as much as I love the one sitting here with me now.

I feel like I've been ripped in half. There is one side of me that wants to stay here in his arms forever. Be his happy place. But the other half of me knows what I can give him if I go. Everything he's ever dreamed about.

"We should play flip cup." The idea forms at the same time the words leave my lips.

"Really?" He gives me this one-eyebrow look that makes me want to abandon the idea and instead smuggle him down to the sex cave, but I hold steadfast and stick to my plan.

"Yes." I practically jump from his lap. "I thought you loved flip cup, or at least you did the last time we were at one of these parties."

Dax takes my hand and tugs it until I climb back into his lap. He kisses a trail from my collarbone to my ear and whispers, "Confession time. I actually despise playing flip cup. But it was the best plan I could come up with at the time to get you to hang out with me."

My heart picks up speed in my chest. "You were into me that night?"

He plants a soft kiss on my temple. "I think I was half-smitten from the moment we met."

"You liar."

I try to jump from his lap again, but he anticipates my escape and locks his arms. "Fine. Maybe not the very first meeting, but when I watched you take down half a pitcher of beer at curling, I was intrigued. Something clicked early on with us. I can't quite explain it."

He kisses me slow and deep, then his tongue intertwines with mine, and we go from sweetly kissing to heavy petting. When his hands find their way up my thigh under my dress, I can tell that he's also considering a quick trip to the sex cave.

But we can't.

Sex will muddle my head and screw with all my thoughts, and I'll make excuses to stay and then watch him grow more miserable. I need to stick to the plan. It needs to go down tonight. No deviations, no excuses.

"What do you want to do?" he asks, eyeing the door to the basement.

"I think it's time we did some shots."

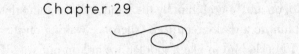

Chapter 29

DAX HAS FIVE levels of drunk.

Level one, his eyes get all glazed, but he's otherwise normal. Level two, he gets unusually loud. This is immediately followed by level three, where he gets unusually quiet. Level four, he loves hard—anyone and anything. Level five, he blacks out behind Dougie's couch and doesn't wake up until morning.

I was aiming for a solid level three with my suggestion of shots. Quiet Dax is chill and won't ask too many questions when I start carrying out ancient rituals. However, I overshoot. Or I under-estimate the amount of scotch he'd consumed before my arrival, and now we're deep into level-four territory, and there is no way I can carry a level-five Dax up Aunt Livi's stairs.

"We need to go." I hand Dax a glass of water and one of Brandon's low-carb bagels.

"Why, Gems? The party is just getting started." It's not. Half the guests have left because they're over thirty and live in fear of the two-day hangover.

The rest are a combo of guests nearing their own level fives and sober companions like me, making eyes at their Uber apps.

"My aunt called. She needs me to check on something at her store."

He grins. His eyes are half-closed. "Anything for you, Gems." But instead of following me out the front door, he turns and heads back toward Dougie's kitchen.

"No, no, no." I grab him by the hand. "We're going this way." I lead him to a dark-green Jeep Cherokee waiting on the street. After I buckle him in like a toddler, we are on our way. There's little traffic as the driver chooses the quieter residential streets instead of the main ones. Dax grows suddenly quiet, leaning his head against the window with his eyes closed. I watch him as the light from the streetlamps illuminates his face as we go by, and an ache blooms in my chest. This is it. Really it. We're going to climb those steps and undo all the trouble I've caused and tomorrow? Who knows what we will be?

His hand finds mine in the dark as if he can sense my unease. "I love you, Gems," he whispers, his head still resting on the window. I settle into the little nook under his arm and wish that this wasn't the last time, with the little hope I have left. That I'm doing the right thing. That I'm not making the worst mistake of my entire life.

The car pulls up in front of Aunt Livi's bookstore. It takes three shakes to wake Dax, but he stumbles out into the street, then, with a second wind, hops onto a light post, makes a full spin around, then jumps down, landing surprisingly gracefully on his feet. When he straightens, his hair flips into his eyes, and he flashes the most genuinely beautiful smile.

I love him. I love him so much it physically hurts.

"Whatcha thinking about there?" I ask.

He saunters over and pulls my hips to his, kissing me hard without waiting for an answer.

"About how much I fucking love you."

"Oh, you fucking love me?"

"Well, I love you, and I love fucking you, and I think we should get inside and deal with whatever it is we're here to deal with so we can go back to your place and get on with the loving." He licks, then nips, my earlobe. "And then the fucking."

Tears brim the edges of my eyes and threaten to fall. I turn away, pulling him by the hand, not wanting him to see but also knowing how little resolve is left in my tank. The longer I put this off, the more likely it is that I'll chicken out and it won't happen at all.

I fit my spare key into Aunt Livi's lock as Dax's hands slip a strap from my dress off my shoulder. He kisses my bare collarbone as he presses his erection into my back.

"We can't." I can't.

I'm teetering on the edge. Ready to call this entire thing off. When I finally get the door open, I have to stop. The bookstore is filled with candles, casting a soft yellow light throughout the room.

Kiersten. Or Aunt Livi?

I don't know if this ambience is meant to entice me to stay or set the mood to go.

"Whoa." Dax steps into the store behind me. "What is this? Another top-five Gemma Wilde sex fantasy?"

I wish that was what this was.

"No. Not sex. I need your help with something."

Aside from the candles, everything Kiersten promised to set up is here. The book is laid out on the counter. Next to it are the candle and yarn. The chicken is sitting in a red Tupperware container next to the cashbox, and as I pick it up, a yellow sheet of lined paper falls, landing on the exact spot where the burned linoleum should be. There's no mistaking my aunt's dainty hand-writing.

Sometimes the best risks are the ones you make with your heart.

Deep breath.

"Come here." I extend my hand, beckoning Dax to join me on the spot where this all began.

"Things are going to get a little weird for a few minutes. I need you to trust me and go with it."

Dax nods but doesn't say anything. I wonder if some of the alcohol has worked its way through his system, and he's reverting to quiet-drunk Dax.

I pick up the candle and hold it to another lit flame, watching the wick ignite.

I close my eyes and push out every thought except for one. "I wish I never did this love cleanse in the first place," I whisper out loud.

This is the point where I should stop, but the words keep pouring from my mouth. "I wish I never tried to change the past. I wish Kierst gets the life she deserves. I wish you happiness, Dax."

I reach for the ball of yarn and hand it to him. "I need you to tie my hands together."

He pulls a string from the ball but gives me an unconvinced look. "I *knew* this was a weird sex thing. If you're into it, I'm into it."

He winds the yarn around my wrists twice and then ties it with a knot.

It's time for the kiss. To seal our fate.

I close my eyes. "I need you to kiss me, Dax."

"Now we're getting to the good part."

I can't see him, but I can feel the smile in his voice, and when his lips hit mine, a million emotions pour out of me. The fear that I'm making a huge mistake. The longing to stay here where he's mine. The guilt. The desire. The frustration that I still don't know why all of this happened, why I'm here, or if I'm even supposed to be going back. But the emotion that trumps them all, that bursts from my chest like a freaking glittering rainbow, is the love I have for this man. This might be the biggest risk of my life, but I'm ready to take it.

"I know this probably goes against some universal law, and what I'm asking may be impossible, but if you can, try to hold on to even a small shred of this. How good we are together. How much I love you. How much I wish I could turn back the clock and love you just a little bit longer."

He opens his eyes, his brows pulled low in confusion. "Of course I'm gonna remember. I didn't drink that much. I love you too."

My heart clenches so hard it feels like it's holding my body hostage. It's as if it's shouting, *Stay, or I refuse to beat another beat.*

"Cut the cord." I squeeze my eyes shut.

"What? Why?"

"The scissors on the table. Cut the cord. Now. Please, Dax."

"Okay, just give me a second."

I hold my breath, listening to the scrape of its metal blades on the linoleum.

"I love you, Da—"

Blackness.

Chapter 30

I WAKE UP in a strange bed.

No.

It's not a strange bed.

It's my old bed from my lakefront condo, but the sheets are different. They're patterned with teeny tiny bouquets of wildflowers.

I've never seen these sheets before.

But the yellow water stain above my head is very familiar. It looks vaguely like the *Mona Lisa*. And I had this very thought only a week ago when I was lying in bed waiting for my alarm to go off.

A week ago.

I'm in my basement.

I'm not supposed to be in my basement.

I fly out of bed at Usain Bolt speed. It's definitely my basement apartment. The low ceilings. The soupy smell. Frank. Hanging in the shower. Acting like his normal spidery self.

No.

No, no, no, no, no.

Something has gone wrong. I'm supposed to be back. This isn't back.

I search my nightstand for my phone. It's not plugged in where it's supposed to be. I rip the covers from my bed and search under it, around it. The bathroom. The kitchen. My desk. It's not here.

I have no way of contacting the outside world.

Fuck.

I need to find out what happened. I need to talk to Dax.

There's a pile of clothes next to my bed. They're not my costume from last night. I actually have no memory of wearing them recently, but I don't have time to dwell. I throw them on, grab my purse, and sprint out of the house, trying to figure out where I went wrong.

I had the candles. We did the hand-binding thing. We didn't do anything with the chicken, but the chicken has always been an unnecessary item of flair. Nothing makes sense.

I hit the asphalt of my front driveway and stop in my tracks. Parked in front of my house is my car. The gray Volkswagen Golf GTI Sport I bought after my first annual commission.

In my old life.

I make a full circle. Just to make sure it's not an auto doppelgänger. But there's no question it's my license plate. My favorite Aritzia sweater is tossed on the front seat.

What the actual fuck?

I reexamine my keys. My VW key is on the chain. This doesn't make sense, but what the hell. Time is of the essence. I unlock the doors, climb into the driver's seat, and challenge every yellow light all the way to Aunt Livi's store.

She doesn't answer my banging on her apartment door, and the store below is still locked up tight. With no other ideas, I let myself in with my spare key, hoping it will hold a clue to what the hell is going on. The store looks the same. But there's no evidence of the night before. No candles. No yarn. No chicken.

But there is something.

It's just the wrong thing.

What the hell have I done?

I run my fingers over the burned linoleum. The scar from our first attempt at the spell.

It's here. My car is here, but so is my basement. It's almost as if I've melded my two lives together. Or am I in a third timeline? How many timelines are there?

Abandoning Aunt Livi's, I cross the street, heading north down James, and when I hit the block where Kicks once stood, my heart bursts into a million happy pieces.

It's still there.

Its shiny window sports all of Dax's beautiful creations. I press my nose to the glass, and although the inside is dark and empty, the shelves are well stocked with inventory.

This is good. This is really good.

I knock on the door in case Dax is in the back office, but he doesn't come out. Which makes sense. It's still early, and it's Sunday, right? Who the hell knows. All I care about is that I've done something right here.

But why the hell did I wake up in my basement apartment? Have I created some sort of weird hybrid world?

I stare around at the near-empty street, wondering what I should do next. If only I had my phone, I could call Dax, Kierst, or even Aunt Livi. They could tell me if I still have Dax. If I still have Wilde Beauty.

Wilde.

I practically run the block and a half.

My heart quickens when the painted white bricks come into view, but as I get close enough to see inside my window, I'm not prepared for what is inside.

Nothing.

Absolutely nothing.

No shelves. No perfectly curated array of clean beauty products. Just empty space and a realtor's sign stating PROPERTY AVAILABLE FOR LEASE.

Wilde is gone.

It hurts. Even though it was my choice, and that choice was the right one, my soul aches at the sight of the sad, empty space. I stand for a moment and mourn the loss of my beautiful dream until I remember that reality is still wonky and that more important matters need my immediate attention.

Like finding Dax.

My feet keep moving. It's as if they have a mind of their own this morning. And they carry me halfway into Brewski's before I realize it. Coffee is always Dax's morning priority before he does anything meaningful. My eyes skim the sitting area and those in line before determining that he isn't here. I'm about to leave when I hear a voice call, "Grande oat milk latte, right?"

I turn and meet the eyes of my man-bunned barista.

"Snake," I call loudly enough that his eyes widen, and he takes a step back.

"Uh, yeah."

"It's me, Gemma with a *G*." I point at my chest as if it isn't obvious whom I am speaking about.

"So no oat milk latte?"

"Yes. Absolutely yes. And I need you to answer a question for me."

His eyebrows rise as he punches in my order without looking.

"Did we ever make out? On New Year's Eve? In a garage, I think?"

He scratches his chin and stares up at the ceiling. "Not that I can remember, but anything is possible. Maybe we should make out now and see if it makes me remember anything."

"No!" I shout with way too much force for someone who has yet to have coffee. "But thank you for clearing that up."

I wait for my coffee. Once it's in hand, I down half, then nurse what remains as I speed-walk back to my car.

The most important thing now is to figure out what's going on with Dax and me. However, if I have created some sort of hybrid world, I should probably figure out if he knows who I am ahead of time. There's no need for another shoehorn incident.

I hop into my car and drive to Kiersten's house, praying she has my answers as I sprint up to her walkway and knock furiously on her front door.

It opens a few moments later, revealing Kiersten in her fluffy pink bathrobe.

"Oh, thank god." I throw my non-coffee-holding arm around her neck and squeeze. She looks the same. She smells the same. She even pries my arm from her neck with her usual "For the love of god, what is wrong with you, woman?"

I push my way inside, my hands clutching my half-drunk coffee.

"No latte for me? Tell me why I'm letting you in at this ungodly hour without a caffeinated offering?"

"I love you, Kierst." The words fall easily from my mouth. "You are amazing and wonderful and I appreciate you more than you'll ever know and I'm going to make it all right, I swear."

She holds my head between her hands and sniffs my breath. "Are you still wasted? I cut you off before midnight. You should have sobered up by now."

"I was with you last night?"

She turns, heads toward her kitchen, grabs a glass from the cupboard, fills it with water, and hands it to me.

"I'm surprised you're up this early. I thought you'd spend the day in bed."

I drink the water because hydration feels like a good idea.

"I need you to humor me. Why did I get drunk last night? What exactly happened?"

Kiersten rolls her eyes but takes my empty water glass, refills it, and hands it back to me. "You were all creeped out about your new place. You didn't like the smell and didn't want to spend the night alone, and so you came here and downed half a bottle of pinot. When you got into my tequila, I cut you off and sent you home in an Uber, which I paid for—you're welcome, by the way—because you couldn't find your phone. Trent found it this morning when your alarm went off, reminding you to go and water Dax's plants."

Dax! I know Dax. "Where is he?"

"Trent? He went swimming at the Y. Why?"

"Not Trent. Dax. Where is Dax?"

Kiersten thinks for a moment. It's the longest, most agonizing five seconds of my life.

"The Magnet River? Or the Magawan River? It's something like that. Up north somewhere. Why are you asking me this? You're the one who told *me* he went camping with Dougie."

"Why?" Dax hates camping. I once made him go glamping, and he lasted a night before he got sick of the bugs and the lumpy beds.

"Well, you told me that he was acting all weird, and then he told you he needed some time away to clear his head."

"So we're friends?"

Kiersten grabs my head between her palms and stares into my eyes.

"What are you doing?" I ask.

"I'm checking to see if you have a concussion."

"Is that how you're supposed to check for a concussion?"

Kiersten lets go of my head. "I have no idea. But your eyes look fine. What the hell is going on with you, Gemma?"

Where to even start.

"If I tell you, you won't believe me for at least three and a half weeks, and even then, you'll only be eighty percent on board."

Kiersten's eyes narrow, and I wonder if she's debating taking on the mental effort to listen to my entire story. "Yeah, let's save this story for another day. But at least promise me you're okay? Physically. Emotionally. All of the above."

Am I okay? "I think so."

This seems to satisfy her.

"Well, I'll get you your phone then." She leaves and returns a few moments later with my silver iPhone. I scroll through my messages. There are a few from work. A handful from friends. And there's a bunch from Dax that I remember, leading right up to the night of the love cleanse. Then they sort of drop off and get very weird.

Got your messages. Sorry. Busy week. Talk soon.

Another busy week. I know I owe you a coffee.

Won't make curling again tonight. Tell everyone I'm sorry.

Going away for a week or two. Any chance you can water my plants while I'm gone?

My heart tanks.

The tiny shred of hope I had that we might be in love in this reality is gone. Things are weird. I can tell by these texts and my responses. Dax is avoiding me.

My knees give out, and I'm grateful for my strategic standing spot as my butt hits Kierst's sectional with an audible *thwack*.

I have to remind myself that this was supposed to happen. Dax and I were supposed to have gone back to being friends. It is what I wanted, right?

"You are starting to worry me, Gems." Kiersten sinks down next to me, her cool hand finding my wrist.

"It's nothing. I'm just in love with Dax. And he is not in love with me, and it's just a little bit overwhelming right now because although this was the plan, I didn't quite account for how bad it was going to feel."

The waterworks come. I don't even try to stop them. There's no point. The tears fall, coating my face and the backs of my hands as I attempt to gain some semblance of composure.

"Well, at least you're admitting it now." Kiersten's hands find my back, rubbing slow, comforting circles.

"You knew?"

"I think everyone knew."

"Even Dax?"

"Well, maybe not Dax, although I have reasons to believe your feelings may not be so unrequited."

"But he left. And I don't think we're on the greatest of terms right now."

Kiersten produces a wad of Kleenex from within the pocket of her robe. "You and Dax have been through a lot lately. You ended a relationship. It takes time to grieve. And collect your thoughts. It wouldn't have been good for the two of you to fall into bed immediately."

She makes a point. Not one I really want to hear right now, but a tiny consolation. I'm starting to piece together the last four weeks of the life I missed. But there are still some gaping holes I need to figure out or explain, like: "Why the hell am I living in the basement?"

At this, Kiersten starts to laugh.

"What?"

"Aunt Livi and I call it your mid-twenties crisis. About a month ago, you decided that you were done living a life you didn't love anymore. You quit your job. You listed your condo. You moved into the basement because you claimed you needed to save money. When we questioned you about it, you told us you were working on something big. Your secret project."

Wilde Beauty.

"*Our* secret project." The words feel right the moment I say them. I grab her hand and hold it in mine. "I'm starting my own store. It's going to be beautiful. Clean beauty products. I'm going to work my ass off until I get it right. And you're going to market it. Launch your business with me. This time we're doing it together."

Kiersten goes very still. "How did you . . ."

I wave her off. "It's a very long story. The important thing is that I'm not gonna screw it up. Or take you for granted. I meant what I said earlier, Kierst. I owe you everything and I'm gonna make your dreams happen alongside mine."

Her eyes narrow. "I'm going to say thank you but I'm still very confused."

I throw my arms around her again and squeeze. "I will make an attempt to explain the best I can later, but right now, I need to go."

"Where?"

"To Dax's place. To water his plants." To solve another missing piece of the puzzle.

Kiersten walks me to the door. "It's gonna be okay, Gems. I have a feeling it's all going to work out."

Again, I get an eerie sense of déjà vu. She said the same thing less than forty-eight hours ago. In a different timeline. In a different life.

A feeling settles over me. At this moment, I know that no matter where I am, my sister will always be there for me.

I reach my arms around her waist and lay my head on her boobs. "I want you to know I love you with my whole heart."

She strokes the back of my head. "Let's take this as a learning moment, and maybe next time lay off the tequila."

Chapter 31

TEN MINUTES LATER, I'm pulling up in front of Dax's building.

God, I missed owning a car.

Dax's spare key is on my Dr. Snuggles keychain, exactly where it should be.

As I take the stairs up to his apartment two at a time, my heart seems to boom louder with every step.

First floor. *Kaboom.*

Second floor. *Kaboom.*

Third floor. It's a drum line all the way down the hall to his door.

This is it.

I have a plan. If I walk in there and it looks like Dax's old place, it means everything worked out as it was supposed to. His store is still a huge success. I haven't screwed it all up for nothing. If it looks like it did in the other reality, well . . . I haven't quite figured out what I'm going to do in that case.

I slip my key into the lock, but as I go to push the door open, a last-minute thought crosses my mind and I freeze in panic.

What if Dax decided to come home early? What if he's in

there now? What if he has continued dating that vet's assistant for the last month and is half in love with her already?

They could be in there.

They could be naked.

His big beautiful penis could be in her magical vagina and I could be walking into something I'll never, ever be able to unsee.

The idea makes me want to throw up.

I knock. "Hello, it's me, Gemma. Everybody decent in there?"

There's no answer. Still, I cover my eyes as I push open the door. "Still Gemma here. I'm coming in. Speak now or forever make things awkward."

I splay my fingers enough to see his far wall. The painting he bought at last year's Art Gallery of Hamilton auction hangs on the wall and there are no naked bodies.

This is a good sign.

I continue my half-hindered glance around the room.

The big screen he insisted was an integral pièce de résistance for any bachelor pad is on top of the Pottery Barn console. The tan leather couch that cost as much as I take home after taxes in a month is sitting on top of the genuine Persian rug we drove all the way to Toronto to buy from a guy who only sells them by appointment from a warehouse in the furniture district.

These are all very good signs.

I breathe out a long sigh of relief. He's okay. The store is okay. I made the right choice.

As my heartbeat returns to an even, steady rhythm, I settle into the second task I came here to do.

Grabbing a juice pitcher, I fill it with water and get to work on the plants along the windowsill, then fill the jug a second time to tend the plants in his bedroom.

But as I step through the door, my heart completely stops.

His bed sits perfectly made. Not a single crinkle in the sheets.

Even though he's supposedly been gone for days, the room still smells like him. Irish Spring soap and the faint scent of his cologne.

I'm struck by this terrible feeling. Like longing or homesickness or grief. It's hollow. As if someone has scooped out all of the good memories from my chest and thrown them splat on the floor in front of me.

See this? It isn't yours anymore.

I have this urge to climb into his bed and suck in all the Dax-like smells that still linger on his pillow. To slide between his sheets and close my eyes and pretend he's there beside me. As if at any moment he'll roll over, lace his fingers through mine, and remind me that we're forever.

However, my tortured thoughts are interrupted by the sound of keys in the door, and my fight-or-flight mammalian brain takes over until it dawns on me that thieves don't use keys. But Dax does.

Every cell inside of me is on edge as the lock flips, and I steel myself for the conversation I'm about to have. The one I should have had years ago.

He doesn't notice me at first. He's too absorbed in the actions of throwing down his leather weekend bag and tossing his keys into the little porcelain dish on top of his bookshelf. I stare at him from the doorway like a creep. Eyes appreciating, heart longing, everything below that lusting after the man who has always been my other half.

"Hey." The floor creaks beneath my feet as I step forward. Dax whips around at the sound, grabbing a shoehorn with his hand and raising it above his head.

"Jesus Christ, Gems. You scared the shit out of me."

I hold up the still-full water pitcher. "I'm here for the plants. You asked me to—"

"Yeah, sorry. I know. I was just thinking about you, and then you appeared out of nowhere. I wasn't sure you were real for a second."

"You were thinking about me?"

He drops his eyes to his bag, which he shoves to the side with the toe of his boot. "Yeah. I was up north. Needed a few days to clear my head. But I was going to call you when I got in. And then you were here."

"I've been thinking about you too."

There's a sudden tension in the air. It's heavy and thick. As if we both know that a conversation is about to happen that will change everything. It becomes a game of chicken. The first one to talk lays their heart on the table. Open. Exposed. Where anything can happen. And I don't hesitate for a second to do it.

"I love you, Dax." The words come easily. I've had a month to practice. "I am totally and completely in love with you. And I know you're probably standing there ready to remind me that I spent the last four years with someone else. And you're right, I did. But I've had a lot of time to think about it, and I think I stayed with Stuart so long because he was safe. He was easy. And losing him would not devastate me."

A hard lump forms at the back of my throat. I swallow hard and continue.

"But losing you would. And I think I was afraid that if I loved you, one day you could change your mind, and we wouldn't be Gemma and Dax anymore, and I couldn't risk that. But then I had a small glimpse of how it would feel to not have you in my life, and it made me realize that you are my person, Daxon. And I want to be with you. Even if it means I might lose you one day."

I pause to breathe. To regroup. Maybe even to see if Dax will hint at how his side of this conversation will go. But Dax doesn't move from his spot by the door. He doesn't move at all. As if my sudden and unexpected confession has frozen him in place.

"What are you thinking?" I finally ask him.

"A lot of things."

"Are they good things?"

His answer is a tentative half step forward. Then a deep breath. Then another. "I spent the last week thinking that maybe we needed to stop being friends."

A sharp pain shoots through my chest as I face my worst fear. "You did?"

Dax swallows. "It's just too much."

I can't breathe. I can't even form words, like *You're wrong* or *I can fix this, whatever it is. I'll do whatever it takes.* I open my mouth to attempt, to try, but Dax is faster.

"I couldn't handle pretending. Waiting for the next Stuart to come along and watch you love him and not me. So I just didn't think we could be friends anymore."

"Dax—"

"But the idea made me sick. Fucking miserable. Dougie made me come home early because he couldn't look at my sad face any longer. But when I walked in here just now and saw you here in my apartment, I knew I'd deal with a hundred more Stuarts if I could keep you in my life. I love you too much, Gems. And you're never gonna lose me."

My lungs draw air with ease. As if a thousand-pound weight has suddenly been lifted from my chest.

"So this means . . ." I'm almost too afraid to say it.

"It means you better get over here and kiss me because I have been waiting four years for this."

It's all the invitation I need. In a beat, I'm across the floor and in his arms.

There's no hesitation to our kiss, no timid brushing of the lips. His tongue melds perfectly with mine as his hands wind their way into my hair. Like they've done it many times before.

Almost as if they've remembered.

I think we kiss for hours. Who the hell knows? Time and reality are skewed for me lately. When he finally pulls away, his lips are slightly puffed from what may have been the most epic make-out of both our lives.

"That was really good," he says, still cradling my face in his palms.

"I was going to say incredible, but if we want to stick with good, I'm willing to put in the practice."

He places another soft kiss on my lips, but when he pulls away, his brows are pulled low.

"What are you thinking?"

He pauses for a moment before answering. "Just that it didn't feel like a first kiss at all."

I still don't fully understand what happened this past month. Why the universe chose me, chose us for this second chance.

"Yes, I'd have to agree."

Chapter 32

6 months later

"HELLO, GORGEOUS."

I'm talking to the floor. But it's a hardwood floor. It could use a sweep and possibly one of those buffing machines you rent from Home Depot, but none of that matters because it's *my* wood floor. And *my* empty aluminum shelves that are soon to be filled with lemon-scented beauty products and a dream four-and-a-half long years in the making.

"I have brought sustenance." Kiersten props open the front door of my store with her hip and holds up a doughnut box. The bell that chimes above her head is a sound I have missed. A memory from literally a lifetime ago and one that I haven't heard in six long months.

I pull a Boston cream from the Nana's doughnut box, take a sip of still-hot oat misto from Brewski's, and stare out at the beginnings of Wilde Sisters Beauty 2.0. The 2.0 part is silent. I say it only to myself, in my head, as I have decided that my sister and my aunt and even Dax aren't quite ready to live in a multi-reality universe.

I chalk up my time in Other Gemma's life as a strange dream

or a vivid hallucination that taught me a few life lessons I needed to learn.

"I feel like we need to make a toast." My sister raises her coffee cup. My coffeeless aunt holds up her book.

"To Gems. For finally growing a vagina and making her dreams happen. I love you. I wish you every success and me an endless supply of fancy face cream." She lifts her coffee even higher. "And to me and my brilliant mind for dreaming up the perfect marketing plan to ensure Hamiltonians are lining up to get inside."

"Hear, hear!" cheers my aunt as I embrace my sister. For the last six months, things have been different between us. Better. I'm trusting in my abilities to solve my own problems, and that's given her some room to focus on her own life.

The bell above the door tinkles once again.

Mr. Zogaib pops his head and only his head in, which is a weird contrast to Other Reality's Mr. Zogaib, who had no problems invading my space when he was on a quest for moisturizer.

"We still on for later, Olivia?" he asks Aunt Livi, whose casual smile indicates she's not at all surprised by this question.

My jaw drops, as does Kiersten's in perfect sister synchronization as we clue in to what is going on.

My aunt fluffs her silver curls. "Yes. I'll send you a text when I'm done with the girls."

She winks. Mr. Zogaib turns tomato red, and Kierst and I close our mouths, only to have them fall open again as she throws a second wink in our direction.

Mr. Zogaib slips out as Kierst and I exchange *What the hell just happened there?* looks while my aunt acts as if it's just another day in the neighborhood:

"So . . ." Kierst finally speaks. "Are you gonna tell us how long that has been going on?"

Aunt Livi shrugs. "Oh, we've been seeing each other for years. But it hasn't gotten hot and heavy until the last few weeks."

"Aunt Livi!" My voice matches my shock.

She, however, waves me off with an eye roll. "Oh, poodle, I'm old, not broken."

I have questions. Lots of questions. But the doorbell goes off yet again and the face that appears in my doorway is familiar, as are the emerald eyes of the man who will forever be my best friend.

"I came bearing coffee, but it looks like you don't need me." Dax eyes my cup, which I proceed to chug, then hold out my hand for caffeine deposit number three this morning. I smile a little as I read the name scrawled on the side: *Gemma with a G.*

"I think that barista has a thing for you." Dax puts his arm around my shoulders. "He gave me one hell of a dirty look this morning when I ordered. I'm kind of afraid to drink my coffee."

He leans in and places a kiss on my temple, his hand traveling down my back until it rests on the waistband of my jeans. His pinky finger slips beneath the fabric, and although its actions remain in the realm of PG-13, the look Dax gives me implies he has a plan for that pinky finger later.

"What time do you think you'll be home tonight?" he whispers so only I can hear.

Our Dax and Gemma telepathy is still working wonderfully, possibly even better since I moved into his place three weeks ago.

After our love declaration and the making-up-for-lost-time sex-fest that followed, we agreed that as badly as we wanted to move things along, it was probably best that we took our time shifting from best-friend Gemma and Dax to relationship Gemma and Dax.

We still had a boatload of sex. But I kept my basement apartment, and we dated for almost four glorious months before deciding that it was silly to keep two places if we were spending every night together and that my rent could be repurposed to get Wilde Sisters Beauty off the ground.

"I have a bunch of inventory coming in this afternoon at two," I tell him. "Kiersten is going to help me until three, but I may be here late—unless you want to stop by and help?"

Dax's eyes immediately flick to the back-office desk. It was too big to move, so the previous tenant left it behind. When I first showed Dax this place, he called it the perfect sex desk, and I guess tonight we will find out if that's true. Ideally twice.

"I have a private client coming in at six, but I'll come by as soon as he's done."

Dax's store was doing well before I traversed through space and time, but after I returned, I formed a curling alliance one Tuesday with Sunny and the Hammer Curls. Not only is Sunny now our new shared BFF, but she also introduced us to her new husband, pediatric nurse Andre Cortez, who happened to grow up with a certain Toronto rapper who now exclusively wears Dax's shoes.

Everything is exactly the way it's supposed to be.

Wilde Sisters Beauty may not be at the same level of success it was in the other timeline. Still, I'm enjoying every second of building it up to its potential.

"I gotta run, but I love you. Text me if you need any heavy boxes moved or spiders killed." Dax gives me one last kiss and a butt squeeze.

"I think Kierst has me covered."

I've been babysitting my nieces and nephew every Tuesday night so Kierst could take up CrossFit. On cue, she flexes her muscles. "These glutes were made for lifting."

"And I prefer to form alliances with my eight-legged friends."

Dax waves to Aunt Livi and my sister, and as he opens my door to leave, I call out to him.

"I love you, Daxon McGuire."

He turns, flashing my favorite smile in the whole world. "I love you, Gemma McGuire."

"Slip of the tongue?"

He shrugs, the smile still on his face. "Maybe? Or maybe I have plans."

Acknowledgments

I THINK THIS might be my favorite part of the whole process: thinking back on the wild ride that is publishing and transforming a late-night what-if into an entire book.

Emma Caruso, you get me and all the woo girls that live inside my head. I knew from the moment we met that you were the right editor for this book, and if you didn't subconsciously hear me muttering from across borders as I worked through our many, many edits, I will tell you now what I chanted over and over to my computer screen: You are right! This is better! How are you so good at this?

Bibi Lewis, you are a superstar agent and a magical book whisperer. I picture the inside of your brain like the Beautiful Mind meme, dissecting my drafts and pulling out exactly what is needed to make them complete. You are a joy to work with. I feel incredibly lucky to be part of Team Ethan Ellenberg, and I look forward to sending you many more "This is good, right?" emails.

The Dial Press and Penguin Random House team, you are damn fine at what you do. Taylor M., I'm so sorry I still don't know how to use a comma (and very grateful you do). Whitney Frick, Avideh Bashirrad, Cindy Berman, Diane Hobbing, and

Debbie Aroff, it's been an absolute dream to work with you. Thank you for all your hard work putting *This Spells Love* out into the world.

I could write another entire book on all of the incredibly talented authors who have taken time to read, advise, critique, listen, and send incredibly inappropriate imagery over the last few years.

Katie Gilbert, my writing soulmate, you are so talented it makes my head hurt. I think about how far we've come from our days as baby authors and laugh, then cry a little, then laugh again. I would not be here without your constant kind words at every single step of this journey.

To the Boners: Aurora Palit, Christina Arellano, Jessica Joyce, Mae Bennett, Rebecca Osberg. Publishing can be hard on the heart. You were my lifeline in the toughest parts, pulling me out of the rough waters with snail dicks and Joshua Jackson in a cable-knit sweater.

My first readers (this title does not do you justice, let's instead go with dear friends), Amanda Wilson, Blue, Kathryn Ferrer, Mae, Maggie North, Sarah T. Dubb, and Shannon Bright, you made me feel funny and smart. Your ideas made this book so much better. I hope you see your fingerprints on these pages.

To the SmutFest 2.0 community, you are my people. You bring joy (and some very fine smut) into my life every day. Thank you for being my safe space. Toronto Romance Writers, there's clearly something in the water up here. We the North! And we know our romance. You've been a welcoming and supportive community from my very first meeting. Extra thanks to Hudson Lin for the retreats that gave me time and mental space to bring this baby into the world, and Farah Heron and Anya Simha for answering my endless publishing questions.

Noel and Dave, my loving parents, who told me I could be

anything I wanted to be (as long as I got a business degree first). Thank you for telling me every day that I was smart, making me carry the ski bags, buying me Baby-Sitters Club packs every time we went to BJ's, and setting the perfect example of what a happily ever after looks like.

Howie Wabb, you made it easy to write about two sisters who will always and forever have each other's backs (and also hate owls, even though they made me cut that part out).

To Andrew, your penis obviously inspired all the sex scenes. (I'm only writing this because our kids still refuse to read books without pictures.) Love your guts. Thanks for giving me the space to do this.

My sweet boys, if you're reading this, you've probably read the paragraph above. Sorry about that. But I hope I'm setting a good example of what a loving relationship looks like. I'm incredibly proud of you and can't wait to see what you become (after you get your business degrees). Also, a big shout-out to my very kind MIL, Cathy, for all of the free babysitting.

To my girls. If you're asking yourself, "Does this mean me?" the answer is yes. If you've made it this far in the acknowledgments, you are clearly one of the gems in my life who have been cheering and cheersing me all along the way. I am blessed to have a life filled with smart, talented women who inspire and push me. Love you all to pieces.

To every reader who has given this book and its debut author a chance, thank you! I hope I made you laugh or hug your sister.

And, finally, to Joshua Jackson and whoever knit him that damn sweater.

This Spells Love

Kate Robb

Dial Delights

*Love Stories
for the
Open-Hearted*

A Conversation Between
Kate Goldbeck and Kate Robb

KATE GOLDBECK is the author of *You, Again,* an enemies-to-friends-to-lovers debut about a commitment-phobe and a hopeless romantic who clash over the years—until friendship and unexpected chemistry bring them together. She lives in Atlanta, Georgia, where she loves bantering with her partner, falling asleep to British audiobook narrators, and scratching dogs behind their ears.

Instagram: @kategoldbeck

KATE ROBB is the author of *This Spells Love,* a whimsical friends-to-lovers debut about a young woman who tries to heal her heartbreak by casting a spell to erase her ex from her past—but she wakes up in an alternate reality where she's lost more than she's wished for. She lives just outside of Toronto, Canada, with her family, where she spends her free time pretending she's not a hockey mom, and she aspires to one day be able to wear four-inch heels again.

Instagram: @kate_robb_writes

Kate Robb: So I will admit that I haven't seen *When Harry Met Sally,* which inspired your novel. I feel like it's a romance sin.

Kate Goldbeck: Wow! I actually love when people haven't seen it.

KR: Did you always love the movie, or was this a recent thing? How did you go from the movie to writing the book?

KG: It's actually a movie that I identify more with my parents. My mom had the VHS, so it was just something I grew up with. But I would watch it with her and think: Oh, this is dating. This is what it's going to be like when I'm an adult and I live in New York City. So I wouldn't say it was a touchstone for me, but it was always something that was in my head, because it was so quotable. But it wasn't until much later in my life, when I got into Reylo fan-fiction, and decided to try writing *When Harry Met Sally* fanfic that I read the script and watched it a bunch of times. Then I started to appreciate it as a quintessential romcom and understand how brilliant Nora Ephron was, because she was able to weave specific anxieties into this timeless story that rings true thirty years later. What about you? In reading your book, it reminded me a bit of *Sliding Doors* but a completely original take on that idea and the multiverse romcom. Was *Sliding Doors* part of the original inspiration?

KR: No, actually. The idea for this novel came from the night that I met my husband. I had been planning to go to a bar with friends, but then another friend invited me to a charity ball at the last minute. I decided, why not? I'll get dressed up and go to this thing. It seemed like a very inconsequential decision at the time. I didn't even think about it, not like I had thought about other questions like: *Where am I going to go to school?* Or *What am I going to do with my life?* It was just *What are my Friday-night plans?* I was faced with two sets of plans, and I chose one over the other. But from that choice, I ended up meeting him and eventually we got married, and we have a family now. And it definitely spiraled my life in a completely different direction than if I'd chosen the other set of plans. I don't know if we would have met if those hadn't been the circumstances. Perfect time. Perfect place. I think the stars just aligned. And so that was sort of the idea that this grew from: What if you had a chance to go back and do something different with your life? If you took a slightly different path, would you end up in the same spot? Or would you just be a completely different person in a completely different place? And what are the consequences of that? When I started telling people about the book, *Sliding Doors* was an easy example from pop culture to describe the idea of "different path, different life," but the book is definitely a separate vibe from that movie.

KG: What does your husband think of the book? Has he read it yet? Is he allowed to?

KR: I will let him eventually. It's me being weird, but it's hard! You put yourself on a page and you're wondering: Is someone going to judge me? Or are they going read into this? Will they think it's terrible and then not want to tell me? There's so much vulnerability.

KG: It's definitely weird. I remember the exact moment when I let my primary partner read my book. I was just so hyped-up and nervous. We've been together for more than ten years. We've shared everything. But there was something so raw and vulnerable about letting him read it. So I completely get that and I'm very, very careful about who I've let read it. I *just* let my parents read it because I wanted their help with the proofreading. But I was looking at their notes after, and I thought "Oh my God, my parents have read all of this." They probably have so many questions. They're probably wondering, like, what parts of this came from my life? I was a little mortified. But I think it's almost the hardest to let the people who are closest to you read the story, not knowing what they're going to take away from it. There's so many things you can learn about a person from what they've written, far more than what they'll probably say to you in a normal conversation.

KR: Yeah, for sure. I think I'm nervous for my sister to read it, because my book has a sister relationship in it. It's very different from our relationship, but I think you take tiny little tidbits from your life, even if the characters are not based on anyone or real events or anything that's happened to you. There are always little pieces that kind of find their way in. How much of your book is based on your life?

KG: I think a lot of it is based on moments in my life with my primary partner. We had a bit of a false start ourselves. We went out on two dates, and then I kinda ghosted him. I just didn't think I could handle anything at that time in my life. So we did not see each other for more than a year. We finally reconnected when I wanted to return a DVD of his, and we had what we call our "second first date." That's when we start our anniversary from. We've always had a little bit of that second chance. A lot of the banter in the book is basically me imagining how we talk to each other. A lot of the locations are just places from my life. And a lot of the anecdotes are mine. Little moments of what it was like to be a single person and some of the bad, bad dating stories I had.

KR: I wish I had written more in my twenties and included my terrible dating stories.

KG: Same.

KR: I used to write emails to my sister and my mom about my terrible dates, and I wish they still existed because, like, I could just write a whole short-story anthology about hilariously bad dates. But now they weave their way into my romances.

KG: Yeah, totally. It pays off later.

KR: In reading your book, it felt like you spent a lot of time in New York City, like it was a place you knew very well.

KG: Yeah, I spent most of my twenties in New York City. It's definitely where I became an adult. Not that I really feel like a total adult, but it was many years of trying to date, moving from apartment to apartment, always trying to find a better deal and never having enough money, despite working seven days a week, because I mostly worked in museums and non-profits. So much of this book is based on those memories. Speaking of which, as someone who wants to be Canadian and wishes she lived in Canada, I loved the setting in your book of Hamilton, Ontario, as well as Toronto, and the details you brought to life. As an American reader, it was all so delightful. As a Canadian author, did you ever feel pressure to set the book in America rather than Canada?

KR: I grew up in Hamilton, and it's so nostalgic for me, so I wanted to honor that. It's a place I love, and it felt like the right setting for the book. But it's funny. I hang out with a lot of Canadian romance authors. And I think, for a while, there was pressure not to set books in Canada. But lately, that's been changing. Like I have heard from some readers that it's the reason they liked the book so much. Because it was Canadian but not a stereotypical portrayal of Canada with . . . I don't know. Maple syrup.

KG: They're not running a maple syrup farm.

KR: Exactly. Hamilton is a very urban city with amazing restaurants and antiques shops and record shops and occult shops, and all the cool clothing stores. I wanted to capture all of that. And the "Canadiana" is just kind of sprinkled in.

KG: Like curling! Is curling a typical recreational activity for you or . . . ?

KR: Okay. There are hard-core curlers up here like my grandparents. I did not grow up curling regularly, but it's one of those things that, you know, you do in high school, as a unit in phys ed, like you go to the curling club, you tie a plastic bag around your shoe, and you learn how to curl for two weeks. Then you do it as a corporate team-building thing when you get your first job. It's definitely part of our Canadian culture, but we're not curling-obsessed, I would say, except for a small niche group.

KG: I kind of wanted to do it too. Honestly. Like, it seems kind of fun like bocce but on ice and like with a broom.

KR: That's exactly it. There is a ton of local beer leagues you can join to curl. A lot of people go to bonspiels on the weekends where it's just like an excuse to drink all day and get together and play a really fun sport. I have friends that do that! So I knew enough about curling. I know how to play. I had to look up a few terms, mostly so I could just make them kind of sexual puns for one scene. . . .

KG: Very important.

KR: It's my favorite scene. Now, one of the main characters in your book is an improv comedian. Did you do a lot of improv yourself?

KG: I have dated a lot of comedians, and I've always been really interested in the women who are able to hang with it. I think it's gotten better in the past few years, but it's a really hard place for a woman to thrive. When deciding what Ari's job should be, I felt like I wanted her to do something that was going to be really difficult, which requires somebody who can just totally roll with the punches, who's very spontaneous and really funny.

KR: And there is so much humor in the book, but it's also an emotional roller coaster. Both up and down. Where did you get the inspiration for the breakup in the book?

KG: I think part of that roller coaster is because this story started as fanfic. You post chapter by chapter, and you grow this built-in audience, and you have to take them up and take them down, leave them on a cliffhanger. But as I got into writing this book, I think I often felt I was arguing with myself, because I see both of the characters as aspects of myself, even though they're so different. They're arguing about things I feel that are deeply personal to me. Do you want to be in a committed relationship? How stable do you want to be versus how much freedom do you want to have? Just a lot of the internal struggles that I've had with myself over the course of my adulthood and often feeling like there are no right answers.

KR: How else do you think writing fan-fiction affected how you approach telling a story?

KG: I come from the film world. I had written some plays and tried to write a romcom screenplay. So all of my knowledge about how you build a story comes from screenwriting books and screenplays. But being in the fan-fiction community really helped me understand how to craft a longer narrative, because I had never tried to do that before. And I don't think I would have written as much as I did if I didn't feel like I had an audience. I had people who wanted to see what was going to happen next, and that was so encouraging. I don't know if I would have ever been able to write this book if I hadn't started that way. Was this your first book or had you written other books before? It doesn't really seem like a debut to me. It seems like somebody who knows what they're doing, and I'd love to know how you go about it.

KR: This was my third attempt at a book. The first book is so bad. I will save it. So one day, I can give it to people and make them laugh and show them that you can get better at things if you try. I saw a clip of Ed Sheeran on some talk show where he says how talent isn't something you're born with, it's something you need to develop. They played a clip of him playing guitar and singing earlier in his career, and he's genuinely terrible. It was the same for me. I get better with every book. My first book is like that clip: genuinely terrible. And then I loved the next book I wrote, but it wasn't the right time for it. But it was a good learning experience for me. And then with this one, I had an idea. I knew how it ended before I even sat down to write it. I had the plot in my head. And it just flew out pretty quickly.

KG: Was there any time you had to kill a particular darling? Where you had to get rid of an entire character or scene you really loved?

KR: So . . . I really hate owls. And there was this rant about owls in one scene, how they're the absolute worst, and our editor eventually had to say . . . I just don't think this rant really fits here? But other than that, no. I'm definitely an underwriter. I had to build out things a bit more, like the sister relationship, to make the story fuller. So I think I'm not one to kill darlings but add additional ones. What about you?

KG: Oh, there's literally almost nothing that hasn't been touched or transformed in this book. There are a couple of characters who were some of my favorites that had to go for different reasons. But there was a whole sequence where Ari worked as a comedian on a cruise ship . . .

KR: No!

KG: Yup. There was a whole cruise ship section, but it just seemed like a bridge too far, and so eventually I cut the whole thing, and that's probably one of the biggest changes. But maybe I'll save it for another book, because I do find cruise ships really fascinating. I did a lot of research. I've watched so many "cruiser" channels on YouTube. My YouTube recommendations are screwed forever.

KR: I love it. I actually started to write a story about yachties, because I have always wanted to be one. I thought there could be so much good scandal that would happen on a yacht. So I do understand the love of the cruise ship culture.

KG: And we also agree that, as you wrote in your book, pants are the worst.

KR: And tequila. We both have excellent taste in tequila! Each of our characters drink Casamigos.

KG: And both of our books are pretty spicy! How did you approach incorporating spice level into your book?

KR: I think steam in romance books is having its day right now. People are looking for fun stories and then some hot sex.

KG: Yeah, I feel like it can be weirdly controversial sometimes, but I do think that when you're writing romance, there's something nice about the story "paying off" in a way that you can actually describe without just emotion. It's satisfying for the reader. There's plenty of books I love that have zero steam, but I find that when people can skillfully portray sex and intimacy, it really helps to drive home the development of a relationship. And I think that was perfectly done in your book.

KR: And I think with my book, there's lots of things that wouldn't really happen in real life. Let's hope. You don't do a spell and wind up in an alternate reality. But it's fun to imagine, and then I also wanted to deliver with fun, satisfying, steamy sex as well.

KG: You know, reading your book reminded me of the 2000s era of romantic comedies, like *13 Going on 30*, or *Just Like Heaven*. Where there was a sprinkling of fairy dust and somebody could live a different aspect of their life. It brought back a lot of those vibes.

KR: It's funny you say that. When I wrote this, we were smack-dab in the middle of the pandemic, and those types of movies were all I wanted. I couldn't read; my brain just wanted to watch movies where I already knew the ending. I just wanted that predictable comfort of a little bit of whimsy. That was my mind that when I wrote this: I don't want to be here. I just want to escape. I want something that makes me happy the entire time I'm reading it.

KG: Absolutely. That's what made it so easy for me to just fly through it, because I was enjoying every moment. Is that what you look for when reading romance too? For me, as a reader, there's nothing better. There's no better sign than when I can just read something straight through and don't even want to take a break to eat a sandwich. I just want to keep reading. That's the sweet spot for romance, because it just feels right to read.

KR: Yeah, I love to get my heart torn out. I love angst. Sometimes. But sometimes I just like easy, enjoyable reading. And I think that there's a whole bunch of different types of romance books out there, and you can choose your adventure. What are you in the mood for? What's your kink? What's your trope? What are you feeling tonight? And you can find something excellent for every different situation. That's why I love romance.

Aunt Livi's Moonlight Margaritas

Some nights require a strong cup of tea. Others, a brisk walk or a quiet moment of reflection. But when the moon is just right, sometimes you get a night where the perfect potion is one of my famous moonlight margaritas.

For the sage-infused tequila

1 ½ cups Casamigos Reposado Tequila (the handsome George Clooney really does make a delightful tequila, but any reposado will work)
3 sprigs of fresh sage (promotes wisdom and healing; also gives a lovely little zip!)

For the margarita

2 tbsp sage-infused tequila
1 ½ tbsp lime juice
1 tbsp orange juice
1 ½–2 tsps Agave (to your taste)

For the Rim

Mix equal parts sugar, orange zest, and salt (I like a nice coarse sea salt for its purifying and healing properties)
1 wedge of lime

Directions

Pour your tequila into a glass jar and add the sprigs of sage. Seal and store in your refrigerator to let it steep for 24–48 hours (the longer the trip, the bigger the zip!).

Rim your glass using a lime wedge and the salt/sugar/orange zest mixture.

Combine the margarita ingredients with a few cubes of ice in a blender and blend.

Garnish with a sprig of sage, lime wedge, or orange slice.

Drink, dance, and share all your troubles with the moon.

Kiersten's Anytime Margaritas

Jose Cuervo
Kirkland Signature Margarita Mix

Directions

Mix according to the day you've just had.

Gemma's guide to getting over a breakup (that doesn't pose a threat to the time-space continuum)

Note: None of the below methods are scientifically backed. They're merely the result of trial and error. Interpret, add, and subtract to the list as you wish.

- Designated cry time (I recommend a nice solid hour)
- Watching YouTube videos of people returning to their pets after long periods away or teens getting into college/university (any *Queer Guy* episode will also work)
- Long walks
- Eating doughnuts
- Eating doughnuts while taking long walks
- Petting dogs
- Don't hate me . . . exercise (especially if you can yell or swear while doing it)
- Hugging your sister (can substitute a friend, pet, or family member and even some therapists)
- Therapy
- Keeping a journal
- Singing "All by myself" by Canadian legend Celine Dion (DO NOT, I repeat, DO NOT make a TikTok)
- Get your hair done
- Buy something that makes you feel fabulous
- Write a list of all the ways you ARE fabulous
- Write a list of all the ways your ex is NOT fabulous
- Burn the list (taking the appropriate fire-safety precautions)
- Remind yourself that you are a magical unicorn, that this moment is the beginning of something wonderful to come (even if you don't quite know how it will unfold yet)

KATE ROBB dated a lot of duds in her twenties (among a few gems), all providing excellent fodder to write weird and wild romantic comedies. She lives just outside of Toronto, Canada, where she spends her free time pretending she's not a hockey mom while whispering "hustle" under her breath from the bleachers, a pinot grigio concealed in her YETI mug. She hates owls, the word "whilst," and wearing shorts, and she aspires to one day be able to wear four-inch heels again.

katerobbwrites.com
Instagram: @kate_robb_writes

The Dial Press, an imprint of Random House,
publishes books driven by the heart.

Follow us on Instagram:
@THEDIALPRESS

Discover other Dial Press books and
sign up for our e-newsletter:

thedialpress.com